FRANCES FAVIELL
A HOUSE ON THE RHINE

FRANCES FAVIELL (1905-1959) was the pen name of Olivia Faviell Lucas, painter and author. She studied at the Slade School of Art in London under the aegis of Leon Underwood. In 1930 she married a Hungarian academic and travelled with him to India where she lived for some time at the ashram of Rabindranath Tagore, and visiting Nagaland. She then lived in Japan and China until having to flee from Shanghai during the Japanese invasion. She met her second husband Richard Parker in 1939 and married him in 1940.

She became a Red Cross volunteer in Chelsea during the Phoney War. Due to its proximity to the Royal Hospital and major bridges over the Thames Chelsea was one of the most heavily bombed areas of London. She and other members of the Chelsea artists' community were often in the heart of the action, witnessing or involved in fascinating and horrific events throughout the Blitz. Her experiences of the time were later recounted in the memoir *A Chelsea Concerto* (1959).

After the war, in 1946, she went with her son, John, to Berlin where Richard had been posted as a senior civil servant in the post-war British Administration (the CCG). It was here that she befriended the Altmann Family, which prompted her first book *The Dancing Bear* (1954), a memoir of the Occupation seen through the eyes of both occupier and occupied. She later wrote three novels, *A House on the Rhine* (1955), *Thalia* (1957), and *The Fledgeling* (1958). These are now all available as Furrowed Middlebrow books.

BY FRANCES FAVIELL

FRANCES FAVIELL

A HOUSE ON THE RHINE

With an Afterword
by John Parker

DEAN STREET PRESS
A Furrowed Middlebrow Book

A Furrowed Middlebrow Book
FM6

Published by Dean Street Press 2016

Copyright © 1955 Frances Faviell
Afterword copyright © 2016 John Parker

Cover by DSP
Cover drawing by Frances Faviell

First published in 1955 by Rupert Hart-Davis Ltd.

ISBN 978 1 911413 81 3

www.deanstreetpress.co.uk

For my Sister Gerry

I

THEY WERE peeling potatoes under the acacia tree. There was such a huge mound that it would take Katie and Moe at least two hours to finish them all; and when they were done there would still be the onions to do. Katie always tried to leave the onions to Moe. Her own hard almond-shaped eyes were delicate, the onions made her cry. Katie's child Peppi was crawling under the old garden table in the dust of the yard. He wore a single cotton garment and was, as usual, filthy. He was one of those babies who always seem miserable, as if he sensed his unwanted-ness.

Moe was smoking. Her thick tawny hair needed washing. It hung in her black eyes as she unhurriedly peeled, dipping the potatoes into a pail of dirty water and then throwing the skins anywhere on the ground. Katie eyed the litter.

"Pa'll be mad if he finds those peelings on the ground when he comes back, Moe," she observed disinterestedly.

"Let him be mad, then," yawned her mother, cigarette in her mouth as she worked.

"Oh well, Krista or Anna'll clear it up—they're as bad as Pa for that sort of thing," said Katie.

"Krista's getting real pretty—she'll be a beauty when she's filled out a bit more—she's so childish still."

"It's time she *did* fill out—she's almost eighteen!" There was something vicious in the way Katie said this.

Moe looked at her sardonically. "The late-ripened apples are the sweetest," she said. "You were an early one."

"Krista's just plain dumb," snapped Katie, throwing a long piece of peel angrily over her shoulder. "For eighteen she gives me a pain in the neck."

"We don't know how old she really is—that's the fact of it. Sometimes she looks about twelve, and when she's serious and quiet she could be eighteen and more, couldn't she?"

Katie wasn't listening. Her child, Peppi, had seized one of Pa's young chickens in his fat hands and was trying to throttle it. The hens ran about all over the dirty untidy yard looking for food. Moe had cut a hole in the fence so that they could try their luck in the garden next door, but that hadn't been a success because the British family next door had a cat. The cat had eaten several chickens and Pa had been furious. He would be very angry if this small bird was throttled, and Moe, suddenly launching herself upon Peppi, tried to rescue it. The child would not release his hold on the bird until she smacked him, and his roars rang through the garden.

"You hit him too hard," screamed Katie; "he's only two." Her heavy face was red with anger as she looked sullenly at her mother. Moe calmly lit a fresh cigarette and continued her potato-peeling.

"You'll have to pay for that wretched bird—he sets such store by them—it's dead."

"And where d'you think I'm to find the money? You know what I earn—nothing."

"You're getting it from somewhere. D'you think I haven't noticed all your new bits of finery?"

Katie paled and instinctively put her hands up to her ears from which dangled the new gold hoops she had recently bought. The screams of the child had changed from fear to anger, anger at the woman who had hit him. He stopped bawling suddenly, as children do, and picking up a stick struck out at Moe's bare legs.

"Bad Moe, bad bad Moe," he shouted.

Moe laughed, pushing him away as unconcernedly as one brushes off a fly. He lost his balance and went rolling in the dust. Katie got up and spat at her mother.

"That'll do, leave him alone, you'll have all the neighbours out here. Look, the windows are opening already."

While Moe stared up at the many windows in the upper stories of the once lovely house, Katie leaned over and took a cigarette from her mother's packet.

"Take the child in—and leave my cigarettes alone. If you can buy gold ear-rings you can buy your own cigarettes!"

Katie picked up the screaming Peppi and took him into the house.

"And come back quickly and finish these spuds, you lazy slut!" her mother shouted after her as, putting down her knife she leaned back, stretching like a cat on her hard wooden chair.

It was already hot. The sun made a golden dusty curtain where Peppi had stirred the sandy earth of the yard. Moe stretched out her legs and flung her shapely arms above her head, yawning as she relaxed from her work. The sun's voluptuous warmth penetrated her thin dress and her face took on a dreamy softer look.

She closed her eyes and leaned her head back on the chair. It was very pleasant in the garden. She felt glad to be alive. She did not notice the litter and the untidiness around her, or the inquisitive heads peering out from behind the curtains upstairs. And so she sat, relaxed and still, until Katie came back from having put Peppi to sleep. She was not surprised to be told quite mildly to finish the potatoes. Moe was like that. Furious and raging one minute, warm and comforting the next. She even gave Katie a cigarette before she went herself from the brilliant sunlight into the dark house.

In the large room, once an elegant salon, where Moe now slept with her husband Joseph, she flung back the wooden shutters and stood for a time looking at herself in the spotted stained mirror. What did *he* see in her? With all these young fresh faces, why choose hers? What did he find in her? She didn't know. She could see no good reason for his choice.

In the looking-glass her rather coarse vital face with the turbulent vibrant hair stared back at her. She was fascinated by it. Not because it was her face but because *he* liked it. She dabbed some powder on it carelessly, and passed a lipstick over her large generous mouth. Her dress was damp with sweat. She flung it off and went naked into the hall lobby where she splashed cold water over herself. She was drawing a cotton wrapper round her fine strong body when she turned to find Katie eyeing her critically.

"You're going in to *him* now?" asked the girl curiously.

"I am. You go and get on with the meal—and don't you forget what I said about the boys. Keep them away from here. I *do* draw the line at them knowing I'm in here."

As she spoke she opened the door of a small darkened room next to hers and Joseph's. The sleeping form of a young man was visible on the bed; but before the door closed again Katie had heard the sleepy but ardent greeting of Rudi the lodger, and had seen his arms stretch upwards for her mother.

With a shrug of her young shoulders Katie returned to the zinc tub in the garden and toiled away for an hour or so; then she went indoors again and came out with a portable radio set. Presently the lilting strains of a sentimental tango filled the air. Putting down her knife the girl hitched up her skirt, gave her full hips a twitch, and with a curious defiant grace began to dance in rhythm to the music.

She danced unconscious of anything ridiculous or unusual in her surroundings, of the dirt and dust of the yard. The hens scuttled away in terror as her dance became wilder and wilder. Upstairs, faces peeped again out of the windows at the girl who danced so shamelessly at noon in full view of the road. They were hostile faces and condemnatory eyes. For although they belonged to refugees from the East, unpopular enough in the village, this family who lived on the ground and first floor of the great house were hated even more. They were known as the "bunker" family because of their having spent four and a half years in a "bunker," or air-raid shelter, under the cathedral in Cologne. The miserable yellow dog watched the dancer mournfully from his chain in a corner of the yard. Behind her three rows of washing swung lightly in the breeze.

Across the road in the little white house almost hidden by weeping willows the Frenchman had come home for his noon-day meal. His car door slammed, and as he turned to shut the gate he caught sight of the girl dancing. He stood there for several minutes watching her, his cigar in his mouth. The bright merciless midday sun showed up the state of dilapidation to which the once-imposing house had come. The rubbish and filth of the once lovely garden, the broken toys littered about, the bicycles pushed against the toppling fence, the broken hen-house, the neglected flower-beds trampled down by the heavy boots of the boys—all were highlighted. The house itself with paint peeling off, tiles missing from the roof, and its pretentious pillars pitted with the marks of gunfire as was its face, looked forlorn and neglected. Against it the figure of the girl was vibrantly alive as she turned, swayed and dipped, oblivious of everything. Nothing could detract from the beauty of the acacia tree whose proud flowering dominated the scene and apologized for everything else. Its exotic scent filled the entire garden, and the little summer house, once the pride and delight of the owner of the house, was almost hidden in the exuberant wealth of its foliage.

The Frenchman noticed all this as he stood there smoking. Nothing escaped him. His sad, rather cynical eyes took it all in before he turned on his heel and went in to his disagreeable old French housekeeper. She never ceased to grumble, to pine for her native country, to curse the Germans around them. Today her master was tired of her. The Comité des Forges was giving trouble. There was all this Ruhr-Saar business working up. There were days when he hated coal with a deadly loathing. Today was one of the days. He cut her grumblings short and told her to go back to France. Her ceaseless complaints about the dampness of the village on the Rhine which gave her rheumatism made him realize the futility and uselessness of life. He hated that. He wanted to see youth, hear youth, and be with youth for a while. Like that red-haired girl over there in that filthy garden. She was young, alive, full of life—just as the exuberant laughter of the mother excited him, so the daughter's dancing for the sheer love of it satisfied something in him. Let the old hag go back to France and do her grumbling there.

"Bring the food!" he shouted. He would enjoy this meal knowing it was the last time he would hear her creaking boots and be irritated by the innumerable wrinkles in her black woollen stockings.

So engrossed was Katie in her dance that she failed to mark the arrival of her brothers. They came tearing in from school and work like a pack of ravenous dogs, shouting, quarrelling and swearing. They stopped short at the sight of their sister dancing and taunted her unmercifully.

"You've got Hank's new radio set!" screamed Karl. "Just wait until I tell him tonight. Look at Katie's red face, Hans, it's the same colour as her hair. Ha. Ha!"

"She's practising for next year's Carnival!" jeered Heinz. "Our lovely little sister—I don't think!"

Katie turned on them furiously with a large wooden spoon which she had seized from the table, returning their jibes with furious blows and imprecations. They dodged the spoon, teasing unmercifully; then, at her threat of no food, they reluctantly desisted and retired to the summer house. Shaking with anger and mortification she switched off the radio and sullenly set about preparing their midday meal.

Slowly the windows upstairs closed one by one. They had all been flung open when the battle began in the garden. Katie hated the days when the twins, Hans and Heinz, came home for the midday meal. The other three boys, Robert, Karl and Franz Joseph as well as her own small Peppi she could manage, but when the twins, great lumping mischievous lads of sixteen, came home too, the place was bedlam. There was trouble every day now. Katie could not control the twins as Moe could, and Moe no longer cared. Since the lodger had come she had left everything to Katie. If Hank had been at home he would have wielded his authority. Without exception the boys feared him.

All the time that his father had been away at the war Hank, young as he was, had ruled his brothers and sisters without mercy. He worked now at the ship-repairing station in the great bend of the Rhine which formed a natural basin for the work. It was too far for him to get home at midday. Katie missed his help. He was terrifically strong, and he was cruel. She kept insisting that the twins take their food to the factory with them, as Hank did, but Moe was too indifferent to back her up, and Pa—he also seemed indifferent lately.

Katie glanced at her son Peppi asleep on the old settee in the big kitchen which served as their living-room. His dirty tear-stained face had the cherubic charm of an angel, and in his sleep his filthy little hands were turned palm upwards as if in supplication. In repose his face was amazingly like that of the young Belgian who was his father. She could see Henri's face as he lay asleep under the willows by the river. She could see the same gold tips to the dark lashes on Peppi's cheeks, the same smooth brow in sleep. Peppi would be dark later, as Henri had been.

Three years ago, that was. Katie had been only fourteen, and Peppi had been born before she was fifteen, long after Henri had returned to his own country. She looked at Henri's child without any particular affection. Peppi was a burden. Until he was three he could not be placed in any nursery school. Since Rudi, the lodger, had come to the house, Moe had flatly declined to look after him as she had done for the first eighteen months of Peppi's life. Katie had been able to go out to work then. She had earned good money in the big laundry near the station. Moe might say that Katie was lazy, but give her work that she liked and she was second to none. They had been pleased with her there. Now she was obliged to stay at home, and to earn her keep by doing all the housework and most of the cooking. She hated it.

All the others, Anna, Krista, Hank and the twins, could buy themselves new clothes, shoes, bicycles and radios—in fact everything they wanted. They earned well in the factories. Everyone could do overtime if he chose. But because of this brat Peppi, she had to slave all day at the endless washing and cooking. Whenever she thought of Henri now she just spat. Ach! she loathed the thought of him. He had got what he wanted and all she had got was Peppi. Henri had gone back to Belgium without thinking of her or of the results of his love-making under the willows. What was the use of Moe saying that as she, Katie, had paraded the village in one of her frocks and a pair of her high-heeled shoes, the young Belgian sentries could not have known her age? The one who had seduced her had thought she was at least eighteen or more. Ach! how she hated the thought of Henri now. It made her sick. She loved Leo, the great blonde lad who worked at the repair station with Hank. Now, there was a man! He was worth a thousand Henris. But Henri had been able to give her food three years ago, and she had been very hungry then. Now there was plenty for everyone, and hunger nearly a thing of the past—a mere memory. But Henri lived on; he was here permanently in Peppi his son.

Leo had a motor cycle. They were all the rage now. Hank wanted one. He would get it too. It gave a youth class to own one of the new gleaming machines. Everyone knew what they cost; but Leo and his friends had ways of making easy money. After Leo found that he could trust her, he had tried her out. She had been slipping out to help him for some time now, and he had shown her how she also could get a rake-off from their profits for herself. She was able to have some of the money denied her from laundry work by Moe. She had been slipping out at night now for over three months, and no one knew except Hank. You couldn't keep anything from Hank. He twisted your arms, flattened your nose, or dug his strong cruel fingers into the nape of your neck until you screamed for mercy.

Hank had met her creeping back to the house at dawn one morning when he himself was returning from setting rabbit-snares by the river. When he had heard about Leo's gang—and he had forced it out of her by giving her "the works" as he called his tortures—he had insisted on being let into the whole thing himself. Katie had been terrified of Leo's displeasure, but to her surprise Leo had been rather pleased. He could use another tough one, he had said. Hank *was* tough. He had proved that all right. Hadn't he been the head of the gang that had waylaid cyclists on the Grüne Ring at dusk and coshed them while the others stole their purses, wallets or even bicycles? Wasn't it Hank who had been the leader of the gang of boys who had gone round putting insulting letters in the doors of the Occupation? Hadn't he led the gang who had painted notices telling the Occupation to go home? Leo had been delighted at this new acquisition. On his advice Hank had disbanded his own gang. Things had got too sticky. Besides, the Occupation were on their way out now—or at least it looked like it. Hank had so far proved a success, and Leo was pleased with Katie. Tonight she and Hank would slip out as usual and join the others as the usual meeting-place.

At the thought of the coming evening her spirits rose again, and she began singing. After the raid planned for tonight was safely over she would have Leo to herself. She loved Leo. She loved him passionately and jealously. He was king of the gang and could pick and choose. All the girls wanted him. She had seen his eyes on the others, Maria, Leila and Trudi. She was not blind, and she knew that his feeling for her was transient and as nothing to the violent passion she had for him. He was cruel, too, and quite ruthless in attaining his own ends. But tonight would be hers. He had said so. She would have to arrange about Peppi. Krista would take the child to bed with her. Krista was soft and dumb. At the thought of Krista's love for children Katie's lip curled.

The boys' meal was ready. She shouted to them to come and get it. Her red hair gleamed in the sun as she stood there waiting for her brothers to emerge from the summer house. Shrieks and giggles came from them but they did not come out. Her thoughts were still on the coming evening. She would wear the new frock Leo had bought her. She hated her red hair. While Moe's was a lovely tawny treacle colour and Anna and Carola were blonde with black eyes, her hair was a brilliant red. In this village they thought it shameful to have such hair. People with hair that colour were not to be trusted, they said. Katie had endured taunts and jibes all her life about it. The Belgian, Henri, had loved it, had run his hands through it and said it was beautiful; and it seemed that in America and England there were film actresses with hair of this hateful shade. Katie loathed it. She wanted it black. The first thing she intended to do when she had enough money was to have it dyed.

The four boys, charging suddenly out of the summer house, broke ruthlessly upon these reflections and almost knocked her down. She set about getting them served. Hateful things, brothers, she thought as she watched them snatching the food which had taken her so long to prepare and gulping it down so as to make sure of a second helping. Food, food, food. It was endless. So many mouths to fill. In the evenings Pa, Hank, Anna and Krista added to the number. Krista helped to prepare it, certainly, but Anna considered that paying a share towards the household expenses more than justified her having her meals set before her. She would not lift a finger to help Katie unless Moe or Pa ordered her to do so.

Most of the food had disappeared before Katie realized that her youngest brother Franz Joseph was missing. He was a fat sturdy sloe-eyed rascal of four who attended the convent kindergarten next to the church by the river. He had a constant habit of straying, as some dogs have. The villagers were accustomed to hearing strident cries of "Franz Joseph! Franz Joseph!" from early morning until dusk fell.

"Where's Franz Joseph?" she asked sharply. "Didn't you fetch him from the kindergarten, Robert?"

The child had apparently come home as usual and then disappeared again. Katie was furious that no one had remembered to keep an eye on the wanderer.

"Go and call him!" she ordered. "He's probably miles away by this time."

No one moved except Robert. Ever sweet and docile, he went off, sausage in hand, and in between bites howled out his brother's name much as the mongrel dog Lumpi howled when tied up and left alone to guard the house. Katie went and listened at the door of the lodger's room. There was complete silence. She supposed they were asleep.

I I

JOSEPH GOT TO the factory to find that he had what they called a free day. His name had been on the notice-board amongst those whose output called for special reward, but he hadn't seen it. Anyway, he didn't want a day off and said so to the foreman. He didn't care about this new notion of the worker management's to encourage the rebuilding drive. A good workman liked to work; he needed no reward except his pay. That was Joseph's view, said the foreman. Others thought differently. Times were changing.

Changing? They *had* changed. What a fool the man was if he thought Joseph hadn't noticed that.

"I don't want the day off," he said dourly, pulling on his dungarees. "I've come in as usual and here I'll stay."

But he wasn't allowed to stay. He was surrounded by his teasing mates. "Old Joe don't want his day off," they laughed. "Too many blooming kids in his home! Go on home, old chap, and get busy—your wife'll get another medal yet!"

This oblique reference to his wife having received a medal for having more than ten children infuriated him. He had been rather proud when she had worn it to Mass every Sunday with all the children walking behind her. Today he did not take kindly to the chaff round him.

"Shut up! That's enough!" he said roughly, and they fell back in sulky surprise. Joseph could usually be counted on to act as the butt of many jokes and sallies.

"Anyone want my sandwiches?" he grunted as he removed the dungarees. "I'll get a hot meal today." That started them off again.

"Good old Joseph! Get a steak man, a good red steak! That'll help on the good work. Seven sons! Make it eight, man, make it eight! Eight soldiers for the European Defence Array. Ha, ha, ha!" He did not answer them and their voices followed him as he passed out of the checkgate, where the timekeeper teased him about his not having wanted his free day.

"Mind your own business!" shouted Joseph. The man looked after him in astonishment. He was usually only too ready for a chat on the ever-burning topic of Rearmament and the European Defence Army. After all, to a man with seven sons the matter had some importance. Wasn't he always complaining that with no army, no kind of military discipline, the present-day youths were insufferable? And today the papers were headlined with the subject and the upheaval the question was causing in the whole of Europe.

Joseph went and sat on a bench under a chestnut tree in a street off the main one where the factory lay. His mind was in a turmoil. He had wanted to smash his fists into the silly grinning faces of his work-mates. It had been all he could do to keep them off the timekeeper. He looked at his hands. They were large and strong yet curiously gentle. He had never wanted to use them for violence before. Not even in the war. What he had done he had done reluctantly under orders, never from love of violence or killing. Never, until now. Beads of sweat were running down his face, not from heat, but from some emotion which still swept him, and which he now recognized as hate. He *hated* them, all of them, and the grinning old fool of a timekeeper most of all.

He took off his cap and shook himself impatiently, then relaxed on the bench under the chestnut tree. The chestnut flowers swayed slightly in the breeze above him. The pattern of their leaves as he looked up through half-closed eyes moved him strangely. The fact that beauty was impressing itself upon his mind was beyond his understanding. He only knew that he had suddenly seen a chestnut tree, not just as a tree, but as some moving living force, and that somehow he got comfort from it. The sun glinting through the spreading leaves reached him on the hard bench. The sky deepened its blue. Looking up, the chestnut blossoms were strong thrusting candles pointing up to the heavens. Hundreds, no thousands of them. Whenever he rode down the street in the tram these blossoms jerked his gaze from the dirty noisy traffic, the gutters, the dust, the petrol fumes, and the creaking oily tram-lines—up, up to the blue heavens.

At the very end of the street, far above the candles, the two spires of the cathedral pointed even higher up to the vaulted blue. Joseph's eyes were caught and held by the spires. They dominated the landscape for miles round the town. He could see them from the village where he lived now with Moe and the children. He'd pictured them often when he had been away fighting, and when he had been a prisoner. He'd visualized his family after their home had been demolished in the bombing, safely sheltered in the bunker under the cathedral's massive foundations. Everything else might be swept away in dust, as indeed it appeared to have been each time he came back on leave, but the cathedral had stood solidly, a monument to God in the midst of a shattered town. Every time he had gone into action on the interminable campaigns, no matter how exhausted or utterly dispirited he had felt, his last vision had always been of these spires, twin fingers pointing up to the God who was surely looking after his family safely housed in the shelter under His church.

The great clock boomed out the hours, but Joseph sat on as if drugged. His thoughts raced round in contrast to the immobility of his body. Why didn't he go home? That was the normal thing for a man to do on a free day. Why not? He pushed away the nagging certainty about Moe. He didn't want to face it. He *knew*—and yet he didn't know. He was too dispirited to care much. Once he knew for certain he would have to take positive action. *Action*—he hated the word. He had heard it too often. What had happened to Moe? What had made her change so much? Was it because he had been away for so long? Or was it Carola? What was it?

Thinking back it seemed to him that she had changed from that day when the child had suddenly sickened. Only a headache and lassitude—then suddenly she could not use her legs then the rest of her little body became useless. By the time she had been rushed to hospital Carola was desperately ill with the dreaded poliomyelitis. And Moe seemed to think somehow that it was *his*, Joseph's, fault that her favourite child was stricken down. He went now impulsively to a telephone call-box and rang up the hospital where she still lay helpless. It was not visiting day. No, he was told firmly, he could not see her now. She was having treatment, and it was the time when the specialists came. They were sorry, the Sister answering the telephone was apologetic, she would tell the child her father had telephoned, but rules were rules. If he liked to come this evening, he could see her. Joseph rang off without promising. He was disappointed. In this turmoil of mind for which he simply could not account, the sight of his little daughter might have calmed him. She was of a sweet, patient disposition, and lay there without complaint. To no one would Joseph have admitted that it cost him a tremendous effort of will to bring himself to visit her. The sight of her suffering brought back so many vivid recollections of the war. Of children lying just as she lay now, but motionless or apathetic from hunger, not from paralysis. Greece for instance—that had been Hell. Something he would never forget.

He returned slowly to the seat under the chestnut tree and took out his pipe. Why was he in this agitated state of mind? What had made him almost want to curse the Sister who had regretfully refused him the sight of his child? She was a nun, a woman to whom the child herself was devoted, and for whom Joseph normally felt awe and respect.

The great clock of the cathedral boomed out twelve long deep strokes, and he got up. Knowing that his workmates would soon be swarming out of the factory, he moved, as if impelled, towards the building itself. Under its deep foundations had been the home to which he had come on his few army leaves, when he had bribed the attendants to be allowed to creep in with his wife on the women's side of the shelter.

He went through the garage at the back of the great church and down to the bunker. Still open, years after the end of war, the sexes still segregated, a dour-faced woman attendant asked him roughly what he wanted. The place was clean and smelt of disinfectant. When his family had lived here it had smelt only of dirty humanity. Disinfectants had been non-existent and water very scarce. He wondered who the place was used by now. Students, hikers and mostly refugees from the East who did not want to go to any of the organized centres, he was told. Accommodation in the town was still at a premium in spite of all the rebuilding. Travellers stranded without a bed for the night often slept here. Joseph shuffled up the steps, back through the garage to the front of the cathedral and followed the stream of tourists and sightseers up to the main entrance.

The noise coming from all the scaffolding in the square was deafening. Everywhere one looked there were workmen perched up on scaffolding, hammering, chipping, drilling and hauling up bricks. Even in the faintly-scented gloom of the chill church the sound of rebuilding could be heard. It was impossible to get away from it. One woke to it first thing each morning and heard it last thing when the night-shifts with their great acetylene flares took over. Clank, clank, clank, went the hammers. Chip, chip, chip, the chisels. Build, build, build, the bricks, as they were unloaded from the lorries and passed by human chains up to the scaffolding. Even Sundays were not free from this nuisance in the devastated town. And not even here in God's house. The work was going on behind a false screen erected to shut off the damaged end. The knocks and thuds came through the barricade like muffled ghostly echoes as the builders strove to repair the interior beauty of the noble edifice whose fair outline had been almost untouched.

Joseph was swept ruthlessly forward by gangs of schoolchildren and their teachers, caught in a swirl of chattering noisy brats being taken over the church. Trying to disentangle himself he pushed as relentlessly as they did, only to find himself one of a group of tourists being given information by a guide.

He did not hear one word of the man's monotonous talk; he was shaken again by the same violent emotion that he had felt for his workmates. He hated these people, *hated* them, unreasonably, violently and urgently. Breaking away from the goggling faces and the rubber-necked listeners he passed his hands over his wet face, then wiped it with his handkerchief.

He was in a chapel, quite alone. It was the lovely chapel of the Crucifix. He sat down blindly, then knelt, fixing his eyes on the head of Christ of the Gero cross, but to his dismay he could not pray. He was still shaken with this horrible, wicked emotion. Gradually the tumult began to die down. He felt curiously limp, almost as if he had been running or taking violent exercise. As he got up a man came into the chapel.

"They say that Crucifix is a thousand years old," he said to Joseph. "They say the date's on the back and it's nine hundred and something. Think of that, when everything new round here has gone up in dust."

Joseph said nothing, but he turned and looked again at the Gero cross.

"I've come a thousand miles to see it," said the man. He moved forward and fell on his knees before the carved figure, sublime in its sculptured suffering.

Out in the main aisle Joseph was caught up again in a stream of sightseers; they were making for the Treasury and he was pushed and shoved in their midst to the entrance where one paid a fee. He followed the party into a world of wealth and beauty of which he had never dreamed.

Wonderful objects which the devout had given as offerings for use in the church. Given to God. Golden caskets full of price-less jewels, caskets containing relics of the saints. From one to another the visitors hurried and pushed and craned as the guide pointed out each exquisite treasure. Crosses, chalices, rings; scep-tres set with gems of world-wide fame given by names renowned in history for the glory of God's house. Down in the vaults there was four times as much again, there was no place to show all the wealth, said the guide. Joseph hated the man for harping on the value of the objects. For just as he had realized the beauty of the chestnut trees, so he now awoke to the breath-taking beauty of these man-made objects. But what about storing up these treas-ures? Wasn't there a verse about not laying up treasures on earth where thieves could break in and steal? Hadn't Christ himself said that? How could the priests reconcile that with all this wealth? They *could*. They could explain everything. All those questions he used to ask the old priest when he had been a boy—they had all been explained. Or had they?

It was a long time since his mind had questioned anything. In the army one just didn't. A man was there to obey, promptly and blindly. Perhaps that was why he had accepted everything as it had come all these last years—ten years doing blindly what one was told was a long time. None of his lot had understood what they were fighting for. What they *did* understand was obedience. Stand, they said. Attention, they said, listen, they said, march, march, march—take cover—throw, throw, throw—fire, fire, fire—take cover, take cover and so on and on in country after country. They had killed and killed. Why? For what?

The sharp clang of the hammers on stone brought back the crack of rifles just as the heavy reverberating thuds of masonry being moved recalled vividly the guns and hand grenades. He hadn't been wounded, not once during those appalling campaigns, and not one of his family had been lost or injured in the continuous heavy raids on the town.

What was the guide saying about the enormous wealth of the cathedral? As he thrust away the thought about not laying up treasure, another and much uglier one took its place. Had all these priceless objects been lying here while people starved at the end of the war? What about "Sell all that thou hast and give to the poor"? Even as he considered this he heard the guide saying that the treasures had not been there. They had all been buried far away for safety, and the Allies had been very helpful about getting them all back to the cathedral. Not one object had been lost. Well, even if they had thought of selling them there would not have been any food to buy with the money.

And now the tour was ended, and again he was being hemmed in by the surge of tourists and children. He tried to say a prayer of apology for his lack of grace as he was carried by the sheer weight of the crowd to the door and pushed out into the hot sunshine.

The man who had spoken to him in the chapel was mopping his brow outside.

"Phew! What a crush!" he grumbled. "If I had known it would be like this I'd have got up very early and come before the crowds got in."

"It's only recently been opened again, on account of the bombing," said Joseph. "They say it's always like this now, except during services; it's quieter then."

He was still violently agitated. What was the matter with him? Was he ill? He stood uncertainly on the cathedral steps facing the station. The sun shone on the gay umbrellas of the terraced cafés at the side of the cathedral, on the flags fluttering from the station, on the scaffolding of the new buildings shooting up all over the ruined square, on the great flock of pigeons fluttering round the travellers at the busy station entrance. He had seen it all before. Seen it every day when he came in and out to the factory. Today it was as if he saw it all for the first time. But why? Why just today? Because he had a free one? But every year he got a whole free week. He was puzzled. I'm outside it all somehow, he decided. It's all exactly the same, only today I have just seen it as if for the first time.

He was hungry, and went and sat at a table outside a small cheap café off the square. He couldn't read the scrawled menu— his eyes were no longer as good as they had been, and spectacles cost money. When the waiter came he asked for the dish of the day. When it came he ate without tasting the food.

"Enjoy it?" asked the young lad who came to clear away. The restaurant was almost empty and he lingered to chat with Joseph, whom he knew by sight.

"Ever been in the Treasury in there?" asked Joseph, jerking his thumb in the direction of the cathedral as he picked his strong teeth.

"Ach! All that stuff! Makes me sick. I don't believe in having all that wealth lying idle. Why don't they sell some of it and use the money to help the rebuilding? What's the use of the treasure if the church falls down?" asked the lad contemptuously as he flicked the crumbs from the table and threw them to some pigeons.

"It's stood up for a thousand years although everything else has gone," Joseph said sourly. "Why should it fall down now?" He remembered Moe saying something similar recently and it had infuriated him. Yet he himself had just been thinking along the same lines.

"It's had a good shaking, that's why," said the lad, who was bending over trying to coax the pigeons nearer. Joseph hated him too now, and thought how satisfactory it would be to send him flying with a neat kick in the pants.

"Seen the Circus?" asked the waiter, straightening up suddenly to admire the legs of a young woman who was passing. "There's some grand trapeze artists, a lot of dwarfs—tiny little creatures—and a peach of a lion-tamer! She's a smasher!" He blew an imaginary kiss in the air. "Just my type—large, blonde and decorative!"

It was only two o'clock and Joseph didn't know what to do. *Why* didn't he go home? He thought longingly of the shady trees in the garden. He was already hot and tired from doing nothing. He was far more tired now than after ten hours of fitting nuts on to bolts. He felt a strong reluctance to go home—Moe was not expecting him. Was it fear of knowing for certain?

He would go to the Circus. He had enjoyed circuses with Moe and the children before. Today he could scarcely sit through the trapeze act; the performers could not grip him any more than the clowns could amuse him. He looked in astonishment at the people round him laughing immoderately. But when the lions came on he sat forward tense in his seat. The great cats excited him terrifically. Not the blonde over whom the waiter had raved. He wanted her silly head to be crushed when she put it between the huge jaws. A violent excitement assailed him at the sight. He wanted to hear their teeth crunch on her pretty simpering face. Bite her—bite her—crunch her face! he breathed, sweating with excitement at the hope of her being mauled.

When it was all over and the great cats were sitting docilely on their stands again, and she was bowing and acknowledging the applause, he was deeply ashamed. He, father of eleven children, had actually been praying that this woman, who had never harmed him, should be mauled, wanting her beauty disfigured and ruined. He was horrified. When everyone else had got up and crowded to the exits he sat on until an attendant told him sarcastically that if he wanted to see the show over again he would have to buy another ticket.

He went out and found his way behind the circus to the ground where the beasts were kept in their cages. The largest lion had sad yellow eyes. Joseph stood by its cage, fascinated by the almost human misery in them. He spoke softly to the creature in sympathy, and it rubbed its tawny head against the bars of the cage as if it understood.

"Get away there! Get away from those bars!" an attendant screamed at him, and in a moment he was being bundled off without ceremony. For a second Joseph thought of smashing the men's faces when they released him at the barrier. Then his hands fell to his sides.

"You might have been badly hurt," said one of them in a mollifying voice. He saw Joseph's fury.

"It liked me!" said Joseph angrily. "It liked me."

"Just hark at him!" jeered the second man. "Liked him—liked him! He'd like you all right, but inside, see? Why, that beast'd have your arm off in a second! Get out, now, get out!"

Joseph saw nothing of the square as he went wearily to the tram halt, nor did he hear the cathedral clock striking five. As he sank down in the stuffy tram, and waited for it to move off, he was blind to the shining river with the sunlight making long shadows from the brand new bridge. He did not see the newly-painted steamers waiting for the evening tourists, the busy barges chugging up and down the wide traffic way. He saw only a cage—the cage with the lion . . . then the wire cage in which he had been a prisoner. He had been just a number in that cage. He hadn't rushed frantically at the wire posts beating desperately at them in a frenzy as Peter and some of their companions had done. No, he had accepted confinement in the same sad apathetic way as that lion. Men and lions, caged, caged. In a cage, in a cage, in a cage, went the creaking wheels of the tram. Build, build, build . . . he could still hear the sickening thuds from the huge block being erected near the halt. In a cage, in a cage . . . he dozed off, he was tired. The conductor woke him roughly, asking for his ticket. Joseph dozed off again and did not wake until the tram reached the village where he lived with Moe and the children.

III

Krista ran quickly towards the factory gates, her heart beating wildly. Then she pulled herself up sharply. What was she running for? As if she were catching a train or being pursued! She stopped short and tried to get her breath as she came to the turnstile.

"Steady now," said the old timekeeper. "Anyone would think the devil himself is after you. There's no need to hurry for a young man—he can always wait!"

From his look and the wink he gave her she knew that he meant Paul. Would he be there? He would not. She would not look. But she found herself turning her head to that piece of wall against which he always leaned whilst waiting for her. He *was* there. Her heart turned such a somersault that when he called "Hello there" at the sight of her she could not say a word. She just stood there with her heart thudding in such beats that she could hear nothing else.

He took her arm and took her away from the crowd of hurrying girls and women. Her fellow employees turned, smiled and chattered, but not maliciously. They all knew him, or at least knew him by sight. He was Krista's American. Not that there was anything unusual in the fact. Hundreds of girls had American or British boy friends now. It was just that Krista was different. It seemed right somehow that she should have a foreign admirer. Lots of them thought that she was foreign herself. Her story had got out all over the factory. The girls considered it romantic and wonderful not to know one's age, name, or parentage. They made up all kinds of incredible stories about her. She might be anyone. She had "class". All were agreed on that. She wore her clothes differently, simple as they were, her head was poised proudly, her hands and feet were small, her ears and brows delicate. When they looked at the thick necks and ankles, the broad thighs and shoulders of her fellow employees, they felt that she was someone of another world. Her voice, light, warm, and full of tones, was something which was so much a part of her that few of them realized its charm. They only knew that they liked to talk to her and to hear her talk.

She spoke with a difference so subtle that they could not put it down to anything except an unusual accent. She was clever, too, and very quick in the extension classes which the perfume factory provided for those who wished to learn languages. The speed with which she was mastering English and French amazed them as well as her teacher. To them Krista was a romantic figure. Shy and gentle, she had that suggestion of helplessness and sweetness which drew out the best in all around her. They adored her, protected her, helped and petted her in a way which they never dreamed of doing to anyone else. She accepted it gratefully, always with a delighted surprise.

They had been watching this affair with the American. From a shy friendship from which she had hung back it appeared to be developing into something serious. He was a "steady," a regular boy friend. What would her foster-father say about it? His devotion to her was common knowledge. When she had first come to the factory he had brought her each morning on his way to work, and she had waited for him every evening. Now he no longer did that. And her foster-sister Anna came in and out too. She worked in a sweet-factory near by. All the girls knew Anna. Large, blonde and comfortable, she sometimes came during the lunch hour. The American had been hanging around several times a week since Krista had met him last February at the Carnival. He was tall, quiet, and very attractive. The girls were entranced with this romance blossoming under their eyes, but impatient that it never seemed to get any further. She never made any "dates" with him, it seemed, never went dancing or walking or on the river or to a cinema, as they did with their boy friends.

"Shall we go down on the tow-path?" Paul asked her now, squeezing her arm as he hurried her away. "Or what d'you say we go drink some coffee and eat somewhere?" He spoke German easily but with a marked accent. Krista was learning English at the factory class.

"Tow-path," she said decidedly. "I haven't long tonight, Paul; I've got to get back. Moe and Katie are both going out; it's my turn to put the boys to bed."

Paul was disappointed. "You're always in this hurry," he said. "Why can't you make a proper date with me like other girls do?"

She was stricken not only at the tone of his voice, but at the mention of other girls. Did he have other girls then? The idea suddenly hit her, but she said carefully, "It's because of father—I've told you, Paul."

"But your sisters, Anna and Katie—they do as they like, they get around places; why just this nonsense over you?"

"I've told you he's afraid for me. He always worries if I'm late home."

"But he can't keep you cooped up there all your life. How old are you?" he asked abruptly, and was immediately dismayed at the look on her face.

"I told you," she said quietly, "I don't know."

He could have kicked himself for his lack of perception in asking the question. She had an almost morbid reluctance to discuss the mystery of her parentage or origin.

"Forget it," he said quickly, drawing her closer to his side. "I'm sorry. Let's go right down to the water, shall we?"

"It's all right," she said, smiling suddenly. "It doesn't matter. I must be about eighteen. Pa found me on his birthday, the 31st of May. We always keep that as my birthday too. It'll be here soon. We reckon it as my eighteenth."

"But that's next week," he said excitedly. "Krista, we can't go on like this. I see nothing of you except for these few minutes after your work. Why can't you come down the river with me on your birthday? We could take one of these steamers to Königswinter or Godesberg and climb up the Drachenfels. Have you ever been up there? It's wonderful!"

They had gone down the steps to the water's edge and stood there looking at the river craft. The barges with the flags of many countries, the new pleasure steamers to which Paul was pointing, were fresh in their coats of paint and their gay striped awnings. The paddle steamers passing swiftly brought waves lapping at their feet on the steps, and from the pleasure boats came the drifting sound of lilting music, the chatter of voices, the clink of glasses, and laughter. It was hot. There was going to be a heat wave, the papers said, and the local urchins were already swimming from one moored barge to another, their shrill thin cries echoing across the water as they dared one another to fresh deeds of valour.

"Why can't you come?" he urged her, pulling her against his side, and turning her so that he could look into her face.

"It's difficult," she said flatly. "Oh, you know I want to come. . ." her voice trailed off. How could she tell him that she wanted it so much that it seemed the one thing in the world which mattered to her? She was shy as well as proud.

"What's he got against me? I'm not a thief or a criminal or even a liar. I'm just an honest guy—that's all. What's the matter with me?"

But she didn't want to talk about it. He saw that. She turned her face away and looked at the cathedral spires. In the soft evening light they were veiled in a rose-grey glow. Lights were already showing from some of the ships and flashing from the long new bridge over the Rhine. The blossoms from the heavily flowering lime-trees on the tow-path gave out a sweet heady perfume which mingled sharply with the smell of the water. Paul looked down from his height at the soft blurred outlines of her young face. The colour of her hair, her skin and her eyes seemed to melt into each other in this light. The eyes in sunlight were grey, and clear as a child's, the curve of her short upper lip and mouth still immature, but there was strength and determination in the small rounded chin.

He put both his hands on her shoulders and turned her face up to his. "*Are* you coming down the river with me on your birthday?"

"Yes," she said faintly. The river and the lights swung away into space as he kissed her.

"But it's wrong, it's wrong!" she said violently when he released her, and burst into bitter weeping. Paul was startled. He simply could not follow her. What was wrong? Why shouldn't he kiss her? What was the matter with that? He couldn't know that he was the first friend she had ever had. That he was the first person except for her foster-family with whom she had ever gone out. She tried to tell him this now. To him it was incredible. He couldn't take it in. To him she was so attractive that she must surely have had boy friends before. That she had never been kissed he had discovered very quickly. It had taken him weeks to overcome her refusal to allow him to touch her. What he could not grasp was that the easy boy-and-girl friendships in the States were something unknown to this girl. They appeared to be known to other German girls and boys—to her sisters certainly—but not to her. And it was all due to this wretched foster-father who kept her almost locked up.

"Well, in the factory then—there must be someone there. D'you mean to tell me that none of those young supervisors ever makes a pass at you?"

The burning colour which flooded her face was his answer. There was one apparently who made himself a nuisance. "Just let me get my fists on him. I'll teach him to make passes," he said furiously.

"I'd lose my job then, and I love my work at the factory."

"Well, he'd better take care. You keep away from him."

"I do," she said laughing. "Oh, don't let's waste time talking of *him*. What about this river trip? It'll have to be on Saturday. Oh, here's Anna coming."

She pulled herself away from Paul's arms as Anna's large solid figure approached them.

"I must go now."

"But you *will* come on your birthday?" He still held one of her hands firmly.

"It'll have to be Saturday. I can't come on Sunday—it's Pa's birthday too. I must be home for that. We always have a tremendous celebration, and this year Pa will be fifty. It's a special one!"

"O.K. I'll fetch you from the factory?"

"At one o'clock."

Anna, the eldest of the family now at home, came up smilingly to them. If she did not find Krista at the tram terminus she would walk along the tow-path to the next halt. She knew Krista was often there. She looked at the two of them. That she had intruded into their private world she could see. But Pa would be mad if Krista wasn't home on time. Anna loved Krista, and for this alone Paul liked her. She greeted them warmly, taking in the younger girl's flushed cheeks and shining eyes.

"I am trying to persuade Krista to spend her birthday with me," said Paul. "Can't you help me, Anna?"

"But I *am* coming," protested Krista. "I've promised."

Anna looked anxious. "Not on the Sunday?"

"No, the Saturday," said Krista quickly.

"That'll be all right then." Anna was obviously relieved. "The birthday's actually Monday, but of course we'll all be working then, so we are keeping it on Sunday. Pa would never stand for her being away on his birthday."

"But it's Krista's birthday too!"

"I wouldn't want to miss being at home for Pa's," said Krista quickly.

"And don't tell him you are going out with Paul on Saturday," advised Anna.

"Oh, I *must*." There was positiveness in Krista's voice.

"No—if you tell him you won't get there." Anna was firm. "Tell him you're working overtime, or that you're coming out with me to some friends."

"Yes . . ." Krista was doubtful. "But Anna, I can't. I've never lied to Pa. Somehow I just couldn't."

"Silly," teased Anna. "Life's so complicated that small fibs are a part of it."

"I can't," said Krista. "If he asks I'll tell him."

"Don't be a little fool." Anna was rough but affectionate. "If he asks I'll tell the lie myself. You keep quiet. He's not really interested in anything lately—haven't you noticed it?"

"Yes." Krista's voice was troubled.

"Well, that's O.K. then," said Paul. "I'll fetch you at one o'clock. We'll go and eat some place and I'll bring Bob's car to pick you up."

Krista still looked doubtful. Anna laughed. "Come on", she said, taking Krista's arm, "you'd better get home. You're doing the boys tonight, aren't you?"

"Aren't you coming too?"

"Only as far as the next halt—I'm meeting Eric there."

They wandered up the steps again and reached the halt on the main road. Here the two girls said good-bye.

Paul stood looking after the tram as it rumbled and creaked away from him. What was it about this girl? He just didn't know, couldn't put his finger on it. She wasn't really beautiful in the accepted way. When his friend Bob had asked him what she was like he had said slowly, "She's not so much to look at—I mean she's no Marilyn Monroe or Jane Russell. She's small and soft, and there aren't all those curves, but I like the way she looks. I guess it's just that. The way she looks at me—that's it."

Bob had been intrigued and had wanted to see for himself. When he waited for Krista one evening with Paul he saw what his friend meant. When Krista had come hurrying out in her jersey and skirt and bare legs, looking shy and startled at this friend of Paul's, he understood. She had *something*, as they said. Something indefinable but terribly attractive. In her loose jersey her slim childish figure had more charm than the flaunted curves of the average young woman. Bob had been very attracted himself.

"I'll tell you what it is about her," he said shrewdly, "she's still got the threshold look, and that's something we don't meet so often. Most of them have crossed it. That's her pull on you, Paul."

And yet she lived with that terrible foster-family who were said to be completely going to pieces because of the mother. He thought of his meeting with her. He had seen the mother at the Carnival. Dressed in a cowboy's dress with a wide-brimmed hat and riding breeches which set off her fine hips, she had looked incredibly young with her brilliant colouring and laughing eyes. She had been hanging on the arm of a sleek, dark young man she called Rudi. This was the young man who was said to be causing all the trouble. He had seen the sister Katie. Now there was a bad one, thought Paul. That flaming hair, that white, white skin, the wide mouth—like her mother's—and the bold black eyes. But she could be a beauty. If she knew how to dress and slim down a little. But she wasn't like Krista. There was something hard, cold and calculating in her smile of invitation. He remembered vividly that scene on the Rosenmontag in the decorated streets of Cologne. Krista had been standing there with the woman they called Moe. She had looked like some small wild field flower blown there accidentally. She had looked terrified when the wine-filled revellers had snatched at her in passing.

He had met the father—the man she called Pa. He had liked him. But *he* hadn't liked Paul. That had been obvious. He resented him. Whether because of the girl or because of the Occupation Paul didn't know. Both perhaps. It was all damned difficult; but the fact remained that just to spend twenty minutes with this girl he would, and *did*, wangle himself leave whenever he could. Bob was good about that. He was always willing to change duty times, lend his car, so that Paul could drive the twenty kilometres or so to the factory.

"You've certainly got it bad this time," he had said; "and for keeps if I know anything."

Paul went now and sat moodily in a café and thought what was the best plan to get around Joseph. His time in Germany was getting short. He wanted something settled about Krista before he left. Something about Joseph attracted him. He was a quiet thoughtful-looking man with a puzzled unhappy face. He seemed to Paul to have known better days, and to be well informed on things about which one would expect him to know nothing. After all, in a country recovering from the upheaval and devastation of war one could never tell. The man could have been anything.

Paul had taken Krista home after the Carnival. It was late and she was dead tired. But although Joseph had thanked him for looking after her and bringing her home, he had seemed annoyed that she had not stayed with Moe. Krista had said nothing about the young man who consorted with her foster-mother. Paul had been received politely but coldly by Joseph, and he had neither been asked to stay then, nor to come again.

When, almost a month later, he had been driving near the factory, he had gone in and inquired for her. He knew only her Christian name—that was the rule of the Carnival. She had introduced Joseph simply as "father," so that Paul did not even know her foster-parents' surname. He did not know then that they *were* foster-parents. He had been astonished at the size of the great house in which the family lived. Krista had quickly explained that it was not theirs, but one which had been requisitioned for homeless people who had lost their own homes in the bombing of the town.

He knew that she worked in the great perfume factory, and he had found it without difficulty. The old doorkeeper had laughed when he had asked if there was a girl working there called Krista. He said that there were over a thousand girls employed in the perfume and cosmetics halls, and how should he know all their names? But when Paul described her, he had smiled and said it must be their "mystery girl"; and he had told him the story of Krista's being found unconscious by Joseph on the night of a terrible air raid on Cologne. He felt sure that Paul meant *that* one, he said. When the girls came hurrying out after the six o'clock hooters sounded Paul had scanned each face anxiously; but when she *did* come, he knew long before she reached him, recognized her immediately by her quick light step and the poise of her head on her slim neck. She was not like anyone else. She was quite different. That was it. At the carnival she had been wearing some kind of fancy flower-girl costume. It had suited her admirably and he had been agreeably surprised when she had told him that the woman called Moe had chosen it for her. Now she wore a grey jersey and skirt, and she seemed to him infinitely more attractive in these simple clothes as she came running out. When she saw him her grey eyes lit up immediately in unmistakable pleasure. She was exactly as he had remembered her.

"She's got something—she's not like the others," the old doorkeeper had said. He reckoned it was the result of her terrible experiences in the war. In his opinion she was a girl probably brought to Germany with her parents who were doing forced labour for the Nazis. She did not look German, he said—everyone was agreed on that.

Paul reflected on this now as he sat in the café. If she had no memory whatsoever of any life before that night of the air raid, then whatever she had suffered before that could not have affected her. He realized now that part of her attraction for him could be this mystery about her, but he had known nothing of it when he first met her. It had been a month before he had been able to look for her again because he had been sent away unexpectedly on Frontier duty. Since then all he had seen of her were these stolen minutes by the river. She was always terrified of being late home. The others—Anna, for instance—did not seem to care whether their father was angry or not. Nor did the one they called Katie. No, it was only Krista, and she was frightened of her foster-father. That first evening when he had waited for her outside the factory she had gone with him to a cafe. She had been late home then, and Joseph had been upset. Since then every time he saw her it was the same story. She must get home—she could not stay—Pa would be worried. There was this one thought in her mind—not to be late home.

Paul was an orphan himself, and the story of Krista's being found by Joseph and never identified moved him very strongly. He had been brought up in a large State orphanage in the Middle West. He had worked from the time he left there until the recent death of an uncle had left him with money for the first time in his life.

As he left the café and walked back to the town to meet Bob, he thought of the night when Joseph had found and carried the child Krista through the blazing square to the shelter under the cathedral. His first impression of Joseph had been correct. He was all right. He *must* be to have taken this unknown child into his already overcrowded family. No one had offered the boy Paul a home, although his parentage was known, and his father and mother a respectable young couple who had been killed in a car accident. He had grown up in the loneliness of a large orphanage, and yet there were relatives who could have taken him in. That uncle, for instance, who had died leaving Paul his money. Why hadn't he given his sister's child a home? That would surely have been better than saving the money and perhaps salving an uneasy conscience by leaving it to the boy at his death? That Krista was unusually devoted to her foster-father Paul realized. What he did not yet appreciate was Joseph's almost unnatural love for Krista.

IV

As HE TRUDGED, hot and tired, up the road from the station to the village, Joseph saw its ugliness. The hideous little station itself, with its heaps of slag and brickets wept over by three smutty willows. The tiresome barrier across the level-crossing, the silly face of the grinning clock, then the stark grey slate houses each side of the grey cobbled street, the post office, the miserable little grocer's and baker's and the tobacconist's. He noticed them all. Surely this was the ugliest village on the banks of a river famed for its beauty. Everything was smutty and dirty from the fine layer of coal from the great bricket factories. Even in winter the snow was grey a few minutes after it had fallen.

The fields were rapidly being lost as more and more commercial enterprise sprang up in the great post-war drive for prosperity. As he walked he could hear the eternal clang, clang, clang, of the workmen repairing the war-shattered suspension bridge, and hear their whistles and shouts from the floating raft on which they worked. There had not been a bridge left in the country at the end of the war. Those which the retreating armies had not blown up the advancing ones had shattered. Build, build, build; there was no getting away from it, it was everywhere one went, and yet a man could not get a home for his family. They were not building homes but factories, shops, cinemas, bridges and banks. If a man wanted accommodation for more than two he must provide it himself. The refugees were crowding in from the East, and living-space was strictly rationed to so many square metres per person. Just as in the prison camps each man had been supposed to have a bare minimum of space.

There came to him suddenly as he trudged, a vision of the Bavarian village where he had been born. The little church perched on the summit with its onion dome, the cool placid mountains behind, and the sweet smelling pines and the tender green of the grass. Strange that he should think of this now. In the thick of the war he had thought of the cathedral with its spires as if it were his home. And now as he passed the narrow eyeless houses he thought of the friendly whitewashed cottages in one of which his childhood had been spent. He saw his father, a strict man who ruled them with the stick, sitting toiling away playing the church organ, saw again the skis and skates he mended for the visitors in winter.

He hated the dirt of this river village. As he turned into the one and only pleasant lane, lined with weeping willows, he could see the large house which the local housing authorities had requisitioned from the absent owner. Here he had lived with Moe and the children ever since they had been forced to leave the bunker under the cathedral. There had been nowhere large enough to accommodate his family in the town. Eleven children, and Krista whom he had adopted made twelve, and now Katie's brat Peppi. Fifteen people to house!

The owner of the property was in prison for war crimes; but his wife came frequently and made terrible scenes about the condition of her property. Moe would shout at her and she would shout back, and finally someone from the housing office would have to be fetched to ask the woman to go away. Moe did not care in the least—she rather enjoyed a battle. She had not asked to be put in this great house, she said; she had just been sent here; but Joseph felt a deep shame whenever the woman came and wept because her husband was being kept in prison by the Occupation and her home had been taken away from her.

He knew that the property was deteriorating under the abuse of his unruly brood of boys, and at times he would insist that it be tidied up and cleared and swept, but, as Moe pointed out to the owner's wife, there were other tenants upstairs. Why should their family be blamed for everything? She knew that her family were hated and distrusted by the village, that they were called the "bunker" family in derision of their having lived for so long in one. Their neighbours looked upon them with the same contempt as they did upon the miserable refugees flooding the place now, and regarded them as foreigners just because they came from the town. Moe did not care in the least, but Joseph had always minded this hostile feeling. He was a friendly man at heart, and liked to be on good terms with his mates, although he was clumsy at showing his good will.

Everything his family did was criticized and commented on by the families upstairs. The house had two bathrooms, and running water in the bedrooms: but even so things had been so unpleasant with the families from the East on the two upper floors that another kitchen had been installed upstairs. Since then there had been peace. Peace at least as far as the cooking was concerned.

As Joseph approached the house it looked peaceful enough, if untidy, in the late afternoon sun. He knew that he was envied by many for the spaciousness of his temporary quarters but after all, the house built by the owner for his own family now housed thirty-seven people! Whereas the house next door, almost as large, was occupied by a British family who had only one child. What could they want with all those rooms? And, what was worse, the child was away in England at school, so there were really only two people for the whole house.

He noticed the acacia tree with the same start of surprise as he had the chestnut tree. It was as if a skin had been peeled from his eyes, giving him the clear vision of a child. The dog whimpering on its short chain barked a greeting to him, and thinking of the lion still, he went over and set him free. He ran round in circles with joy, and Joseph noticed with anger several weals on his back as if he had been recently beaten. In one of the front flower-beds his son Franz Joseph and Katie's son Peppi were making mud pies in the place in which he had recently planted young wallflowers. He raised his hand to smack the boy, then let it fall again to his side. What did it matter about the wallflowers? The whole place was in a mess. The child knew he was doing wrong, and hastily began trying to smooth back the tumbled earth round the up-rooted plants. His impish face was dabbed with mud.

Joseph went into the house. It was deadly quiet. No sign of Katie or of Moe. He looked into the sitting-room, then into the horribly littered kitchen, then into the bedroom he shared with Moe. Outside the small slip room which she had given the lodger he heard a sound . . . then Moe's giggle . . . and then the deep chuckle of the lodger himself. He rattled the door loudly. It was locked. Heaving his weight against it he forced the loose latch and burst into the room.

They had thought it was one of the boys trying to tease them by rattling the door. Moe had called out telling whoever it was to go away. As he burst open the door they lay there in the tumbled bed, Moe, his wife, and Rudi, the lodger, looking astonished at the sight of him. Astounded, not embarrassed—that was what infuriated Joseph. For a split second he stood staring at them.

"Why, Joseph! What's brought you home so early? Is anything wrong?" faltered Moe.

"Get out!" he said quietly; then, as she did not move but just stared open-mouthed, he shouted, "Get out of that bed!" and as she stumblingly obeyed at the violence in his voice he saw that she was naked.

She fell on her knees before him, terrified at the fury in his face. "Joseph, Joseph!" she cried.

For answer he spat full at her white body, beautiful still, in spite of so much child-bearing.

"Slut! Slut! Filthy slut!" he spat at her, and went out of the room, slamming the broken door behind him without a glance or word for the man cowering in the bed.

He shook so much that he could scarcely control the movements of his body. He had suspected this for some time, imagined somehow that she lay with the lodger, a man almost young enough to be her son. That was why she had brought him back from the Carnival last February. Why then did the actual proof of his fears move him to such violent emotion? Was it anger, disgust, or sheer contempt which shook him so? He didn't know. His stomach heaved, and with difficulty he kept himself from retching. He went outside to the yard and put his dry mouth under the tap there, and as he did so he trod on the heaps of potato peelings.

"Pigs! Pigs!" he muttered, leaning against the fence; then, as he heard movements in the passage inside the house, he went blindly out of the gate, ignoring the cries of Franz Joseph to come and see how he'd tidied the flower-bed. He turned back towards the hideous station at which he had so recently arrived, passed over the level-crossing, and went down the ugly street to the beer garden by the river.

V

WHEN THE TRAM started Anna said to Krista, "He's in love with you all right. What about you?"

Krista said miserably, "What's the good? Pa will never hear of it."

"What's it got to do with Pa? It's *your* life—yours and Paul's."

"I can't go against Pa's wishes," Krista said positively and flatly.

"Then you're a fool!" Anna's voice was contemptuous. "Make the most of your chances. No one is going to help you if you won't help yourself. I tell you, Krista, something will have to be done about Moe. The children are beginning to notice. She's quite shameless. I'm not standing for the little ones knowing what's going on. They know far too much as it is."

"But what can we do?" Krista asked unhappily.

"Speak to Pa. He seems to be blind. Everyone knows except him."

"No! no! Please don't, Anna. He's so unhappy lately. There's something on his mind."

"Maybe it's Moe. Maybe he *does* know. It's time he took notice."

"I don't think it's that. It's much deeper. He seems to be so terribly depressed and apathetic about everything. Have you noticed how he doesn't bother about grumbling at the boys any more—he never makes them clear up everything as he used to? He never teaches us new songs or trains us in part-singing any more."

"Pa doesn't like me." Anna said it as a matter of fact without the slightest resentment. "He's never really got over Gabrielle."

Krista said nothing, but she pressed Anna's hand. Anna had been in love with a young Englishman. There had been a baby, but Gabrielle had died.

"Anna," asked Krista, after a few minutes' silence. "Did you love him?"

"Yes," said Anna quietly. Her dark eyes misted over. "I loved him, and he'd have married me if Pa hadn't made such a fuss."

"Did he, George, I mean, know about Gabrielle?"

Anna shook her head. "I never told him. There wasn't much chance. Pa sent him about his business too quickly."

"But why did Pa dislike him so much? I liked him—we all did."

"Because he was one of the Occupation, but chiefly because he was a soldier, I think."

"Then don't you see how hopeless it is for me and Paul?"

"*Don't* tell him. That's my advice. Look where it landed me." Krista looked even more miserable. Anna was impatient.

"Haven't you got any will of your own?" she asked sharply. "Don't you want to get out of this mess here? D'you want to live for ever in such a way? You're pretty—more than pretty—you must know that. Take your chance while you've got it. That American's a fine man. He'll marry you if you play your cards properly. Don't be a fool like I was."

Anna's words, although meant kindly, threw Krista into greater confusion. Did Paul really want to marry her? He had never said so. True, there hadn't been much time for talking seriously. There was always this awful rush to get home before Pa got back. She was longing to talk to Anna. There were a lot of things she wanted to ask, but she was too shy, and Anna was already getting up to leave the tram.

"Well, bye-bye then. . . ." Anna was gone, waving gaily to her. Krista could see Eric waiting for her. He was fat—not tall and handsome like Paul—but he was a good steady man. Anna was taking no chances this time. She meant to be married.

Robert and Franz Joseph were hanging over the level-crossing barrier as Krista stepped out of the tram. Their chins were resting on the wood. She called anxiously to them to get off before the gate swung back. The fascination which trains and trams had for them was so strong that the man who worked the crossing was sick of chasing them off. Robert, usually a very obedient child, was deaf where trains and trams were concerned.

"You're late, very late," he said reproachfully as Franz Joseph seized Krista's hand and began dragging her up the road. "Franz Joseph and me met three trains and two trams—you weren't on any of them."

"Because I was on this one," she said laughing. She saw from them that something was wrong. Robert had a sensitive little face. He was quite unlike Moe's other sons. He was the only one with blue eyes. The only one who was what his brothers called "soft." He had been born after the end of the war, and was now nine years old. Joseph loved this rather frail-looking son better than all his other strapping ones. But Robert was not one of Moe's favourites. She had no use for weakness, or for book-learning as she called it. A man should do a man's job, she said, not sit about with clean hands. Her sons had all been sent out to work at thirteen when they left school. The old schoolmaster had pleaded for Hank and the twins to stay on. They were intelligent, he said. But Moe was adamant and overruled Joseph. Robert, at nine, was showing such unusual promise that Joseph had resolved to enlist the aid of Father Lange in the matter. He wanted at least one of his sons to have a chance to better himself.

As the boys tugged her up the dusty road Krista heard scraps of what had taken place earlier in the evening. It had only just happened, according to Robert about an hour ago. But one never knew with children—time was nothing to them. It was only just beginning to mean something to Krista. Since she had met Paul. She questioned Robert sharply, and he looked aggrieved at her tone. Krista was never cross, never impatient. That she was in an agony of apprehension he couldn't know. Apparently Pa had come home very early. Moe had been with Rudi.

"In the little room, with the door locked," Franz Joseph had added. Pa had broken in the door, which was loose anyhow, Robert had said with the detail which children love, and there was no lock on the door now, it had fallen off and the door was splintered. Moe was very angry and was raging round the house in a terrible temper. She had struck Robert and Franz Joseph. They were upset at the injustice of it. They hadn't done anything wrong at all. Moe had hit them as she passed, just for nothing.

Where was Pa? Krista asked this as she began to hasten her steps. She must get home quickly.

"He's gone out. First he was furious—shouting—then he said nothing—not even good-bye," said Robert, and began to cry. Robert adored his father.

"It's very bad of Pa to break the door," said Franz Joseph. "If I break something he's very angry. He was angry because Peppi and I were playing mud pies in the wallflower-bed, but when I tidied it all up and put the plants back in the soil he didn't even look! He just went out of the gate!"

"And Moe was furious with Katie," sobbed Robert. "She said it was all *her* fault. That she should have been 'on guard.' Oh, Krista, why didn't you come home? It would have been all right if you'd been here."

And she had been with Paul. She was late because she had stayed talking to Paul. Being kissed by Paul. She was overwhelmed now with remorse, just as an hour ago she had been overwhelmed with a terrifying feeling that she was walking on air—that there was no reality in the world, in familiar objects, that there were only she and Paul and the wonder of just that. Just as her feeling for him was a sweet terror because she wanted to run away at the same moment as she wanted his kisses, so now the knowledge that she must get home and find out the worst conflicted with the temptation to turn round and escape it all. She tried to calm and comfort the two little boys, and soon they were chattering of something else.

She was thinking of Pa. It was for him that she feared. She loved him with complete devotion. Was it because of him that she felt this terrible guilt every time she met Paul? Or was it just that Pa didn't approve of the friendship? For she *did* feel guilty. Was it the feeling itself which made her guilty? Was this sweet terrifying weakness which Paul caused in her wrong? She had wanted to ask Anna, but she had been too shy. They were always talking and giggling and telling smutty stories at the factory. And at home Moe and Katie did the same. Anna was not interested. She just said nothing. They never talked like that when Pa was home. He had always been strict about such things. The boys had had to mind and obey him. When he had come home and found the yard untidy and littered with potato-peelings and their toys all over the place he was mad. They'd had to clean everything up. The yard had been swept and tidied, the steps washed down, and the toys and bicycles put away. Pa was very particular. Every boy had to scrub his hands and his face before meals. Pa had inspected the row of hands held out to him, had looked at the neck and ears of each boy, pulling up his hair and raising his chin to see that nothing had been scamped. He had insisted that every member of the family sit down at table for meals, whether it was round the kitchen one, or out in the garden under the acacia. How good and orderly he had been. He had tried to keep these great boys under control. *Had*. But lately it had been different. Hank had control. Pa had lost it somehow, had lost his strength and energy. He didn't seem to care any more. And now this. *This* was something which Krista knew had been thrust away at the back of her mind for some time now. But it had been in the forefront of

Anna's. She had spoken of it tonight. "We shall have to do something about Moe," she had said. Something about Moe! Well, it was done now. It was too late.

What had happened with Hank and Joseph lately? There was a terrible tension between them. Was it because Pa would insist on taking money from their wages every Friday? Hank resented that. He had protested violently. It was ridiculous to think of building this house of which their father dreamed, he said. It would cost so much money that they could never save it. It was a dream, and there was no place for dreams in the world, said Hank. Moe thought the same and backed him up. There had been some terrible arguments. But Pa always got the money out of them in the end. They must have a place of their own, he insisted.

"Haven't you brought us any sweets?" Franz Joseph's voice broke in on her thoughts. She found some in her pocket. They could buy them cheaply in the factory canteen, and the little ones looked forward to them.

"Hurry, *do*," she entreated as they lagged behind to share out the toffees in the tree-lined lane. How sad the willows looked in spite of the sun, their tender green trailing down limply in the dust. The street was dirty and littered with paper from the factory at the corner where cardboard boxes were now manufactured.

Katie stood at the broken gate, knitting. Her face was sulky, and her hard black eyes had a gleam of secret joy in them. She looked with distaste at Krista's slim figure as she came in with the two little boys hanging heavily on her arms. They wouldn't dare hang on *her* arms like that. Krista was soft and they knew it.

"Go on in. Moe wants you," she said, jerking her head in the direction of the sitting-room, rarely used except on Sundays. Her voice was ominous. Krista was going to get into trouble. Katie was delighted. She had had just about enough of Moe. Let Krista get some for a change.

In the prim room with the heavy lace curtains—the only room boasting such a refinement—and the red velvet tablecloth, and the photographs of Grandma and Grandpa on the walls, Moe sat smoking. Her face was dark and set.

"You're late again—and on the one day you should have been home. You knew I wanted you early tonight!" she greeted the girl harshly. "You'll have heard from the boys—your Pa came home

too *early* and now you're *late*. Where've you been?" She looked
curiously at Krista's flushed face and at a new quality in it.

At the censure in the angry voice Krista began to stammer, as
she sometimes did when she was frightened.

"Paul . . . he came to the factory . . . you know . . . the American friend at the Carnival . . . I . . . I . . . I. . . ." She broke off at
something in Moe's face.

"So that's it! Our little saint is human after all. So you've got
yourself a young man, have you? Katie said so. I didn't believe her!
Just wait and see what Pa'll have to say to that. Did those brats tell
you what's just happened? Don't look so disgusted. If you've got
a young man you'll soon know what it means! Oh yes, *you!* You,
with your child's body that's beginning to change and your white
neck with your head so high! You're the sort that men like all
right. Make no mistake about that, my pure Miss! Just you wait,
you'll know what it's like to be tormented—and my God, you'll
get it bad when you do!" And she burst into fits of laughter in
which there was hysteria, and the next minute was sobbing.

Horror froze Krista into immobility again. She was shocked,
not only that Moe was saying these things or that she was trying
to excuse her own shame, but that what she said brought home
to her the very thing of which she had been thinking. She wanted to comfort Moe, to put her arms round her as she did round
the children when they were unhappy. She tried to bring herself
to do so, but all she could do was to whisper, "Don't Moe, please,
please, please."

Moe's insinuations had brought a wave of real nausea, and
a new fear of this "thing" of which they were forever talking.
This was the thing which had produced Peppi for Katie, which
had made Lisa get married so hurriedly three years ago, which
had made Anna so unhappy and which now tied Moe to a man
young enough to be her son. She had tried to close her mind to
its significance—deliberately not understood all those references
and stories—but there was no getting away from it. It got you in
the end. Paul! Was this what he wanted from her? The thought
was terrifying. Was this why she felt guilty? She thought of the
exquisite snatched moments by the river. The scent of the limes
and the strange smell of the water would be for her forever mixed
with that first agonizing happiness. No! No! She could not bear
that this frail loveliness should be shattered by Moe's horrible

words. Scarcely knowing what she was doing, she turned and fled from the room, saying that she would go and look for Pa. She did not hear Moe's strident jibe that Joseph could come back for *her*, Krista; that he'd always had a hankering after the saints.

She ran out of the house, past Katie still staring over the road at the Frenchman's house and down the path to the village as if pursued by devils. Her heart was hammering again, her ears ringing—not with that last taunt, but with those other words of Moe's. "Your child's body that's beginning to change . . . your child's body that's beginning to change . . . you are the sort that men like all right . . . you . . ." Behind her she heard running footsteps, but she did not turn. Over the level crossing and down the ugly cobbled street she ran, and across the waste land to the river. Villagers looked after her in astonishment as she ran with her hair flying in a cloud. Her whole being was in a confusion so great that she scarcely knew what she was doing or why she was running. The white misery of her face shocked them. They hurried one to another to say that there was fresh trouble in the Bunker family again, and to speculate as to what had made the usually happy and serene Krista into an almost demented fugitive.

Behind her, stumbling to keep up with her swift feet, and breathing in great tearing gasps, ran the little boy Robert. "Krista . . . Krista . . . wait . . . wait . . ."

Some of the villagers tried to check him and find out what was the matter. They disliked Robert less than any of the other boys in the family. But he would not stop and, brushing them off, went pounding on until his arms were caught by a strong pair of hands, and the keen eyes of Father Lange regarded him as he panted and coughed in the priest's firm hold.

"Steady! Steady! Why are you running after Krista like this? Don't you see that she doesn't want you just now? If she did she would wait for you. Now then, what's the trouble, Robert? Come along and tell me."

The priest had just passed the beer garden and had seen Joseph sitting there drinking. He wasn't drinking beer, either, but spirits, which he couldn't take. Father Lange had allowed Krista to run past him with blind eyes. He knew where she would go—to the river. Later she would go to the church. He was not worried about Krista.

The bunker family were a source of endless trouble to both Father Lange and the schoolmaster. No matter what was wrong, whose hens were stolen, whose windows broken, bells rung, or flowers and vegetables picked, the crime was invariably laid at the door of the bunkers. Interest in the doings and misdeeds of this large family sometimes reached fever heat in the village, and it was usually the priest who calmed the angered villagers.

The family were loathed with a vicious undeserved hatred, all except the girl Krista. Her strange story was known to them all. Here she was looked on as a wonder—almost as a saint. Pitied and admired by neighbours who thought that her fate in being adopted by such a family was a tragedy, the priest himself knew that Krista was happy. She loved her family, was devoted to them. The villagers would not have believed him had he said so. How could they believe it when they had made up their minds that the whole family were bad?

Father Lange was used to all this and more. He merely smiled. Sometimes he checked them sharply for their uncharitableness— the bunker family themselves knew far more about charity than they did, he would tell them. Now he saw that there was fresh trouble he remembered something which the schoolmaster had mentioned to him. What was it? That the boy, Robert, had something on his mind. Something which was taking his attention off his lessons. Usually his show pupil, Robert had recently been coming to school looking like a ghost, with great dark circles round his eyes and a mind which wandered all the time. Remembering this, and looking at the child's obvious distress, the priest decided to see what comfort in the form of ice cream would produce.

"What about sitting down and cooling off," he said, still holding the boy's arms. "It's terribly hot—let's go and see what our friend the baker can find us in his ice-machine," and he took the still panting child into the baker's shop.

V I

KATIE OPENED her window very cautiously—Anna slept heavily, but she had a maddening habit of waking when least wanted to—and swung herself down on to the grass. She closed the window to within an inch of the sill and crept round the silent house to the glass sun-room built on at the side, in which Hank, Karl and the twins now slept. She tapped on the glass three times. A window opened and Hank's head appeared. He was a powerful lad of eighteen, with a coarse brutal face and his mother's bold black eyes.

"The old man asleep?" he asked.

Katie nodded. Joseph had had to be dragged, pushed and shoved home after Krista had found him drunk in the beer garden. She had come running in a frenzy, begging them to come and help her get him home. Joseph was a heavy man, heavier still when drunk, and it had taken the entire family all their strength to steer him through the village street.

On rousing from his drunken stupor he had become fighting mad. Hank had hit him unmercifully. Pa was always like this after spirits. If he stuck to beer he was just sad. Normally a gentle man, when intoxicated from schnapps he became violent. Hans and Heinz had held his arms whilst the others, Moe included, had literally pushed him step by step, roaring and shouting, to the house.

The village had looked on in shocked silence. Joseph had been known to drink before, but only on permissible occasions, such as the Carnival, skittle contests, wine festivals and birthdays, when everyone was permitted to be as merry as he liked. This was just an ordinary week-day. He was shouting for Rudi and threatening to break his neck, unaware that one of those shoving and supporting him from behind was the lodger himself.

At the garden gate he had completely collapsed and they had carried him in like a corpse by his feet and head. Moe had removed his coat and his boots and he had fallen at once into an uneasy sleep. Rudi had been concerned.

"Poor devil, poor devil," he kept repeating, looking down at the unconscious Joseph. He was a pallid young man who wanted no trouble, and his lack of courage irritated Moe suddenly.

"Oh, shut up," she had snapped. "What's done is done."

Rudi had gone off to his night shift and said that it would be safer if he didn't return. Moe remarked calmly that she would arrange other accommodation for him, that everything would blow over. Rudi wasn't to worry.

She had chased the family to bed and lain down in her usual place beside Joseph. She saw no reason to do otherwise. Anna and Katie had seemed astonished.

"What's he got to grumble at?" she had said to them fiercely. "He's never been deprived of his rights. He's here at night and Rudi's here in the day, so what?"

The girls had offered no comment. Krista had already been despatched to get the little ones to sleep. They had all been out at the gate in their night-shirts watching for Pa.

All of this had been less than two hours ago. It had been an unexpected nuisance, and Katie listened anxiously at the door of her parents' room before daring to creep round the house.

"They're both asleep," she assured Hank.

"It's a bit risky, but we can't change our plans. If we had a telephone, now . . ."

"Don't be a fool—are we going or not?"

Hank went and opened the door of the sun-parlour. It had been a kind of conservatory, and Moe still used it for her plants. They were on the shelves all round, mixed up with the boys' belongings. When she watered her geraniums she thought nothing of watering their most treasured possessions; and if they would not get up when the alarm clock went off in the morning, she would use the watering-can remorselessly to fetch them out of bed. Hank hated the place. It was always damp, too light, too cold in the winter and too hot in the summer. Being made entirely of glass, there was no privacy at all—one felt forever on show. He resented more than anything having been pushed out of his small slip room for the lodger.

He listened. "Moe's restless. I can hear her turning in bed. Blast her and that wretched gigolo." He swore viciously. "Of course we're going. We can't let Leo down. He'll be in the lane any moment now. Here's the meat for the dog."

"Doped?"

"Of course," he answered impatiently.

"Last time you put too much stuff on it—the brute slept till late afternoon and Moe was suspicious. That brat Robert kept telling her the beast was ill."

"All right, don't keep on about it. Alfred must have made the stuff too strong. A good thing if he had never woken again—it's dangerous getting past him going in and out. Pa *will* have him tied so close to the house."

"He always hears Leo's machine, no matter how far away he stops the engine."

They listened, holding their breath. The house was dead quiet except for the deep regular snoring of Joseph. The twins, awake, demanded eagerly to be let in on the job. Hank was impatient to be off. "Don't wake Karl! I've told you, not this time," he snarled. "Leo has to test you out first. This is no child's play, it's the real thing."

He was aware that his two brothers were rapidly becoming a menace to him. Had it not been for Moe and her blasted lodger they would never have found out about the gang. When Hank had slept in the small slip room it had been simple enough to creep in and out of the window. She had made him turn out for her lover. Well, now that was over, or at least it looked like it. Tomorrow he would move back to the small room.

He had been counting the notes which he had to hide under a loose board in the summer-house floor when the twins, who had trailed him there at dawn one day, had come upon him. He had beaten them up mercilessly to make them swear secrecy. Now he made use of them. They had to keep guard for him and Katie. They had to whistle the "all clear" for them to return. Later he intended to make more use of their physical strength.

They watched him now pulling on his black jersey with its hood that almost covered his face, his black tight trousers, rubber-soled shoes and black woollen gloves. All the gang wore these dark garments when on a "prowl" as they called it. They watched him pick up his bicycle chain wrapped tightly in a woollen stocking and twist it round his waist and place his jack-knife in his pocket. The twins watched him in admiration. They feared his brute strength and his cruel mind, but they admired and envied his courage and daring.

Leaping lightly down from the window he hissed, "Close it, you b—s, and mind you don't keep me waiting when I come back. Only one of you is to sleep—the other must watch."

When their brother and sister had gone, the twins looked at each other. They listened for the sound of the motor cycle and presently it came, faint but unmistakable.

"Hans," said Heinz, when they had drawn lots as to who should sleep first, "he's bloody strong, but do you realize that we two together are stronger?"

Hans nodded. The same thought had just occurred to him. Hank was either too stupid or had forgotten that the link between these identical twins was so powerful that their reactions were simultaneous. Had they but united against him that night in the summer-house they would have defeated him.

Katie was at the gate waiting for her brother. A dark cloak with a hood was wrapped round the flashy dress Leo had given her as her share of the last job. Her legs were now in nylons and her hair tied back with a ribbon. The lids of her eyes were smeared with green stuff, her lashes stiff with mascara in an overpowdered face. Her mouth was a scarlet gash. She looked at least twenty-five.

"Fixed the dog?" muttered Hank.

She nodded. "He's all right. Getting used to the stuff. He didn't stir, just ate it without getting up."

"If he makes any noise when we return he's getting the bicycle chain," swore Hank. "Where's Leo?"

"Hist! Step back in the shadow," whispered Katie as a large car swept round the corner and came to a halt at the next door gate. A light was burning in the porch of the Englishwoman's house as she and the Englishman let themselves in with a latchkey. The car, driven by a chauffeur, turned, its headlights sweeping on to the boy and girl crouching in the hedge. The driver stopped and shouted, "Hi, you love birds, choose a safer place. I almost ran you down." He backed the car and returned up the road. The lights in the upper stories of the house came on, but the one in the porch was not extinguished.

Hank cursed the house and its occupants. Houses of the Occupation kept the porch lights on all night. He and his friends made quite a bit removing the bulbs and selling them.

The sound of an approaching motor cycle was apparent; then the engine was switched off and the machine coasted down the slight slope and came to a standstill at the end of the tree-shadowed lane.

A slight cry, like that of a nightjar, came from the motor-cyclist and was answered by a similar one from Hank. They waited in silence for a minute, then crept up the lane, and both mounted the pillion of the motor cycle. Katie was wedged between the two lads, her cloak tucked round her legs, and the hood, like those of her brother and Leo, pulled down almost over her face.

The motor cycle stopped before a bomb-shattered derelict shelter marked "dangerous" on the river bank, and was pulled up on to the tow-path in the shadow of the trees. The rest of the gang were already waiting for their leader inside.

The lad Leo, as powerful as Hank, but slimly built with the coiled strength of a panther, saluted the waiting members of his gang with a curious gesture made before the face with the right hand. They responded, one by one, with a similar gesture; then at his signal, all sat down on the floor on old car cushions piled against the one sound wall of the place. The entrance facing the river had been completely shattered, and was closed up with boards of wood. Each member of the gang raised these boards and squeezing past, replaced them after entry. There was no light; the moon streaming in from the shattered roof lit up the young faces grouped round their leader.

"All set?" he asked softly, after he had given them some detailed instructions. "Everything clear?" His voice was unpleasant, with an undertone of menace, and the clear green blue eyes in the clean sun-tanned skin were hard and merciless in spite of the mobile and pleasant mouth. "We'll just go over it again. You, number one," indicating Hank, "will go with three and four to the house. Approach it from the back—the side door of the sun-veranda is your point of entry. Cut the shutter slats with these———" He handed them a small sharp saw and a knife. "Then the glass with this," showing a round stone wrapped in a chamois leather. "The key is inside the door—the old fool of a woman always leaves it there. Put your hand through the hole you've made and open the door. Pass the carpets and rugs out to numbers three and four, who will find the car waiting at the tradesmen's entrance. The silver is upstairs in the front bedroom, the first door on your right when you've reached the landing. Wrap the silver in the rugs and bring all the pictures from the downstairs and landings. Some of them are good. We don't know which. Bring them all. Get all the clothes from the woman's and man's wardrobes, and all trinkets. Replace the shutters after you've finished, and keep your gloves on all the time. Numbers two and seven will keep guard at the back entrance. I'll take watch on the front one and the main road. Numbers two and three will load the stuff into the car and then come with me to the landing stage. The others will disperse separately, and assemble here later on. O.K.?"

There was a murmur of assent and Leo got up. "I'll get the car. Number five, you'd better come with me. It looks less suspicious to see a man with a girl at this hour of the night."

Katie got up and followed Leo out. On the opposite side of the road was an all-night garage. The hand on duty was one of the gang. He indicated a saloon car standing by the petrol pump. Leo took the proffered keys.

"Don't be too long," warned the garage lad. "My shift ends at five, and the car must be back an hour before that so I can clean it."

Katie climbed in beside Leo and they drove over to the shelter. There was not a soul about and the others piled in the back of the car, some of them on the floor. Katie was shivering with such intense excitement that she could scarcely breathe—not only from the thought of what they were about to do, and not from fear of what they risked if caught. It was the proximity of Leo which caused her shivering.

He turned suddenly and looked at her with dislike. "Pull your hood over your face," he snapped, "that blasted hair of yours will get us all copped yet."

She shrank at the tone of his voice and obediently pulled down the hood.

An hour later the car drove down to a small landing stage further up the river. An old barge with the Dutch flag was moored there in the shadow of the thick trees. At three hoots from the car horn two men appeared on the plank they used as a gangway. The rolled carpets full of loot were carried down the path and stowed on board in a cabin. The elder of the two men was a foreigner. He nodded approval when all the stuff was safely on board.

"All right, boys. Well done. We'll have this sorted out and got rid of—you'll get your share on our return trip, same as usual. We'll be back some time next week. Same time, same place? We'll send word by the usual method. O.K.?"

Leo and Hank assented. They would get the message at the ship-repairing yard. It would be passed in code under name of some repair needed. They didn't really like having to trust these men to pay out their correct share of the sale, but they had no choice. The loot had to be disposed of safely, and not in this town. The river was the obvious answer. They had met these men while doing their repairs, and so far it had worked very well. Tonight was their fifth transaction. Last time, for instance, they had been especially lucky, and all the gang were to be richer for the proceeds of the sale of jewellery they had unexpectedly found in the house of the new millionaire baron who had made, like hundreds of others, a fortune out of others' shortages and necessities. Hank and Leo felt no scruples at stealing. Their companions at the yard were constantly telling them that the money was just as much theirs as his. Homeless from a very early age, living for years in the company of similarly placed people of all types, the children had thieved and scrounged whenever they had been hungry—and that had been almost always.

The papers lately had been full of the great fortunes amassed so quickly by those profiting from the new prosperity. Hank had listened to Leo's views on the subject. He did not question these men's methods of acquiring fortunes; he envied them and was determined to imitate them by any means in his power. He wanted money—Hank wanted money—they all wanted it. Money meant power to buy what they liked, do what they liked, go where they liked. "Get rich quick"—that was the motto all around them now. Well, they could do the same; they *were* doing it. Already they had, every one of them, been able to buy some of the things for which they had been craving.

The proceeds from the sale of the jewellery were to be paid out to the gang tonight. Leo went into the cabin and returned later with his pockets stuffed with notes. The younger of the two men on the barge was looking appreciatively at Katie's hair and painted mouth.

"Coming on board for a little swig? I've got some good Bols."

"No," barked Leo, following his look, "we've got to get the car back by four."

"Pity," said the man, winking at Katie. "I'd have liked it. Good journey back, then . . . and until next time."

Leo and Katie took the car back to the garage after dropping the others at the hide-out. Then they joined the gang assembled there.

Now that the job was successfully ended, Leo pulled Katie openly to him in the shelter. His hands caressed her in the darkness as they leaned against the rotten wall.

"You did damn well," he whispered. The admiration of the other man, his open attempt to attract her, had increased Leo's desire again.

Hank produced some schnapps which they had found in the house they had just robbed, and in glasses also plundered they all solemnly drank, choking over the unpleasant raw spirit and pretending they liked it as much as their leader obviously did. "Only one," he snarled, as Hank reached a second time for the bottle, "this stuff'll give you away quicker than anything when you're not used to it. It's dangerous."

He filled his own glass again, then, going outside, hurled the bottle and its contents into the river.

"Fool," said Hank sulkily, "that's dangerous too." He was beginning to like the stuff—it gave him a hell of a kick.

Leo began counting out the money. They received their share more or less equally, with the exception of Hank who, as number two in the gang, got almost as much as the leader.

"Well, you've all got your share," finished Leo sharply, when the notes had all been distributed, "and now get out—all of you. Remember, keep your mouths shut. Take care where you keep the money—understand?"

All assented. "Then get out," he snapped, his eyes on Katie. A ray of moonlight streaming through the damaged roof caught her white face. The brilliant hair was dark now in the shadow, her eyes large and mysterious. Gone were the rather spiteful lines of her sharp face. She was almost beautiful.

"We'll meet as usual next week, you'll get your signal in the usual way—see?"

They filed out, each making the secret sign of the gang as they left. Hank did not move.

"You heard me? Get out!"

"Where to?" demanded Hank nastily. "Go on—get on with it . . . that's nothing new to me. I'll keep guard at the entrance for you."

"Don't smoke," snapped Leo, "you'll give the place away. Go over to the garage and wait for us there."

"No fear!" retorted Hank. "And get noticed hanging around the place at this hour of the night? No, I'm waiting here . . . with my back to you, of course."

"Hist!" warned Leo. "Someone's coming!"

The stolid steps of a boatman came down the path, followed by a drift of cigar-smoke. The moon was suddenly hidden in a pile of cloud. There was complete silence.

"O.K. He's gone. Go ahead. You've got exactly fifteen minutes."

He stood with his back to the couple on the dirty floor of the shelter, wishing that he had enough money in his hoard under the summer-house floor to buy a motor cycle of his own. Then he would no longer be dependent on Leo for transport. He had already learned all about Leo's machine. Engines presented no difficulty to Hank. They responded to his touch as to a magnet. His great hands were deft with machinery. He knew that at the shipyard he was highly prized, in spite of his youth, because of this. He began calculating his money, and working out just how many more weeks must pass before the pile of bank-notes under the summer-house floor would buy him a motor cycle.

V I I

JOSEPH AWOKE to Moe's shakings. She was standing over him in her cotton wrapper, her hair a loose mass, her face shining from its daily scrubbing with cold water. She had flung open the shutters admitting the merciless light.

"It's after six! Get up, get up!" she was shouting.

He sat up and pushed a hand over his stiff face. His whole body ached and hurt as if he had been beaten. His mouth was dry and vile. In the middle of his forehead a gong was striking with each breath he drew.

He looked resentfully at his wife's freshness and energy, and distaste of her deceptive cleanliness swept over him. He glanced at the place beside him in the bed—still warm from her body—and knew that she must have slept beside him as usual. He *hated* her, hated her sly black eyes and that vicious hair.

"Marry a woman with blue eyes and hair that is either very dark or very fair," his mother had told him and his brothers. "None of the in-between colours are to be trusted."

He put one foot to the ground and the floor rose up to hit him. He reeled back on the bed. "I'm sick," he moaned.

"You've got a hangover," she said brutally. "A nice spectacle you made of yourself all through the village last night—it took a regiment to drag you home."

She fetched a cloth and cold water and bathed his forehead, and then held out a cup of strong coffee to him. "Here, drink this black—it's the real stuff, not ersatz; it'll do you good," she coaxed. He wanted to strike the cup out of her hand, but he began to retch and heaved himself off the bed and lurched over to the basin.

He put his head under the tap and let the cold water trickle over his forehead. A set of clean clothes lay on a chair. There was no sign of the ones he had worn yesterday. Moe stood looking at him as he strove to get control of his stomach.

"Get out!" he said.

He couldn't remember anything of the previous evening except for that picture of Moe and Rudi. There was a vague recollection of Krista . . . her anxious face through the mists of alcohol and of Father Lange pleading with him to stop drinking, but of getting home or of how he'd got home he hadn't the faintest idea. What he *did* remember was the cause of the drinking, that damn lodger! That sleek dark Rudi whom she'd brought home from the Carnival last February.

"Where is he?" he shouted suddenly, lifting his face from the water. "Where is he?"

She didn't pretend not to understand him.

"At work!" she said flatly. "Work has to go on . . . for him, for you and for me."

"Come here!" he said roughly. The habit of obedience to the male was still strong in her. She went over. He put his wet hands round her full thick throat and her eyes flickered before his. Then as a fresh fit of retching seized him he released her and leaned again over the basin. She watched him dispassionately, a little smile on her face as she stroked her bruised neck. She had seen Hank do just the same to the girls' necks. Well, now she knew where he got it from.

"Better hurry," was all she said, "you'll miss the tram."

She heard his lumbering movements as he put on the clean clothes—the sudden thud as he slipped once. She brought fresh coffee. "Drink this—the other was wasted."

He got the hot fluid down somehow, then sat down on the bed and pulled on his boots. His face was grey but she saw that already he was regaining control of his stomach and head. The second hooter sounded from the great factory where the twins worked.

"Half past six!" she said, and at the same minute the alarm in Hank's and the twins' room went off and there were sounds of their getting up.

Joseph picked up his cap, brought in by Franz Joseph from the garden where it had fallen last night. It had rained, and the cap was soaking wet.

"If *he's* here when I get back tonight I'll break his neck—and yours too!" he said as he reached the door.

Moe shrugged her shoulders and went to get Katie out of bed. She lay on her back dead asleep with her wide mouth open. Her mother leaned over and examined her face curiously. She noticed the green stuff on her eyelids—the mascara which had run down one cheek, the lipstick still on the mouth and the faint red smears on the pillow. Peppi was not in the bed with her, he was with Krista again, she supposed. Katie must have been out again last night, that was evident from the frock flung over the chair and the make-up still on her unwashed face.

Moe's face expressed her distaste. She was fastidious about washing. She washed everything in the house regularly, there were always at least three lines of clothes out each day; and she washed her own body just as thoroughly. All the boys were scrubbed in the bath by Joseph at least once a week with a hard brush, and no less vigorously than the clothes. Moe would throw refuse or potato peelings cheerfully on the ground and leave others to deal with it, but where personal hygiene was concerned she had definite standards.

She flung the covering off the sleeping girl. "Get up, you lazy good-for-nothing!" she screamed, and as Katie opened dazed and sleep-logged eyes, "and wash that stuff off your dirty face! You've been out all night again! If you bring any more brats here you'll be out on your backside, make no mistake about that."

She went over to the bed in which Anna slept and shook her roughly. "Time to get up!" she said, more kindly. "Hurry now."

Katie, who had been in bed only two hours and a half, pulled the bed-covers up and lay back again.

"I'm not getting up yet," she said sullenly. "Let them get their own breakfast."

"You'll get up and fast!" shouted Moe, pulling the clothes off again and heaving Katie out by her shoulders. "If you choose to work all night that's your own business, but you're not going to get out of your work here. Come on now, *out!*"

"You can talk," grumbled Katie mutinously; "look at what *you've* done!"

Moe folded her lips tightly.

"Shut up!" she said tersely. "I don't want any remarks from you. Get up and be about your business—and see that your face is washed or I'll clean it for you."

She slammed out. Anna, already half-dressed, stood yawning before the open window pulling her jersey over her head. Her good-natured round face was rosy with sleep, her dark slate eyes darting curiously from her sister to the crumpled dress on the chair.

"Have a good time last night?"

"Yes," muttered Katie, "but I'm dead beat. I'm absolutely done in!"

Anna was brushing her hair. All the family had the same thick strong hair as their mother. Anna's was of a beautiful pale straw colour.

"Like to cut in with our gang?" suggested Katie as she stood in her slip. Anna noticed that her sister had not even removed her under-things but had slept in them. She was lucky indeed Moe had not started on that.

"No thanks. I earn all I need at the factory," said Anna, swinging the hairbrush vigorously. "I don't want anything to do with it. Your jobs are too dangerous for me."

"We're on to something new. We can use some good lookers like you!" Katie purposely flattered Anna, but Anna was not to be drawn.

"No thanks, Katie. Talking of good lookers, Krista's going to be the beauty of the family. You should just see how the men in the trams are beginning to eye her."

"Krista!" Katie spat the name contemptuously. "Father's little angel! Did you hear how he kept babbling about her when he was drunk last night?"

"No," said Anna comfortably, "I was too busy looking after your Peppi and Franz Joseph. Krista's all right, she's a good kid. You're only too glad to dump your Peppi on her night after night; and she does it willingly."

"*You* should talk! You're the lucky one. *Your* brat died."

"Shut up! Shut up!" said Anna fiercely. "I wanted mine . . . I loved Gabrielle . . ." her voice broke off. "Don't mention her again or I won't do another thing for Peppi."

"Hurry up, you girls," screamed Moe. "Am I to do *all* the blasted work this morning?"

"Where's the sainted Krista?" retorted Katie. "Isn't she helping?"

"I'm here—in the kitchen!" Krista was standing at the table cutting up long loaves. She had already been down the street to the baker's to fetch them. The boys were supposed to do this, but they were never up in time, and it was usually Anna or Krista who went. Beside her were a dozen mugs waiting for warm milk or cocoa and she was keeping an eye on Peppi and Franz Joseph who were quarrelling violently over some bricks on the floor.

Moe, entering suddenly from chivvying the boys, sent both children flying with a sweep of her strong arm and planked Franz Joseph outside the door where he promptly set up a loud bawling.

"That Katie, she should be doing this, she doesn't earn her keep, the lazy bitch. D'you know where she goes at night?"

"No," said Krista, her eyes on the pile of bread which was not yet high enough. There had to be sandwiches for Pa and Hank as well as for Anna. Krista's factory had a canteen at which the girls ate at tables with lavender cloths and flowers on each one.

"You had her brat last night; didn't she tell you where she was going?"

"No, Moe, she didn't."

"Does she give you anything for looking after Peppi?"

Krista said in astonishment, "But Katie has no money, Moe. She has no chance to earn any."

Moe laughed unpleasantly. "She's getting money from somewhere. Haven't you noticed all her new bits of finery?"

As Krista said nothing she went on: "She goes with that young Leo from the repair yard down the river. I've known it for some time." She did not add that she had been afraid to reprimand Katie or to tell Joseph in case Katie told Joseph about Rudi. Well, now it didn't matter. Joseph knew. There would be no more fear either of her or Hank. They'd get an earful from her now.

Hank came stumbling into the room at that moment. His eyes were bloodshot and heavy, his hair rough and his clothes pulled on anyhow. He needed a shave, his dark hair grew quickly. Moe didn't mind about that. Joseph sometimes omitted to shave in the winter mornings, as did many workmen.

Hank slumped down at the table and snatched a round of bread, plastered it with jam and shouted:

"Coffee. I want coffee this morning."

"Maybe you do, but you're getting cocoa," said Moe calmly.

Hank looked up, astonished. "I want coffee," he asserted loudly, "and it's coffee I'm getting. You take enough money from us."

"You get coffee only on Sundays and in the evenings, you know that."

"I get coffee when I want it," shouted Hank, thumping on the table and upsetting the mugs of milk poured ready for the children. "You made coffee this morning. I smelt it."

"That was for Pa—he had a hangover."

"Well, I want some too. *My* head is swimming."

The two pairs of bold hard eyes stared at each other. Then Moe went and fetched the coffee-pot.

"I could do with some myself," she sniggered to ease the tension. She had just made the discovery that she was afraid of Hank. Afraid of her own son. And just as she had decided that she need have no more fear in future because Joseph knew.

"You've made a damned lot of trouble for us," said Hank coldly, "and if Pa goes on drinking we'll have the police come nosing round here. That won't suit me at all, d'you hear? You tell Rudi to watch his step, and you watch yours."

She stared at him in amazement. How dared he talk like this. He was getting impossible. He wanted to rule the house.

"Hank!" she said sharply. "Don't you talk to me in that way! What is it you're doing that makes you so afraid of the police? Where d'you go at nights? Katie's dead beat this morning. I've kept quiet all this time because of . . ." she faltered.

"Rudi! And now the old man knows, is that it? Well, if you think that makes any difference you'd better think again. It's *too late*, see? I'm in pretty deep, see? And so is your precious Katie, and what's more I'll drag the whole of your brood in with me if you as much as open your mouth to Pa. Give me the coffee."

He swallowed it noisily and went without knocking into the room where Katie and Anna slept. Katie, still in her slip, was attempting to do her hair.

"You little fool! Look at your face. You'll give us all away! Come here!" He dragged her by her red hair out of the room and, half dressed as she was, pulled her under the tap in the yard. Still holding her, and regardless of her screams, he held her neck so that her face came under the full stream of cold water. He scrubbed her face viciously.

Her screams brought the upstairs people to the windows and the children all running out in various stages of dressing. They thought it wonderful fun; none of them liked Katie, she was mean and sharp. Moe stood leaning against the doorway still in her wrapper and watched unprotestingly. She would have liked to have done the same thing to Katie herself, but had not the energy or courage this morning. Hank had taken his father's place during the war years and had chastised his younger brothers and sisters. Willi had been older, but he was like Joseph, gentle and against the use of the stick. Hank had seldom been without some weapon with which to keep the children quiet in the bunker. Had he not succeeded, they would have been turned out long before they actually were.

Moe looked on now unperturbed while he spouted water down Katie's bare neck and arms.

Krista came out and put a restraining hand on him.

"Hank, please let her go . . . please . . . look at her clothes . . . please . . ."

Moe caught sight of all the refugees gaping out of their windows.

"That's enough, Hank!" she said sharply. "Let her go and come and finish your breakfast. You'll all be late this morning."

Hank released Katie with a violent movement which sent her spinning across the yard. She picked herself up, soaked, her streaming hair hanging down her face red from scrubbing, her slip and legs dripping with water.

"You'll pay for this, Hank," she screamed. "I'll tell Leo. He'll take it out on you for this," and flinging away from them all she rushed back into the house with Moe's roars of laughter and Hank's rough guffaws ringing in her ears.

"Oh, dear, she looked so funny! So funny, with all that stuff running in streaks down her red face!" gasped Moe as she resumed her own cup of coffee.

There were tears in Krista's eyes as she began putting the sandwiches in the lunch tins. The twins had come out to witness their sister's discomfiture, and now still giggling, were trying to swallow their milk quickly. Anna, dressed and looking placidly unperturbed, said quietly, "One of these days you'll over-reach yourself, Hank . . . Katie's not a person to trifle with." She picked up her shoulder satchel, into which she put her sandwiches.

"Coming, Krista? You've eaten nothing again. Bring a piece of bread to eat in the tram. Here, I'll take it for you. Come on now, Katie can finish the other sandwiches—she's done nothing. We must be off!"

Krista picked up Peppi who was clinging to her legs, and kissed him and Franz Joseph. Robert was already at the gate.

"Come home quickly, Krista," he begged; "I don't feel safe when you're away."

"Silly," she teased. "There's nothing to be afraid of. Hank's away all day, and you're going to school." But as she turned to wave at the little face looking anxiously after her at the gate she knew that she was very afraid herself. Afraid of what? Of Hank? Of his arm-twisting, his bending back of one's fingers, his pressing down on one's neck or nose? She suffered it all herself as each child was the object of his attentions, even if her own body had never been touched by him. She was used to that. That was an old fear. No, it was a new fear, a much worse one which was assailing Robert as well as herself. The fear of what had happened last night. Even Karl, a stolid stupid child, was uneasy. Franz Joseph was fractious today instead of his usual impish mischievous self. Peppi howled miserably, and Robert was a bundle of nerves.

She smothered the fear. There was always something to be pushed away until one had to face it. Sometimes when she actually *did* face it she found that it was no longer there.

Anna was calling to her that the tram was coming and that if she didn't hurry the barrier would come down and she would miss it. They travelled together every day to the town. Anna in her chocolate factory didn't get out until later than Krista. She had longer hours and it was harder work than Krista's.

Krista felt ill. Her inside kept rising and having to be thrust down again. She had not slept. After they had got Pa to bed she had had to soothe the children and then done as Katie had asked, and taken Peppi's sleeping form from her bed into her own, but even with the warmth of his little body pressed against her own shivering one she had lain awake.

She had heard Katie slip out, then the suddenly hushed barking of Lumpi, then the faint throb of a motor cycle. Hours later the same sounds heralded their return. What did they do? Where did they go? She knew instinctively that it could not be for any good purpose that they crept out in the night and returned with the dawn.

The clanging bell of the approaching tram and the shrill warning from the level-crossing barrier hurried her to a run and she was panting as she caught Anna up; together they dashed through the barrier just as it was coming down.

"Here's your bread!" said Anna. "Come on, eat it. You'll feel bad at work on an empty stomach."

Krista took the bread but she couldn't swallow it. Her face was paler than usual this morning and her eyes were heavy. Her heart almost burst with anxiety for Pa and with shame for Moe. But Moe didn't seem to care, that was what was so awful. She just behaved as usual this morning, as if nothing had happened yesterday, as if Pa had never broken open that door on her nakedness and shame. What would happen? What would happen to them all? She began to cry.

"Krista, Krista, everyone's looking at you! Try to stop, *do*!" Anna's bulky form pushed itself in front of the weeping girl. Anna was rough and lazy, and in some ways stupid, but she loved Krista. There was something she admired in her. She couldn't have said what it was, but she knew it was something she would never have herself, any more than Katie or Lise would. In the strangest way she wanted to protect the girl as she did the children. She could not look on unmoved while they were hurt.

She stood stolidly in front of her while Krista with a great effort of will controlled her sobbing then, when a passenger got out she took the place beside her.

"Don't go on like that," she said roughly; "they're not worth it, can't you see? The only thing for us to do is to get away. You must marry, Krista, and get away. That's what I want to do. There's no more fun and games for me. Gabrielle taught me that. I'm going straight. That's why I won't have anything to do with their night prowling. I mean to get away from here. There's someone interested in me just as that young American is interested in you, Krista." Her voice trailed off as she greeted an acquaintance who had got on to the tram. She saw with relief that Krista's composure had returned. Her face was calmer and although tear-stains were visible there was no disfiguration of her pale beauty.

But Krista dared not let herself think. If she did she would weep again. Last night her anguish and horror had been so great that she had run to her favourite place by the river, a little bay with sand by the breakwater, where in summer they bathed and the children paddled. Amongst the tall reeds she had lain and wept and wept. Her child's world had been shattered and in that one evening she had grown into a woman.

Marriage . . . marriage . . . marriage. Anna was talking again about marriage. You must marry and get away . . . there's somebody interested in *me* just as that young American is interested in *you*. . . . Paul? Was that what he wanted from her—marriage? Or the thing which Rudi and Moe had been surprised in? Her fingers closed again on her rosary as Anna began to chat with her friend. "Our Father," she began, "which art in Heaven, hallowed be Thy Name . . ." *Thy* Name! But *her* name? What was her name? She didn't know. Suddenly it seemed to her terribly important that she know her name, although all her life with the family who had adopted her had been one long fear lest she be taken away from them. She had been terrified that her memory would come back and that she would be claimed. For she loved them. That was it. She loved them all. They were *her* family. She didn't want to go away from them, she didn't want to be married, she had no one else but them.

"Here we are," said Anna briskly, jumping up as the tram approached the great railway bridge where she had walked with Paul only last evening. "And you haven't touched the bread. Give it to me if you don't want it. I can always do with some more. Bye-bye for now, Krista. Don't worry, it'll all blow over . . . like it always does."

She followed Anna from the tram, her face drawn and serious and began walking quickly in the direction of the perfume factory. On the way one of the young supervisors caught her up. Most of them had been women when Krista had first gone there to work but gradually they were being replaced by men. This one was in the department where the finest face cream had to be hand-mixed.

His glance went slowly over her. "Getting tired of the cream-mixing?" The hand-mixing department was not popular. It was too messy.

"No," she replied quietly, "it's all in the work."

"I can get you shifted if you say the word." He looked at her slim bare legs as he spoke.

"It's all the same to me. I'll be shifted anyhow next week. I'll have done my month there, thank you."

"As you will," he said sourly. It was true then what the other young supervisor had told him when he had mentioned Krista. That the girl might be a smasher to look at but she was dumb from the neck upwards, that was what he had said. He looked at the bent neck over which the colour was flooding, at the soft curling hair and the grace of the young body.

She had something. There was no doubt about that. Well, they said that those who looked so innocent were the worst. He didn't agree about this one. She was just dumb! Why, there was not another girl in the department who'd have missed an opening such as he'd given her. He felt affronted, and walked ahead of her through the check-gates and into the factory without a word.

VIII

THE RIVER divided the village, the bridge had been destroyed in the war; but there was a ferry over to the other side. A path through some waste land led from the main village street to the towpath. Seven poplars stood in a line along the water's edge and beyond them lay the church. To the right the tow-path wandered through some still lovely wooded country to a wide bend where the ship-repairing yard loomed up stark yet beautiful with its cranes, masts and tall chimneys. There were always numbers of vessels in for repair.

The little area round the church was a haven amongst the noise and smuts of the side where the factories flourished. The church itself, large, severe and whitewashed inside and out had a big squat dome and a small spire with a weathercock on it. Round its walls were indifferently depicted the Fourteen Stations of the Cross. Behind the altar was a fresco which was far older than the wall paintings. It represented two angels with wings spread, holding aloft two sprays of lilies over the infant Jesus. The colours were fading, but the painting had quality. The angels, as Robert said, resembled Krista. She might have been the model for one of them, the other could have been her twin sister. The windows were of plain but very old glass. The priest's house was next to the church, the old disused graveyard of which went almost down to the water's edge. Beyond that was the convent; where the nuns ran a kindergarten for very young children.

If one wanted peace it could be found further down the tow-path towards the repair station. Beyond the sandy bay beloved of bathers and children, and the little breakwater always occupied by fishermen, a path led off the main one up into thick woodland. Here the silver birch trees met the thick undergrowth of willow weeds and made a screen from all passers-by. One could lie in the willow weeds amongst the cow parsley and the meadowsweet, the blue chicory and the marguerites, and still see the river and the tow-path but not be seen oneself.

Joseph came out of the church, his mind in a turmoil again. It was Friday evening and he had been to see Father Lange. The priest had urged him to forgive Moe her infidelity, indeed had insisted on it. Why should he? Because he himself hoped for forgiveness, said the priest. But why? Moe was nothing but a disgusting whore who had been fouling her own nest. Why then had he come here, asked the priest—to justify his own attitude? Was Joseph himself so much above reproach? Had he never committed adultery himself, asked Father Lange remorselessly. When Joseph had mumbled that during the war when he'd been abroad there'd been some women, of course, but that was different, the priest had said sternly, in what way different? Adultery was adultery, there were no degrees in it.

Joseph thought that there were. There had been some excuse for him because he had been away from his wife. Moe had no possible excuse. She had been committing adultery and at the same time living with him, her husband. It was filthy, vile and revolting. He couldn't forgive her.

Had she given up her lover? asked Father Lange; and Joseph had been obliged to tell him that he had threatened to break her neck if she didn't. Father Lange had himself interviewed Moe. He did not tell Joseph this, or that Moe had given him no such promise. She had not been to Mass for a very long time now. Gone were the days when the entire family had walked behind her every Sunday morning, even little Peppi and Franz Joseph. Now she never came; Hank had told the priest that he no longer believed in religion. Joseph came intermittently, as today, for instance. Krista and Anna brought the younger children without fail. Lately the twins had been absent from the party. Krista had told him that they refused to come because their brother Hank had told them that religion was all rubbish, no one believed that stuff in the modern world.

The village was buzzing with the story of the terrible scene when Joseph had surprised his wife with the lodger. The upstairs tenants of the house had heard everything and had embroidered and spread the story. What about the children? Father Lange had asked. Didn't Joseph realize his responsibility to them? If Moe had failed in hers, then it was all the more urgent that Joseph should take control. The first step was to find out where his own fault lay.

Joseph was furious. He left the church without making his confession. His mind was still filled with hatred of his wife. The past few days had been black, both at work and at home. He had not suffered the taunts and jibes of his mates who were astonished and affronted by his surliness. He usually took a great interest in the midday discussions on politics. The men invariably got on to this when eating their food. The elections were due in the near future and feelings were running high. Would the Federal Chancellor get in again? Joseph was anxious that he should, but many of the men wanted a change. They wanted a man who had been under no influence from the Allies. Notwithstanding the admission that the present Chancellor was putting the country on its feet again there was amongst the workmen a feeling that they should have a man who had never taken part in a Puppet Government. Joseph was known to be a staunch supporter of the

Chancellor. Now, when asked by his mates for his opinion, he would answer sullenly that he had nothing to say.

At home he had scarcely spoken at all, except to order the boys, half-heartedly, about their evening duties when he arrived home to find the usual appalling muddle and mess in the yard and house. Moe, once so proud of her spacious home after the squalor of the bunker for so many years, seemed to be getting more and more indifferent. When any of the children tried to placate him and make him talk he snapped roughly at them. As for Moe, he didn't know if she were still seeing that unspeakable young man because he had not addressed one word to her since that morning after he had been drunk. He had told her then that she could sleep in future in the room she had given her lover. He did not want her in his. What was the use of Father Lange saying that unless he forgave her he himself could not hope for forgiveness? There was no comparison between his own small lapses and her cold calculated infidelity. She had brought the young man home after the Carnival as a lodger in spite of Joseph's protests that they were already too large a family and were not allowed lodgers in a requisitioned house. She had brought him and installed him there with one purpose, and one only. His being on night work had made it so easy.

Joseph could not get over this, or the fact that the lodger was only a few years older than their eldest son, Willi. It was revolting and unforgiveable, yet the priest said that he must love her. He must cast out hate from his heart and replace it with love; until then no one could help him.

Turning from the church, he stumbled along the tow-path. His head ached, his back ached. He felt for the first time in his life that he was old. Soon he would be fifty—half a century, said the boys admiringly. Pa had lived for half a century! He was ten years older than Moe. He had married her when she was a slip of a girl like Krista. A spitfire, a wild, slim gay thing who had enchanted him. Why had she grown as she was now?

Krista would celebrate her birthday with his. He had found her on his fortieth birthday, lying on a pile of charred bodies, that night when the town was ablaze. Ten years ago. The family had planned all kinds of celebrations for the joint festivity. He was revolted at the irony of it. There was to be an excursion down the river ending up with fireworks and a sing-song in the garden afterwards. He would tell them tonight that he wouldn't go. He would go to the hospital and visit Carola. Sunday was visiting day, he knew. He would go there alone, or perhaps with Krista and Robert. He couldn't bear the proximity of any of the others, they looked too much like Moe. Carola didn't, nor did Robert. It was then that the thought about Robert struck him. The boy was completely unlike all the others. He was small, slim and his bones were delicate. He had blue eyes and an oval pointed face. All the others were like their mother. Robert had been born the year the war had ended. Some months after. If Moe was unfaithful now, hadn't she assuredly been so then, when he was away for so long?

He turned off the path in his agony of mind and sat down in the thick lush grass where the bank sloped down to a curtain of willows. The boats were already showing lights, their colours reflected in the swift water. The floating raft used for repairing the bridge was alight with twinkling lamps although it was barely dusk. He watched the vessels passing, the ones upstream with a slow painful progress, the ones down, rapid and easy. One should always go down, he thought. If one went against the stream, the currents one encountered were like those of this great river. At work, for instance, it was the same. Do as the others did and you were all right. Decide not to, and you were up against it immediately. Take the Trade Union. They wanted him to join it. He must, they said. There was no alternative. Trades Unions were new to Joseph, something which the British had introduced again into their zone. They had been banished by the Third Reich before the war. Now they were all on the *go* again. He would *have* to join. He didn't like it. Some of the men were going far from his own beliefs, and indeed from their own former ones. They had definite rights now, and they demanded them.

The tow-path was deserted at this hour. Later, when it was darker, it would be full of lovers in the thick shadows. He sat there watching the flow of water and something of its steady calm power slowly reached him. His mind was less violently perturbed. Strange how things like trees and water could help him. He hadn't found this help in the church today.

The evening sun caught a figure coming towards him. Her cloud of hair was lit up like a halo, the edge of her face was rimmed with light, and it seemed to Joseph that she was one of the angels behind the altar come to life as she came slowly towards him. She wore a white jersey and a pale skirt, and in that light the indeterminate colour of her hair and skin were blended together into something so ethereal and unearthly that Joseph could only stare. The grass was so long that lying as he was resting on his arm she could not see him. She passed so close that her skirt almost touched him and there was a look so troubled, so remote and poignant on her face, that for a moment he could not bring himself to utter her name. She went by like a wraith and when he called "Krista" she turned, startled, and her movement revealed the lovely line of hip and breast, unmistakably that of a woman. Joseph, still staring at her beauty, realized with a pang that Krista was no longer a child.

She sat down beside him in the grass, putting her arm through his with a gesture so utterly confiding that he again felt that pang of something like anguish.

"Where are you going?" he asked gruffly, to hide his emotion.

She said simply, "To church—it's Friday night."

"What have you been doing out here?"

She looked away from him to the river, her face troubled and confused.

"Well?" he asked gently.

"I . . . I . . . wasn't ready to go to church." She stopped. "I . . ."

"Is it Moe?" he asked. "Because if so, there's nothing you can do about that; it lies between her and me."

She shook her head and tears began trickling down her face.

"Not only that, though of course that too. Pa, there is something I want to ask you. Has everything possible been done to discover who I am?"

Joseph was too startled to answer. That Krista herself should bring up this question astonished him. She had always so obviously disliked the subject that he had invariably ordered it to be dropped when one or other of the family brought it up. He had adopted her chiefly for the reason of her strange terror that she might be taken away from them. When officials had come after the war had ended and order was beginning to be restored, the most searching questions had been put both to him and to the child herself. She had been repeatedly examined by many doctors to try and enable her to remember the smallest clue as to her former life, for she had never recovered from the deep amnesia caused by the blow on her head.

She had been frantic with anxiety lest she should be taken away. The Child Tracing and Repatriation Officers had questioned Joseph at length as to every detail of his finding her. They had, it seemed, made endless inquiries and efforts to discover her identity without success. Her age and description did not tally with that of any missing child on their lists. That her parents or relatives had been killed on that night with thousands of others seemed obvious. He had been allowed to adopt her. There were only too many orphans filling the homes.

He said slowly, "Why do you ask? You know that everything was done when I applied to adopt you, Krista. Nothing came of the inquiries."

"What will happen if I should want to marry? My parents' name? I mean my name. I've no birth certificate?"

"They'll issue you a new one in our name, they told me so," he said shakily. He was so upset that he could scarcely speak. Somehow the thought of Krista marrying had never entered his head. But why not? Of course she would want to marry. She was growing into a beautiful girl, hadn't he just noticed it?

He said violently, "Have you some young man, too, like the girls are forever finding? I thought you were different."

As always, at any show of anger or violence, she shrank and seemed to withdraw into herself.

"Well," he repeated, but more gently, "have you a young man? Out with it!"

And then she began telling him about Paul, in a stumbling uneven flow of words. She could never talk when she was upset. She told him how she felt whenever she saw the American and that she couldn't understand why, but she had thought that perhaps it was wrong to feel such a delirious happiness whenever she saw him. She wanted to be with him and at the same time she wanted to fly from him. Why? She was puzzled and frightened. Joseph listened with rising fear and dismay as he watched her usually still face alight with life as she told of Paul and her meetings with him, he felt such a blinding hatred of this young American that in comparison all his other hatreds were as nothing.

He got up abruptly as she finished and said violently, "Krista!" His voice terrified her by its harshness. "You're doing wrong! You feel unhappy because you know it's wrong. You must give up this man—he means no good by you. You don't belong to his world.

He wants the same as all the others do. He's just having his bit of fun. Look at Katie and that Belgian, and Anna and the Englishman—they both went away and left them with a child. You're not like the others—give him up before it's too late. Think of Katie and Lise too. Now I understand why they are so—*she* must always have been a slut and I, the fool, didn't see it."

"No, no," protested Krista, "Moe's not bad! She's good, she *is*. She's had to work so hard and to bear so many children, and you were away so much and it wasn't easy in the bunker; it was awful, the people kept complaining about us and telling her we were too many. Even when she's angry she doesn't mean it, she forgets it at once. Look how the boys love her! Even when she *is* angry and hits them they don't mind, they know she doesn't mean it really."

He had never heard her so vehement before. Her pale face was flushed and her eyes brilliant as she defended Moe.

"She's been good to me, she has! Always, always." She was sobbing now. "And she never misses going to Carola. No matter what is on, or *how* she feels she always goes to Carola. She finds the money," she sobbed. "Every week she finds it somehow. She goes without things herself. Carola never goes without anything. Have you ever seen Carola's face when Moe visits her? It's lovely. Sister Edith says that every time Moe goes there she seems to give some of her vitality to Carola. Sometimes when Moe comes back she cries for a long time—and sometimes she never says a word, she *can't*."

"Moe cries?" asked Joseph in astonishment. He hadn't seen her moved to tears for years now.

"Yes, she does, and the Sisters say that she will be the one who will make Carola walk again. They told me so," insisted Krista.

Joseph was silent. He was amazed at the perception of the girl. Had he really been as blind as Father Lange said he was? He thought of that day only a few days ago when his eyes seemed to have been opened. The day he had seen the chestnut tree and the lion as if for the first time. Good things and bad. On that day he had seen only the bad in Moe, and yet the thing which he saw had been going on for months before that. She was the same person, it was just that he *knew* now.

He hadn't visited his little daughter for weeks. Shame filled him now at the thought that, after being refused permission on his free day, he hadn't again tried to visit the child, or even to inquire when he might. The nuns were good and the hospital very human. Then into his mind came once again the horrible picture of that tumbled bed and the two shameless ones in it. He pushed away the thoughts of his sick child and said angrily, "That's enough, don't go on trying to excuse Moe. There's no excuse for her. Don't mention her name to me. I loathe the thought of her. And *you*, you look to yourself with this young American. He means no good to you. If I see him hanging round you I'll send him about his business."

He had never spoken so harshly to Krista before and she quailed at his anger.

"Promise me you won't see him again," he insisted.

"I'll tell him that you don't like our friendship," she said at last. "I *must* see him again to tell him so and to say goodbye."

"But you'll break with him?"

She nodded.

He looked at her gratefully and pulled her roughly to him. They sat so without speaking for a while. Tears were trickling slowly down her face. "That's right; you're a good girl, Krista," he murmured awkwardly, "you're not like the others, you're different . . . you're not for that."

Even as he said this she felt a strange relief, a kind of peace steal over her. Pa was right. She hadn't been really happy since the friendship began. She had been restless and ill at ease. Her tears ceased, and when he looked at her again her face was calm in its immature softness.

"That wretched Carnival," Joseph was saying. "She met *him* there, and you met this Paul there. There's not going to be any Carnival for you next year, for any of you."

At the mention of the Carnival Krista's mind went back again to those days last February. In a way it had been through her that they had gone at all. When she had taken home her first week's wages from the factory and showed them proudly to Moe, begging her to take it as she wanted to begin repaying something of what she owed her foster-parents, Moe had refused to accept the money. After Krista's urging she had said, "Well, I'll tell you what I'll do. I'll put all this towards a fund for the Carnival. We'll all save for it, but this, your first wages, shall start the fund. But you must give Pa his bit towards his house. He sets so much store by that. The rest shall go for the Carnival."

What fun they had all had laughing and teasing one another about the costumes they should wear. They had all been sitting round the kitchen table to which Pa and the twins had joined an extra piece to make room for them all. Ah! how lovely it had been when they were all happy together as they were that evening. How Moe had laughed, throwing back her head, and that hoarse throaty chuckle of hers made everyone laugh with her. They had all sung to the boys' accompaniment on their harmonicas, Moe's husky contralto leading them. Pa was always their conductor at their concerts. He knew a lot about music and taught them how to control their breathing. His father had been a skilled organist, and Pa had a deep fine bass voice himself, just as Hank was going to have later. They had sung descants, part songs, rounds. They all loved music, and on summer nights under the acacia, and in winter round the great stove which they had to stoke strictly in turn, the singing would be kept up long after the rest of the village slept. That had all been before the Carnival though. Before she had met Paul. Before Rudi had come to live with them.

She thought now of the Carnival with mixed feelings. It had been like fairyland with the ruins hidden and blanketed with flowers and flags and the absurd and lovely costumes in the wild processions. But some of it she hadn't liked. She had been frightened too. With the barrels of wine in the streets there had come a change in the faces of people one had known. The wild behaviour and their unbridled lust and zest for excitement had terrified her. Moe had laughed at her and teased her, especially over the Weiberfastnacht which had outraged Krista. The custom of the women taking over the town to molest the men went back for hundreds of years, she said, and who was Krista to think it disgusting?

But after she had met Paul it had been wonderful. He had looked after her, protected her from those hordes of wild revellers catching at every woman's skirt. That he had been American hadn't mattered at all then. In the Carnival one took on the role of the costume one was wearing, not for one day, but for the whole Carnival. That was one of the nicest things about it. Visitors came to it from all over the world; but there was no identity and so no nationality. Only an occupied country could really appreciate that, thought Krista, accustomed to hearing endless grumbling and arguments about the failings and foibles of the countries which occupied hers. But now it was all different. Paul was one of the Occupation, and Pa was angry that she felt as she did about him. He wanted her to give up the friendship; and in her anguish at hurting him she had agreed. What had she done?

Someone was coming along the tow-path whistling loudly, and the tall lithe form of Leo came into view. He was on his way home from the repair yard. His fair hair was long and thick, and he wore a dark blue jersey which set it off, and dark blue dungarees. In his hand he held a coil of rope with which he was practising lasso-throwing as he walked. The rope caught the heads of the meadow-sweet and the blue chicory and was crushing and cutting them off as he swung it. With a dexterous whirl he cut off a marguerite and threw it so that it landed in Krista's hair, then stared insolently at her as he said good-evening to Joseph. Joseph felt the lad's eyes on the girl beside him and gave him but a curt greeting.

As Leo's footsteps died away Joseph said, "That's the young fellow Katie's going with. I don't like him. He's been in trouble with the police."

Krista shivered. She had seen the hard eyes and rather thin lips and the bold insolent air. She was thinking of the motor cycle in the night and the long absence of Hank and Katie. Should she tell Joseph of her fears? He was looking intently after the youth, with such misery and bewilderment that she knew it was impossible to add to his worries. She would keep it to herself. Should she tell Father Lange? He was kind but lately she had shrunk from talking to him. Why hadn't she told him about Paul? Was it because, as Joseph said, it was wrong?

She got up. "I'm going to church, Pa," she said. "Are you coming?"

"No," said Joseph violently, "I've no use for church at present."

"I will pray for you," said Krista with a serenity she did not feel.

The beauty of the evening had suddenly gone. A chill wind was blowing up with the swift current of the river. The sky was a heavy grey now and the seven poplar trees on the way to the church were swaying violently. The dark green water glowed with diesel oil from the vessels on it. Throwing a scarf over her head Krista went into the church.

The scent of lilies and incense drove out the fumes of the diesel oil and the organ playing softly calmed her anxiety. She began to pray, her eyes on the altar. Presently a small figure joined her and a small voice whispered.

"Wherever have you been, Krista? Me and Franz Joseph have been looking for you everywhere. We're getting ready for Pa's and your birthday on Sunday."

I X

SATURDAY! She sprang out of bed and without disturbing the little boys opened the green shutters. The room looked on to the back garden. The trees dripped miserably through a curtain of rain. Krista was dismayed as she looked at the heavy sky. What would they do if it was still raining? Would Paul still want to go on the river? And what would she wear? She had a new dress. It hung in the cupboard ready to put on. But if it was going on raining, what then?

She went to consult Anna. "Wear it," advised that sleepy young woman as she finally sat up in bed. "It'll probably clear up and you'll be sorry you haven't got it on. Take a coat or a jacket though. It gets cold on the water."

So she put on the dress. She considered herself, or as much as she could see in the small square of glass. Was it all right? She did not care for bright colours and in spite of Moe's advising her to get a really gay summer dress she had chosen this one of soft blues and greys. It seemed to her that she looked drab and insignificant in it, but she preferred it that way. The point was, would he? There were so many pretty girls in so much more attractive dresses. Anna, standing yawning in the doorway, was amused that Krista was showing interest in her appearance. It had taken Paul to do that. She was putting the chain and little gold cross with the name "Krista" on it round her neck. It had been on her when Pa had found her that night, and was the only clue to her identity.

As she turned from the looking-glass she caught sight of one of Robert's shoes. It was sticking out from under his bed and was sole upwards. She picked it up. It was sopping wet. When Robert had been put to bed it had not been raining. It had been a lovely evening. She looked for the other shoe. It was equally wet. His socks were soaking and when she examined his jacket it had obviously been out in heavy rain. She showed them to Anna, who whistled in astonishment.

Krista bent over the sleeping child. His fair hair was in close tight curls. It had been wet and had dried in the ringlets which he hated. She was mystified.

"Wake him up and get the truth out of him," whispered Anna. "I don't like it. *What's* going on in this house?"

Krista woke him. She hated to do so, but he had to be at Mass: Father Lange counted on Robert. He had obviously been out in the night, but she had not heard him go. It had not rained until after she had gone to sleep, and that had been very late. She had stayed awake thinking with mixed delight and terror of today.

"Robert, Robert," she said gently, putting her hand on his warm little body. He sat up. He was immediately and absolutely awake as only children can be. Holding up the shoes and socks she asked him, "Where did you get these so wet?" and was horrified at the sudden fear in his face. The bland sleep-washed look was replaced by one of acute anxiety and apprehension. He looked a little old man.

"I don't know," he said flatly, and lay down again.

"Robert," she tried again, "you've been out, haven't you? Where've you been?"

"I couldn't sleep," he muttered resentfully, "so I just went for a walk."

"Where?" she pursued remorselessly.

"Along the tow-path," he said vaguely.

"Did you go out after the others?" Then as he did not answer, she said sharply, "*Did* you, Robert?"

"No, I just went on my own." There was a pink tinge spreading over his delicate face. It had a transparent look this morning. He couldn't face her. She knew he was lying. But hadn't *she* lied too? Hadn't she promised Pa that she wouldn't see Paul, except to say goodbye, and wasn't she intending to spend the whole afternoon and evening with him? Even if she didn't tell the lie, Anna would lie for her. What was happening to them all? They all had some underhand affairs on—*all* of them. What made them lie like this?

"You can't go to church in those wet shoes," she said quietly, "you'll have to wear your best ones."

"Suppose Moe notices? I'll have to say that Peppi poured water from her watering-can on them."

Krista was sickened at the ease with which he invented the excuse. Robert, the most truthful little boy in the family! She said gently, "But that isn't true, is it?"

"It could be," he said obstinately. "Peppi's always doing it and Moe only laughs."

She let it pass. "I'll get you some other socks. And don't wear that damp jacket. If I were you, Robert, I shouldn't go walking about alone in the night. There are sometimes unpleasant people by the river."

She did not miss his quick look of fear. But he said nothing. He kept his head down staring fixedly at the floor, then looking up suddenly, remarked brightly on her new dress.

"You'll get that damp too," he said shrewdly, "it's not the sort of day for it."

And this was Moe's comment when she came into the kitchen presently. Moe was always up early in the mornings, and always cheerful. All the others except the very small ones appeared in varying degrees of wakening and dressing, resentful at having to get up. Moe laughed and sang as she bustled about admonishing everyone to hurry and get a move on. She might be in her wrapper still, but she was always washed and combed and her skin shone with health and vitality. She looked at Krista's dress out of the corner of her eye. "Is that the birthday dress?" she asked, attacking the loaves with a huge knife. Krista nodded shyly. "Is it all right?" she asked anxiously.

"Hmm!" said Moe appraisingly. "I should have thought a cherry-coloured one, or even a yellow—but I don't know that you aren't right. Those faded colours suit you."

"Faded? Does it look faded?" Krista's voice was worried.

"Of course not, silly. It's only my way of describing those soft colours. Think of it. Tomorrow you'll be eighteen! You may be nineteen! But I don't think you are. I've had enough children to know. I always said you weren't more than eight when Pa found you."

They were cutting up bread, side by side, at the long table.

"Moe," said Krista tremulously, "thank you. Thank you—for all these years, I mean. I can never repay it." There was a hint of tears in her voice.

"What's the child worrying about now? Who wants repayment? You can't repay love. That's something none of us deserve, but if you get it, take it and be thankful." She patted Krista's arm affectionately. "You're one of us. One of the family."

"But I *do* appreciate it. That you took me in when you already had so many."

"Here, don't let's get emotional! It's too early. Wait until the birthday, then we'll all weep. You know what they say about us Rhinelanders? We are built too near the water. And the tears turn on and off too easily. And now Pa wants to build a house right down on the river. You know he's got an option on a piece of that waste land? It's an exorbitant price but he's set on it."

Krista was surprised. Pa no longer confided all his hopes and dreams in her as he used to do. What had happened to her loving intimate relationship with him? She treasured it above all.

"That fellow Peter he's so fond of has got a friend, Franz, who's a builder. He's bought that waste land. If Pa can find the lump sum as a token payment he'll start talking about building. I don't like it. People like us can't afford to be saddled with debts hanging round our necks. What's the matter with *this* house? It suits me."

"Pa's afraid that the owner will come back. We'll be turned out then. Nearly all the British have gone now. There's only the family next door."

"There are still thousands of them all round Bonn. And it doesn't look as if they'll ever settle all their squabbles."

Krista longed to confide in her that she was going out with Paul. The fact that she was deceiving Pa lay heavily on her conscience. True, she had told Pa that she must see Paul to say goodbye. But she didn't need all those hours to do it in. She opened her mouth to tell Moe several times, but the words stuck in her throat. Moe would laugh, or certainly tease. She didn't mean to hurt, not in the least. It was just her way of looking at such things.

When Katie came in she noticed the new dress immediately. "What are you wearing *that* for," she said. "It's a beastly day—you'll look a nice sight with that full skirt clinging round your legs in the rain."

"They're good legs anyhow," said Anna quietly; "much better than yours or mine."

"They won't be improved by wet clothes hanging round them," retorted Katie spitefully, "and I shouldn't be surprised if the colours don't run when it's wet!"

"It'll be the shop who'll be surprised if that happens," snapped Moe, "for they'll be getting a visit from me. Run, indeed! It's a washing dress. You're envious, that's all."

Robert came apprehensively into the kitchen. He was wearing his best jacket and shoes. Moe looked at him sharply. "You look seedy," she said. "Come here." She examined his face, felt his hands and forehead, and made him put out his tongue. He insisted nervously that he was all right. Moe couldn't forget Carola. She hadn't taken much notice when Carola had seemed lethargic and later complained that her legs wouldn't walk. She took no chances now.

"Did you run all the way to church and back?" she asked the boy. Robert assented. It was the easiest way. She had made up her mind that she had found the cause of his pallor. "You're a good boy," she said. "Come and get your breakfast."

Just as Krista was rushing off with Anna, Katie called, "Both back to midday meal?"

"No, neither of us. Preparations for tomorrow."

No more was said. It was accepted that everyone might have some secret for the double birthday.

"Have a good time—and make the most of it," called Anna to Krista as they left the tram, "and no backing out, or hurrying back, mind. I'll do the necessary for you."

Never had a morning seemed so long. She had finished with the cream vat. Now she was on the filling of the perfume bottles. The dainty glass containers came up in tens under the machine and were automatically filled. She had to watch very carefully so that not one drop of the precious liquid was wasted. It was all she could do to keep her eyes on the filler. She was so much on edge that it was a torture to have to sit there for the four-hour morning shift. The great clock in the airy work hall ticked so slowly that it seemed to have been purposely slowed up to lengthen her ordeal. With each tick the word Paul seemed to sound in her ears. Paul, Paul, Paul, until she longed to throw one of the cut-glass bottles at it.

"Have a sweet?" Her companion thrust a chocolate in her mouth as she bent, intent, over the filler machine. "My boy friend got them for me from the NAAFI. He's British. Good, aren't they?"

Krista couldn't answer—the chocolate was too large. She smiled her thanks.

"Your boy friend's an American, isn't he?" went on the girl. She was small and dark with hazel eyes and pretty teeth. Krista nodded. "He's a good looker," she went on, "isn't he? So's mine. I'm getting engaged soon. Mother said I could be engaged to John as soon as his people wrote to me. His mother wrote this morning. I've got the letter here in my pocket. I'll show it you. You read a bit of English, don't you? You'll *have* to if your boy's American."

"Doesn't your mother mind your marrying an Englishman?"

"No, she likes him. She's only sorry that I'll have to go and live in England. But you can't have everything, can you? I can't get married until my young brother's left school and can help mother a bit."

"You've no father?"

"He was killed in the war."

"How old are you?"

"Nineteen," said the girl, stuffing another chocolate in Krista's mouth, "and John is twenty-two. I suppose we'll have to wait another year until my brother's left school."

At last the hooter sounded and, without waiting one minute beyond wiping the machine properly and turning everything off tightly, Krista was out of the hall and into the cloakroom and the first to take off her overall. Unpinning her hair, which had to be worn up at work, she combed it anxiously. It seemed to have no colour at all. It was shining now with the light from the glass skylight on it. She peered anxiously at herself and frowned.

"It's all right. You look sweet," said an older worker, laughing at her anxiety. The sun blazed through the skylight. The rain had washed everything and the world had a new tender look as she ran out of the gate. There he was. In the usual place, leaning against the wall. A feeling of intense happiness filled her at the sight of that motionless figure. She felt suddenly so light that there was no street, no pavement under her winged feet as she ran to him.

Bob's car was round the corner, and they were just in time to catch the boat. The old boatman hurried them on board, laughing as they came panting up the gangway when he sounded his little warning bell.

Lunch was on deck, under the striped awning. Sitting by the boat rail at a table for two Krista had a vision of the long table at home. It would be noisy and filled with squabbling, chattering, and laughing, the clatter of plates and dishes and the eternal wrangling as to whose turn it was to fetch and carry. For in this glorious sunshine she was sure that they were eating under the acacia. Pa would be home. It was Saturday. Suppose he asked where she was?

"What's the matter?" asked Paul, watching the changing moods on her sensitive face.

"I was just thinking that Pa will probably ask where I am." Her voice was regretful.

"Look. This is *our* day. Can't you forget that tiresome family for once? There's only you and me this afternoon, so just relax, will you?"

"I'll try," she promised, laughing.

She was so entranced with everything that Paul was touched by her naive delight in the simplest things. The boat, the music, the water, the journey which he had made so many times, all enchanted her. He looked at her as she sat there with the breeze blowing the soft tendrils of hair all over her brow. The sun caught one outline of her face, the rest was in shadow from the awning. She was utterly lovely. About her was always a faint sweet perfume from the factory, and although she was unaware of it from constant proximity, Paul had come to connect it with her. It seemed part of her. A delicate flower scent—just right for her.

They passed through the village and she was excited to see her little breakwater and her sandy bay from quite a new angle. The woods with the silver birches where she loved to lie when it was hot; the marguerites and poppies, the blue chicory and the great masses of rushes all seemed touched with a new magic today. Even the water itself was mysterious and compelling as she gazed down at its translucent depths. Here, in the middle of the stream, it was different. She had never seen *this* water before, only its surface from a distance. And the church! That gave her immense pleasure as she viewed its white shape and its tower and weathercock. The seven poplars seemed much more beautiful from this side of the water.

"Eat your food," urged Paul. He knew that she left home very early and that this was long past her usual lunch hour. He urged her to drink with him. She didn't want to drink wine. They drank it at home at the week-ends—and at the wine festivals. There was always trouble afterwards. But she wanted to please him and she obediently drank.

"Happy?" he asked her.

She smiled. "It's so lovely I can't believe that it's real. It's more like a dream." And that was what it really was, she thought. Soon I shall wake up, and there will be Pa and Katie and that lie I told. For Anna would tell it for her and that was the same thing. But she pushed it away now. The day was Paul's. Hers and his. She had promised him.

Disembarking at Königswinter she was as excited as a child at the beauty of the landscape, at the gay little shops filled with souvenirs for the tourists, at the horses standing there with the old-fashioned carriages. In her pleasure Paul himself saw it all as if for the first time and realized its charm as he never had before. She was delighted at the ferry boats which took the cars across, at the crowds of visitors in the wide street by the river which had the air of a seaside town. He asked her suddenly if she had ever seen the sea. She was astonished. "How could I have? I've never been away from this piece of the Rhine," she laughed, and asked him if it was really like the pictures and films of it.

They began the climb up the Drachenfels. Up the long stony path winding through groups of little tourists' shops and cafés, stopping all the way to drop their coins gaily in every peep-show they passed. All the fairy tales were here—Snow-white and the Seven Dwarfs, the Little Elves and the Tailor, the Sleeping Beauty, Hansel and Gretel, Red Riding Hood—all of them.

"Oh, oh, I must bring Franz Joseph and Robert here!" she cried in delight. "They'd love it all." And the donkeys, standing patiently in their long lines waiting for the lazy sightseers who did not want to walk. Krista adored them and fed them with apples from her jacket pocket. Paul offered to hire her one to ride all the way up if she wished, but she was horrified at the idea that one of these small sad creatures should carry an adult, and looked with disapproval at the heavy giggling young women sitting on the patient beasts. Only by reminding her that they would pass them again on their way down could Paul get her away from them. She loved animals. All animals, she said. And birds, too—she had a tame robin, she told him, and several tits. But Hank killed birds. Her face as she told Paul this told him much more about Hank; but he insisted on her promise being kept. No talk and no thinking of the family. Had he any idea how difficult it was? How could he have? She was very perceptive, and sensed that in his lonely life he had never had to consider the effect of his actions on anyone else. She was part of the family. He would not see that. Didn't want to admit it. But she *was*. They were part and parcel of her childhood, her whole upbringing. She couldn't forget them; not for long, at any rate. She was surprised at the number of times she had put them out of her mind since she had known Paul.

The path was steep but not too steep. It was now very hot, but after the rain it was pleasant; the way led through trees and glades checkered with sunlight. Ferns grew in the crannies of the old grey boulders and small rock plants which Krista recognized with pleasure. Her old schoolmaster had been a keen botanist and had taught her all their names. They wandered hand in hand, and it seemed to the girl that there were still wings on her feet.

Afterwards when she thought about that day she could not remember the actual sensation of a single footstep. She seemed to have floated up, past the little chalet huts with the wooden benches outside under the trees where the boys and girls sat drinking lemonade and raspberry juice, past all the side-shows, and the cave where the dragon lived, from which the mountain took its name. Into all these they went, enjoying the simple delights offered in return for a few coins; and so up the last steeper climb to the large restaurant perched on the side of the mountain where they sat drinking coffee before they made the final stretch to the summit.

They stood there then by the great rocks where so many climbers had carved their names, and looked down at the little island in the middle of the Rhine, at the newly-built American Headquarters, at the evidence all round of the importance of the new capital and its surroundings. Amongst the lovely green of the woods, the flashing sunlight on the river with the range of dark hills behind it held Krista speechless. She just looked and looked.

"I like it up here," she said at last. "It's wonderful! It makes me feel very small."

"You aren't so large," Paul smiled.

"I like to be in a big quiet place," she went on. "I don't like noise. I hate it when people shout. It shrivels me up. That's why I often go down to the river, and lie in the reeds there. I can only hear the water and the birds. When it rains I go into the church. That's the same. The feeling's the same. Robert's like me. He hates noise. When people shout at him he runs away and hides."

"But no one shouts at *you*?" Paul's horror was apparent at such a thing. He flung himself down on the hillside and pulled her down beside him.

"Only Katie. She shouts at everyone. But she's unhappy. She loves Leo and he's tired of her. Hank is always teasing her and taunting her about it. Poor Katie."

"Now then, no family. Remember?"

She laughed up at him. "I'm sorry. But they seem to come into everything."

"Don't I come into your thoughts at all?"

She flushed. "Of course. Too much. *Far, far* too much."

"Really? You mean that? You *do* think about me?"

"All the time," she said simply.

He tilted her face up to his and searched it questioningly. The clear grey eyes met his unflinchingly, and there was in them something which filled him with joy.

He kissed her mouth. A long, long kiss. He had never kissed her like this before. He had never dared.

To his delight she did not resist as she usually did, but met his approach with the first feeling she had shown him. He put his arms round her slight body and held her close. She stroked his face, and when he turned her mouth to his again her long lashes veiled her eyes. Should he tell her that he loved her, that he wanted her? Would she be frightened? With a wisdom born of his love for her he sensed that he must walk very warily lest he lose all the ground he had gained in these last three months. She was less apprehensive of him, less alarmed at his caresses up here than she was by the river, but the slightest mistake might send her flying off. When he thought of how easy it was with most girls, he wondered at his own patience. But hadn't he always known that she would be different? Wasn't that part of her attraction for him?

Even now she suddenly pulled herself away and said shakily, "No, no, it's wrong."

"But why? What's wrong?" He was gentle but persistent. "I love you. I wouldn't harm you. If you love me you must want me to kiss you. Don't you?"

Her voice was low and troubled. "Of course I do. I *do*. Really. But I'm frightened. I'm frightened of love—if this is it."

"It's frightening all right, but unless you have some courage you'll never *know* how wonderful it is. Look, what do you think you were born a girl for? So that you can love and be loved and have children. You love children, don't you?"

But at the word children he saw that he had made a mistake. Katie. Lise. Anna. All of them. Had they all loved like her? Anna had loved. Her baby had died. She pulled her hand away from his. "It's wrong. Pa said so," she said flatly.

"Krista," he began, "listen to me. You *must*. You've got the wrong idea. How can you help it? That family of yours have blinded you to all the lovely natural things in life—to friendship, companionship and love between men and women. Your foster-parents—don't judge everyone by them. All marriages are not like that. And the girls. Don't judge by them. They had bad luck. Times were difficult—we don't know what temptations there were. Forget all that and think of *us*. We can have it all different. The world lies before us—look at it down there. Isn't it lovely? Don't you think we were meant to be happy in it?"

"Father Lange said that." She looked at him through the thick fringe of lashes. "He said God wanted us to be happy. But . . . why . . . why . . . are Pa and Moe, and Katie too . . . so terribly unhappy? Even Anna . . ." Her voice stopped.

"Krista." Paul felt his way more carefully now. "That's what I mean. You've got to leave all that out. You *must*. You aren't meant to put other people's lives straight. They must do that for themselves. No one can help you and me. We've got to take our chance. But if we don't, it may never come again. Not like this. If we love one another, nothing else matters. *Nothing*. Get that straight. Love is something which you can't order on a plate. It just serves itself—or doesn't—whether you're German or American. We must just take it—it may never be offered us again."

Krista was silent. What had Moe said this morning? Something strangely serious for her. "You can't repay love, but if you get it, take it and be thankful." Wasn't it much the same as what Paul was trying to tell her? She put her hand in his and her trembling began to subside.

"Don't you trust me?" he asked her.

"Yes, oh yes. I *do*. It's not that. It's me. I'm frightened. I don't know myself any more."

"Who does? It's one of the things which make life so exciting. Finding oneself through another person. That's how I'm finding myself—through *you*. It's wonderful. If only you'd give it a chance."

"I will," she said tremulously, "I will. But it frightens me."

"We'll get married. And have our own home. I've never had a home. Never. All my life in places with hordes of others. Never any privacy. But now it can all be different. We'll have a home. One of our own."

But at the word "married" Krista was filled with apprehension again. Not at the idea of marriage, but marriage meant asking Pa. He would never, never agree. "Paul," she began, "I can't marry you. Pa will never allow it. Never."

"But why not? What's to stop you? You're not his daughter!"

Not his daughter. Not his daughter. Whose daughter was she? She would never know.

"*I'll* talk to him. That's my job, not yours. So don't go getting yourself all worked up about it."

"No, no, Paul. Don't! I beg you not to. We must wait. Not *now*." There was such urgency in her voice and such anxiety that he was upset.

"What difference does it make *when* I do it?" he demanded impatiently. "He won't like it anyhow. You said so." And when she looked away with misery on her face he said angrily, "You don't love me." But at her stricken look he was immediately contrite. "Forget it," he said, pulling her into his arms. "That was mean of me. I know you love me." She clung to him now, and in her sudden unwonted kisses there was a new warmth and sweetness. He sensed in them the promise of surrender. Tempted as he was by her yielding to press further with this success, he knew that he could not. And with this knowledge came a sense of furious frustration, a sickness of the whole wretched situation. Why, he couldn't even talk easily to her because of this damned language barrier. He was obliged to use the very simplest words; his German, fluent and adequate for everyday use, was hopeless when it came to these issues. He pulled her head down on to his shoulder and, stroking her soft hair, tried to talk calmly to her. He wanted to explain that there was a difference between love and lust; but when he tried the words stuck in his throat. What was the difference, anyway. Weren't they sometimes almost the same thing? Now, for instance. He loved her with all that was best in him, and yet he wanted her. And he could have her—he sensed that. He was stronger than she was. But because of his love for her he couldn't.

He tried haltingly to explain his feelings, trying to show her that what she saw every day in that family was not real love. But she cut him short. How did *he* know? He had never lived in a family. They did love each other. They *did*. He was exasperated but blundered patiently on, and the intent anxiety on her face made him very gentle. She was only a kid. He felt much older than his actual years when with her. He meant Moe and Rudi, he explained. Pa and Moe, Katie and Leo. And all the time that he was searching for words he felt how superfluous it all was when he could have taken her in his arms and shown her what he meant. And her eyes, troubled and searching, upset him. She was sure that her foster-parents had once loved each other—that they still did in spite of everything.

"It's not always the same," he said hesitantly. "The love's there all the time, but things hide it, blot it out like clouds do the sun—but it's there, it must be."

But what had happened to her foster-parents? Suppose the same thing happened to this feeling she and Paul had for one another? What then?

"We have to take that risk," he said decisively. "It's the same for everyone. If you're not game to take a chance, then love is not for you—or me . . . And now do you understand what I'm trying to tell you? That I love you, Krista, more than anything in the world? Aren't you willing to take a chance?"

But now, as always, she jumped to her feet. It was late. She must go. It would take them hours to get back. She *must* be home by ten o'clock. Paul took her in a strong hold and forced her to face him.

"*Are* you going to marry me?" he demanded.

"I don't know," she said miserably. "It all depends on Pa."

With an abrupt gesture he released her.

"Paul. Wait a little. *Please.* It'll all come right if only you'll wait a little. Don't speak to Pa. Not yet."

"All right, if that's the way you want it," he agreed grudgingly. "But don't let it be too long. I'm not as patient as those donkeys down there."

"It won't be long," she promised. She took his arm in a new trusting way which delighted him. It was the first time she had done so.

"It's lovely here," she said, her eyes on the beauty around them. "It's like being out of the world, above it all. Why can't we live on the top of a mountain?"

"Because no one would carry up the necessities of life," laughed Paul, kissing her. They began the long descent of the great hill. All the way down they passed young lovers in the evening sun. Far below them lay the river; and on it the white steamer waiting to carry them back to the world.

X

"HOHE ZOLL *Er leben, Hohe zoll Er leben,*" sang the lusty voices of the children under Joseph's window on the morning of his birthday. He had slept heavily, exhausted by his mental conflict. At first he thought that it was still very early and was preparing to shout at the singers to cease their noise when he realized that what they were singing was a traditional birthday greeting.

The watch by his bedside said eight o'clock. The shutters were closed but the window was open, and through the slats the long shafts of yellow light were making a pattern over his un-shaven face. As he caught sight of himself in the mirror hanging crookedly on the opposite wall, he was struck with the effect of the sunlight and shadow. He looked like a striped creature—a zebra or a tiger. He was amused with his discovery and moved from side to side to get the effect from every angle.

Moe, coming in with a tray, was struck with his extraordinary postures and wondered if he were going mad. In the mirror he saw her reflection and stopped moving as if he had been caught doing something shameful. She wore a striped print dress and it struck him as funny that while he was watching the stripes of sunlight and shadow she should come in wearing a striped dress. He burst out laughing. She was so startled that she almost dropped the tray. Her hair had been washed for the birthdays and shone with an extraordinary brilliance.

Putting down the tray, she flung open the shutters revealing the twins, Robert and Franz Joseph singing lustily while Anna, Karl, Hank and Katie accompanied them on mouth organs. Krista, celebrating her birthday too, was not taking part.

"There!" said Moe gaily, "look at them wishing you a happy birthday. And I wish you one too, Joseph."

Joseph grunted. He could not bring himself to thank her for the luxury of breakfast in bed or her good wishes. He did not see how he could avoid speaking to her if he accepted these birthday celebrations. He found it hard to be gracious to the children. They trailed off somewhat feebly when they saw his taciturn face.

"Happy birthday, Pa," they chanted when their song was finished.

"Thank you," was all he could get out. He had an insane desire to fling the tray at their round open mouths. To see them all staring at him through the window was too much. He felt suddenly as that lion must have felt with all those silly spectators gazing at him. As he had felt when his guards had stared at him through the wire cage of the prison camp.

"That's enough, shut the window!" he said sharply. Moe saw that he was still in a bad mood, and slamming the windows, told the boys to go away and went out of the room.

"Keep quiet for a while; maybe he'll be more amiable later. He certainly isn't much like a birthday boy," she grumbled to them.

Joseph had been drinking again the previous evening, and the children assumed that his bad temper was due to that. The twins sniggered and imitated the swallowing of a glass of liquid, but Robert slunk away to find Krista. He had painted her a picture for her birthday. It was a picture of the two angels in the church, and above them he had made a picture of Krista herself. All three had the same face, and all three had halos. Only the two angels had wings, however. He showed it to Moe apprehensively. She was quite astonished.

"Did you do this all by yourself?" she asked. He nodded. He had done it at school and one of the boys had lent him his paint-box to colour it. Moe determined that this Robert should have a paint-box of his own. She thought this painting remarkable.

"But Krista shouldn't have a halo," she protested. "Only angels and the Holy Family have those."

"Krista *is* holy!" insisted the child. "So I gave her a halo too. She looked sort of naked without one."

Moe laughed heartily, flinging back her hair and whooping with joy. The idea that a halo could make one less naked delighted her. Robert was affronted, but she assured him that she thought the picture lovely and that he'd better find Krista and give it her.

Krista and Anna were busy with the bedding which they were hanging out of the windows to air. It was a beautiful morning, and Moe was not in the least upset that the neighbours would be scandalized by their doing this on a Sunday.

Normally, Hank would still have been in bed, for he was now over eighteen and considered that he could do as he liked because he earned more than his father did, but he had got up to join in the birthday serenade. He was so furious at his father's lack of appreciation that he considered going back to bed again. He looked round the garden, heard the birds in the trees and went to find his catapult. He was hoping to get an air rifle soon. He would not be satisfied until he had killed every bird in the place.

Joseph couldn't understand how a lad of his age could be earning such high wages. He earned more than a skilled workman like himself. Even the twins were getting what was in Joseph's estimation a very high wage. They worked in the big rubber factory further along the river. Anna and Krista both worked longer hours and for much smaller wages than the lads, but they were getting far more money that Joseph's father had ever earned.

It was all an enigma to him. Here were these striplings, inexperienced and callow, able to buy all the luxuries which he, Joseph, had never been able to afford. They would not hear of saving, and resented the amount which he insisted each one should contribute weekly towards building a new home. No, they were not going to save! They knew what had happened to two generations of savings. They were going to spend theirs. Moe encouraged them in this. She could never forget her little sum reduced to infinitesimal value with the advent of Currency Reform. Much better if she had bought a piano with the money as she had always wanted to do. Moe saw no reason why the children should not buy themselves clothes, bicycles, and musical instruments with their own money. Joseph, still supporting the younger ones, never seemed to have money for anything, and yet he worked far longer hours than they did. It was something which his mind just couldn't take in. Where did all their money come from? For they spent it and yet always seemed to have plenty. The whole river trip and celebrations today, as well as the royal feast they were to have, had been paid for by the children. Hank had supplied most of the money, it seemed.

He looked without appetite at the tray before him in honour of his birthday. In a miniature vase was one huge red rose. He held it to his nostrils and the exquisite perfume held a nostalgia which was unbearable. Such roses as these, big, dark red, like cabbages, had grown in his mother's garden in the Bavarian village. For years he hadn't thought about his mother, and in the last few days she had come several times into his mind. Was he getting old? He was fifty today. A landmark in a man's life. More than seven years of it wasted by the war. *Wasted*, he thought bitterly.

He couldn't eat the food on the tray. It nauseated him this morning. When Krista, sent in by Moe to see how the wind was blowing, wished him a happy birthday and kissed him affectionately, he pointed to the rose.

"From you?" he asked gruffly.

She nodded. He had often told her about those roses in his mother's garden. What had made her find just such a bloom for today? He knew where she had obtained it. Robert went sometimes to help a young market gardener who was experimenting. They said he was a wizard at growing things. The river soil was good and he was making his land pay.

Krista had bought Joseph a tie. She gave it him now very shyly.

"Come here," he said.

"You must never leave me, Krista. You hear? *Never*, never. I can't spare you . . . you must stay with me." His voice was quite excited and the girl was frightened.

"It's our birthday today. Give me your promise that you'll finish with this young American."

"But, father, I promised you only two nights ago," she faltered. She had been trying to pluck up courage to tell him that Paul wanted to marry her.

"But I want to hear it again," he said violently. "There's no hope for me if you go . . . I am damned . . . damned. . . ."

"Father, father," she cried, bewildered by his strangeness. "What do you mean? You're good, you're not damned . . ." She began to shake and could not stop herself. Her foster-father was looking at her with eyes that were so unhappy that they were indeed those of one in torment. She couldn't withstand that look and sank weeping by the bed.

"All right, Father," she said between sobs, "I'll say good-bye to Paul."

"You're a good girl," he said again, "too good for all of us. Bless you, child."

"Eat your breakfast. Moe will be upset if you leave it," she begged, and at that moment Moe entered the room. She looked from Krista's wet eyes to Joseph.

"The children have bought you a present," she said. "They're coming to give it you."

She went to the door and motioned to the boys outside. With a flourish of mouth organs they marched in carrying between them a brand new black Sunday suit, which they laid on their father's bed.

Joseph was stupefied. He had never managed to save enough for a suit since he'd come home after the war. His old clothes had been destroyed with his home, and he had made do with his uniform dyed, and one suit he had bought second-hand which he wore on Sundays. Where had they got it?

"We had your old suit copied," they said gleefully, "and if it doesn't fit anywhere the tailor will soon alter it for you."

"But the money?" he urged. "How did you get so much money?" Suits were an exorbitant price. He couldn't understand it. He fingered the fine black material, noting the silk lining, and the fine finish of the thing. He could never have afforded such a suit himself. He thrust it away.

"*Where* did the money come from?" he insisted.

Moe chuckled. "Ask the boys!" she said. "They're all earning big money now, so are the girls. Always a rise, always overtime, they're on the way to the top. Get rich quick! Why, we'll own a house like this yet!"

"Not if they spend like this!" retorted Joseph. "Spend, spend. Just look at the bicycles, radios, boots and new clothes—and now *this!* Why couldn't you have put the money towards our own house? What's going to happen when the Peace Treaty's signed and the owner of this place comes back?"

"They're giving you their bit towards that," protested Moe. "This is extra—they're getting rich, all of them." Her voice insinuated that he, Joseph, alone of those who earned their living, was not doing the same.

"We saved the money—we did really, Pa," insisted the twins. "Hurry up and put it on."

Hank had said nothing. He stood lounging in the doorway looking at his father with a contemptuous smile on his face. He wore a loud-checked red-and-purple shirt, open at the neck, and a pair of very tight pale fawn trousers. He was chewing gum, now a universal habit taught the youngsters by the Occupation troops.

"You can sell the damned thing if you'd rather have the dough," he said out of the side of his mouth; "he doesn't like it, boys."

"Try it on," urged Moe, who had come in with Katie. Katie's eyes were as scornful as Hank's. She knew Joseph had never liked her. She detested him. She was the only one who had not contributed towards the suit. Hank had paid the bulk, but each of them, even Franz Joseph, had given his mite.

But Joseph was looking at the gift in a stunned way. The world was upside down. Parents should give their children clothes, not the children the parents. The suit did something to his pride. He hated it. He looked at his arrogant insolent son lounging there and he knew suddenly that this lad despised him, yes, *despised* him. When Joseph had come home after more than seven years' absence broken by only a few rare leaves, this boy had resented him. In him Moe had invested the authority which the father should have had. Joseph sensed that she had done this because of Hank's great physical strength and his sheer brutality. Hank despised him, Joseph, because he was incapable of keeping control of his family. Despised him above all because of Moe.

They stood grouped there in the doorway now, watching him. He looked at them as if they were strangers. How had he come to have all these children? Begotten without thought, without love. Were they just the results of lust? The thought was loathsome to him and yet . . . why did it have to be like this? One was lonely . . . got married . . . and suddenly there were all these growing people belonging to you. Why had he never realized them as persons? For now they *were* and they terrified him. He had brought all these people into this world—a world which was already upside down—and he knew nothing about them at all. What were they thinking of *him* as they waited for him to thank them for their gift?

He hated the suit. *Hated* it. He swallowed hard trying to say something, then, seeing the anxious expectancy on their faces, the breathless apprehension in Robert's, who sensed that his father was not pleased with the present, he managed to thank them in a heavy stilted way. It was no use, he could not find any pleasure in their gift, but rather shame—shame that these striplings could give him such a thing. It was all wrong. The world was mad, utterly mad when children could and did earn more than their parents.

He saw the disappointment on the younger ones' faces and hated himself for his mean inability to be grateful. From Hank's contempt to Moe's secretive smile, from Krista's anxiety and Robert's almost agonized expectancy, he looked from one to another and he just could not say the words they were waiting to hear.

"Get out, all of you, if you want to see me in it," he shouted at last; and, relieved, they all withdrew.

But Moe was muttering angrily to herself. Was he going to keep up this battle indefinitely? She had said she was sorry. She had abased herself to him. She had sent her lover away. True, he was only a few doors away down the road, but she hadn't as yet made any attempt to resume her illicit relations with Rudi. Had Joseph been decent and forgiven her she might have given him up for good. She had been frightened by Joseph's violence, not for herself but for her lover. Hank's threats had frightened her for the children. But this belly-aching misery had been going on long enough. Moe could never keep up a quarrel or anger for long. She couldn't live like this. He was like a great dead whale now. Ever since that day when he had surprised her with Rudi he had been like this.

Looking at him now in the bed, she realized with a shock that he was already old. He looked spineless and lifeless on this, his birthday. He might at least make an effort to enjoy the day for which the children had planned so much. Lifeless, that was the word. Well, and didn't she know that? She wanted to pull him from the bed and force some of her own tremendous energy

into his sapless veins. She was suddenly frenzied with rage at him.
The great miserable lump! She made up her mind suddenly. She
would *not* give up her lover—and she would make no secret of it.

What did it matter to her if Joseph taunted her with the fact
that Rudi could almost be her son? That was their own business. Rudi had young girls enough to choose from; he was a
good-looking fellow and he was earning big money. God knew
there were superfluous women enough in the town, but he had
chosen her, Moe. She corrected herself, not "Moe" to Rudi. He
never used the loathed shortened form of the maternal term. He
called her by her Christian name, Margarethe, which Joseph had
never used since the birth of their first child. To Joseph and the
family she was "Moe"; the name she resented rang in her ears all
day for a thousand things. To Rudi she was Margarethe, not just
wife or mother, but a person. When he spoke her name softly, the
years fell away and she was young again, an eager flame of a girl.

At the thought of his strong limbs and the violence of his
love-making she was exultant and at the same time filled with distaste for the man lying there in the bed. Ach! What did that dead
lump of clay know of love like hers and Rudi's? Rudi took her
away to a world of pleasure which in all these years of childbear-
ing she had never known existed. She looked at the man in the
bed now as if he were a stranger and went silently from the room.

XI

THEY WERE ALL in the kitchen when the flowers came. They
had assembled for the midday meal and were arguing whether or
not the table should be carried out into the garden. The day had
turned hot and sultry, and although the door into the yard was
wide open there was no air.

The girls stood holding the dishes of food while the boys,
having over-ruled Moe, were lifting the table to take it out when
Robert, who had been swinging on the garden gate, came rushing in followed by a youth. "Flowers! Flowers! Look, just look!
For Krista for her birthday."

The youth held out a great flat basket tied with ribbons and
covered with cellophane. He also held out a book for Krista to
sign.

When she saw the flowers Krista's heart gave such a jump that she dropped the dish of beans. It crashed to the floor, but so great was the excitement and interest over the flowers that no one said a word. The beans lay amongst their feet and the pieces of broken dish.

"Sign the book, Krista, the boy's waiting."

"Fancy delivering flowers on a Sunday," cried Anna. "I know who sent those."

"Special order, special delivery," grinned the youth, mounting his bicycle which he had left against the fence, "and Happy Birthday, Miss."

Tremblingly she signed her name and, urged by the excited family, ripped off the cellophane covering. She was speechless at the beauty and magnificence of the flowers. They lay in a gold basket—masses of exquisite bluish-pink roses and pale creamy-coloured carnations. None of them had ever seen such a basket of flowers except in the windows of the great florists in the town.

"There's a letter—look!" shrieked Robert. "Open the letter, Krista." But the small white envelope contained only a card. "Happy birthday to Krista. Paul."

It was seized avidly and handed round the family from one to another. Katie looked scornful but the others were delighted.

"I told you so!" cried Anna. "He means it seriously, Krista. Aren't you lucky? Oh, I'd love someone to send *me* flowers like this." She buried her face in the fragrant blooms. "I've never seen such a lovely basket."

Krista stood silent. She couldn't speak. Her heart was thumping again and such a wave of happiness enveloped her that the dirty yard and the dusty garden with the group of curious faces vanished. She saw only Paul's face when she had told him how Pa had found her on his birthday, and that they had given her that same day for her own birthday. He had sent her these wonderful flowers, arranged for them to be delivered specially on a Sunday because it was her birthday.

She could not bear the ring of interested female eyes, the curious stares of the boys. She wanted to be alone with the flowers.

She bent down to begin retrieving the mess of beans to hide her emotion. When she looked up again Pa was there.

He stood staring at the flowers.

"Who sent them?" His voice was harsh.

"Krista's American," said Moe quietly. She was overcome herself by the magnificence of the golden basket and the quantity of flowers. She handed the card to Joseph.

Krista went on clearing up the broken dish and fetched a brush to sweep up the beans.

"Krista!" She looked up, startled by the voice.

"Throw them in the dustbin."

There was a gasp of amazement from the children. Then Moe said angrily, "This is *too* much. Throw them away! You must be mad, Joseph. What's wrong with Krista getting some flowers on her birthday? It's the proper gift for a birthday—especially for a young girl. Take them indoors, Krista, out of the sun. Put them in the shade somewhere until we've had our meal."

"Throw them in the dustbin," repeated Joseph, his eyes on Krista.

She went very white, then gathered up the basket in her arms.

"No, Pa, I can't do that, they're too beautiful—it would be wicked." Her voice was only a whisper. "I'll take them away—I'll give them away—but I *can't* throw them in the dustbin."

"No, no, don't throw them away!" There was a chorus of horrified protest from everyone—even Hank.

Krista took the basket into the house. She put it in the dark cool parlour, knelt down by it on the floor and buried her face in the flowers. Tears flowed down on to the roses. She couldn't stop them. When urgent voices summoned her to come and eat she wiped them hurriedly with her hand and went out into the garden.

The family were all round the table. At the head two places were marked for her and Joseph. Their chairs were decorated with green boughs and marigolds, their names formed on the table-cloth with tiny rosebuds from the rambler rose in the garden.

Joseph was already in his place. He looked unhappy and out of the picture as Krista took her seat beside him. He avoided her smile. His face had a hurt, surprised look. She put her hand timidly on his arm but he brushed it away.

"Bring the food," he said impatiently, "let's get on with it." The boys poured out the wine, bought by them for the occasion. They raised their glasses—even Franz Joseph and Peppi were given some—"To Pa and Krista, Happy Birthday!" they toasted them.

Krista smiled tremulously and thanked them. As she raised her glass she saw only Paul's face, Paul's eyes, and heard only Paul's voice. "Happy Birthday to Krista! Happy Birthday to Krista!"

But Joseph ate in silence, barely acknowledging the toast in his honour and glowering at each child in turn as they committed some small misdemeanour or other until Moe could stand it no longer. He was wearing the new suit. Twice he had taken it off and put it on again. The children had commented on the way it fitted him. They were delighted.

"I must say, you're a nice person to toast," she burst out. "Not a 'thank you' or a smile, not a word for the suit. Not many fathers have children earning enough to give them a present like that—it cost a small fortune."

"It would have been better to put it towards a home," he said sullenly. "What are we going to do when the Peace Treaty is signed? And those flowers, they must have cost a fortune too. It's not right—so much spending, spending . . ." He looked round the table. At the bread, the butter . . . butter was terribly expensive . . . at the meat, the wine and the fruit. He couldn't understand it. In his home in Bavaria meat had been a luxury seldom enjoyed, wine almost never. Pastries and sweets such as those on the table today had been something far beyond his mother's budget. Before the war he and Moe had been very poor. There had been only his pay and all those mouths to feed. They had lived chiefly on bread, potatoes and onions, and had never thought of anything better. Then there had been unemployment—and hunger—until he had joined the army. During the war the children had known little else but hunger. Now they got meat frequently; and all kinds of small luxuries, not once, but often. They paid their share towards the food and they wanted these things. They were no longer content with bread and potatoes and onions. These still formed their staple diet but they wanted and got additions in the form of meat, fish, sausage, fruit and cakes.

"Eat while we have it," Moe would say. "Who knows when we'll have to go without again?"

"Spend while you have it," was another of her bits of advice. "It's no good saving—you'll only lose it all as thousands have done."

Joseph looked at her now. She was eating apple strudel which she had not made herself as his mother would have done, but which she had fetched from the baker's early this morning. She was piling whipped cream on it, as were the girls. The bowl of cream was in the middle of the table and everyone helped himself from it with his spoon. He watched her smack her lips over the goodness of it, saw her encourage the little ones to take more.

"Eat more, eat some more," she would urge them; "who knows what'll happen tomorrow?" The last bit would be solemnly divided into so many tiny portions. Nothing was ever left on the plates. If one child could not have a second helping on Sunday then he was the first to get it on Monday. Moe was scrupulously fair. The children knew this and appreciated it. Everyone got his or her share. She saw to that. Joseph thought of his sister's family starving in the East Zone.

Hank was stuffing himself with cream too. The children seemed to Joseph to be like animals as they seized this, snatched that, and talked with their mouths full. Had they always been like this, or had he only just noticed it? He thumped on the table suddenly.

"You eat like pigs!" he shouted. "Like pigs; and in the East Zone there are thousands of people starving."

They stared open-mouthed at him. Was Pa really going mad? They laid down their spoons. His was untouched, as was his apple strudel.

"Go on eating, children," said Moe. "Your father's not feeling well . . ."

Hank got up. He flung the wine in his glass over his shoulder on to the ground.

"That's to your damned birthday," he jeered. "Happy Birthday indeed. You're a misery! Come on boys, let's forget it and go down the river." He went off with the slouching gait of one of his favourite film stars.

Krista sat pale and miserable. She could not swallow her food. It was the flowers which had upset Pa. She knew that. Paul's lovely roses and carnations had brought misery to this birthday.

But it was not of the flowers that Joseph was thinking as he sat at the birthday table. He was thinking of the suit which was indeed as the shirt of Nessus to him. He hated it, *hated* it.

When they were all seated in the motor-coach the suit seemed to Joseph to burn into his flesh. It was not only that he disliked all formal clothes—it was something far deeper.

It had taken the family a long time to persuade him to go through with the day's planned festivities. A deep brooding had fallen on their father, evident to all of them. He had been like this sometimes in the evenings ever since he came home from the prisoner-of-war camp in France. He would sit there thinking; and when they spoke to him he just didn't hear. Sometimes he would mutter to himself; and the word "shame" was one they frequently caught over and over again.

"It's just the war," Moe would say. "As if *we* didn't have enough to put up with. Why, he never saw a bomb in that last French camp and we were being glutted with them all day and all night. Supposing I just sat and thought about all those deafening, screaming bombs, why, I'd never get up again."

Hank had taken tickets for the whole family to go on a tour of the river valley to Bonn, the new seat of government. They were to see the Chancellor's house and the President's house, and the new colony towns built for the allies. Joseph didn't want to go. He said he was tired.

"Tired on your birthday!" jeered the boys. "Snap out of it, Pa: we've paid for the tickets."

In the end he had been persuaded. Hank had been quite conciliatory. Krista had said that she had never seen the town where the Chancellor lived: she would like to see it with Pa. In their best clothes, the boys with their cycle-club woollen caps gay with large coloured pom-poms, and Moe in a dashing new hat with forget-me-nots on the brim and Joseph in the new suit, they set off in the early afternoon. Katie had to stay behind; someone had to look after Peppi and Franz Joseph, whom Hank had refused to take. Krista offered, but the idea was shouted down. It was *her* birthday! The motor-coach trip was for her as well as Pa.

Katie was furious and stood at the gate to see them go. She was so angry that she would not wave. As she turned to go back into the garden she saw the Frenchman opposite beckoning to her. She knew about him. He had no wife and made do with a series of housekeepers. The last one had walked out on him this week. He was going to ask her if she could find him someone.

She would like to go herself. She liked something about the way he looked at her.

"All alone?" he asked her. His pronunciation of her language amused her. She pointed to the children.

"Come over here and bring them," he called. She went in and locked up the house, and snatching up Franz Joseph before he could stray, took Peppi and him across the road. The little white house was almost hidden by the weeping willows flowing over it. On his veranda were cane lounging chairs, cushions in gay colours, a gramophone and drinks in long glasses. He had two small puppies.

"Sit down," he invited Katie with a smile. He seated her in one of the chairs, put an exciting green drink in her hand and showed Franz Joseph how to work the gramophone. "Play all those," he explained to the delighted little boy, giving him a pile of records. "He can't hurt it, it's so old."

Katie lay back.

"Put up your feet," said the Frenchman. "And now tell me why such a pretty girl as you hasn't got married."

Katie stared at him. "Pretty? I?" she said, astonished. "With this hair."

"It's beautiful," he said, taking a long strand in his hand. "In France, properly dressed and made up, you'd be a riot!" He contemplated her between quizzical eyes, smoking hard at his cigar. "Tell me, is this child yours?" pointing to Peppi. Katie took a sip of the green drink, choked a little, and began telling him about Henri.

Presently he asked her about a housekeeper. Did she know anyone for him? She longed to take the job herself, but Moe would never permit it. She needed Katie too much at home.

"Is it a big house?" she asked, although she knew it was tiny.

"Come and see for yourself," he offered. "It's quite small and a friend who works with me on the Comité des Forges sometimes sleeps here, but I'm alone now since my old housekeeper went back to France." They went upstairs. Peppi and Franz Joseph were entranced with the gramophone. The records lasted a whole hour. They were still playing them when Katie and the Frenchman came down again.

The motor-coach sped down the lovely river road through hills and villages gay with flowers and flags for the summer tourists, then up and across the hills and back by another inland way to the water again. When they came to anything new or of any special interest the driver stopped the coach and, standing up with a large megaphone, delivered a short lecture on the subject.

Down the banks of the ever-widening Rhine they at last reached, after many stops to buy the badges and caps of each small village, the famous Lorelei rock in the middle of the stream where the siren had lured the sailors to their deaths. Here they all got out and listened to a long recitation about the legend. Krista was entranced, so was Moe. They all knew the song about it, and stood there staring at the rock while Hank took photographs of them with it in the background. The road along the river bank was crowded with cars and motor-coaches whose occupants were all doing the same thing. Hank had taken a number of photographs before Joseph noticed that his camera was a new one. He was about to protest at this evidence of further spending when he heard Hank remark that it had cost more than the suit. He was too stupefied to say a word. Where *did* the money come from?

When they reached Bonn they stood staring at the white residence of the Chancellor. Moe was furious.

"He's only got one daughter," she said angrily. "What does he want with a house that size?" And it was the same when they came to the President's.

"We have to pay for it," sneered Hank. "With our taxes."

"Shut up," snapped Joseph. "Would you have our Government representatives living in hovels? They've been put there by the people. It's their right."

When they stood staring in at the windows of the white ugly houses forming the colony of the Allies, some of the occupants came to the windows and drew the curtains across, but one Englishman came out of his house and said sarcastically, "Would you like to come in and see the inside?"

Sarcasm was unknown to Moe. She accepted gratefully. She had an insatiable curiosity about other people's houses, chiefly because she was never invited into any but the Englishwoman's next door.

The man seemed surprised, but he stood aside for her to enter. He seemed astonished when the whole family followed. They tramped up the stairs, and down to the cellar, through the garden, and when there was nothing more to see were obliged to say good-bye. Had the motor-coach horn not been hooting loudly they would have stayed longer, for the Englishman offered them some tea. Moe was so delighted that she could scarcely speak.

"Go outside and tell the driver he must wait," she shouted to Hank. "After all, we are nine people! Something to be reckoned with. Tell him he must wait."

The Englishman asked if they were all one family. When he heard that there were three more at home and two married ones, he was speechless. Hank came running back to say that the driver would not wait. He had twenty-five other passengers and would not wait for nine. Moe reluctantly got up; she was desolate that she could not stay to tea with the foreigner. He, however, seemed relieved. To find unexpected tea for nine guests would have upset the cook who was upstairs dressing herself to go out.

He stood at the door of his house laughing heartily as they drove away. It had made his dull Sunday afternoon. They, the Allies, lived like pariahs in this colony of brand-new ugly houses with their own shops, schools, even their own church—it had been fun to be invaded by such an extraordinary family. The mother, with the ridiculous hat and the fine vivid face, had told him the story of the afternoon's excursion with such gusto that he could still hear her rich throaty voice as she gave her opinions on the size of the President's house, and still more on the Chancellor's.

Joseph was angry that she talked so volubly to a stranger. Hank would not speak at all. He had another of his violently anti-Occupation days. They had been astonished when he accepted the invitation to enter the house.

As they were coming away another motor-coach drew up, and its load of passengers got out and stood staring over the fences of the gardens and in at the windows.

"How rude they are," Moe said. "It's a shame to behave like that." She was unabashed when Joseph said that they had been doing exactly the same.

"He won't ask *them* in," she said triumphantly. "Look, he's drawing his curtains." She turned and waved gaily to the Englishman who waved back with a grin.

Late in the night, when the house was silent after the evening's sing-song into which Joseph had been persuaded, he got up. He slept alone. Moe was still in the slip room. He went to the window and saw that it was a dark heavy night. He put his raincoat over his nightshirt and pulled on his boots. He moved very quietly in the sleeping house. Taking the new suit from the cupboard he climbed with it in his arms out of the window.

The dog, accustomed now to the nightly prowlings of the children, gave only a short suppressed growl as he came out. Joseph loosed him and, hushing his delighted whimpers, stole to the gate. He made his way through the silent village street to the river. In a deserted spot on the tow-path under some thick willows he rolled two heavy stones on to the suit, tied it with cord, and attaching another heavy stone to the cord, he dropped the bundle in the deep water. It sank quickly. He stood there for some time watching the little eddies of bubbles where it had sunk.

The dog stood with his ears cocked, watching too. Suddenly he jumped into the water and began frantically trying to find the bundle.

"Come out, come out," urged Joseph, and scolded the dripping creature when it stood again on the path by him. He patted the thin miserable flanks. He felt a melting affinity somehow with this cowed creature whom he knew the boys ill-treated.

The suit was gone. He felt better. Cleaner in some queer way. It had been a horrible experience wearing it at all. As he passed the bridge he saw with a rising anger the great flares and powerful arc lamps of the night shift as they toiled at the clanking machinery, repairing the bridge. Almost four o'clock and men were working—and for what? For money? So that they could buy new suits, radios, bicycles and cars? So that they could stuff themselves with food and wine? Or were they working for a new bridge? A new bridge to accelerate the economic life of the new country being built all round him? A new country which was to be ten times better and greater than the one which the last disastrous war had shattered?

Headlines of the newspapers glared before his eyes . . . Great Trade Achievement . . . New export market captured . . . Output beyond all hopes . . . Japanese market ours . . . Huge Brazilian Orders. He thought of the weekly talks in the factory on output. More output, more and more. Hadn't he had that accursed free day because of his own increased output? And why had he achieved it? He didn't know. Was his own work for the acceleration of the rebuilding of his country? What was this extraordinary haste, this relentless rushing towards another crisis? It affected them all. They were working, working harder and faster—and for what? Money? Was that it? The country must have money . . . send out the exports to bring in the money. Build, build, build. The hammers were like death-blows in the still night. A large May bug hit him on the forehead. He brushed it frantically away although it was a sign of luck. An owl hooted in the drooping trees. The dog howled suddenly.

Across the river flashed the moving lights of another night shift working on a great building. They were hammering at the new factory shooting up like Jack's beanstalk against the dark wide river-bend. The shouts and whistles of the workmen drifted across the water on the still air. And even the river was not quiet now. Trains of barges were already coming down the waterway carrying some of those urgent exports to other countries. The sky was beginning to lighten. Far away the clock of the cathedral boomed out four slow deep strokes.

XII

THE SIXTH housebreaking expedition brought trouble to the gang. They had completed five successful raids without encountering any difficulties from the inmates of the houses, or the law, and they were growing careless and over-confident. They would laugh and joke every time they passed a policeman. What fools the police were. Why, it was easy hoodwinking them; the idiots were just having circles run round them by a pack of youngsters. On the sixth prowl, the first two to enter the chosen house were surprised by the caretaker. He was an old man but he was no coward, and he put up a fight for his master's possessions. Hank, who had entered with Alfred, another important member of the gang, lost his head at this unexpected obstacle. When he could not fell the old man with his fists he pulled out his heavy bicycle chain and struck again and again. Even when the defenceless old body had fallen lifeless in a pool of blood Hank went on striking with a ferocious maniacal look on his face. Katie, who had followed closely on the heels of the first two, stood watching him in horrified fascination. She remembered Hank stamping and hitting at some small creature exactly in this wild way when he had been a child.

Leo, behind her, screamed to him. "Stop it! Stop it! You fool, you'll kill him, and then we're for it."

The boy Alfred, frantic with fear, dragged Hank's arms from the body. Hank, panting a little and with a queer brilliant light in his usually dull eyes, calmly replaced his weapon under his belt and ordered the others to make it snappy. The old man had not had a chance to cry out; Hank had struck too quickly. With the exception of the twins, keeping watch at the gate on this their first adventure, the whole gang were now standing looking silently at the caretaker.

Hank bent down and cold-bloodedly went through the old man's pockets. He found, as he had hoped, a bunch of keys. "Saves us a lot of time and trouble," he said. "We needn't break anything open."

Leo was gazing in horror at the body on the floor. He knelt down and listened for breathing. There was none. He felt for a pulse as well as he could with his gloved hand. Then he stood up.

"You've done it," he snarled. "He's a deader."

"Rubbish," snapped Hank. "I didn't hit him hard enough."

He looked round at the ring of hostile faces accusing him silently, and began furiously to justify himself.

"If I hadn't got at him he'd have reached the telephone, you fools and he'd have seen both Alfred's and my face. We'd thrown back our hoods. Eddie's slipped up on this—he swore there'd be no one in the house. I had no choice . . . We're all in this—understand? *All* of us. Now get going or the evening's wasted."

Leo, quickly pulling himself together, gave some short sharp orders and the house was hastily ransacked. They worked noiselessly in their rubber-soled shoes and gloved hands. Tonight they were even more noiseless—as if they feared that the dead man on the floor might hear. Leo's face was a greenish white as he stood by the quiet figure. He was thinking of all those months he had already spent in prison. He was not only older now, so that he would be dealt with as an adult, but this was murder. *Murder!*

Surely the old buffer must be alive. He bent down again and tried to find some sign of life but there was none in the grey face and wide open mouth. The eyes stared sightlessly at him. Suddenly he felt as if a cold draught had passed over him, although the sweat was pouring down his face. He thought he was going to fall and steadied himself with a hand on the table.

Hank, coming back at that moment, snapped, "Ready? All right. We've got a damned good haul tonight. No wonder they left this old fool to guard it, and look what I've found,"—showing a Luger to Leo—"it'll come in useful for us."

"Is it loaded?"

Hank nodded.

"Hand it over," ordered Leo, whose colour was coming back.

"No, finding's keeping," sneered Hank, putting the gun into his belt.

"Hand it over," repeated Leo quietly, and there was something in his quiet voice which made the brutal Hank shudder. Slowly he removed the revolver and handed it to Leo.

"I'm the head of this gang. Understand? *You* did the killing. You did it alone, but the law of the gang is that we're all in this together. Now . . . any marks anywhere? All got gloves on? What about the keys? Put them back in his pocket, Hank. Now then, give me a hand, number five, and help me roll him under the table. With this dark red tablecloth and the chairs round the table he won't be found in a hurry. Good thing the carpet's red too. It'll all soak in, probably won't show at all. Replace the shutters and listen for the all clear after I've contacted the twins."

They got away without incident and the stuff was loaded on to the barge again.

"Good load tonight," commented the man who admired Katie. "Must be some toff who had all this stuff."

"Made it all off other people's stupidity. He's a politician," snapped Leo. "Deserves to lose it."

"True," agreed the older barge man. "This'll be our last trip for some months now. We'll be back next week with your share; then don't expect us again. We've autumn business coming along and that'll keep us in Holland for some time."

When the gang met separately as usual later on in the shelter, Leo called the roll carefully. The twins had seen nothing of the murder of the old man; they had merely been keeping watch at the gate armed with a whistle for emergency. Now they heard of it with terror. Leo made a short statement to the gang. Then he ordered each in turn to swear the oath of loyalty.

"This is bound to get about; there are so many robberies that they pass, but this is murder. Understand? *Murder.*" He looked at Hank as he repeated the word. "It just depends on how soon the body is discovered. Now remember—any crime like this, committed in our raids due to obstruction, is a crime shouldered by us all. Now, swear the oath, all of you."

When it came to the turn of the twins they hung back.

"Swear it!" snarled Hank. "You miserable cowards, you worried me enough to come. You worried me sick. Well, now you've had a bellyfull and you're in it with us. Come on, swear the oath or I'll sling you both in the river and you won't come up again either."

Katie had watched the murder of the old caretaker with a fixed glassy stare. She had been too frightened to protest. Hank's ruthlessness had opened her eyes to what she had done. It was she who had brought him into this, and now seeing him strike so savagely and with such an appalling lust for killing on his brutal face, she was terrified. She shrank from him in horror and was sitting as far away from him as she could. Leo was cruel but he was careful, not brutal. Leo thought things out and hurt one in another way. For instance tonight when she had clung to him he had said: "That's a good-looking sister I saw with your father last Friday night on the tow-path. She's a nice little bit. It's about time you introduced her to me. That's the sort I like. The ones who look like angels give me a double kick!"

She had been sick with jealousy and hatred of Krista and determined that she should never meet Leo. Now, when she moved closer to him in the corner of the shelter, he brushed her away impatiently, telling her to get up and take the oath like the rest of them.

"And what if I don't?" she asked sullenly. She was still shaken from what she had witnessed in that house, and being the gang leader's girl she thought she had the right to exemption from the oath.

"Swear the oath and make the sign," said Leo in a dangerously quiet voice: and without further protest she repeated the words required of her. It was as she raised her now ungloved hand to make the sign before her face that she began to recoil in horror. Her hand was red with blood. She had helped to roll the old man under the table. She stopped in the middle of the last vile words of the oath and pitched forward in a dead faint.

When the commotion was over, and Leila and the twins had revived her with a swig of brandy stolen from the house, they had all been commanded by Leo to take off their black gloves and those whose hands were blood-stained had washed them in river-water fished up in an old tin by Hank.

They were all silent now. Fear was in them; and Leo suggested breaking up the meeting and getting home. They left separately as always, slipping out one by one, and calling softly if it was all clear for the next to emerge. The last to leave, as always, were Hank, Leo, and Katie. None of them spoke. Leo neither touched nor looked at Katie, who could barely stand up on her feet. Wedged in between the two lads she could not bear her brother's hands round her body—her gorge rose every time she had a vision of his face as he killed. The twins had gone on ahead on their bicycles. It was dangerous, and made the return doubly so, but they had no choice. Two of the gang were absent owing to illness and the twins had taken their place as look-outs. Eddie had not dared to keep the car lent them by the garage-hand long enough to take the twins home. They had come and must return on their bicycles.

They reached home before the others, having cut across the fields, and in putting away the cycles woke Robert. He left his bed and came to see what was happening. He was stupefied at seeing the twins out in the early hours of the morning. That Hank and Katie went out sometimes he knew and worried over—but now the twins too. They silenced him roughly with threats, and fear for themselves lent them an untoward brutality. Robert, accustomed to good nature and fun from these two brothers, shrank back.

"Get back to bed," threatened Hans; "and forget you've seen us. If you open your mouth to anyone—*anyone*, mind you—we'll shut it for you for good."

Robert stole back to the room he shared with Franz Joseph and Krista. She was awake and asked him fearfully where he had been, but the child, whose teeth were chattering in spite of the warm night, replied that he had only been to the lavatory. Krista tucked him up in the truckle bed he shared with Franz Joseph.

"What is it?" she whispered. "Tell me, Robert. What's the matter, darling? *Tell* me."

"Nothing, nothing," he insisted, turning resolutely over to the wall.

Krista went back to her bed but she couldn't sleep. She was waiting for the sound of the motor cycle which she knew would come soon now, for she had heard it earlier in the night and Katie had left Peppi with her again. She pressed his little head on to her shoulder. What *was* it they did in the night? Why didn't they ask Moe for a key? Were they afraid of Joseph, who would never have allowed it and who liked all his family to be in bed early?

She tossed and turned, listening for the sound of the machine which heralded the return of the night prowlers. She knew that Robert wasn't asleep either and that he was listening as keenly as she was. Presently it came faintly, and then shortly afterwards the sounds of Hank and Katie returning very cautiously.

Katie and Anna's room was next to hers and later in the dawn when she had fallen asleep she was again awoken. This time the sound which woke her was of sobbing. It came through the wall, and Krista knew that it was Katie. She got up quietly and tiptoed to the closed door, then opened it gently and entered.

"Katie?" she whispered, "Katie, what is it? Are you ill?" But the only answer from the tumbled head buried in the pillow was a muttered "Go away, Krista, leave me alone—" and there was in the whisper such a fierce insistence that she crept back to her room without another word.

Katie was careless by nature—as careless as her mother, but neither as generous nor as clean. Those black woollen gloves saturated with the blood of the old caretaker were left by her on the window-sill of the room she shared with Anna. Anna, good-natured, and, if it did not involve too much trouble, kind, was washing some woollen things, and seeing the gloves lying there, swept them up, to find them damp and sticky. She rolled them up with some garments of the children's before she sorted the things out for the washtub.

When she picked them up again she saw that the children's white vests had red stains on them—stains suspiciously like blood. Separating the gloves from the other garments she examined them carefully, then placed them in a basin of cold water.

The water was immediately stained red—the red of blood—and as she moved the gloves about with a wooden spoon it became deeper in colour.

Anna went to find Katie. She was disturbed. She looked first at her sister's hands, but there were no cuts or wounds on them. "Katie," she said abruptly, "your gloves are covered in blood. What on earth have you been doing with them?"

To her astonishment Katie turned a burning red and panic showed in her eyes.

"Where did you get them, you meddlesome creature?" she screamed furiously. "Prying into my affairs—give me the gloves . . ."

She followed Anna to the bathroom where she saw the basin of red water and the gloves soaking in it. Her face went pale. Anna thought she was going to faint. She knew Katie's inability to see blood without this nausea.

"You wore them two nights ago when you came back so late, or rather so early. Oh, yes, I'm not always asleep. What on earth were you doing?" Then as Katie did not answer, but stood staring at the reddish water, a headline in the local paper swam before Anna's eyes. "Murder of caretaker during owner's absence. Burglary causes caretaker's death". The evening papers had been full of the finding of the old man's body. His daughter had arrived early in the morning and could obtain no answer to her bell. She had noticed the cut shutter slats and had fetched the police.

Why should this particular paragraph jump to her mind exactly now? Anna didn't know why, except that when she had pointed it out to Krista last evening and had remarked jokingly that Katie and Hank had been out that very night, she had been astonished at the sudden pallor of Krista, who had said agitatedly, "Anna, we *must* find out what they do and where they go. They are going more and more often, and Katie always has plenty of money now—she never used to have a penny of her own. Last time the twins went too—Robert saw them come back. He wouldn't tell me at first because they threatened him until he was terrified."

"Leo gives her the money—she's his present fancy. Don't be silly, Krista, I was only joking." Anna laughed reassuringly. "They go to some low dive in the town and dance. You know how Katie loves it. You've seen the clothes she wears. She takes Hank as a blind, that's all."

But something had registered in Anna's mind even as she reassured Krista. What was it? That Hank was not the sort to be used as anybody's blind, and that he loathed dancing—could never be coaxed to join in the fun when Pa sometimes taught them Bavarian folk dances in the garden. He always insisted that it was silly and preferred to play or clap for them. She could not really believe that he would even enter such a place as a dive connected in any way with dancing.

Now, again, the panic in Katie's eyes brought back that paragraph to Anna's mind. For Krista had talked about the crime—the owner of the house was a friend of one of the owners of the factory. He was frequently there, was actually known to several of the employees. Thus the whole horrible crime had been discussed over the filling, sealing and labelling of the bottles of perfume at the chain-belt table at which Krista was working this month.

Anna looked mistrustfully at Katie. Doubt was beginning to creep into her lazy mind.

Katie saw this. "It was one of the boys. He fell off his motor cycle and cut his leg. I helped to hold the cut together until we had torn up some handkerchiefs to bind it," she said defiantly.

"With your dirty gloves on?" jeered Anna. "What about our first-aid classes? It was the night that old caretaker was bumped off—sure you weren't holding him?"

This chance shot produced such an effect that Anna was startled. Katie's face went even paler; her eyes were frantic as she faced Anna.

"Shut up! Keep your big mouth closed!" she shouted. "Give me that basin."

"Why, Katie! Whatever's biting you? You look mad! Here, take your beastly mitts. I don't want them. They've ruined these vests and Moe will be furious."

"And so I will," shouted Moe, sweeping in on hearing her name. "Wasting time gossiping here when there's so much to be done." She looked from one to another. "What's all this? You two are always quarrelling. Take after your father, both of you always disagreeable." She stopped short at the sight of the blood-stained water in which the gloves still lay.

"I just thought I'd do her a good turn by washing her gloves which she left on the window-sill, and look what they've done to these vests," said Anna angrily. "*I'm* not disagreeable. *She* is! I asked her what she'd been doing to get all that blood on her hands and she screamed like a wild cat and turned green."

Moe looked from the gloves to Katie's agitated face. Into her own face came an expression very like fear.

"Take them and wash them yourself," she said sharply. "And learn not to talk so loudly. And you'll wash out all these vests again. They belong to your brat and it's you who should be doing them, not Anna. You're dirty as well as lazy. You're getting worse and worse since you've taken up with that good-for-nothing at the repair station. Fancy leaving gloves with blood on them. Why didn't you put them in water at once?" Moe's voice was rising and rising in spite of her just having told Katie not to talk so loudly, and she had begun working herself up into one of her rages. They were short-lived but terrifying while they lasted. Now she stamped and shouted round the house, railing at the children, sweeping things out of her path; anyone who crossed it got a swinging blow from her strong arms. A few minutes later she would pick them up and caress them. They never bore her any ill-will—it was just Moe.

Katie bore the brunt of this rage now without a word. She was thankful that her mother's outburst had taken Anna's mind off the gloves. She was terrified lest Hank should hear of the affair. He would be furious with her for her carelessness and she would pay dearly for it. She took the gloves, holding them with the tips of her fingers as if they would bite her, and covering them with soap powder began resolutely to rub them. The face of the old caretaker with his wide-open mouth and eyes had never left her since that night. Now, seeing his blood again on her hands, she began to retch.

Anna, returning from a skirmish with Moe, watched her dispassionately.

"If you're going to have another baby you'd better have it somewhere else," she observed without emotion. "Pa's in no mood for any more; he's turning real queer. Sometimes I think he's going mad. You'd better watch your step."

"Shut up! Shut up! Leave me alone!" screamed Katie. As her efforts to overcome the nausea broke down, she pushed her sister violently out of the way, and rushed to lock herself in the bathroom.

XIII

MOE WAS dressing herself to visit Carola. Every Tuesday and Friday afternoon she put on her best clothes and went to the hospital which lay outside the town. The nuns who tended the child spoke of her as an exemplary mother. She never missed a visit, and she was never late. For Mass, expeditions, for trains and trams, Moe was never on time, and would arrive untidy and panting; but for Carola she arrived as soon as the great clock boomed out the three strokes which meant that visitors could enter the wards.

Carola would lie with her face turned towards the door through which her mother entered. The nuns would arrange her like that, for she was still paralysed. On the stroke of three Moe would come in, full of smiles and caresses, and with her bag and pockets full of sweets and fruit for the child. Sister Mayella and Sister Ruth loved to watch the little patient's face as her mother came through the door.

It was for her mother that Carola had first smiled—even her face had been paralysed. It was for Moe that she had recently moved one leg—the smallest fraction, but she *had* moved it—and the good sisters were convinced that it would be Moe who would make Carola take her first step when her helpless limbs were finally freed from their encasing plaster. They welcomed Moe's visits, just as Moe loved to come. To the nuns Moe was a good mother and a good woman. She obeyed all the rules and never smuggled forbidden things to her child. She was never upset or allowed herself to appear upset before Carola. The child came first. Always.

As she dressed herself—she always put on her Sunday best for Carola—she called Katie to her. Katie had been out of sorts lately. She neither scolded nor sang, never danced, and she was not eating her food. Moe had overlooked none of these things. The girl came unwillingly at her mother's insistent call.

Moe, putting on a new hat with feathers in it, looked at Katie in the mirror. Yes, there was no doubt about it. There were the little tell-tale blue shadows under the eyes, her belt was just that much too tight, and her jersey strained over her big breasts.

"Are you pregnant?" Moe asked harshly, and as the revealing colour spread over the girl's face she turned on her furiously.

"Who is it this time? Why can't you be more careful? We can't have any more brats here."

Katie's flush faded and a white misery took its place. "How far is it?" demanded Moe remorselessly, her eyes sweeping Katie's body.

"Two months." The words came unwillingly from the girl's lips.

"Will he marry you? Or is he tired of you?" came scathingly from Moe. "You don't know how to keep a man—you never will. You're all over them like treacle. They're sated before they've begun."

"Shut up! Shut up!" screamed Katie. "You don't know what you're saying."

"I know well enough what Pa will say to you!" retorted Moe sharply. "He'll tell you to clear out! He's not as good-natured as he was. He's turned real sour lately."

She put the hat on at another angle and prinked at herself in the mirror. Before Rudi was her lover she had never looked in it. Now she wondered all the time if he saw her as the mirror reflected her.

"Like it?" she asked more amiably.

Katie flattered her gratefully. She was frightened at what Moe had just said about Pa turning her out. There would be no mercy from Leo, and who would want her with Peppi and an unborn child?

"You'd better see what you can do about it," went on Moe more mildly. "You're only seventeen now—and two children will be a double burden on you." She picked up her gloves, satisfied now with the hat.

"What d'you mean?" asked Katie sullenly.

"What I say," snapped Moe impatiently, spraying herself with some toilet water which came from Krista's factory. She liked to smell nice for Carola, who always sniffed appreciatively. The child could still smell, and hospital smells were not always agreeable.

Noticing Katie's woebegone face, she relented. She could never be angry for long. She put a hand on the girl's shoulder. "No use worrying, that won't get rid of it. You must get him to marry you. Cheer up—I'll look after you."

As she went out of the gate she called to her not to forget that she must collect Franz Joseph from the kindergarten. "And see you're not late or he'll stray away," she shouted again, leaving Katie staring into the mirror.

Punctually as the third boom from the clock died away the doors of the hospital were flung open for the visitors and the very first to enter was Moe. At the sight of her mother Carola's pale face was illuminated with a joy so vibrant that Sister Ruth felt choked. Down the long room came Moe, brave in her new feathered hat, her arms full of packages, flowers and fruit. Perhaps only her lover knew her like this, as with infinite gentleness she put her arms round the little girl and stroked her face with fingers that shook.

"Did you bring Robert?" asked the child, after all the surprises in the parcels had been examined. Robert, nearest in age to Carola, had always been her inseparable playmate.

"He'll come on Sunday with Krista—he had to go to school this afternoon." Moe thought with a pang that the child's voice was even weaker today.

She had given up bringing Franz Joseph, in spite of Carola's pleadings. He had a habit of disappearing and of being found in some ward quite far away where he entertained the patients until forcibly removed by one of the nuns. Franz Joseph's faculty for disappearance was extraordinary. In spite of his robust and very sturdy little person he could slip away under one's very nose.

Carola lay with her hand between Moe's two strong worn ones. She could move all her fingers now, and traced the veins and lines in her mother's hand lovingly as if she would learn to remember and treasure even those when she was alone again.

"Father Lange came," she said suddenly.

A shadow passed over Moe's face.

"He wants me to have my first communion soon."

"You're too young," said Moe firmly. Had she not been with the child she would have said it angrily, but as always, she controlled her voice in her presence.

"I'm nearly eight. Father Lange doesn't think that's too young, and the sisters would like that too. So would I . . ."

"But my darling, you can't get up yet. You must wait until you get stronger." She did not say "Until you can walk" because in her heart she did not think that her child would ever walk again.

"Father Lange says that the Bishop will come here and do it—there's another girl and a boy, too . . ."

An ominous pang shot through Moe's heart. This could surely mean but one thing, that Carola was not going to get better.

She felt furious that, unknown to her, the priest had discussed such things with the child. But then she reflected that she was at present on no terms with him to discuss anything with her—neither was Joseph. The child in the next bed was listening avidly and said now: "Carola won't go to heaven unless she's had her first communion—I've had mine, so I'm safe."

"That's simply not true," said Moe calmly. "You can ask Father Lange yourself . . . he will tell you that all little children go to heaven."

The thin, pinched-looking child shook her head. "Oh no," she said positively. "We are born in sin. Carola and I want to be on the safe side. We confess our sins to each other. We each pretend to be the priest in turn. We do not," she finished proudly, "give absolution unless we are truly sorry."

Moe was shocked, but Sister Ruth, coming in at that moment, was quite unperturbed.

"I don't think they ought to pretend to be the priest," insisted Moe. "It's not right."

"If you had to lie in this room day in and day out for months you would pretend *anything*," said Sister Ruth calmly. "And the first person to understand would be the good father." She patted the little girls' heads affectionately.

The moment Moe dreaded was the one when she had to steel herself to get up, say good-bye calmly and walk away. It would have been so much easier to walk out without a backward glance at the little figure in the bed whose eyes never left her—so very much easier than to have to keep turning to wave and smile as Carola expected her to do.

None of Moe's children had ever been ill beyond the usual colds and ailments of childhood. She herself had never been ill in her life, nor had Joseph. In the face of this terrible thing which had fallen on Carola she was helpless. When the child had first been struck down she had been in a fury of anxiety. She never doubted the skill and care of the doctors at the great hospital. She had given all her spare money for prayers for the child's recovery. She had gone to the Black Madonna whom everyone knew could work miracles, and spent hours on her knees praying for life and energy to be given back to the helpless limbs. Krista had done the same; so had Joseph.

No miracle came, and in place of faith had come anger, anger at God who could strike down an innocent child. Surely of all her children Carola was the most blameless. What was the use of Father Lange rebuking her so sternly for her refusal to accept God's will? Resentment had taken the place of faith, anger the place of love, for the child had lain in this bed ever since.

Carola had been in hospital for six months when Moe had met Rudi at the Carnival. She had had several chance adventures during the days of the blitz on the town. Joseph had been away, and everyone else did the same. After Joseph came home she had never thought of such things—until she met Rudi.

Rudi had made friends with the family. The extraordinary thing was that they liked him, and he liked them all. He was quiet, slept all day because he was on a night-shift which paid almost double. He was pleasant and he gave no trouble. It was when Moe conceived such a passion for him that she cared for nothing else that all the trouble started. She dominated everyone by her sheer vitality and high animal spirits. She fascinated him as she did many others by her abounding exuberant joy in life, her thrusting vibrant love of life itself. Among other women of her age, tired and worn out by the struggle for existence in a devastated country ravaged by a recent war, she stood out like a great flaming poppy amongst tired marguerites.

In her new-found happiness she was utterly shameless. As for her religion—something which she had always accepted as a necessary part of life—she didn't care now about that either. What had God done for her? Allowed the enemies' bombs to destroy the home for which she and Joseph had striven and worked, and then struck down the most sinless and innocent of her children. Why should Carola have to suffer? Why not Anna, or Katie, or Lise—all three guilty of the sins of the flesh? She gave up the struggle to understand and abandoned herself so wildly to her lover that she lived almost in a dream of desire into which the children and the everyday chores were as bubbles on its surface.

She knew that she was wicked and she didn't care. It was only here in this quiet ward with the serene-faced nuns and her most loved child that she felt any vestige of guilt. Only this child's patient resigned little face could give her this feeling. The face of the famous Black Madonna, once the most beautiful thing in the world to her, could not move her to a sense of sin as this child's could. When Carola spoke of the possibility of her first communion Moe had been overwhelmed with fear; not only because it meant that the doctors might have abandoned hope, but because it meant that she must herself soon come to terms with God. When Joseph had spat at her naked body she had felt only contempt; but when Carola looked at her with eyes of love she felt more naked than when he had dragged her from her lover's bed.

XIV

THE ICE CREAMS which Robert had enjoyed with Father Lange had elicited for the priest the fact that the child was terrified by his older brothers: by something which went on at night and in which, as far as he could make out, most of Robert's family seemed to be involved.

The boy's reluctance to talk was obviously due to fear. Father Lange had no illusions about Hank. He knew him to be a cruel, brutal lad who would hurt any creature smaller and weaker than himself. Katie he knew also as a spiteful, rather mean-natured girl. She was loose, not because she was warm-hearted and could not refuse like so many girls, but because she wanted gain from her body's favours. The Belgian, for instance, whom she considered to have treated her shamefully, had been extremely good to her in the matter of gifts of food and money, to say nothing of perfumes and cosmetics which he got from Belgium for her. The priest got to know all these things. It was impossible not to know them in such a village. As to her having been seduced at the age of fourteen, had Father Lange not known her real age he himself would have put her down as twenty-five now. At that time she looked quite twenty.

Since this new horrible affair of the lodger, the family no longer came in a bunch to Mass each Sunday. That had been something which the villagers had watched in silence. For say what they would, they were a fine brood of children as, dressed in their Sunday best, they followed their parents through the village street. Even the little ones had been in the flock, shepherded by the older ones. Fifteen of them, and all one family; not many could boast that, certainly none in this village.

Now this solidarity which the priest had applauded was a thing of the past. Now only Anna, Krista and the four little ones came. Willi and Lise were married—both no sooner than they should be—and Carola lay in the hospital.

This family, always a thorn in the flesh to the village, were now rapidly becoming the focus of violent ill-feeling. The villagers here, once ardent Nazis, were proud, arrogant and self-satisfied. One saw that by the way they treated the wretched refugees billeted on them. If they were forced to have them in their homes—every house had to be measured, and where there was extra space after each member of the family had been accounted for, refugees were sent by the housing authorities—the resentful householders had a thousand ways of showing their annoyance. They could, and did, make life a burden for the homeless. Turning off the water, the gas, refusing them access to the bathroom or lavatories, locking the door on them, tying string across the stairs so that they would fall—all these and a thousand other petty miseries were endured constantly. The priest, listening to a daily recital of these examples of man's inhumanity to man, was sometimes depressed. Often he thought that the bunker family was the most charitable of them all. Moe never complained of her neighbours, and no beggar was ever turned from her door. Since the extra kitchen had been put in upstairs there had been peace. If she resented the contemptuous attitude of her neighbours she never said so. Only when the owner's wife—the woman who had formerly lived in the big house—sometimes came and abused her, did she shout back, and Moe, when roused, was not to be under-estimated.

She was hated far more than Joseph. Joseph, who now had to be dragged and carried through the street dead drunk from time to time, was a spectacle which shocked and outraged these river villagers, and for which they blamed Moe. From the first they had never liked her. Anyone who had actually lived for four years in a bunker with all those children was something below their understanding. No one in this village had actually lost his home. That it had been in the line of actual fighting as the Allies advanced had been terrible enough. There were shrapnel-holes all over the houses, but they had been spared the horrors of bombing, although they had seen the fires of the blazing town every night, and heard the bombers in great droves going over them to drop their monstrous loads.

Decent people lived in houses—they got them somehow. Just as they had no pity for the homeless bombed-out people from the town, neither had they any for the refugees now. Let them stay in their own East zone. Weren't they occupied here too? Was it their fault if the victors had cut the country into four quarters and they happened to find themselves in the worst one?

After a time, when the bunker family had started their week-end evening concerts in the gardens, the villagers had gone to the authorities and complained. They had got no satisfaction. Then they had the idea of urging the British family next door to them to complain to the Bürgermeister. He would listen to the voice of the Occupation, they said. But the British family said that they were not disturbed by the noise, and nothing would induce them to complain. The Frenchman who lived in the little white house under the weeping willows, and who managed the coal in the district, also insisted that he was not inconvenienced by the concerts which the bunker family sometimes kept up until the early hours of the morning.

Father Lange was heartily sick of hearing of the misdeeds, the rudeness, the noise and the unsatisfactory behaviour of the most tiresome family in his parish. In fact he would no longer listen. The latest rumour, for instance, was that certain members of the family went out in the early hours of the morning and did not return until dawn; that there was something sinister going on there. Knowing the family and the village, the priest put it down to amorous adventures of the elder ones. Both Anna and Katie had borne illegitimate children whom he had baptized. He came to the conclusion that they were using the boy Robert as a look-out to let them in and out of the house. He decided wearily that he would soon be baptizing more little bastards with black eyes, but nothing worse than illicit love ever entered his head.

He was therefore surprised when, returning just before dawn one morning from administering the last sacrament to a dy-ing-woman, he found himself nearly run down by a motor cyclist in the dark lane. Father Lange was carrying a torch and flashed it on the rider. To his astonishment there were three people on the machine. They were dressed in dark clothes and with a sort of hood which children wore on their mackintoshes—Capucin hoods. The light from his torch shone full on the face of Hank, and revealed clearly Katie's brilliant red hair under the hood which had slipped back as she clutched at the driver when he swerved to avoid the priest.

"Stop! Stop there!" he shouted furiously, but the machine, which had been coasting, began to function again and, gathering speed, went on down the lane.

It was with a very thoughtful face that Father Lange returned to his little house by the church. He was alert and observant, and in spite of the shock which his near-accident had given him, he had made a mental note of the number of the machine.

X V

FRANZ JOSEPH had the soul of an explorer. He played alone, he wandered alone, liking his own company. Too young for school he was taken every morning by his brothers to the kindergarten kept by the nuns in the convent next to the church on the river. His merry monkey face with the black mischievous eyes and big laughing mouth made him a great pet of the good sisters there.

He was fond of wandering through the village and worming his way into strange houses and gardens, so great was his desire to explore the world which lay outside his home. He had twice been found in the laundry near the station, and once even watching the dentist, whose house was near their own, removing a lady's tooth. He had hidden behind a screen and only been discovered when he had clapped his hands in appreciation as the tooth came out. The dentist had been amused when the boy explained that as the door was open he thought he could come in, but the lady had been very annoyed.

The house next door was one to which he could always go provided the Englishwoman was there. The horrid girl who usually answered the door always told him roughly to go away, but if the Englishwoman was at home she usually invited him in. He liked to stand and look at all the queer things in her house. They were all so different from those in Moe's house. There were lots of pictures there, while in Moe's house there was only the one of the Lorelei.

"Moe doesn't have one like that!" he would say after gazing in rapt silence at some picture or object. "Hers is much better than yours."

He said it as if to reassure himself that it really was so. He was too young to understand that the fascination which the objects held for him was their beauty. Like his father he loved beautiful things—bright colours, flowers, butterflies and beetles. Of all the boys this child was the one most like his father. In childhood Joseph had had the same merry acceptance of life, the same exciting desire to see and explore for himself the enthralling mysteries of the world. At a time when this child should have enchanted and compensated him for much, Joseph was too utterly shaken by life's struggle to notice him.

The English lady had become a great friend of Franz Joseph. She would often give him sweets. If she forgot, he would say, "Have you any sweets today?" and she would take the box or tin from the glass-cabinet in the corner and open it gravely.

"How many may I take?" he would ask, looking anxiously at her.

She would laugh and tell him, five, ten, or perhaps more: it depended on the size and variety.

He would choose them solemnly and slowly, counting them out and savouring the lusciousness of each one. She would replace the box in the cabinet and say, "Well, Franz Joseph, and what do you say?"

He would bow gravely, click his little heels as he had been taught by the nuns and say, "Thank you."

Sometimes he would tell her various bits of news and gossip of the family, or of the village. He knew a great deal because he got around so much. Sometimes he would only look at things, or she would show him pictures of her little boy. Sometimes he just went and asked for the sweets, or in season apples or pears, and later in the autumn for walnuts which grew on the large tree at the bottom of her garden. He had told her all about Carola in the hospital, and one day she had given him a parcel for his sister. Moe had been astonished and delighted when he had brought it home. He told her about the Englishwoman's cat and dog who were great friends and slept together in a basket and ate from the same bowl. She had a little boy, he told his mother, but she had sent him away to school in England. He lived in the school and slept in it. "Fancy that! Horrible!" said Moe. She had heard that the British sent their children away and kept dogs in their place: now here was proof of it!

Franz Joseph usually called next door on Fridays; that was the day of the week when the Englishwoman renewed her stock of sweets. He knew exactly when she came back from shopping and all the parcels had been taken in from the back of the car. He knew to a nicety when the girl who answered the door would be out, because if he climbed the tall poplar by the acacia he could see everything that went on in his own and her house. He loved to climb to the top of the poplar and, hidden in its leaves, peer through the windows of old Fräulein Schmidt's room upstairs. She was like the old witch in *Hansel and Gretel*, always stirring something evil-smelling in a pot on her gas-ring. The window through which he could look into the Englishwoman's house belonged to the room in which she painted pictures. He would watch her as she mixed the colours on a wooden thing and she had lots of brushes. One day she had looked up and had been startled to see the little monkey-face so close to the window-pane; but she had opened the window very gently and told him to be very careful not to fall.

"Can your little boy climb as high as this?" he had asked, and she had nodded and said that in the summer holidays he would come home and Franz Joseph could see for himself.

"From England?" he asked. And she said, "Yes, on a big boat from England."

After that he had often climbed up and watched her painting, until one day the horrid girl who did the cleaning had caught him peering into the room. She had shouted so roughly that he nearly fell: told him to go away at once: that he was a rude inquisitive boy. Franz Joseph had been very hurt.

"The Englishwoman doesn't mind," he had shouted; "she likes me, I tell you."

But at that moment his father had come home and looked up, hearing the shouting in the tree. He had been very angry.

"She's quite right, it's very rude to look into other people's windows, and if I catch you doing it again I'll beat you."

Although Joseph had never beaten any of the children and Franz Joseph had climbed the tree again, he had not dared to peep into either Fräulein Schmidt's or the Englishwoman's windows again.

The day that Moe set off for the hospital after questioning Katie about her pregnancy, Franz Joseph had one of his exploring moods. Kindergarten was over at half past three when he was fetched by Moe or Katie. At four o'clock the nuns stood in the garden of the convent handing over the last little ones to their respective families. Franz Joseph had been making a paper boat in the handwork class. Sister Elizabet had taught them to make paper cut-outs with blunted scissors. Franz Joseph had only just been promoted to scissors, but he had made the best boat in the class.

He held it in his chubby hands as he waited with Sister Elizabet at the convent gates for Katie. The boat had opened new visions of the world to him. Already he could see it sailing up the great river which Pa had told him went in one direction to Switzerland and in the other to Holland. He just could not get there fast enough to try it out. The tow-path was to him the scene of many glorious adventures. Here, lying on his stomach in the tall grass he would travel, an intrepid adventurer, through the jungle and swirling waste waters in a canoe made of bark. The reeds became huge tropical trees, the insects great jungle beasts.

The river was strictly forbidden unless someone accompanied him. But today Franz Joseph's soul was already far away with his boat. Vivid pictures of the jungle which the nuns had shown him fired his imagination. He couldn't bear to wait to begin the great adventure. When Sister Elizabet's attention was taken off him by Sister Gertrud, who had come to ask her something, Franz Joseph ran up to them saying, "Here's Katie—I can see her, good-bye, Sisters, and God be with you." which was the farewell they were taught in the kindergarten.

He ran off up the road as if he had really seen someone coming for him. Sister Elizabet called good-bye and thought no more about it. She was astonished when ten minutes later a hot and impatient Katie arrived to collect her brother.

"But you came for him ten minutes ago!" she protested. "He saw you coming down the road."

"Well, he couldn't have—I've only just come!" retorted Katie crossly.

Sister Elizabet was loath to think the child had lied.

"You're very late," she said reprovingly. "Have you come straight from your home?"

Katie replied sulkily that she had not. She had, in fact, come from the repair station. She had been upset by Moe's questions and on the impulse had rushed off to try and find Leo. He was working on a boat and she had not been able to see him.

"Well, hurry on then," urged the nun. "The child will be back home by now."

She locked the iron gates carefully after Katie and went to tidy up the garden after the children's games there. She was a little worried about Franz Joseph; the Reverend Mother might think that she had been negligent in not looking for herself to see if Katie was outside the gate as the child had said.

Katie went home angrily. She would give that lying little beast something to remember when she got at him. She hurried up the main street and entering the garden called loudly for her small brother. Robert and the twins had just come in and she asked if they had seen him. They had not.

"Go and look for him at once," she shouted at them. "The little devil has gone off again."

When Karl came in she sent him off too. The boys were tired and hungry and departed grumbling. It was hot and dusty, but Katie was merciless. They must go. She herself had to prepare the evening meal before Moe returned from the hospital. She had slept all the forenoon instead of doing it then.

When Anna and Krista got back from the town the child was still away and Moe was at home raging about the missing boy. As usual it was Katie who took the full blast of her fury. It was Krista who suggested inquiring next door. She knew that Franz Joseph sometimes went there. She had seen the Englishwoman frequently. Now she was stirred with a curiosity to speak with her. She spoke the same language as Paul did, or almost the same. She was invited in. No, Franz Joseph had not come as usual for his sweets. They had not seen him today.

"You're Krista, aren't you?" said the foreigner. "I know all your names."

"You've seen Carola, too, haven't you?" said Krista. "Isn't she lovely?"

"Carola's a lovely child," agreed the neighbour, "and very like her mother."

Krista was astonished. It seemed a far cry indeed from Moe's florid beauty to the little waxen face with the gold curls and dark pansy eyes lying in that white hospital bed.

"Let us know if you don't find him. We'll run round in the car and see if we can find the rascal," said the Englishwoman.

Krista pondered over the likeness between Carola and Moe. She herself could not see it . . . and yet sometimes when Moe sat dreaming with a cigarette, wasn't there something of Carola in her? When her eyes were soft and her mouth relaxed, wasn't it true then? Was this why Moe loved this child so much more than any of her other daughters? Did she sense in this dreamy, sweet-natured little girl the child she had once been herself?

She took a bicycle from the yard and rode through the village main street to the river. Franz Joseph loved the river. A child whom she had questioned told her that he had made a beautiful paper boat at the kindergarten that afternoon. When she reached the tow-path and the going became too rough she was forced to dismount. She was wheeling the machine and calling out the boy's name when Leo came swinging along the path. He barred her way with his long arms outstretched. His smiling mouth belied the intent look in the blue-green eyes. They travelled up Krista from her feet to her hair and a great burning flush swept over her at what she saw in his look.

"Let me by," she said bravely; "I'm looking for Franz Joseph, he's lost."

"Put down your bicycle!" he said without taking his eyes from her face. "I've been wanting a little talk with you for a very long time."

The bicycle slipped from Krista's hands and slithered down in the grass across the tow-path. One wheel grazed her leg as it crashed down, but her fear was so great that she did not notice the pain. Speechless, she began to tremble. The sight of this excited Leo. The bicycle lay between them, and as he stretched out his arm to grasp her she broke away in a panic and fled up the bank into the little wood. He came crashing after her. He was tall and lithe, in splendid training from running and swimming, and she realized with terror that she had put herself into further peril by fleeing into the wood. Here there would be less chance of anyone coming to save her. On the tow-path there would always be the hope of someone coming along hearing her cries. She turned quickly, and began running back down the slope trying to reach the open again, but the trees had been felled and their stumps were hidden in the long grass. She tripped heavily over one and fell headlong.

With one bound her pursuer reached her, and before she could move had flung himself upon her. He lay with his hard body pressing hers into the soft grass and his cruel face laughing down at her. With frenzied terror she hit out blindly at him, but catching both her hands in one of his own strong ones he pinned them down. One agonized scream came from her before his other hand clamped down on her mouth.

She lay there with her heart almost bursting from her, helpless and terrified whilst he pressed his weight on to her. He was bruising and crushing her mouth, her hands held in a merciless grasp, when through the thick undergrowth crashed Robert followed by the twins. Without hesitation Robert hurled himself upon Leo, hitting valiantly at his face. To defend himself Leo was forced to release Krista's hands and mouth. Her white shocked face brought the twins to Robert's aid. They did not like Leo, although he was their chief.

"Let her go!" commanded Heinz, while Hans and Robert tried to haul Leo's steel-taut body off the girl. He got up slowly, cursing them, and stood looking down at Krista; then, as she did not move, he pulled her roughly to her feet. She shrank away from him. His eyes glowed strangely and his hands were twitching.

"We were only having a bit of fun," he said. "No need to make a song and dance about it."

Hans went up to Krista. "Has he hurt you?" He could not bear the look on her face. Katie and Anna could look out for themselves—they'd have scratched and bitten—but Krista was different. She was utterly defenceless in the face of violence. At school the twins had protected her, and although Leo was the chief of their gang they had gone instinctively to her help.

With a tremendous effort of will the girl pulled herself together to reassure Robert. She was still trembling, but she could see his anxiety. She pulled him to her side.

"It's all right, Robert. I fell over a tree stump, and Leo fell over me," she said hesitatingly. "Have you found Franz Joseph yet?"

They had searched everywhere, he said, but no one had seen him: what should they do now? They went down the slope to the tow-path and Robert picked up the bicycle.

"I knew you were here when I saw it lying there," he said, "and then I heard you scream, Krista, so I came quickly."

She was squeezing his little hand as if she could never let it go. Heinz and Hans looked curiously at her. She appeared quite calm again, but her pallor was frightening. It was going to be damned awkward if Leo started his tricks on Krista. Katie was another matter: she could look out for herself; but Krista! No, they were agreed on that. As Robert and she went off with the bicycle Leo said quietly to the twins, "Keep out of things which don't concern you or you'll find life rather unpleasant."

He smiled as he said it, and his tone was very light, but they were under no illusions as to what he meant. Leo was not a person to be interfered with. The twins would pay for having interrupted his intentions today. Leo was not head of their gang for nothing.

A cry from Krista told them that the missing child had been found. He was lying on his stomach completely absorbed in an ant-hill. The rushes hid him completely. A paper boat floating far out in mid-stream had given the clue to Krista.

"You must have heard us calling," said Heinz angrily. "We came quite close to you."

Franz Joseph shook his head. "No, I didn't hear anything at all. Only ships' sirens and birds," he insisted. "And I didn't see anybody but the ants."

Heinz was angry at the trouble the child had made for them all. He did not mention the unspoken fear of each of them that he might have fallen in. Every year the number of drowned was high. A treacherous current made swimming dangerous unless one knew how to zig-zag to avoid it. The older lads swam every evening in spite of the danger, and every summer there was a race to see who could swim across the wide river first. Leo had won it easily both last year and this. He was a magnificent swimmer and diver. Hank was as strong, but lacked the style and skill of his chief. A child who fell in would have no chance whatever against such a strong fast stream. The water was deep, and large steamers could navigate quite close in to the banks.

Heinz picked up his small brother and shook him roughly, hoisted him up on his shoulder and told him he was in for trouble as soon as he got home. Moe was waiting for him, said Hans. Franz Joseph set his dirty little face resolutely. He didn't care. It had been worth it. It had been wonderful by the river with no one to keep telling him not to lean over the bank. He scrambled down from Heinz's back and ran up to Krista. He put his hand in hers.

"You won't let her beat me too hard, will you?" he asked anxiously.

But Franz Joseph did not get his beating. Joseph was at home, sitting waiting at the head of the table.

"What's happened to Krista?" he said, after one look at her face. The marks of Leo's fingers were round her bruised mouth. There was a silence; then she said lamely that she had fallen over a tree stump.

It was Robert who said, "That Leo fell on top of her—he wouldn't let her get up."

"Leo?" said Joseph sharply, his eyes on Krista. "What were you doing with Leo?"

"I met him on the tow-path when I was looking for Franz Joseph." The words came unwillingly.

Joseph looked at Hank who had just come in late from work.

"Tell your friend to keep away from Krista." His voice was furious. "It's enough that he's always with you and Katie. I don't like the fellow."

Hank, who had sat down without a word, took the plate handed him by Katie and began eating. He did not answer his father. The meal was unusually silent. They were all exhausted from the heat and from hunting for Franz Joseph.

When it was over Hank called the twins, and taking the air-pistol which he had recently acquired told them to come and shoot birds with him.

"What's the row about Leo?" he asked, as they left the house. The twins told him. They were uneasy. Hank's face was dark. To his brothers' astonishment he was furious with Leo.

"Let him wait till I get at him," he said. "Isn't it about time we told him where he gets off?"

The twins were silent. They were thinking of the old caretaker. Leo had something on Hank now. As they walked across the fields Hank was in such a rage that he couldn't speak. The face of Krista was revolving again and again in his mind, and each time he visualized it his hatred of Leo grew.

X V I

IT GREW hotter and hotter. The willows every day more tired and smutty, the grass more limp and scorched. On the great river the summer season was now in full swing. Tourists were filling the town and the villages along its banks. The grapes were ripening, and soon there would be the wine festivals to encourage even more visitors. As the pleasure boats drifted down the current, so the long line of cars raced parallel with them on the riverside roads.

Prosperity was returning again. The hotels were full. Money was pouring in. The beer gardens and restaurants were a riot of noisy drinking and singing in the evenings, and the lilting music of Strauss could be heard everywhere on the water.

Against all this frenzy for pleasure, for eating, drinking and love-making which seemed to be filling the population, the steady sound of the hammers and bricks never ceased. Working long shifts, men slaved at the new buildings. Whole new towns had grown up for the Occupation along the river. Huge new buildings for their own Government had shot up in the little town now decreed the capital. The great white building which was the seat of the new Government—the democratic one this time—which now dominated the once pretty and modest little town of Bonn, had already become a regular Sunday sight-seeing tour. Motor coaches brought loads of curious sightseers who peered and stared in at the windows and took photographs while eating and drinking their picnic food. At the entrances of the homes of the Chancellor and the President armed police stood guard, and the new flag flew. For a long time there had been no flag. The Third Reich one was forbidden by the Occupation. When the Chancellor, whom they called the "old man" and who came from the great town itself, rode out from his house, motor cyclist outriders cleared a path for him and brought up the rear. The country was out of the mire again. Gone were the days when the roads were swarming with the uniforms and cars of the Occupation. They were almost negligible now, and the country's own cars, made in its own factories, were not only on the roads but winning the races abroad. The sports teams, fed adequately again, and so able to train, were holding their own with the world. Gone was the shame of defeat. It only remained for the wretched Peace Treaty to be signed for the army to be formed again.

Leo and Hank had a friend who worked as a waiter in one of the small but popular waterside restaurants with terraces overhanging the river. This lad, as brutal as Hank but far more vicious, told of foreign tourists wandering down the river late at night, their pockets filled with bank-notes, looking, like the population, for pleasure and romance in the environs of the town.

The cafés, restaurants and beer gardens catered especially for just these wealthy business men. Their terraced gardens were gaily painted. The tables were discreetly shaded by day with gay umbrellas; at night Chinese lanterns and fairy lights lit the diners against their background of massed flowers and water. With the moonlight on the river and the changing lights of the passing vessels, it needed only a discreet orchestra playing Strauss waltzes or gay drinking songs to put the tourists in the mood for romance or adventure. The waiters and restaurant-owners would ply them with the wines of the district and blinded with moon-light, flowers, and music they could readily be persuaded to the delights of amatory dalliance. The girls, like the wines, were famous.

Eddie, the lad working in the restaurant which this year seemed to have become the popular one of the moment, had been watching with greedy eyes the huge wads of notes which some of these foreigners flaunted after sampling too much wine. He had observed how easily the girls of the town could lead the men off afterwards, and his avaricious soul could not bear to see such opportunities lost. He belonged to the gang—in fact he was one of the most useful members, and had it not been for Hank being brought in by Katie, he would have been number two. Being employed in such a fashionable restaurant he was a mine of information, and it was from him that the gang learned when certain families would be away and their houses empty. From him came the tips on when to plan the raids.

It did not suit Eddie at all that, owing to the absence of the two bargees for some months, there would be no money coming into his pockets. He had expensive tastes, and his tips did not cover them. When Leo and Hank came to him for advice on how to find a new "fence," to their astonishment he was for finishing with housebreaking.

"Small fry," he said contemptuously; "and look what a trouble it is to get rid of the stuff afterwards. Those two men swindled us right and left, and what could we do about it? No, there are too many in the gang for profit. Let's get on to something bigger. We can do it now. We're old hands. I've got a plan. We don't need more than us three, and perhaps Alfred, but we need dolls—good-looking ones for this plan of mine. We can start with Katie and Maria of course, but we shall need more, so that we can use a fresh girl each time. I tell you, boys, this is money for jam!"

The three repaired to an unfrequented part of the river bank to discuss the plan.

"We'd better use Katie first," suggested Leo, "she's seen one killing and she's hot stuff. But we can't use her too often. She's noticeable. Maria's all right, but she's not every man's cup of tea. We don't want them too striking—they'll be recognized too easily."

"I don't like it," said Hank bluntly. "I don't trust skirts—they're all soft and they're all fools."

"Stay out then," snarled Leo, "but Katie's in this—she's just the one; so's Maria."

"It's money for jam," insisted Eddie. "All you've got to do is to be on tap—understand? It's no use your being out in the village when the right sap comes in. You've got to be in a place where a phone-call will have you here on the dot. You can use my place—it's on the phone and the landlady's never in."

He smoothed back his curly hair which was of that burnished gold that elderly spinsters love. It was a pity that the lady tourists never came out alone at night. If they came they were usually Americans and in parties of at least four. Eddie would have liked to have reversed the proposed roles and played decoy to some of the well-padded lady tourists. His landlady, for instance, was already completely under his thumb. She doted on the orphan lad, calling him her long-lost son and lavishing affection on him. He was biding his time and enduring her ridiculous attentions. The house in which he lodged was hers. He meant to get it, but he was playing his hand slowly.

Hank stuck out for some time. He didn't like this new idea of the girls being used as decoys for the rich tourists to be robbed. Leo and Eddie were adamant. It was a damn good idea—if Hank was yellow he could stay out. Hank's strength was useful to them. They really needed him but they were not going to give any such sign. Leo knew that he held the whip hand. Hank was a *murderer*, he seemed to have forgotten that.

The three youths, in their open-necked shirts with their skin bronzed, and their muscles hard from work and exercise, drew the eyes of many women as they strolled back along the river towards the restaurant where Eddie worked. He had suggested showing them the lay-out of the place—the exits to the river, the whole show—before the place got busy. He was on duty tonight, and took his friends round the terraces, pointing out the darkest tables—those under the lime trees—and how easy it would be for the girls to decoy the half-intoxicated men to the dark tow-path at the rear of the place. Here, under the thick weeping willows, the boys would take over. The tourist would be stunned, robbed and left hidden in the shadows—or if necessary rolled into the river.

"What about the proprietor?" asked Leo, who was no fool. "If he's about it'll be impossible."

"He's old, and goes home early, the girl must appear to have come at the tourist's invitation. When I phone I'll say which table—they're all numbered—and she must just walk boldly in and join him. She'll give us the signal when he's well under."

Hank's mind was too simple for such cunning. He was accustomed to get all he wanted by sheer brute strength. Eddie and Leo, however, were planning details enthusiastically. They were contemplating the addition of drugs to the wine. It would make it all so much quicker.

"Rather risky, though," said Eddie; "drugs can be traced more easily than a cosh."

"Not through Alfred," insisted Leo; "he gets us the stuff to keep the dog quiet. He's clever and careful. He's more careful than *some* members of the gang have been." He looked meaningly at Hank as he said this.

Alfred worked at his uncle's pharmacy, his sister, Maria, was the decoy whom the boys had been discussing. Alfred was studying to be a chemist while helping his uncle in the shop. A quiet, studious-looking lad, with a moon face, his thick spectacles hid his merciless grey eyes. Alfred was, perhaps, more to be feared than Leo, for he had access to lethal drugs. Not openly, of course. His uncle, a careful well-meaning man who had adopted his nephew and niece when their father had been killed in the war, was very strict about keeping well within the law and giving access only to qualified persons. His store-cupboards were always locked. How could he know that his quiet nephew was a clever locksmith?

"I don't like it," repeated Hank, "it's too risky."

"You're yellow," taunted Leo.

Hank, as he knew, would not take this.

"I'm not yellow," he retorted. "But why stick your neck out? Now if the proprietor himself was in with us . . ."

"I told you, he's old," said Eddie contemptuously. "But his son is young, and the old man keeps him short of dough. He'll come in easy enough with us—the old boy's leaving the night work more and more to his son."

"I don't know if Katie will do it," argued Hank. "She got a knock over that last job—girls are no use on this sort of thing."

"And whose fault was the last job?" sneered Leo. "She'll do it all right—leave her to me. She'll need new clothes—understand? And after each job every one of them must be destroyed. It's no use any of you jibbing at the cost. The clothes are the cop's best means of identification. A girl can do anything with her face or hair and they know it. They rely on clothes."

Hank was dubious. He had not been blind to the effect of the caretaker's death on his sister. Katie had been curiously apathetic since that night. She no longer seemed to care that Leo's passion for her was waning.

On his way home a new idea came to him. He had remembered the interest Leo had shown in Krista. He was still seething with fury at Leo's attempted seduction of her that other evening. The very thought of it made him see red. He didn't know why, but the very idea of Leo having anything to do with Krista made him want to kill his chief. Lately Krista's face had been coming through all his dreams; even during working hours at the ship-yard. He would take care that Leo never saw her again—but at the same time he would use Leo's interest in her to force Katie from her apathy and make her fall in with the leader's new plans.

XVII

THE FIRST TOURIST was decoyed by Maria, not Katie. As the one used in the plot would be the one to receive a share of the money acquired by it, the girls insisted on drawing lots. Maria was the lucky one. She was a dark-browed, luscious type of girl known to every lad in the village as easy. An orphan, she had been adopted with her brother Alfred by the elderly uncle and his wife. The wife was bedridden and in no way able to control her niece. Maria had the same moon face as her brother, but while he was sleepy and lazy she was tempestuous and restless. She had no use for the village, and spent most of her evenings roaming the town.

At eighteen she was already horribly experienced, and easily the toughest girl in the gang. Like all the others, she had learned to steal during the bombing and thought absolutely nothing of it. She had robbed numerous Occupation soldiers of their wallets after they had gone with her to the room she hired with an older girl in the town. Under a complexion of peaches and cream she hid the resilience and persistence of a much older woman. She had been Leo's girl until he had discarded her in favour of Katie's red hair. Now it seemed that he was tiring of Katie. The gang all said that he was crazy about that half-witted girl whom the bunker family had adopted. She would be his next, they said.

Maria, rehearsed and primed for every move by Leo and Eddie, ready for any emergency which might arise, did not make a slip. At exactly the right moment she joined the more than half-intoxicated tourist at his table, ushered there by Eddie. The foreigner was enchanted by her ripe beauty and the boldness of her caresses and overtures. Eddie telephoned the waiting Hank as soon as the old proprietor was out of the way. The son, as he had surmised, had been only too keen on cutting in with them and was a willing accomplice. Hank, waiting in the room Eddie rented from the woman he was slowly and gradually parting from her possessions, came immediately at the signal.

When the foreigner, feeling the effects of the drug supplied by Alfred and put in his wine by Maria, began to get heavy and dazed, it was easy and natural enough for the waiter serving that table to help Maria get him out of the restaurant garden. The waiter, of course, was Eddie. At the rear, in a dark corner, Hank and Leo took over. The man was lugged out under a willow, hit savagely on the head and robbed of his bulging wallet. By the willows was a kind of natural cave in the rocks forming the terrace garden wall. The body was pushed into this. Later, when the restaurant was completely empty, the body was rolled into the river.

The problem of whether or not to kill had been discussed at length by the gang and put to the vote. The majority were for killing. After all, they'd bumped off one man weeks ago and nothing had happened; the argument for killing was too strong. The man, on recovery, might remember not only the restaurant but the girl and the waiter. He had visited the place several times before on his business trips and had made Eddie's acquaintance. This was how Eddie had found out what huge sums of money these business men carried about with them. He had made certain that this one had plenty on him before he had offered to introduce him to a very attractive girl with whom he could spend the evening—and the night if he wished. Maria, on delivering her unconscious charge to the two gang leaders, then disappeared quickly to the ladies' room where she changed her entire outfit before leaving the restaurant.

The sum of money in the wallet exceeded all their hopes, and furthermore it was all in their own currency. The various visiting-cards and identity marks and papers were burned with the wallet. One of Hank and Katie's troubles was where to hide the money. Their hoards were accumulating fast. In the house, where no privacy of any kind existed and no keys either, it was impossible to hide it. They were forced to use the loose board under the summer-house floor. Sometimes when Hank was at work he would sweat when he thought of the children playing in the summer-house. Robert in particular was an inquisitive child. At any moment the hoard might be discovered. He had almost enough for the motor cycle now. If Pa wasn't such a stickler for insisting on that wretched contribution towards the building of the house every week he'd have had it long ago. He doubted if he'd ever have gone into the gang if Pa hadn't taken that money off him every week. It was a damned shame. Didn't he earn the stuff himself? Why should it go towards a house? If he worked late on overtime the old man knew he was earning more and asked for a larger contribution. He did the same with the girls. There was so much work in all the factories that anyone who wanted to earn more could do so. What was the use of working overtime if it all went towards a house? The gang had enabled him to get the money for his longed-for motor cycle in about three months. Had he earned it all it would have taken him three years or more.

The share-out after each raid took place in the gang's hideout. There was trouble at once after the first of the new schemes. In the housebreaking raids everyone had received an equal share with the exception of Hank and Leo, who got double as the leaders. Now it seemed that only those actually taking part each time would get a share. This time it meant that Katie, Leila the twins and two others got nothing. Katie made a sullen protest immediately.

"It'll be your turn next," said Leo. "We only need one girl each time. We won't be able to use you too often—your hair'll give you away too easily."

Katie was furious at this excuse to put her off. In her heart she knew that Leo was tired of her and this increased his attraction for her. Alfred, usually silent and placid, insisted that he be paid his share. He had provided the drug to put in the wine at a considerable risk of discovery and he was not going to be put off. The twins, not wanting to be left out, and becoming rapidly influenced by their fellow members of the gang, gave voice to their indignation but were told bluntly to pipe down by Hank.

The only one who made no protest was Leila, a blonde, graceful girl whom Eddie favoured at present.

"I don't want any of your dough—it stinks," she said flatly. "I came in on this for housebreaking—I'm used to that—but I didn't reckon for killing. I'm getting out."

Leo's eyes narrowed. "Unfortunately you can't," he said suavely. "You're in the gang. You've taken the oath, you must do your bit, and you'll be called on very shortly."

"You mean that I must do what Maria did?"

The repugnance in Leila's voice brought Eddie to his feet. He had been sitting in a corner watching.

"You'll do it, and what's more you'll do it damn well," he said roughly.

"I'm with Katie. I won't do it. You never told us it meant killing each time," she said sullenly.

"So you won't do it either?" demanded Leo swinging round on Katie. "This is the first we've heard of it."

"I'm against killing," she insisted, looking boldly at him.

Leo hadn't intended that the girls should know what had happened to the tourist after they left him. Eddie, always too fond of talking, had mentioned quite casually when the gang had met this evening that the strong current in the river could be counted on to carry the body a long distance, and that it would be far away from the restaurant when it was discovered. There had been a little gasp from the girls, with the exception of Maria, who had never had any illusions. She just went on smoking calmly.

"Put that out," snapped Leo suddenly. "Haven't I warned you not to smoke. Listen . . ." There were footsteps approaching the shelter. In absolute silence they held their breath until they had passed.

The twins had been horrified at hearing of the tourist's murder but they were too frightened to show it. They knew as yet nothing of the length to which their gang leaders would go, but that they were in Leo's bad books over the incident with Krista they could not doubt. Leo seemed to sense some hostility in his gang, for he said suddenly, after dismissing peremptorily the protests over the pay-out. "Every member will now take the oath again. Some of you seem to be losing your grip, and thinking you can get out when you like. Well, there's no getting out—see? Once in always in, and anyone trying to rat on us will get what's coming to him—or her, see?" He looked meaningly at Leila as he said this.

The menace and icy threat in his voice was not lost on any of them. One by one at his command they filed past him, repeating the words of the oath and making the curious gesture before their faces until it was Leila's turn. Her round blank face was unperturbed as she said quietly, "I'm not taking the oath again. I'm getting out, like I said."

Eddie seized her roughly by the arm. "Stow it, you bloody little fool, you can't rat on us now—you know that."

But she stood there mutely, refusing to repeat the words.

"Hank," said Leo; his voice was regretful. "Take her other arm."

Eddie and Hank stood on either side. Her arms were held as if in a vice.

"Repeat the oath," insisted Leo quietly.

Leila was silent. Her face was a closed mask, her lips set. Leo signalled to the two who held her. They twisted her arms until she screamed with pain and sweat ran down her face. The cries rang out on the still air until Leo, fearful that they would be heard, ordered Alfred to put his hand over her mouth or to tie a handkerchief round it.

Alfred, his round eyes glowing strangely behind the thick rimmed glasses, clapped a hand over the girl's mouth.

"How can she repeat the oath with her mouth sealed, you fools," cried Katie scornfully. Alfred took his hand away but no sound came from Leila's bruised mouth. The twins could stand no more, they were not yet used to such brutality. They rushed to Leila and tried to free her, hurting her even more by their clumsy efforts.

"Let her go," ordered Leo suddenly, "and deal with these two bloody idiots."

Leila, released suddenly, fell in a limp heap on the ground. Her face was green-white, her mouth twisted in pain.

Katie and Maria had watched her torture without a flicker of feeling. Now they went and hauled her into a corner as if she were a sack of potatoes.

The twins resisted Eddie and Alfred, fighting violently. They were thick-set and strong and in splendid condition. Leo saw that he was losing control, that the twins were more powerful than their opponents and he called upon Hank to subdue his brothers. Hank refused. He said he drew the line also at this latest stunt of the chief's. He had always thought it was dangerous to trust girls. He saw, perhaps, the red light ahead in the appalling lengths to which Leo was prepared to go. As to murder he cared not at all whether they killed or coshed and left to die. It was immaterial to him, but he saw the risk they ran in antagonizing these girls if they were unwilling to act as decoys, and without decoys the whole scheme was useless.

Watching his twin brothers getting the better of their antagonists he perceived suddenly how strong his own family were in this gang. Leo hadn't wanted the twins—perhaps for this very reason. But he had been short of members after two had left the district and had been obliged to try them out. Hank himself was as powerful as Leo, and far more feared, but Leo was quicker and better educated. He knew more. Katie was easily the leader of the girls, while the twins, he now realized, when acting in unison were the strongest physically of any.

He foresaw a day not too far off when the gang would be under his control through his family. They were accustomed to be ruled by him, and if they were the most powerful in the gang it would mean that he ruled it through them. If Hank had been asked whether he liked his chief, Leo, he would have grunted and said that Leo was all right. In his heart he hated Leo. Hated him for his superior education, his lofty assumption that he was always right, hated him most for his easy conquests of women. For Hank, agonizingly shy, and all too conscious of his ugliness and ungainliness, longed more than anything in the world to be attractive to the opposite sex. When he saw the burning looks which women cast on Leo's slim hard strength, on his gold waving hair, his bronzed glowing skin and the curiously light blue-green eyes, it was as much as he could do to keep his hands off his chief.

His own mottled dark complexion, black eyes and coarse black hair, and most of all his huge ears—over which he had been teased unmercifully at school—were no more attractive than his thickset body. Hank had no graces, no charm, no weapon at all with which to attract women. His manner was surly, his voice harsh, and his gait the shambling one of a lad whose strength had overtaken him too fast for his mind.

He did not obey Leo's order and watched them fighting for a moment. They were getting noisy in their excitement. Leo's order to stop it were ignored, their tempers were up. It looked like becoming a desperate struggle between the four lads when Hank barked suddenly, "Enough! Leave the twins alone", and at his word the fighting ceased. The four stood panting and angry separated by Hank. Leo's eyes met his for just one second. There was something deadly in them. Hank felt uncomfortable at that relentless glare and went over to Leila. He turned her over. She lay inert on the sack where the girls had dragged her.

He bent down and pulled the tumbled hair from her face. Her eyes were closed and something in the expression of the curved lashes on her cheek reminded him quite sharply of Krista. It unnerved him. Leila was opening her eyes now and gazed terrified at him. He lifted her to her feet, but she could not stand and sank down again against the wall of the shelter.

"Get her some water," he snarled. "Go over to the garage and ask Lu for some." Leo protested immediately. No one was to leave the shelter. One of the girls produced a bottle of red wine and some of this was poured down Leila's throat. She gasped and choked and then began to cry. When anyone touched her she winced and whimpered with pain.

"Stretch out your arm", ordered Leo. The right arm came up, but the left one remained hanging limply.

Alfred, with some experience of anatomy from his studies, came over and began feeling the arm.

"Broken", he pronounced laconically. "Now then, here's a nice little mess you've got us into, Leo. What about this one?"

"Let it be a lesson to you, damn you," said Leo, "You see what's coming to you if you don't stick to the rules of the gang and obey orders."

"You've broken her arm, and now she's 'out' for the next job—she'd be some decoy in plaster!" sneered Katie.

"Then it'll be *you* who does the next," snapped Leo. "Now then, Leila, are you ready to repeat the oath of the gang, or do you want the other arm broken?"

Leila got to her feet with difficulty. Eddie moved to help her, but she shrank away from him in horror.

"Don't touch me," she said, and the revulsion and loathing in her voice reached even his degraded mind.

"It's your own fault," he mumbled. "You know the rules— why don't you stick to them."

"Repeat the oath," snarled Leo. He had to assert himself because his pride had received a serious blow when four members of his gang had ignored his orders and obeyed Hank's just now.

In a low voice and with many halts Leila repeated the vile words; then she broke into bitter sobbing.

No one paid any attention to her sobs, but they produced an uneasy atmosphere in the gang. The twins, in particular, were already fed up with the brutality of the recent proceedings; it would take little more to cause them to revolt too. Leo sensed this, and calling them peremptorily over to him one by one insisted on their repetition of the oath of obedience and loyalty.

Hank, watching them and seeing the twins' reluctance when their turn came, stood menacingly over them.

"Want some of the medicine Leila's had?" He thrust his great head under their faces, "Get on with it before I make you . . ."

The time was not yet ripe for his plans and he could not in any case afford to overlook any signs of insubordination from his own family. Leo, after a few curt pregnant words, dismissed them all. The words contained a warning that anyone betraying the smallest item of the affairs of the gang would be dealt with in the threat set out in the oath which they had just taken. None of them, when they had so lightly joined the gang and learned the code, had really believed that those words would be actually applied. The threat mentioned the full penalty for treachery—death.

None of them now, having seen Leo's ruthlessness over the tourist and over Leila, could doubt that he would carry out the threat, no matter which member of the gang was guilty. They filed out silently into the wet warm night after making sure that they were unobserved. None of them wanted to hang about or to discuss anything this evening. Death had suddenly become a startlingly personal possibility.

XVIII

When Father Lange spoke to Joseph about Katie and Hank having been out on the motor cycle in the early hours of the morning, Joseph listened resentfully. He was only too well aware of the villagers' attitude. He merely grunted and said that nowadays the young did just as they liked and would take no questioning about their doings.

Father Lange was angry. "It's your duty to find out what they're doing. I hear it's not just occasionally but regularly that they prowl about when they should be in bed. What kind of a father is it who allows this?"

"It's no use blaming me," shouted Joseph. "I'm no longer the master in my own home."

"And whose fault is that?" asked the priest gently. "If you were to forgive your wife and put your house in order you'd soon have control of your family again."

Joseph shook his head wearily. "It's too late," he said, "I'm tired. There's nothing left in me—I'm like a worn-out shoe. I gave all my strength in those long years away from them ... away from all humanity and decency ... now there's only the shell left. I did my duty to my country. There's nothing left for my family."

"I'm a much older man than you, Joseph," said the priest sternly; "come, man, pull yourself together. I know you're tired,— aren't we all? But they're *your* children, your own flesh and blood."

"Are they?" asked Joseph dispiritedly. "Sometimes I wonder."

He was on his way to work and left Father Lange abruptly. The priest stood staring after him thoughtfully. He liked Joseph, liked him perhaps better than many of his regular, self-satisfied parishioners. The man's puzzled misery, his bewildered inability to adjust himself to circumstances, his reluctance to take decisions, moved him. It might look like weakness to some, but the priest knew better. The man was going through some kind of terrific mental upheaval. He had purposely refrained from reproving him again for his absence from Mass. He saw that at present it would be useless. He did not want to alienate Joseph further, but he had felt it his duty to speak about the adolescents. Their life lay ahead, and whether he wanted to or not Joseph would have to bear the responsibility for them. If Joseph would not do something about them, then he would reluctantly have to do it himself.

The steadily mounting resentment in the village was becoming dangerous. Everyone was saying, for instance, that the girl Katie was pregnant again, and that the mother was shamelessly continuing her affair with the young man; not in her own home, but only a stone's throw down the lane.

He was worried about the twins, too. They were such great jolly lads, with their straw-coloured hair and black eyes, but since they had been under Hank's influence he had seen little of them. Anna was steadier now. She had taken a knock over that child who had died. It hadn't been easy for her. He liked the way she had taken Moe's place and brought the little ones to church on Sundays. Krista was unhappy. There was this wretched business of the American. He saw Joseph's point of view—but at the same time the girl was far too good for any of the local lads. Because he had perceived her innate purity despite her surroundings, he had pleaded for her to stay on longer at school—after all, her real age was not known—until he had been able to get her into the perfume factory.

That had been difficult too. There was always a waiting list because the place had a reputation for its high standard of care and consideration for its employees. They took only girls of good reputation there. Many of them came straight from school, like

Krista, and stayed there all their working lives. He knew that there she would get advantages which she wouldn't have elsewhere. She would mix with girls of a better type than those in her home and village, and she could continue her education in the factory's extension classes. He had seen that both she and Anna kept in constant contact with the nuns at the convent. Katie would have nothing to do with them. The girl wanted to get out to work; she hated being the drudge at home, but with two babies what chance would she have of that? Sometimes the priest thought despairingly that there were no good girls left at all. He thought of the local legend of St. Ursula martyred with eleven thousand virgins and knew that it would be no easy task to find eleven thousand now. The Occupation troops, Belgian, American and now British and French, had all played a part in this deterioration begun by the ill-fated Third Reich. But the fact was that although the women had pleaded hunger as their first excuse, then that they had been ordered to make themselves pleasant to the conquerors, they needed no excuse for sin. It was always there in everyone. And now, with the new capital Bonn near, and its surroundings full of foreign troops, with temptations increased by the revival of the notorious Carnival and constant wine festivals, there was simply no keeping the women from the men. It was not easy for a man with daughters here, and when the mother herself was amoral what could one expect?

The schoolmaster had spoken to him about Robert. The child was growing even more nervous and apprehensive. He looked tired and could no longer concentrate properly. Although Robert was so young, both hoped that he was earmarked for better things than his brothers. Father Lange had taken Robert with him one afternoon on a visit to the large seminary for students for the priesthood. It was a beautiful place, and the child had shown an intelligent interest in the life there. Robert was one of the Father's most faithful servers, and it was of him in particular that he was now thinking.

Joseph went on his way to the station. A small French car came to a stop by him and the Frenchman from the house opposite asked if he would care for a lift. In astonishment he accepted and climbed in beside his neighbour. The Englishwoman next door sometimes gave Moe a lift in her car into Cologne when she was going to visit Carola, but this was the first time anyone had offered one to Joseph. He was pleased. There was no joy for him in his work any more, and something in his defeatist attitude, in the very set of his shoulders, had made the Frenchman notice him. He knew him of course; it was impossible not to know each member of that noisy family by sight. The Frenchman, lonely and bored, spent a good deal of time in the garden watching them.

"I can take you right into Cologne—where d'you work?" he asked Joseph. They agreed on a point at which Joseph should be dropped, and from which he could reach the steelworks.

"I work in coal, with the Comité des Forges," he told Joseph. "It's right that steel and coal should travel together!"

They discussed the factory and its problems, then the Frenchman said, "You have a fine bunch of children; I envy you."

"Have you no children?" asked Joseph abruptly.

"I had," said the Frenchman quietly. "My fourteen-year-old son was shot as a hostage with several other schoolmates during the Occupation of France. My wife died during that period too. Now I'm alone."

Joseph was silent. Then he said, "I wonder you can bear to come to Germany."

"I was sent here," said his companion. He did not tell Joseph that he had accepted the mission for one purpose only, to try and find the man who was responsible for his son's death. He had hunted him down now. He was at the end of his long search; and the strange thing was that the vengeance was already losing its savour. The whole thing was beginning to sicken him. He had vowed to give a champagne party on the day that his son's murderer paid the penalty for his crime.

"I'm sorry," said Joseph, "The war was terrible. I was in France. I was a prisoner there at the end."

"What was it like—bad?"

"No. Better than the endless fighting. Except for the cage. I can't forget being caged."

"I was in prison too; it's the most appalling thing that man can suffer."

They talked of prison camps. Joseph was surprised how quickly they reached the town. The Frenchman spoke good German; he had learned it in a German prison. Joseph spoke quite good French, acquired in a French prison camp.

"At least one good thing came out of our two enforced confinements," his neighbour said as he set Joseph down by the new bridge. "We've learned each other's languages, even if we could have wished the circumstances different under which we did so."

Joseph went on his way slightly cheered. The man had been very decent to him. He was surprised. He worked now like an automaton. He was always at the top of the individual output list. He spoke very little, but thought a great deal while his hands manipulated the complicated machinery. His thoughts ran always on the same lines. Rudi and Moe . . . and now Krista and this American. On the journey to these ends they ran through every kind of general problem—war, peace, destruction, building, bombs, war, destruction, building—in this kind of endless circle. And God? Joseph pushed that problem as far away as possible. He just could not face it.

He had one friend at the factory with whom he had been together during most of the war. This man, Peter, was now as happy as Joseph was miserable. He had been a prisoner in France with Joseph, and they had come back together, Peter to find that his wife and children had been killed in the bombing of the town. Peter had found this ironical. That he should have been through so many violent campaigns without a scratch struck him as ludicrous. He had since married a buxom widow who had lost her husband in the war. They were not going to have any children. No, definitely not. They were both agreed on that. Children nowadays were nothing but trouble. They simply could not be kept in their proper place. It was a world for the young—and didn't they take advantage of it? No, Peter would not contemplate a family. Joseph found this shocking. One should have children. The church said so. Politics were playing a prominent part in the daily life of the workmen now. The elections were in the offing and feelings were running very high. Joseph could not understand how so many of the men wanted a new leader as Chancellor. Wasn't the "old one" good enough for them? Look at what he had accomplished. Why, the country from being a heap of dust and ruins was already assured of a place in the sun again. And it was all due to the efforts of this dauntless old man. How could there be any other party for men of his faith? But they seemed to be able to separate these things successfully in their minds now. Thousands of them wanted a change, and managed to compromise with their religious beliefs.

Peter, for instance, was going to vote for the Opposition leader. What *he* wanted was a new leader. They were all looking for that, but until one emerged Peter was advocating the Opposition party and actually holding meetings supporting it. He was a fluent and witty speaker and the men liked listening to him. Joseph listened too, and what he heard only puzzled him the more.

"Push out the Occupation . . . send them packing . . . give us separate sovereignty. . . ." These were the words everywhere now. Everyone was tired of the endless squabbles of the Allies. First it had always been Russia who would not agree and who was always blamed for their non-agreement; then when the country had been split and the East isolated from the West by the dropping of the Iron Curtain, and the refugees had begun trailing out in a steady stream to wreck the new economy, it was evident that there was trouble between the others as well. France was opposed to the Peace Treaty, but they'd seen how the French fought: they were not afraid of the French. America and Britain couldn't agree either. Were they going to wait indefinitely while their victors quarrelled?

"You can't keep us down," they were beginning to chalk up on the buildings and fences, and that was always the gist of Peter's harangues during the lunch hour at the factory.

"We can't be kept down. We're up—listen boys, we're up! Soon we'll be at the top, the very top!" And they would all cheer and shout.

Joseph was silent. At the top of what? Didn't these fools realize that there was a slide from the top which could lead to the lowest basement? Hadn't they all experienced it? Wasn't that why he was feeling as he did now, why no one had a home, why the children had starved, why there were still not enough schools and they had to attend in shifts, why they were all slaving and striving and building like a great hill of disturbed and frightened ants? He got up when Peter had finished to a burst of applause. Joseph was cheered loudly as he indicated his wish to speak.

"It's no good, no good," he said. "You're all building on nothing and it means nothing if there's no foundation. You don't stop to think—where did it all lead before? It led to this—" he pointed out at the great heaps of debris still waiting to be cleared away—"and to that"—and he pointed far out to the endless rows of still devastated homes.

"Why must you always want to be on top? Tell me that. What's the matter with taking only a part, like every other nation. What are we building like mad for? Tell me that. To have it all smashed down again? For it will be, if you insist on being on top. It's like children, like my Franz Joseph with his bricks. Build it up, knock it down—and so it goes on. Twice already! Do you want it a third time? No. Of course you don't. Then think *what* you're doing, think *where* you're going, and think *whom* you're following."

He sat down to a roar of applause. "Good old Joseph!" thundered those of his mates who were dubious of any new party. Old Joseph talked simply, without Peter's flow of words, but he talked sense. Joseph himself was astonished. What had made him get up like that? He could see that Peter was annoyed and astonished. It was talking to that Frenchman that had done it. He saw that man's point of view too. That man had seen his. They had talked astonishingly easily.

Coming out of work Peter said to Joseph, "You talked a lot of bosh today. What's the good of sticking to that old stuff? The world is moving and we must move with it. We've been kept back long enough—too long. Up and get cracking, that's my motto! Drive out all these Allies and their petty squabbles and let's manage our own country. We've waited long enough!"

"We lost the war," said Joseph quietly. "We must expect what we get."

"Did we?" jeered Peter. "Well, there's always the next round."

His words shocked Joseph. Hadn't Peter's wife and children been killed in the last round, as he called it? Did the man want another war? Didn't the last mean anything to him? Couldn't he see that in the event of another war Germans could be fighting Germans if the East remained isolated from the West as it was at present? His sister's boys, first cousins to his own, would be on the opposite side. That was why so many people were opposed to the Peace Treaty.

Peter meanwhile was looking at Joseph with a new thoughtful air. Joseph was getting queer. There was no doubt of it. But he was well liked. He spoke very seldom—but he meant what he said. Peter determined to work on his friend. He was glib, and his brain worked faster than Joseph's. He and Joseph had endured some appalling hardships together in the campaigns. They had almost starved, almost died from thirst, almost frozen. They had come through it all and in the last, and to Joseph most terrible time of all when they had been in a wire pen, Joseph had been the one who had carried Peter through. Joseph was a good pal. Hadn't he proved that a hundred times?

"No ill feelings, old chap?" he said, seeing Joseph's glum face.

"Of course not," said Joseph in astonishment. And it was true—Joseph had an affinity with this man which precluded any kind of ill feeling or affront. Whereas he felt hate for most people and things at the moment, for Peter, proved comrade of those terrible times, he felt nothing but affection, even love. That Peter did not think as he did either personally or politically, puzzled, but did not offend him.

When he got home that evening he was gentler to Moe. He still hated her, but it was difficult not to like her at the same time as he hated her. She was in one of her softer, more unusual, moods. The children were laughing a lot—they had a number of family jokes and were bantering and teasing each other good-naturedly. He thought suddenly of what good evenings they had had before all this trouble blew up. Father Lange's words of this morning came back to him. He would have to take some firm decisions. Things would be even worse for a time before they were better. It was no use putting it all off any longer. He got up immediately after the meal, and went to the beer garden by the river. Not to drink, but just to get some peace in which to think things out. He had taken to slipping into the summerhouse after the children were in bed. He would smoke his pipe there and enjoy the acacia.

He had three urgent problems, as he saw it. First, Moe. Then Hank. Then Krista. If he were honest with himself and put the problems in their order of importance to himself he would have to place Krista first. When he discovered this he was horrified. The girl who was not his real daughter mattered more to him than his wife or his son. The discovery of this was a shock. Did he still love Moe? Had he ever loved her? Was she right when she had thrown those bitter words at him, "You have no love in you. You never loved me—never!" That was the only excuse she had made for her conduct.

He watched the barges passing by. They were going, many of them to other lands. When he himself had been away all those years he had longed for his fatherland so much that it had become an ache, an agony. For the Rhine in particular, for the Cathedral with the twin spires, for the narrow, chatter-filled Hohestrasse on Saturday nights when one could scarcely move for the crowds of shoppers; for the Schildergasse, for all those small streets and squares which had been a familiar part of home over the years. But when at last he had got back there for good, the whole place had changed and lost its magic for him. The appalling devastation was partly the reason for this, but not the whole reason. He had changed too. It had taken him a long time to discover this.

Those other countries in which he had seen devastation, hunger, and misery—had himself helped to create them—in what way did they differ? People were the same—exactly the same as his own. They ate, slept, loved and died just as these here did. Why then hadn't he cared? Why? Because he hadn't given time to think about it? Or because he just blindly obeyed orders to ravage and destroy? The sight of his own land, his own town, lying in ruins, moved him as those others never had. He got back to this every time he tried to think out the problems of his own family. Somehow these things seemed far more important. But Father Lange had reproved him. Set his house in order before trying to puzzle out the affairs of nations, he had said sternly. But couldn't the man see that the two things were tied up together? Governments ought to provide houses. What was the use of his trying to keep his family together and control them when the hostile tenants in the requisitioned house made life impossible with their endless complaints and gossip? He hated the wave of building all around him not only because it seemed a senseless section of the vicious circle, but because he himself needed a home quickly and urgently before it was too late. He didn't want it for show, or just to boast about its possession. He wanted it for shelter, for some kind of privacy in which to tackle the problem of the children. Was it so much to ask of one's country to whom he had given so many years?

The beer garden was filling up, the drinkers becoming happy and beginning to sing as they waved their beer mugs. "Come and join us," they called to Joseph. One or two of them travelled every day with him in the tram, but they never dared acknowledge him in the village because of their wives who loathed the bunker family. But they themselves did not dislike Joseph when they saw him alone like this. The poor devil looked unhappy. They were sorry for him.

Joseph was pleased at their attempts at cordiality, but he saw Krista coming in the gate looking for him. He noticed the looks of the men on her, saw one of them catch at her dress as she brushed past seeking for him. He got up, calling to her. She had been sent to ask him to come back. They had decided to have a concert. Wouldn't he come and help them? It took Krista all her powers of persuasion to get Joseph to accompany her. They didn't want him, he insisted. He had no place there. They could get on very well without him. But at last he gave in to her and followed her out of the place. As they went up the cobbled street old women and men sat in the open doorways of the ugly houses in the evening sun. Krista could feel their comments burning into her back as she passed each house with Joseph lagging behind her. He came reluctantly and heavily. She sensed that. He had wanted to stay alone thrashing out his problems. Going back with her to the whole family only meant putting it off again.

She noticed that all the spring seemed to have gone out of his walk. He walked slowly, like an old man. And he was only fifty. Long before they reached the house they could hear the singing. It was a song which Joseph did not like, from last year's Carnival, called "Forbidden Fruit".

Joseph stopped dead. "It's no wonder the neighbours complain," he growled. "They're all out of tune." He began hurrying his steps now and it was Krista who had to run to keep up with him.

"It's appalling!" he went on. "Out of time as well."

XIX

IT HAD BEEN a still and lovely evening. Moe had been sitting with them under the acacia tree. She was in one of her best moods, gay, affectionate, soft and almost sentimental. Supper was over, but the table was still uncleared because of Joseph, in case he might like something when he came in. The air was sweet and languorous with the scent of the acacia and the last lilac. With their stomachs full from an abundant meal the boys were all affable tonight; even Hank and Katie were singing and laughing with the others.

"Let's have some proper music," cried Moe. She was sitting with her arms on the table, smoking. "It's no good without Pa," said Hank. He said it flatly and positively. He loved music but was discouraged at his own failure to take his father's place as conductor. He lacked Joseph's ear and his sense of time.

"Where is he?" asked Lise. She had come in as she often did with her husband. He was a short, stodgy, bespectacled electrician and as soon as he arrived Moe invariably found something for him to mend. There was always a plug or contact suffering from the boys' rough handling. Hank was a good engineer, but he would never attend to dull things such as plugs and switches.

"He's probably in the beer garden," said Moe. "Let's hope he isn't drinking again."

"He never used to drink," observed Lise, putting her child on the ground. "There must be some good reason for it." She looked at Moe as she said this. She had been feeding her child as a mother bird does her young, automatically popping bits of cake in it, and was now confronted with a tightly shut mouth indicating that it was full.

Moe did not lose her implication, but all she said was, "That child's had enough, Lise. Don't overfeed her."

Hank went indoors and then came out with a self-conscious grin on his face. "Look," he said. In his arms was a large accordion.

"Ooh! Ooh! What a beauty, where did you get it?" shrieked the entire family.

"Bought it," he said laconically. He was looking at Krista. He found it difficult not to look at her. For some reason which he didn't understand he wanted her approval passionately—more than he had ever wanted anything else. She loved to hear him play. He knew that, and for this reason alone he had bought the accordion.

Lise's husband exchanged a glance with her. "Instruments like that cost all of three hundred marks," he said. "I suppose you bought it on the never-never?"

"No. I paid for it," said Hank still looking at Krista. "The never-never may be all right for you, but I'm a fellow who likes to pay cash down, on the nail."

He began to play an air from the Carnival of the previous year: it was still the most popular all over the district.

> Hätten wir doch das Geld vergraben,
> Das wir über vertrunken haben,
> Hätten wir einen Haufen,
> Ei, wir könnten saufen!

They all joined in and sang lustily, but as there was no one to keep them together the noise was greater than the harmony. Moe got up and with the twins danced wildly round the garden. Suddenly Hank broke into the air from the current year's Carnival—that fatal Carnival which had caused so much havoc in the family. Not only the town and district but the whole country had been singing and dancing to its songs.

> Gute Fahrt kleines Schiff auf dem Rheine,
> Fahre ins Glück und kehr bald zurück.
> Grüss' mir Mosel und Ahr, grüss die Weine,
> Fahre ins Glück und kehr bald zurück.

He played this so well that as Krista listened she was dancing again through the flood-lit crowded streets of Cologne on Rosenmontag. They had danced and danced until they could dance no more, and Paul had taken her home. Their hands had touched in the dance, his arm had been tight round her—but that had been all. He had made no attempt to kiss or embrace her in the reckless way of all those dancing around them. Perhaps that was why she instinctively trusted him, and had slept in the tram with her head on his shoulder all the way home.

The song agitated Moe violently. She had made up her mind to give up Rudi. She wanted to. The present position was impossible. She saw that it could not go on like this. She had been blind, she saw that. She would give up her lover. Having made this decision she felt curiously virtuous, as if it were already done, and kindly disposed to everyone because of it. When, however, Hank began playing that tune "Good voyage, little ship, on the Rhine," she cried violently, "Stop it! Stop it! We've had enough of that thing. Krista, go and see if you can find Pa. Tell him we want to have a concert. Tell him we can't manage without him."

She was terribly agitated. She was seized with a wild longing to go to Rudi again. She knew he would be there—this was his free evening. It was that damned tune. It had dominated all those three wild days last February. And where was Joseph anyhow? He was never at home now. What was the use of her abstention, of all her attempts at reconciliation, of all this good will if he went off every evening and did not even notice it?

Krista got up slowly at her request. She had a dreamy withdrawn look on her face. The music had upset her too. It had brought back the whole Carnival and her meeting with Paul. She had thought of nothing but him ever since that heavenly day on the Drachenfels. She was tormented with the thought that she had deceived her foster-father but knew that by doing so she had achieved a victory over her own fear and mistrust of her love for Paul. Paul had done that for her. She saw now how infinitely patient and gentle he had been.

She slipped out of the garden without a word and went to look for Joseph. The village was growing so fast with the new commercial expansion that two new beer gardens had sprung up. At the third one she found Joseph. He was sitting alone; and there was a lost unhappy air about him which caught at her throat.

As she and Joseph entered the gate the group round the acacia tree put down their instruments, all except Franz Joseph who was banging a saucepan lid in place of a drum. He went stolidly on making an appalling noise. Krista's eyes went to the group under the tree. Her heart gave a sickening lurch, then her breath almost stopped. Sitting next to Moe, with Lise's baby girl on his lap, was Paul. She was too taken aback to move and stood there unable to say a word.

Joseph saw him immediately; ignoring the greetings and shouts of welcome from the children he stood staring at the American. His glance went from him to Krista, who stood white-faced with her hands clutched nervously together at her breast.

"Well, are you struck dumb?" shouted Moe. "This is a nice way to greet a guest. Come on, Krista, and say good evening to your boy friend." She gave a snigger as she deliberately used the popular term. "You look surprised to see him, little innocent—I bet you knew damn well he was coming, you sly puss."

"No! No! I didn't, truly I didn't," faltered Krista. Paul put the child on his lap down as he stood up. He was perturbed as he saw Krista's unmistakable fear. He sensed immediately that he had made a terrible mistake in coming to her home like this. But what else could he have done? He had been ordered away again unexpectedly and the thought of going without seeing Krista had been torture.

"Krista," he began awkwardly. He found it appalling to have to explain to her in front of all these staring eyes. If he could have taken her in his arms that fear would have gone out of her white face, but he had to blunder on. "I didn't know when we went to Königswinter that I had to go away again or I'd have told you then. I've got to go tonight—I had to see you."

"Königswinter! You went to Königswinter with him?" Joseph cut him short. "What's this, Krista?" His voice was deadly quiet.

"Father . . . I spent Saturday afternoon with Paul . . . it was for my birthday . . . I . . ." she stopped at the look on Joseph's face.

"The Saturday before the birthday?" he insisted.

She nodded mutely. Her lie must now come out, and shame was mixed with fear.

"You gave me your word—and you told Anna to lie to me? When I asked where you were she said that you had been working late at the factory and had then gone out with her." His voice began to rise in anger. "You lied to me! *You*, Krista, *you!* You're just like all the others." His voice was bitter.

"Father I didn't mean to lie, really I didn't. But you're always so angry, what was I to do? Paul begged me to go down the river with him for my birthday. That's all."

"And what's wrong with that?" Paul's voice was belligerent; he hated to see Krista so frightened. "What's wrong in my taking Krista out for an afternoon?" He was genuinely puzzled at Joseph's anger and moved protectively towards Krista, who had begun to cry.

She pushed Paul away and said urgently, "I didn't know Paul was coming tonight. I did see him on that Saturday—I told you that I must say good-bye to him. Father, I *can't*. I *can't* give him up." She caught Joseph's arm entreatingly. He shook her off impatiently.

"Get out!" he shouted violently to Paul. "Get out of here. I've told Krista she's not to see you again." He was in a fury now and the veins on his forehead stood out startlingly. Moe said quickly, "Don't shout so, Joseph, don't shout before you've heard everything—and for goodness sake sit down!"

"Krista did *not* know that I was coming here tonight," said Paul as calmly as he could, "but if she had, what of it? What's wrong with my wanting to marry her. Is it so wrong?"

At the word "marriage" Moe's eyes narrowed. The girl *was* deceitful. She had never said a word of this to Moe. If he wanted to marry her he must have spoken of it to her; one would think the first person to tell would have been her. After all, wasn't she the only mother Krista could remember? Moe was hurt, and Krista saw this.

"Has he asked you to marry him?" Joseph asked more quietly. She nodded, unable to speak. To have her emotions and Paul's paraded like this before the inquisitive eyes of the whole family was agony.

"And you never said a word to me. Did you know anything about this?" he shouted again at Moe. She lied cheerfully in defence of the agitated Krista. "Of course, she told me and I was delighted for her. How could she discuss anything with you? You're always in a mood, never want to listen to anyone except yourself."

"You're a deceitful girl! And to think I imagined you were different. You promised me to give this man up; now he tells me that he wants to marry you. And *you*," he was shouting again, "Do you want to marry this enemy of your country's? This man who is here to occupy us and keep us down?"

"Shut up!" shouted Paul now, whose temper was no longer under control either; "I love Krista. She loves me. There's nothing you can do about that. For us there's no nationality—we can't help it if I'm American and she's German. We want to be married. It's people like you who put hate into their children."

As Paul said this he knew suddenly that what he said was true. The children, for instance, they all loved the Occupation soldiers, no matter what their uniform or nationality, they played with them, trusted them completely. It was their elders who would sometimes call them away, with that disapproval and resentment in their voices which would be handed on to the little ones. He looked at the small boys here, still playing desultorily on their instruments. They liked him. All of them, and he liked them. The girl Anna, and Moe too. Even Katie. The two who resented him were Joseph and Hank. And even Hank had been quite pleasant to him this evening.

Joseph could see nothing but danger to Krista. This man wanted to take her away. He said violently, "That's easy for you to say. You haven't fought in a war. You haven't starved and thirsted and bled for your country. Wait until you do, then you'll know there's nationality all right. You stick to your people and Krista'll stick to hers."

"She doesn't belong here! That's just it!" shouted Paul angrily. "She's not of your people—she has no people."

"Damn you! This is the only home she remembers. There'll always be wars. You can't get away with that rubbish about nationality. Get out of here, and leave Krista alone, like Pa says." Hank, who had spoken, rather admired Paul. He liked his quiet air of authority. He envied him his uniform. Until the word marriage had been uttered he had had nothing specifically against Paul. Now that he had said that he wanted to marry Krista, Hank to his own surprise was violently antagonistic.

Paul was unpleasantly startled at this attack. He had been given a great welcome by them all, Hank included. Moe had made him feel at home at once, with her warmth, her rollicking laugh, her overflowing generosity; and the homely but real fun this large family were having until Joseph arrived on the scene were a wonder to Paul.

"Krista", he said firmly. "We can't talk here. Will you come to the gate with me?"

"You can say good-bye to her *here* and *now*. What are you waiting for? There's nothing more to say. Get out!" Joseph was shouting again.

"Pa," yelled Moe, "how can you talk like that? He's our guest, I asked him to stay. If you don't know any better manners, then I do. Sit down, all of you, and finish your wine."

Krista was now so upset and frightened at Joseph's attitude that she couldn't get a word out. Her face was piteous in its wavering between her father and Paul.

Paul caught her firmly by the arm, putting himself between her and Joseph. "We *are* going to be married," he said, looking defiantly at Joseph, "so make up your mind to that."

Moe put down her wine glass. There was a little smile on her face. "Splendid," she said, "Krista's a lucky girl, here's to you both!" and she raised her glass high.

"No!" shouted Joseph angrily, "It's out of the question. Impossible. Get out now and leave her alone. Don't come here again."

Krista found words at last. "Please go now," she begged Paul. "May I go with him to the gate, father?"

"Go where you like. You're like all the rest of them—wanton, wanton, WANTON!" His voice rose to a shriek and suddenly with a violent movement he seized the table leg and hurled the whole thing over.

There was a crash of crockery, and screams from Peppi who was unceremoniously thrown to the ground, where he sat howling with the wine pouring over him and the food and the table-cloth smothering him.

Moe went on smoking. Her drink had been dashed from her hand by Joseph's violence, but as the table had been overthrown at the opposite end, nothing had fallen on her. Her face was white with anger as she watched the girls trying in vain to calm Peppi and Franz Joseph and to clear up some of the mess.

"Go to the gate with your friend, Krista," she said tersely. "I don't suppose he would want to come here again even if he weren't going away."

Hank had been watching Krista. For some reason, despite his limited emotions he was violently agitated. He wanted to kill his father for bringing that stricken look to Krista's face. "That's enough, Pa," he said savagely. "We've had about enough of your shouting; all the neighbours are listening. Sit down and be quiet; or go to bed."

Joseph gazed at his son in amazement. He had never been spoken to like this by any member of his family, in fact never told to sit down or go to bed by anyone. As if it were he who was the child. What were things coming to? He looked round at the ring of hostile faces. They no longer understood their father. When he had come home every night and ordered them to clear up the yard and wash themselves and insisted that they behave properly they had grumbled but respected him. Now he cared nothing for the place, or for what they did. He had somehow got rid of that lovely new suit they had bought him. When Moe had not been able to find it in the cupboard she had gone to the tailor to see if Joseph had taken it there for alteration. But no, the tailor hadn't seen it. She had searched the place in vain. The boys thought that perhaps Pa had sold it to add the money to his fund towards a house.

When Hank spoke so disrespectfully to him he looked at Moe. A year ago she would have either boxed Hank's ears or thrown something at him. Now she sat smoking with a set hard look on her face. The sight of her detachment infuriated Joseph further. "Why you . . . you . . ." He could not find words to express his rage. "I'll teach you to talk to me like that." He seized a stick from the ground.

In a moment Moe got up, picked up a pitcher of water from the ground behind her and threw its contents over Joseph.

"Take that to cool you down," she screamed. "And if you want any more there's the wash-tub full over there."

The cold water shocked Joseph into sanity. He dropped the stick. He was shaking—that appalling red rage had over-whelmed him again. He had felt the same urgent desire to smash Hank's grinning face as he had felt to have that lion-tamer's face crunched. He shook himself as a wet dog does and put his face between his hands. He seemed exhausted and bewildered now. Lise's husband took him gently by the arm, while Anna rushed for a towel.

"Come on in and get dry, Pa," she said soothingly. "Come along. You're all in . . . come on in to bed."

Krista had gone to the gate with Paul. She had not witnessed this last indignity to Joseph. Katie, her spiteful eyes following them, was still clearing up the broken crocks. Moe was calmly totting up the cost as Katie listed them. Joseph was always com-plaining that they were all extravagant. Now he would see what his fits of temper cost.

Anna came out of the house. She pointed mutely up to the windows of the top floors. Heads were all hanging out, the windows flung wide open. Well, and why not? They could see the river from up there and what could be nicer on a summer evening? Anna knew that the beauties of the landscape were but an excuse. Tomorrow the story of Paul's proposal to Krista and the reactions would not only be all over the village, but would be embroidered with lurid colours. The twins looked up too. Put-ting their fingers to their mouths they let forth an ear-splitting imitation of an air-raid siren, still used, but as a fire alarm now.

The windows suddenly banged down but the curtains behind them moved, all except Frau Schmitt's. She was deaf.

The tension was suddenly released. Moe threw back her head and laughed heartily, and the boys joined in.

"What an evening! And it started so well!" she sighed when she recovered.

"It's no use trying anything now," said Hank bitterly. "Pa's impossible. I think he's got a screw loose."

"Don't speak of your father like that!" reproved Moe, but she said it mechanically.

At the gate Krista stood trying to make Paul go away. He wanted her to go into town with him. He was angry and miserable. He did not know how long he would be away from the district. Joseph's behaviour had astounded him; but it had made him all the more determined to get Krista away from the family. Where was the crime in wanting to marry her? Surely her foster-father would prefer that to the illicit unions of his own daughters?

To his pleading that she should write to him Krista turned a deaf ear. She wanted him gone and gone quickly. That Pa could believe she could trick and deceive him was agony to her. Beside this the unhappiness of Paul seemed at the moment of secondary importance. If only he would go quickly she could get back to Joseph and explain to him.

"Please go," she begged, "Pa's right. It's no good. I never thought that it was!"

"I've as much right to you as they have," said Paul angrily. "You don't belong to them. Krista, don't you care for me enough to fight your foster-father? You must see that he's unreasonable over you." He pulled her to him and kissed her roughly and angrily. She struggled to get free, resenting his attentions in sight of the others, but he would not release her.

Robert sprang from the hedge behind which he had been watching the farewell. At the first sign of trouble he had hidden himself. When adults quarrelled and shouted at each other he was terrified, as was Franz Joseph. They had learned to disappear.

"Leave Krista alone! Leave her alone or I'll kill you," he screamed, while Franz Joseph began pummelling the American's legs.

At Robert's cries Moe came running. She began laughing when she saw what was happening.

"Ah! So our little saint's being kissed," she taunted. "Well done, young man! Take another one, now, a bird in the hand is worth two in the bush!" She went into fits of laughter while Krista, white-faced and frantic, pushed Paul away and ran past them into the house. Paul was aghast. "I shouldn't have done that, but she makes me desperate," he burst out miserably. "She seems to have no spirit in her . . . and I'm mad about her."

Moe suddenly became serious. She put a hand on his arm, thinking how attractive were the dark wings of his hair and the steady blue eyes. What an appalling scene he had made for them by coming here tonight. Joseph was besotted with the girl, always had been. He thought of her as his property, his special find. She loved Krista herself, but she bitterly resented Joseph's absorption in his adopted daughter to the neglect of his own flesh and blood. She decided suddenly that the best thing for everyone would be for Krista to marry this foreigner and get right away from her foster-father. What future would there be for her if Joseph was going to behave in this way to every man who came after her? And there would be plenty. The girl was not just attractive; she was growing really beautiful.

"You're in too much of a hurry, silly," she said, laughing again. "She's still a child, whatever you may think; she's not like other girls you know. Have a little patience. She'll come round—she likes you. Did you see her face when she came in and found you here? It was lovely."

"But your husband?"

"Oh, him," said Moe contemptuously; "you can see what he counts for. Who cares about him?" She laughed again.

"Krista cares a lot," said Paul glumly.

"Well, don't look so miserable, the world's full of girls, all just waiting to fall into a pair of arms like yours."

Her roars of laughter angered him, but in spite of his anger he sensed its heartiness and her wish to comfort him as she took his hand and pumped it up and down.

"I only want Krista," Paul said, "and I mean to get her."

"Well done! But true love never runs smoothly. Be off and find a more willing one, and you'll soon have Krista come running—and if you can't find one, come and ask *me*."

Her laughter followed him down the road as he walked under the willows to the ugly station. It had started to rain and looked drearier than ever. His heart was leaden, like the sky, he saw only the white anguished face of Krista and heard her voice begging him to go away.

Hurrying steps behind him made him turn. Anna was pounding after him.

"Paul, wait a minute," she panted. She was a heavy girl and Paul had been walking like one pursued. "Don't be angry with Krista, please. Oh, I know she's upset and doesn't know what she wants. It's all father's fault. He idolizes her. She's a saint to him. You've no idea. He'll never let her go—and she must get away. She must marry and get away from the family. I've told her so. She's just a normal girl like me but father's given her a halo and she's trying to live up to it. Don't you see?"

"But what can I do?" retorted Paul angrily. "You saw how she sent me packing. She wouldn't even promise to write to me, and she begged me not to write to her."

"How stupid you are," cried Anna. "Write to her at the factory, lots of us get letters there, and give me your address at the place where you're being sent. I may need it, you never know."

"You'll help me?" asked Paul eagerly.

Anna nodded and put his slip of paper in her pocket.

X X

LEILA LIVED with her grandmother in a miserable little hovel by the river. The grandmother was wise, with the wisdom of one now dependent on her grand-daughter. She said very little about the fractured arm and accepted Leila's explanation of the accident even if she doubted its truth. She had learned that it did no good to nag at the girl whose way of life appalled her. What else could one expect from a child whose mother had run away with another woman's husband just because her own was missing in Russia? The old woman had taken her grand-daughter gladly and had worked at a laundry to support her. Now Leila was old enough to work for herself and for the last two years had worked at the rubber factory where the twins Hans and Heinz were employed.

They made rubber goods—horrible things about which the young should know nothing in the old woman's opinion. They were now making women's breasts which could be inflated to any size required. Leila had brought some of them home with her, and had demonstrated their correct use to the scandalized grandparent. She had put a tight jersey over them to show how they added to her attractions. The old woman had not minced her words, but Leila had been unabashed, saying that she was glad enough of the money they brought in, and at the same time determined that she would not show her grandmother the very newest kind with a certain improvement added.

The smell of rubber—hot rubber—permeated the once lovely fields and woods for miles. In a strong wind it was wafted right to the village where its pungency caught the pit of one's stomach, but after a few weeks' grumbling everyone had accepted it as they did the employment which the factory brought their young people. It was accepted that this post-war drive brought compensation for expansion in the wage-packets brought home regularly by those who for too long after the war had known hunger and unemployment.

The grandmother made little comment on the fractured arm but the old village doctor made a great deal. He accepted Leila's version of an accident with a wide smile.

"Come off it!" he said. "D'you take me for a fool? Now tell me the truth, how did this happen? And why didn't you come to me immediately?"

Leila had been taken home by Eddie that night and without a word had crept into bed to lie all night in agonizing pain from an arm which next morning was so swollen and black that deception was impossible. The bruising of the entire arm prevented the finger-marks of her torturers being seen. After her explanation of a fall from a motor cycle the doctor had asked for the real one. When she stuck to her story he demanded brusquely to see her back and the other arm; in short, he told her to strip. Her terror was so obvious that he had called in the grandmother and asked her to remove Leila's clothes.

When she stood naked the old man was horrified. The girl's left arm, shoulders and back were a mass of bruises—which could be consistent with a fall—but some of the livid marks on her young skin had obviously been made by deliberate pressure of fingers. The old woman looked on in silence. She knew perfectly well that Leila went out in the night and concluded that she went, as did so many others, to meet a man. But what could she do about it? She was old, no longer able to work, the laundry said she was too slow, her fingers were getting twisted and bent with rheumatism. When she remonstrated with her, Leila had retorted sharply that if she were nagged she would go elsewhere to live and the old woman could fend for herself.

Leila was generous. She earned more than the laundry had ever paid the grandmother for her long day's work. Growing old was a terror when one was alone. Her husband was long dead, her two sons lost in Russia. This girl, daughter of her most beloved son, was her sole source of support until she could claim the old age pension. That was not so easy. She came from the East, she did not belong here.

She loved Leila, had loved her from childhood, but she feared for her since the girl had been mixed up with these flashy young men and that red-haired girl from the bunker family. Leila was often away all night now. The grandmother sensed that something sinister was going on, and had been for some time when this accident occurred.

When the girl was dressed again the doctor said abruptly, "You must come to hospital and have an anaesthetic for that arm. Apart from the fracture, it's been wrenched from its socket, almost—" he looked sharply at her—"as if someone had been twisting it."

He noted her increased agitation as he said this and drew his own conclusions. The police sergeant whose district covered her village was a friend of his. He would say a word to him and have the young woman's obvious ill-treatment recorded.

Leila went into the hospital where Carola was, and after two days there, during which she steadfastly stuck to her story of the motor cycle accident, was discharged with her arm in plaster. As she was coming out she met Moe going in to visit Carola. Moe, with her arms full of packages, stopped, surprised. She didn't know Leila very well but had seen her occasionally with Katie.

"Whatever have you been doing?" she asked.

"Fell off a motor cycle," said Leila laconically.

Moe's eyes narrowed. She remembered those blood-stained gloves of Katie's and her explanation of someone falling off a motor cycle, but that had been some weeks ago.

There was something going on among these young people, something dangerous. She didn't like it. "Was it that Leo's machine?" she asked.

"No!" replied Leila. And that was all. She seemed to have no interest in her own fractured arm—a topic which in Moe's life would have been of absorbing interest.

"You won't be able to work," she said. "How long will it be? Whatever will your grandma do?"

"I can use both hands," said Leila abruptly. "The machine I'm working is easy; I'll be able to use the hand soon although the arm is in plaster."

"So!" Moe looked at the pallid face and the blue shadows under the eyes.

"Where do you kids go at night?" she shot out suddenly.

Leila was taken off her guard. She had no answer ready. "Up the river," she said vaguely, "we just meet sometimes and talk."

"Oh yeah!" said Moe bluntly. "Tell that to someone else."

"Why don't you ask Katie then?" said Leila stung by her tone.

Moe went home and did exactly that. She found Katie lying in the summer-house stretched out on the seat asleep. It was late afternoon and as she lay there utterly relaxed the lines of her pregnancy were already visible.

When the girl awoke at her shakings she was astonished at her mother's question. Why should she ask it just now? She had never made any serious attempt to find out what they did at night. She had been too occupied with her own affair with Rudi. Katie was sullenly silent.

"Oh, I know well enough what *you* in particular have been up to," Moe said, "but what do you *all* do—there are a lot of you going and coming home at all hours. What do the others do? Or do you have combined necking parties?" She laughed her great hoarse laugh. "I've just seen that Leila at the hospital," she explained, and did not miss the flash of fear in Katie's face. "Funny the way you all seem to be falling off motor cycles lately! Who was it you helped tie up when you got all that blood on your gloves?"

"One of the boys—no one you know!" was the quick reply, but her face belied the lightness of her tone. Katie didn't like this subject and would not answer Moe's inquiries about Leila's accident, insisting that she knew nothing about it. Moe did not insist—Katie had to be relied upon to smooth the way for her visits to Rudi. She had resumed the relationship with the young man in spite of his misgivings about Joseph's threats. It was costly, for the landlady where he now lodged had to be bribed. She pretended to be shocked, but Moe had rightly concluded that it was the kind of shock that can be reduced in terms of cash.

Katie was left to wonder how much Leila had disclosed as to the cause of her injuries. That she had told Moe it was from a motor cycle fall indicated that she was using that way out. Katie thought of her persistent refusal to take the oath after she had learned that the tourist had been murdered. She could see that Leo had admired her courage even while redoubling the torture. Who would have thought it of the quiet Leila? Katie had seen her face as Eddie, who had brought it all upon her, approached her after she had been revived from fainting from pain. The horror and contempt on it had been appalling. There was going to be trouble from Leila. Katie wondered if a real accident to that young woman would not be safer for them all. She began to think about a little push near the edge of the river by their hideout. It was particularly deep just there and in the strong current no one with a broken arm would have much chance. She was frightened now, not of Leo or of Hank and Eddie but of Leila, who would bring peril to them all.

It was that very evening that Hank told her she was to take Leila's place. Eddie had let them know that a wealthy tourist had been coming regularly to the restaurant in the evenings and that he had asked Eddie to introduce him to an attractive girl. It had to be tonight, for unless they made haste the best part of his wad of notes would be gone.

Katie demurred at the short notice.

"You always knew it would be at short notice!" said Hank. "That's the whole idea of the thing—we act on the signal from Eddie. He telephoned me at the repair station today. The man is due there tonight for dinner and Eddie has promised a girl. You see you're there or you'll get what Leila got."

"I won't do it," said Katie flatly. "I don't like it either. Hank, please tell Leo it's dangerous. We'll get caught—these men are well-to-do business men—there'll be a hue and cry from the police soon, there's bound to be."

"Getting yellow?" sneered Hank putting his great hands—hands very like his father's—round Katie's neck and pressing hard. "It's Leo who gives the orders, not me."

"But why shouldn't it be *you?*" coaxed his sister. "You're just as clever and stronger than Leo, and the twins would support you—so would I. This decoy business is all wrong. We should have stuck to the housebreaking: it was good enough for everyone until Eddie started this new stunt."

Hank let go of her neck. His face wore a bitter look.

"You know damn well why it's Leo who gives the orders and not me! He's educated and I'm not, see? He can make me look pretty silly when he likes. Why, I can't read any too easily—you know that—I left school at twelve; he can understand anything, and Eddie can speak English and French too."

"That's only because he's a waiter, he picks it up from the tourists."

"Be your age!" said her brother brutally. "It's because he was in with a set of British and Belgian sods before he took up with us. I don't trust that fellow. He's too slick. He let us down over that last business—swore the house was empty."

"I loathe him," said Katie.

"Leo orders you to be there at ten o'clock tonight," said Hank; "look out for yourself if you're not. What Leila got is nothing—a mere flea-bite to what we'll give you."

"Leila's going to make trouble," said Katie. "Moe met her coming out of the hospital today. We'd better make sure her mouth is shut."

"You can see to that yourself, but you'll answer to Leo if you're not on time tonight."

Katie shivered. She didn't feel any too well. Pregnancy did not agree with her. All the time she had carried Peppi she'd been sick, and now it was just the same. Moe said it was her flaming red hair—that people with red hair had fewer skins than others and that there was something wrong with their blood. She herself had always bloomed during her pregnancies, she said. Katie was peculiar.

Soon, thought Katie angrily, she would not be able to get into the tight satin frock which Leo had bought her, then he would notice and that would be the end. If only she could have done something, as Moe had said. The Frenchman was definitely interested. He liked her. She went indoors and took the dress from the cupboard. She couldn't find the belt. It was black with a bright emerald ribbon in broad velvet. Leo had said that it suited her hair. That had been when he had first been attracted to her. Only a few months ago—it seemed a lifetime now. She felt heavy and spiritless. At the thought of having to attract the tourist tonight she felt furious. She was constantly having nausea at the smell and sight of food and to have to eat and drink with him filled her with apprehension. But there could be no let-up. Leo was already tired of her. He would have no mercy.

When she came out Krista was with Hank. "All right. I'll go and see Leila," she said sullenly.

She was worried that she couldn't find the belt. She envied Krista's supple slimness. Krista was growing taller and slimmer every day—or so it seemed to Katie, who watched herself swell in terror.

She hated Krista. Hated her wide grey eyes, her milk white skin, and most of all her lovely soft cloud of ashen hair. She hated her innocent virginal look, she wanted to take her somehow and smirch her in dirt, to soil her beauty and her breathtaking freshness.

Krista was unaware of this. She considered that Katie had been unfortunate. That Belgian had behaved shamefully in seducing her, and then going away leaving her to bear the consequences. Krista was sorry for Katie, endured all her spite and willingly looked after Peppi for her. That Katie was so often snappy and spiteful puzzled her, and that she went out on these night outings alarmed her. She knew that Leo was Katie's boy. She was terrified of him. Since he had flung himself upon her in the grass that evening she had for ever a vision of his cruel smiling face as he had pinioned her hands.

She had been trying vainly to put Paul out of her mind. Since that evening when Pa had behaved so terribly to him she had scarcely dared to think of him. She had been so unhappy at work that the nice chief supervisor had spoken to her. She had said just a little about Paul. The supervisor knew him by sight. He was talked about in the factory. He was too good-looking to escape notice when he leaned against the wall waiting for Krista.

The supervisor had said that Krista was wrong to think that she must give up Paul. She should have more courage and she would find things would come right for her.

But Krista wasn't comforted. Pa had scarcely spoken to her since that terrible evening when he had upset the table and ordered Paul away. She longed to regain the old intimacy, but he rebuffed all her advances. Paul had written to her to the factory:

Krista, my darling,

It's no use saying how sorry I am. Nothing matters to me but your happiness. Write to me, *please*. You haven't promised not to write, have you darling? I think of your beauty in everything lovely that I see. You are always with me, working, sleeping, and waking—because I love you.

Paul.

She read the letter alone on the tow-path where they had so often met. Her hand shook so much that she could scarcely open it, while her heart seemed to explode with the violence of its beating. Why should she feel so lonely amongst all those crowds in the town just because one person was not there? But she did. Every day when she came out of the factory her eyes had gone to that piece of wall against which he leaned until he saw her coming. She knew perfectly well that he wouldn't be there. He was away—hadn't she herself begged him not to come—and yet she couldn't prevent herself from looking for him. "It's the same world," she thought, looking at the familiar square and the Cathedral, the bridge and the river, "but it's as if I were dead. A piece of me died when Paul went away."

She sat down on a stone under the bridge and wept with his letter in her hand. No one took any notice of her. The war and its aftermath had made people blind to suffering—blind or indifferent. There were always trails of refugees on the roads and at the big station. Krista watched them with their bundles and their tense strained faces. Even the children looked old; no one took any notice of them either.

Presently she got up, dipped her handkerchief in the river which was still abnormally high from the melted snows, and bathed her tear-stained face. She put the letter between her breasts, folding it into a small square so that it would not crackle. There was no privacy at home. Robert and Franz Joseph shared her small room, and the entire family rifled each other's possessions.

When she got home Katie spoke rather anxiously to her, asking her to take Peppi into her bed that night. As she agreed willingly, for she was always sorry for Katie who missed so much fun because of her child, she felt the letter next to her heart. The words in it burned. "I think of your beauty in everything lovely that I see." Paul thought her beautiful . . . he thought she was beautiful!

When Katie had gone out she went into Moe's room where there was a mirror. The other rooms had only a tiny square of looking-glass. Moe's had a full-length one which she had removed from the room she had formerly shared with Joseph. Krista stood there looking at herself just as Moe had done on the day when Joseph had come unexpectedly early.

Was she beautiful? The grey eyes stared back unblinkingly at her. She could not see anything attractive in the reflection. In the mirror she caught sight of Moe's amused face. "Well, well, having a look at ourself, are we?" She laughed good-naturedly. She had just come from Rudi, happy in their reunion. She laughed at the girl's embarrassment at being caught looking in the mirror.

XXI

IN THE HOUSE next door the little English boy had come home for the summer holidays. He had another boy with him and the two played a strange game in the garden with a wooden bat and a ball. First they stuck some sticks in the lawn at each end and then hurled the ball at each other, taking it in turns to ward it off with the wooden bat.

Sometimes the Englishwoman played too, and even the father in the evenings. And sometimes a whole lot of British children came out in cars from other places and then they all played this strange game. Robert, Karl and Franz Joseph were fascinated by it. They watched from the top of the fence and asked what game it was. It was apparently called cricket, a name they had never heard before.

The English boys invited them to come and play too, and they jumped down from the fence and soon were quite efficient at fielding the ball and in time Robert and Karl learned to use the bat.

When Hank heard that they had been playing with the British children he beat the two boys unmercifully. "Next time," he said, "you'll get something much more lasting than a beating to make you remember what I say."

When Moe was told what had happened she was for once very angry with Hank.

"I can't help it if they *are* Occupation," she said firmly; "she is good to Carola and that's enough for me. She takes me to the hospital in her car and gives me things for Carola. What do I care if people are foreigners? It's their hearts that matter. Not one person from this village has ever given me anything for Carola, let alone inquire after her. Deeds speak more than words. You lay off, Hank. If the kids want to play next door, let them."

Hank knew better than to argue. One did not argue with Moe. She got into a tearing rage and flung things at you. He had his own way of getting things done.

The next time he caught Robert playing with the British boys he called him peremptorily back, tied him to a post at the bottom of the garden and with a pen knife carved the word "Traitor" on his back. He had first taken the precaution of tying a handkerchief round the child's mouth to prevent his screams from being heard.

When Krista was helping the boys to bed that night Robert did not want to remove his shirt. She saw that it was bloodstained and stuck in places to his skin. Horrified, she fetched Moe.

Moe stood looking at the word which Hank had carved on the boy's back. It had been cut fairly deep. Robert, white-faced and still shivering from pain and shock, was almost unintelligible. It was obvious that he was too frightened to reveal the source of his torture. Krista had elicited that Hank had caught him playing with the little boy next door.

"Don't let Pa see this," was all Moe said as she gently covered the place with some ointment and disinfectant. She knew that Hank was cruel but this shocked her inexpressibly. When she hit out herself it was always in the heat of temper or annoyance, and the children knew it. This was carefully planned and considered brutality.

To Robert she said, "Why d'you like going there so much?"

He whispered that he liked the little boy and that the lady was kind to him and always welcomed him.

"It's natural enough that he should want to go there when they invite him," she said angrily. "Hank will hear something about this from me." She told Robert to keep away and stay in their own garden.

When Hank came in she attacked him immediately. The tortures which he had inflicted on the dog and any animal on which he could lay hands had left her unmoved. An animal was an animal—a child, and his own brother at that, was different. Not that she sympathized with Robert. She had no use for weaklings, but when Hank accused her of going next door and making up to the Englishwoman for what she could get out of her for Carola, her fury knew no bounds. She picked up the zinc bathtub and with her strong arms held it aloft and flung the filthy potato-water over him.

Drenched and livid he caught her, and his great hands gripped her throat. The maniacal look in his eyes left her unmoved. Her own bold steady ones did not flinch before his, and very slowly his hands released their hold.

"So!" she said shakily. "You would manhandle your own mother!"

"It's your fault," he mumbled, shaking the water from his drenched clothes.

"Leave the children alone," she said more calmly. "It's your father's place to chastise them."

Hank spat in contempt. "He's about as much use as a sodden potato."

She did not reprove him. She saw in his eyes his contempt for her. He knew perfectly well that she had resumed her relations with Rudi. He held the whip-hand again. She had known fear when he had caught her by the throat and his great hands had gripped her neck, although she had not shown it.

She took the suit she had soiled with the dirty water and spent an hour cleaning and pressing it, but as she ironed, she began to wonder about Hank. Cruel things which he had done even as a small child came back to her. Horrible things. She had assumed that all boys were cruel—they all teased and tortured animals and smaller children—but some of Hank's recent doings had shocked her.

She had known several foreigners since the Occupation had come. She liked them herself, they were far more friendly to her than the villagers were. Joseph liked them too—provided they were not after Krista, as that young American was. Hank hated them all. He had got his violent ideas from the gang of boys in the village. Moe knew they were the ones who were dropping the notes in every British letter-box at night. The notes told the Occupation to go home and free a house for the people to whom it really belonged. She knew it was his gang who had painted some of the huge notices on the railway embankments and bridges. "Tommy, go home," they said, and on others, "Go home, Yankee."

If he did these things, what else did he do when out at night? She was frightened and the thought of Rudi made her keep silent: she knew that if she opened her mouth to Joseph, Hank would immediately tell him of her visits to the house where Rudi now lodged and she could not forget those threats to the children.

Robert's back did not heal. In two days the whole area was septic. The knife which Hank had used had cut up some worms beforehand. It was Anna who insisted on taking the boy to the doctor, in spite of Moe's begging her to wait a little.

The doctor made little comment as he dressed the now inflamed and swollen back. He asked Robert who had done it. The word was quite clear in spite of the inflammation. The boy wouldn't say. His obvious terror reminded the doctor of the girl Leila who had refused to tell the truth about her arm.

Anna kept silent too. She had brought Robert because she was innately kind, and she could not bear to see him in pain, but she did not want any trouble and was upset when the doctor insisted on driving them home. He wanted to see Joseph, he said.

Shocked and amazed, Joseph looked in horror at his son's back and asked him sternly who had done it. The child would not answer. Joseph gazed round the circle of closed faces of his family. No one would risk incurring Hank's displeasure for fear of similar treatment. It was Franz Joseph who supplied the answer.

"Hank did that," he said calmly, "I watched him cutting. The skin was tough, and he said the knife wasn't sharp enough."

"Let me get my hands on him," growled the doctor furiously. "You'd better see what's going on here, Joseph, there's something

I don't like . . ." and with that he had slammed out after telling Robert to lie on his stomach that night.

"If anyone attempts to touch your back again I will bring the police here, he threatened. And come to me tomorrow morning so that I can see for myself."

He went next door. He knew the British family there. When he told the Englishwoman about Robert's back he thought she was going to faint.

"I shouldn't encourage the boys to come here," he said bluntly. "You see what happens."

"But the mother comes here, and so does the girl they call Krista."

"Ah," said the old doctor. "Krista now, she's different, she's a lily amongst this pig-swill, if I could get her away I would."

"But she loves them," protested their neighbour. "She loves them all."

"No one could love that creature they call Hank," insisted the doctor grimly. "Who else has she but this family?"

"There's a young American," said the Englishwoman, "I've seen him with her once or twice. He looks such a nice fellow."

"She'll never get away from her foster-father," said the doctor thoughtfully. "He dotes on her."

At home Joseph had begun an inquisition as soon as the doctor had left. He had suspected for some time that Hank was cruel and brutal with his younger brothers, but it had been much easier to close his eyes to it. Now, shocked by Robert's back, he started asking questions. No one would answer him except Franz Joseph, an exceptionally intelligent child for his age. From his youngest, Joseph got a fair picture of what had been going on in the house.

It all came back to the same thing—Moe. Moe and Rudi. No matter what it was, it all came back to that. Moe had left the room during his questioning, but with the candour and horrifying clarity of childhood Franz Joseph supplied him with all the details. Finally, asked where Moe was while all this went on, the child had said simply, "In the bed with Rudi."

"Here?" thundered Joseph.

"At Frau Fischer's," was the answer.

So that was it. She went there now. Joseph got up and without a word went out of the house. They watched him go in silence. Krista was at a church gathering. Moe put Franz Joseph across her knee and spanked him for telling tales.

"You're as bad as Hank," said Anna coldly. She was disgusted. "What's the difference? Leave the child alone, he only answered his father's questions."

"Keep your large mouth shut," snapped Moe. She felt ashamed already that she had spanked Franz Joseph. He was regarding her with his black eyes. There was no merriment in them now. He turned shakily away. "I hate you," he said coldly. "You're a bad, cruel Moe," and at the look on his usually mischievous face she was stricken.

She held out her arms persuasively, but he would not go to her. "I'm going to wait for Krista," he said with dignity.

"Watch him—he'll be off again, and we'll all be hunting for him," shouted Katie.

"I shall be on the gate," said Franz Joseph quietly. He set his little mouth firmly, put his hands behind his back and marched off.

Moe went to find Hank. Joseph knew now. She had no more fear of that. He faced her sullenly when she stormed at him about Robert. "The little brat's a sneak and a spy! He's got to learn to stick to his own flesh and blood. He's been spying on us at night."

"Hank. You've *got* to tell me what you're doing. What did you mean when you said you'd drag all of us in?" She caught him by the shoulders and shook him in her anxiety.

"Oh, nothing. It's black market—that's all. Coffee from Belgium—we get it through without tax, but it has to be done at night. It's child's play, and easy money. But if any of you start talking the police'll come down damned hard on us all."

"Katie's in it too?"

"*And* your precious twins. So keep your mouth closed." He picked up his accordion and began to play "Mutterlein," singing the words with an air of sickening sentimentality and laughing at her concern at what he had just told her. He was amused at the ease with which he had deceived her.

XXII

ON THE DAY after Germany won the international football match Hank and the twins came home drunk from the celebrations held by their cycling club. They were brought home by the policeman from the next village. He had been very decent about it, merely giving the parents a warning. They would overlook it this time because of the football match. Every boy in the district was wild with joy. Football was the sport on which they were all mad keen nowadays.

Joseph was furious, and inexpressibly shocked. They were so young, the twins only sixteen and a half. Why, at that age he had seldom tasted beer or wine, and never spirits. Times had changed, said Moe drily, the boys had wine on Sundays and on all special occasions, and as to beer, everyone knew it was mostly water. He was incensed at her anxiety to excuse them and accused her angrily of not caring what they did.

"If it comes to that," she shouted "whom do they get their example of drinking from? From you, of course!" and when he did not answer she tried to provoke him to reply. "Well, what have you got to say to that?"

But he was silent. He saw that it was true and a terrible sense of guilt overwhelmed him. He longed to retort that if the lads took their cue from him what about her? What did she expect from the girls when she flaunted her sordid affair before them? The sight of his sons the worse for drink had brought him up with a violent jerk to what was happening in the home because of this struggle between the parents. They had come home shouting "Up, up with us; and down, down with the Occupation." They were not helplessly drunk but aggressively. That was dangerous and he had been terrified lest their neighbours should hear them. This small corner of the willow-lined lane, once the most elegant of residential quarters, was now almost an international colony. Next door they had the British, opposite the French. Further along the lane the dentist had a Belgian wife, and in two houses next to that were Americans. It all had to do with the coal. Something connected with this Ruhr-Saar question. Joseph discussed it frequently with the Frenchmen who often gave him a lift now. Supposing they had heard the latest toast in the cafés being bawled out by those drunken lads? They had been wildly excited about the car-racing success and now this.

The policeman had said that the news was a tremendous tonic for the whole country. It was a sign that they were recovering their former place in the world of sport. The other would follow, was following, he said. He was far more tolerant than Joseph, who was grateful to him, but horribly ashamed. Moe got them to bed. She was upset too, but she would not let Joseph see that she was. Anna dealt ruthlessly with the twins; she was disgusted, and thankful that Krista was at a cinema with the younger boys.

After the policeman had gone, Joseph and Moe had the first interchange of words on the subject which had lain silently between them all these weeks.

"We can't go on like this," he said heavily. He had not been able to trust himself to speak to her after Franz Joseph's revelations that she now went down the road to Frau Fischer's to visit her lover. He had been so outraged that he had just taken himself off. Now he saw that things couldn't be for ever pushed away. He must have it out with her.

"Look at what's happening to the boys!" he said. "I'll never touch another drop of spirits from this evening onwards."

"Joseph!" she cried, "d'you really mean that?"

He asserted that he did. "I've been drinking to escape from all this mess we're in," he said roughly. "And you—what you're doing—is that for the same reason?"

Was it? She didn't know. But she answered "Yes" mechanically when he pressed her.

"You've got to stop it!" he shouted violently. "You can't really care for a boy like that! It's ridiculous."

She studied him carefully. He wasn't so lifeless as he had seemed. When he was roused like this his face was as hard as granite. It was a strong face but lately it had been as devoid of vitality as Rudi's was devoid of character. She sat there now, thinking what a splendid man she could make from the two of them. Each had what the other lacked. It would have been easy to lie now but she was truthful. She *did* love Rudi no matter what Joseph said. She loved him. She saw his faults; his weakness, his cowardice, his leaning on her, his desire for her warmth and assurance. But when she thought of his childhood, his adolescence, of all that he had told her of his unhappy life, she understood it in some maternal sort of way. And he gave her something, something she needed.

"What d'you get out of it?" Joseph demanded angrily again. She wanted to shout "Love! That's what I get. Love, affection, pleasure. Things you never gave me, never even considered as a possibility for me". But she said carefully that Rudi treated her as a person, not just as a housewife, a mother, an everyday necessity to be made use of and regarded as such. Joseph stared at her as if she were mad. Did she think she was a young girl to have these silly ideas.

"But that's what a woman is meant for," he said in genuine astonishment. "Didn't we marry for exactly those reasons? That you should look after my home and bear and tend my children?"

"That was years ago," she said bluntly; "I was only eighteen. We change, all of us. Times change. Women are not as stupid as they were. We want to be ourselves, not just part of a man's life."

He looked at her in stupefaction. "You've been listening to all these silly talks on the Woman's Hour," he said bitterly.

"What if I have? It helps to get the potatoes peeled. Nothing stays the same. It can't. I'm sorry I've wronged you but you'll never understand." She had burst into tears, a thing she did so seldom that Joseph knew she was genuinely moved.

"I'm no good at words," he said gruffly, "but I thought of you night and day all those years I was away. What's happened to us? *What?*" And when she didn't answer but just sat there with set lips he went on, "Carola started it all. You were knocked sideways by that and I wasn't kind enough. I should have been especially good to you then. But I've changed too. You're right. We change. There are so many things I can't forget. Things in the war. Things I saw—and *did*. They haunt me. They blind me to everything else. And *now* I see it all coming back again. It'll all happen again with rearmament and newer, more terrible weapons. War's like time, it repeats itself. You can't get away from it. Did you hear what that policeman said? The other will follow! Once we get an army it will all start again!"

He put his head in his hands but she had seen that look of helpless acceptance again on his face. She hated it and she hated his absorption in politics. It was all this silly rubbish at the works which depressed him. That Peter; he was always working Joseph up about something the Government was doing or about to do.

"What's the good of concerning yourself with all these matters?" she urged. "They only make you miserable. Why can't you
put it all out of your mind. Forget it all."

"Can you?" he demanded.

"Yes," she said decidedly. "For me every day is a new life. It's
the only way. I learned that during the war, in that bunker. It was
the only possible way to endure it."

"I can't do that," he said heavily, "I'm too old, I suppose."

They went to bed. Not together. But there was a better feeling between them than for a long time. She had the strong intuition that he had forgiven her, that it would not be long before he
asked her to resume their normal life again. Did she want that?
She was indifferent. That was the truth. But it would be better
for everyone if he forgave her. She saw that. She pushed away the
absolute despair which the thought of never seeing Rudi again
evoked in her. There was always something. One couldn't have
everything. Some women managed it. But not her sort.

At breakfast next morning Joseph was gentler than he had
been for a very long time. The small children were excited about
the policeman having brought the boys home last night. Hank
was sullen and silent. The twins were ashamed and very apprehensive. Had they known it, so was Hank. What would Leo say
to this? Had they let out anything dangerous last night? Pa had a
new air of authority too. Did he think that their lapse last night
gave him the right to lecture them like this? Hank stood it only
because he was not sure whether anything damaging had come
out last night. He had to find out. He accepted Joseph's angry
remonstrances quietly. For the moment, that was all. Let him wait.
He forbore to argue or to apologize. He just said nothing. The
twins were upset. The police! They had been brought home by
a policeman! Visits from them in the past had invariably meant
trouble. For bicycles without lamps, for riding on footpaths and
numberless small but punishable incidents. Katie started to defend Hank and the twins by saying that they had learned to get
drunk from Pa. Moe shut her up instantly and fiercely. She was
not going to have the new atmosphere between her and Joseph
spoiled by a brawl this morning.

Later in the morning a message came from next door that
Moe was wanted on the telephone. She knew at once that it
was the hospital. They often sent messages through the British

house. Hank was always furious when this happened. He would get them a telephone of their own soon, he boasted. It wasn't shortage of money which prevented his getting it now, it was the number of lines and instruments installed for the damned Occupation which kept so many German families without one. Moe always laughed. Telephones were not for them she retorted. Why, who would use it? She had never used one in her life until Carola was taken ill. She hated the thing. It usually meant bad news. Lately she had admitted its uses. She could ring Rudi up at his work if necessary from the public call-box outside the post office.

Apprehensively she went next door. The sister in charge of Carola's ward wanted to know if she would come this afternoon at two o'clock. It was very important. She asked frantically if the child were worse and received a non-committal answer that she was not to worry. But she *did* worry. She felt sick with anxiety as she went back.

As she hurriedly got ready to go to the hospital she thought all this over. She had pleaded with Joseph for leniency for the boys. Why, it wasn't so long ago that his own skittles team had won the match for the whole district and he had come home as merry and as noisy as the boys. Had he forgotten that so quickly? This victory was a great event in the minds of lads keen on sport. Surely they could be excused for once.

Katie was out shopping. The child Peppi was playing on the floor in the kitchen. She thought he looked much happier when his mother was out. He was growing into a pretty boy with those large mournful eyes and his dark olive skin. His baby hair was changing from gold to a darker shade now. It had the curious mixed look which some women had from dyeing theirs. This coming child of Katie's! It wouldn't be so bad if the girl liked children, but she didn't. It was horrible. When Katie came back, she told her abruptly about the hospital telephoning.

"I expect she's worse," Katie announced. There was no commiseration in her voice, and she regarded her mother curiously as she said it. It was extraordinary that Moe was so fond of this child Carola. She doted on her. Just as Pa doted on Krista. Katie considered them quite objectively as people. She hadn't the slightest feeling for either of them. But she admired Moe. She liked her assurance, her air of being ready for anything. Joseph she despised.

At the hospital Moe was asked to wait a little. In reply to her frantic question, whether she had been summoned because Carola was worse, she was reassured. What was it then? Was it the question of the Confirmation again? Or were they just putting her off, and Carola was really worse? As she sat in the waiting-room her hopes rose and died a thousand deaths. At last the sister came and took her to the door of the ward. It was not visiting day. That was why she was so apprehensive. Sister put her head round the door. "Ready?" she called.

"Yes, she can come in," came the voice of Sister Ruth.

"Shut your eyes," said the sister gently; "shut them tight and don't open them until I tell you."

In a sweat of real fear Moe did as she was told.

"Look, look now, Moe," came the soft little voice of Carola.

She opened her eyes. Carola, in a wheel chair, was facing her in the centre of the ward. She was dressed in a pink jacket and a shawl covered her legs. She looked frighteningly small and frail in the great chair. But her smile was heart-breaking as she slowly and with a tremendous effort held out both arms to her mother.

"You see?" cried the nuns round her chair, "she can raise *both* arms, and now Carola is going to give you a surprise, aren't you, Carola?"

Several doctors were standing there watching. One of the nuns removed the shawl from the child's legs. Moe drew in her breath sharply—she drew it with such difficulty that it was painful. Carola's wasted legs, as thin and pathetic as her sticks of arms, were strapped to iron supports.

She gave a cry and moved towards the child.

"Wait," said a doctor laying a restraining hand on her arm.

"Come, Carola." The other doctors had lifted the child from the chair. They each took one of her hands.

"Steady," said the doctor standing beside Moe. "Now Carola, *try*, try now. Walk to your mother, try as we have been showing you all these weeks. Come."

The child stood poised, wavering, when the doctors let go of her hands. In her eyes was a terrible determination. The fear of falling was visible on her white face but her eyes, fixed unwaveringly on Moe, were brilliant.

Moe stood motionless. She couldn't move or say a word. She knew she should be encouraging Carola but the shock and relief were too great. With an effort in response to the doctor's low words she held out her arms.

"Come, my darling, come to Moe." Her voice was so gentle that her neighbours would not have recognized it. Her family knew it as reserved only for Carola. Katie had heard it like that when she had listened at the keyhole during those long afternoons in the lodger's room.

At her mother's voice Carola took two steps forward. They were lurching, unsteady steps, but they were steps.

"Splendid, come on . . . come on," urged the doctor standing by Moe.

Carola paled, the fear of falling was now dominant. Tiny beads of sweat dripped down her face. The effort was agonizing. There was absolute silence as the child gathered up her strength again. The children in the beds round the side of the ward were watching breathlessly. Suddenly she took three quick unsteady steps and fell with a little cry into her mother's arms.

Moe clutched Carola to her. Sweat ran down her face as well as the child's, and one of the doctors mopped his brow. Sister Ruth took Carola gently from her mother and put her back in the chair. She lay back absolutely exhausted but triumphant at her feat.

"It's a miracle," breathed Moe. She was weeping unashamedly now. "It's a miracle."

"She did it herself," said the doctor who had stood with Moe encouraging the child, "with patience, determination, and courage. She was determined to walk. Determined to surprise you. She has been trying for weeks now, but she wouldn't let us tell you. She's been having under-water treatment and it's had amazing results. But the real recovery has been achieved by Carola. From her sheer determination to come home to you. Carola's a brave girl. Isn't she, children?" He appealed to the children watching open-eyed.

"Yes, yes," they cried.

"And you must be as brave and as patient as she is and you'll all get better too," he continued.

"And will she really be able to come home?" asked Moe eagerly.

"Not yet," he said quietly, "but she *will* eventually. It won't be so very long now. She's got to walk without those supports first, and that's where you can help us. You can give her the incentive for that extra effort which she can't make for anyone else. You're tremendously important to Carola. Her recovery is largely due to you."

Moe could not speak. The praise of the doctor was sweet to her. Sweeter still were those words, "You're tremendously important to Carola."

"She's one of the most lovable children I've ever treated," he said. "Are all your children like this one?"

Were they? Had they been? Anna had been lovable. The twins were lovely boys, always had been. Katie never. She considered them one by one. Robert was docile and sweet. But there was a reason for his being different, and perhaps for her not liking him as much as the others. Krista was not hers. No, the pick of the whole bunch was this small, frail thing with the gold hair and huge dark eyes. She had pulled at Moe's heartstrings ever since she had been born.

"On Sunday will you bring Pa?" Carola asked.

Moe nodded. If she had to carry Joseph herself she would get him here on Sunday. These days he never wanted to visit this child. Couldn't bear to see her lying there. Now it would be different. He would see her standing on her feet, a thing they had never thought to see again.

Moe tried to thank the specialist as she said good-bye to him.

"Don't thank me," he said, "God has given her back to you. We never thought she would walk again. I may as well tell you that."

A celebration followed, with cakes and sweets for the children. Carola sat in state as hostess. The nuns had invited everyone who had helped in the child's treatment, the doctors, masseurs and nurses. It was wonderful, and Moe came in for a lot of interest and praise. The thin child in the next bed to Carola's, her special friend, was wheeled out next to the hostess' chair. "I won't want Carola to get better too quickly," she said to Moe. "She'll go away, and I'll be left here all alone."

"You'll get better too," said Moe quickly.

"Oh, no," replied the child, "I'm a hopeless case, I heard them saying so . . . my mother doesn't come any more. She can't stand it. I have to stay here until I die." She stated it as a matter of fact. Moe was shocked, but more shocked that there was no denial from anyone.

XXIII

IN THE TRAM on the way back Moe met Father Lange. She began to pour out her news about Carola. But he knew all about it.

"I go there every week," he reminded her gently, "and I knew that you were going to get a surprise today."

He knew of her devotion to this child. God sometimes worked things out in a strange way. Perhaps this child was to be the one thing which would save Moe. He asked her whether she would now agree to the child's confirmation. Mightn't they wait until Carola could walk unaided up the church at home? asked Moe eagerly. He smiled, understanding her wish for this miracle to be viewed by the whole village. Very well, he concurred, they would wait. Suddenly she said abruptly, "You're a good man, Father. I'll try to be better. I will, truly. You've been so good to Carola," and before he could tell her that it was God whom she must please and not him, she was gone from the tram.

She had been away from the house for almost four hours. The hospital was over an hour's journey. When she got in she saw that Joseph was at home. She went up to him at once, full of delight to tell him about Carola, to where he was standing in the yard staring at a new motor cycle which was flashing in the sun. The boys had told him that the machine belonged to Hank. When she eagerly spoke to him about Carola he was scarcely listening and made no comment.

"Where's Hank?" he demanded, cutting her short.

"Call him," she said tartly. She was bitterly hurt at his lack of interest in her news.

Hank came strutting in. He was now quite unabashed about last night. He had decided that the policeman knew nothing. They had given nothing away. When one came to think of it, it was very funny to have been brought home tenderly by one of the blasted police. If only the fool had known that all three of them were members of a dangerous gang. Why it was damned funny! It had been a glorious evening last night. He didn't regret it at all. His only regret was that his head had ached all day. But everyone at the repair station was suffering from the same thing and allowances had been made.

Joseph wasted no time. "Whose machine is this?" he snapped.

Hank looked boldly at his father and said rudely, "Mine, of course, whose did you think it was?"

"Where did you get the money?" demanded Joseph.

There was a pregnant silence, then Hank laughed. "Saved it," he said loudly.

"How much did it cost?"

Hank was not quick enough in lying. Taken off his guard, he stated the purchase price. He was too blown up with pride at his own achievement to be cautious. Power was coming with money, just as Leo had told him it would. Power to buy all things which meant a new world for him. With this motor cycle of his own much of Leo's ascendency over him would go. Hank had not been blind to the effect of his own orders to the gang having been obeyed at the last meeting, while Leo's had been ignored.

When Joseph heard the price of the machine he was dumb-founded. It never entered his head that Hank had actually paid for the thing. He assumed that he had made a deposit and would pay the remainder over a long period. He hated this. It was wrong for juveniles. To him Hank was still a child. He might be earning more money than his father, but he was still undeveloped and irresponsible. The sum of money which the cycle cost would have helped him enormously with his project for the building of a house. If he did not secure that plot soon the option would be up. The matter was becoming urgent. Every day now there were signs that the country was more and more on its feet again. It could not be long before their full sovereignty was restored to them by the victors; especially now that the same victors found it in their interest to confer this. Just like this question of Rearmament. They'd taken every weapon away from them for over nine years. Now it seemed that they were going to get them back again. And why? Because they thought that his country would make better use of them next time? Even Joseph knew better than that. No, it was because it suited the Allies to arm them again on account of Russia. All the men in the factory had been discussing it feverishly. None of them wanted to be rearmed. None of the young men wanted conscription. They were doing very well as they were. Too well, that was the trouble, said Peter. Other countries were jealous of their success in the commercial and export world. An army and conscription would slow them up a bit. They were not such fools as people thought.

The acclamations of joy at the turn of events and the sense of justice with which these new signs of the Fatherland's resurrection were received by the mass meant one thing, and one thing alone, to Joseph. That he would be turned out of this temporary home! He had gone again and again to the housing authorities. He could not forget their chuckles and sneers.

"A house for fifteen people? Impossible!" they had laughed. It had been made to appear shameful that they had such a large family. How quickly they had forgotten the last Government of the Third Reich which had encouraged and subsidized them. Everyone said that the Peace Treaty would soon be signed. Joseph dreaded the day. The owner of this large house which sheltered them would certainly be released from prison then, and they would all be turned out again.

Peter's friend, Franz the builder, had already made a fortune by carrying out shoddy work with shoddy materials for the Occupation houses. No one blamed him for this—indeed they approved. If the Occupation did not trouble to obtain the services of a qualified surveyor or architect to pass the plans, whose fault was that? What did it matter to Peter's friend if the houses which looked so attractive from the outside began to sink soon after their completion? What did it matter to him if the walls cracked and the ceilings sagged and the roofs leaked? He had been paid. He carried out the work to schedule. The houses were up, the Occupation living in them. The builder was far too clever to be accused of fraud or using poor materials. Long before any trouble started Franz had left the district and was carrying on business under another name.

He could now afford to build a few really well-built homes for his own countrymen. The profits from cheating the Occupation should go to that. Because Peter told him about Joseph and his large family, the man had said that he should be one of the first to have a chance. Joseph would have to find quite a large deposit, but the builder would agree to take the rest of the money in instalments as rent. This was a favour—but even so the sum required before any kind of serious discussion could take place seemed enormous to Joseph. He despaired of ever getting it, even with the compulsory help of his family.

When he heard the cost of the motor cycle he was too furious to speak. The suit had been bad enough. That money could have gone towards the house. He had not been able to bring himself to the idea of selling the thing—he had hated it too much. That Hank could spend all this money on himself appalled and terrified him. Where did it come from?

Father Lange had told him that the village were talking about the amount of new clothes worn now by the children in the family. The boots, the new bicycles, the musical instruments. They were all at a loss to understand where they came from. They knew just how much the boys and girls could earn in the factories now—a lot, certainly, but not enough for this standard of life. Their envy knew no bounds, as details of each new purchase were given them by the upstairs tenants of the house.

Joseph's resentment could no longer be repressed. He shouted at Hank, accusing him of selfishness and of an insatiable desire to spend. He accused him of perverting his brothers to his way of life Hank retorted by saying that his father was a nice one to talk, everyone knew what he had been spending on drinking and why should they all save towards a house when he and most of the others would have left home by the time it was completed?

"Left home?" Joseph demanded. What did he mean by that?

They would all want to get away, shouted Hank. Did Joseph think that home was such a pleasant place? They were sick of the fuss and eternal rows going on. They would all get married and leave the place. Joseph was dumbfounded. He had never contemplated their all getting married. Why, Anna, the eldest at home now, was only nineteen. People did not get married until they had a settled job and a place to live in. Hank pointed out that both Lise and Willi had got married without either of these necessities. There was a noisy quarrel, with both Moe and Katie joining in, suddenly interrupted by the arrival home of Krista and Anna. They tried to soothe the angry participants, but in vain. Joseph's mind was made up. He would get control of this unruly family again. Hank had held the reins too long. When Hank now demanded angrily what Joseph had done with the new suit they had bought him, his father, beside himself, shouted that he had put it in the river, which was the best place for it. There was a dead silence. Then Moe said slowly: "Joseph, do you mean to say that you deliberately put that beautiful new suit, to which all the children subscribed, in the river?" Joseph maddened by all those staring faces retorted, "Yes, exactly that, in the river."

"But why?" asked Anna quietly amongst the chorus of protests.

"Because it burned my skin as if it were unclean," said Joseph shortly.

They looked at him with something very like fear now, and Hank with a real fear. Could his father *know* anything? Did he know that some of the money which had bought it had come from those burglaries? No, impossible. Yet why did he say that it burned him? Hank was suddenly in a cold sweat.

Moe asked quietly, "What do you mean, that it burned your skin?"

"Just that. You wouldn't understand. All the time we were looking at the President's house and the Chancellor's house that afternoon the suit burned into me like a hot brand. I could never have worn it again."

Moe looked at him consideringly. She took her mind back to that Sunday afternoon. He had been very quiet. But then there had been all that fuss over Krista and the flowers in the morning. He hadn't wanted to go for that motor-coach tour at all. They had finally persuaded him. On the way back they had left the coach in Cologne and gone to visit Carola. The nuns had made a special occasion of it, because of the birthday, and they had all been allowed in for twenty minutes. Yes, Joseph had been strangely quiet.

She was extremely angry that he had thrown away all that money. The suit could have been sold. What was the use of her saving and scrimping and of his accusing the children of extravagance if he did things like this? She simply could not follow it. She gave it up and said angrily, "You're mad, Joseph, *really* mad."

He sat there glaring at them all like a trapped creature. Even Krista dared not go and console him as she used to do. Their eyes accused him. Their lips formed the word which Moe had thrown at him. That was it. Mad. He was mad.

There came to him suddenly a conviction that he was sane. Horribly sane, and that it was *they* who were mad. He got up to leave them and it was then that Moe said bitterly, "So you have nothing to say about Carola?"

"Carola?" he asked stupidly, "What about Carola?" And she realized that he hadn't heard one word of what she had told him of the miracle of the child's recovery.

With an effort Hank threw off his fear. There was no money left now in the hoard under the loose board. None of his, anyway; the twins and Katie still had some, but not much. He had spent all that hoard on the motor cycle. He had got it through one of the mechanics at the repair station. It was much better so: no questions were asked as to how he had come by such a large sum of money. He was going to try out his new toy. He didn't care what Pa said or what he thought. He didn't like his new bossy manner. Did the old man mean to have his own way again? If so he had another think coming to him. Hank was the master and would remain so. Money talked. There was no doubt about that. And he, Hank, had the money. He took the cycle out into the lane, and watched by the neighbours, tried it out with the twins on the back. They took a noisy turn up and down, and then he sent the twins in to ask Krista to come out and ride pillion. But she wouldn't. She was nervous, she said. Nothing would induce her to get up behind him. Hank was upset and disappointed. Everything he got now he got with a view to Krista's pleasure. He had bought the accordion because she loved music, and he hoped that she would go out with him on the motor cycle. But he had time. She would come; of that he felt sure.

Joseph heard the noise of the engine being tried out, and the twins waved to him as they passed the summer-house to which he had retired. Suddenly Moe's words about Carola struck him. What had she been saying? That the child had walked. She *couldn't*. He was surely going mad. Had he imagined such a thing? He must have—with all this fuss over the motor cycle the words had got muddled. He went indoors. Moe sat alone in the old arm-chair in the kitchen. Her face was expressionless.

"Carola?" he said. "What was it you were saying about her?"

"Nothing that you're glad to hear," she said bitterly. "I came home full of joy to tell you that today she walked—actually walked five steps—and what did *you*, her father, do? Didn't even hear!"

She put her head in her hands and her hair fell over her face as she sobbed. Joseph stood there looking at her. Had he caressed her then, things might have been very different. But he made no move; after a while he turned and went back to the summerhouse.

XXIV

KRISTA WROTE the letter during the lunch hour in the factory canteen. The radio was playing a nostalgic waltz and among the chatter and laughter of the girls round her she felt curiously detached and isolated. She had never written a letter to anyone. There had been no need; except for the family she knew no one. But now she lived in constant dread that Paul would repeat his unexpected visit. It was better to end it all. She had his address he had pressed it on her. She sat there trying to find words—her heart as heavy as the music was light.

"Don't try to see me any more. It's finished. I can never marry you—never. Don't write to me please." She added her love in the conventional form. "But I love him—I will never love anyone else", she thought passionately as she sealed the envelope.

Already doubts as to the infallibility of her foster-father's opinions were beginning to creep into her hitherto docile mind.

She went to drop the letter quickly, before she changed her mind, in the post-box at the big gates. Letters were an event in the family, as rare as a telegram in others. Except for Joseph's correspondence with his sister in the East Zone, letters were few and far between. Joseph was devoted to his youngest sister, who lived under a tyrannous rule, and whenever her letters—often heavily censored—arrived he would be bitter and brooding for days. Moe got cards and notices about Carola from the hospital, and the boys their cycle-club literature. But that was all.

As Krista was putting on her lavender overall in the glass cosmetic-hall, Rosa, her face alight with excitement, came dancing up. She showed Krista an engagement-ring. "Can you come home with me tomorrow evening? We're having a party to celebrate this. I suppose your boy friend couldn't come too? It'd be nice for John—he likes Americans."

Krista was hesitant. "I'd love to come—but I don't think I can. I have to get home. And about Paul. That's all off. I'm not seeing him any more."

"What?" cried Rosa in astonishment. "Had a quarrel? Oh, that'll soon blow over . . . John and I've had lots!"

"No, it's not that. It's my father. He objects. I've promised not to see Paul again." Krista kept her head bent low over her work at the chain-belt table, but Rosa was not deceived. "Why can't you come? My mother wants to meet you. I've told her all about you. She's ever so interested. It's too silly. You've never been to any of our homes, and lots of girls have invited you, haven't they?"

Krista nodded. She had a sudden urgent desire to see what other girls' homes were like. A new and disturbing doubt about her own was thrusting itself upon her. She wanted to know how other people lived with each other. Did they have these tense violent clashes of will, the sudden terrifying upheavals which her family did? Was Paul right when he said that there were millions of happily-married people in the world? That she couldn't judge by hers? She would go! Turning to Rosa she said quickly, "I've changed my mind. I'd love to come, thank you."

"Good! And your boy friend?"

"I can't do anything about him—he's away. Besides, I've just written him telling him not to write or try to see me again."

"How silly of you. Have you put it in the factory post-box? Let's go and ask old Emil if he'll unlock it for us and give it you back."

"No, no. I promised father."

"But why? Besides, he's only your foster-father!"

"Rosa,"—Krista hesitated, then said with a rush—"If your mother had objected to your engagement to John you'd have given him up, wouldn't you?"

"Of course not!" Rosa's voice was scornful. "You can't care much for Paul if you're giving him up as easily as that!"

"Well—what would you have done, then?"

"I'd have gone to the Court and asked permission to marry. Why don't you do that, Krista? After all, they're only your foster-parents."

"It's just because they *are* foster-parents that I can't," said Krista miserably.

"But you won't live all your life with them," protested Rosa. "You'll have to leave them to get married some day—whether it's Paul or someone else. Have they adopted you legally?"

"I think so." Krista was vague. She had persistently refused to discuss or hear anything about the matter. But now it was different. It was suddenly vitally important to her.

"Can't you remember anything at all about your life before your foster-father found you?" pursued Rosa curiously as she manipulated the machine which squeezed the cream into the jars, which Krista would then smooth off with a spatula.

"Nothing," said Krista flatly. Then she said slowly, "But I sometimes dream of a house I've never seen. It's always the same house, and the people in it are always the same people; but although in the dream I know them, I've never met them in real life." She was astonished that she was confiding this to Rosa. For a long time she had refused to contemplate the possibility that the persistent dream might be part of her early life.

"Maybe it's your real home! How exciting! What sort of house?"

"It's low and white—and the roof is of green tiles, and there's a garden full of flowers. It's not like anything I've ever actually seen."

"Have your foster-parents really tried to find your people?"

"Yes. Pa tried everything. And the doctors tried all sorts of queer ways to try to get my memory back. But it's no use. I don't remember anything—not even that night when Pa found me. I had concussion, you see. Something fell on my head. When Pa found me in a blazing doorway I was unconscious, lying on a pile of bodies—all burned. Pa went back after he'd carried me to the shelter—but the whole building had collapsed on to them— there was nothing but a raging inferno."

"If he hadn't rescued you, the building would have fallen on you, too."

"Yes. He saved my life. Moe gave her blood for me—and Hank and Anna gave skin for grafting. I was terribly burned. Just think what I owe them. Now d'you see how difficult it is for me to oppose Pa?"

"You don't owe them your whole future happiness!" insisted Rosa. "You aren't their flesh and blood—even if they did give a little of theirs for you. D'you ever feel that you don't really belong to them?"

Did she? She had always fought the feeling. She had wanted passionately to belong. It was terrifying to be alone—with no roots. But since she had met Paul? Wasn't it different now? Several times lately, in spite of herself, she had had the strangest conviction that her life with the family was really a dream, a dream in which she was on the outside edge vainly trying to get inside. Whereas with Paul it wasn't like that at all. She felt more and more strongly that she belonged to his world—to him.

Rosa looked at her troubled face as she mechanically and deftly put the cream into the jars. "Don't worry. Talk to my mother about it tomorrow," she advised her. "She's not one of these spoil-sports. She'll understand. You are coming, aren't you?"

"Yes, I am." Krista was astonished at herself. What was she doing? Pa would be angry if she were late home again. Should she say that there was a meeting of the factory club? She was shocked at the ease with which lies were beginning to come to her. What was happening to her? To them all? There was something wrong at home. Everyone was on edge and afraid of something or someone. She didn't want to go home now. If it weren't for Anna, who laughed at her fears, she would dread going home still more. Pa was still hurt and aloof with her. He never mentioned Paul—but he watched her, and Krista was terrified that a letter might come, and even more terrified that he might again turn up uninvited. The atmosphere at home now was affecting them all. Something in which Katie, Hank and the twins were involved—and which was turning Robert from a gay fun-loving little boy into a pale jumpy ghost. Robert cried and moaned in his sleep. Twice when she had awoken in the early hours of the morning his bed was empty. When she had remonstrated with him and questioned him he had stuck to his statement that he couldn't sleep and had gone out into the garden. But a child of his age should sleep— and his face belied his glib words. Why didn't she go to Pa or Moe? She had salved her conscience by telling Moe that her boy was not sleeping well. Moe had merely said that he pored over his books too much, and that she had never approved of so much book learning for growing boys.

Katie was more than unhappy now. She wore a look of apprehension as if she were waiting for something. Waiting! That was it. The whole feeling at home now was that of waiting for something. But for what? It was as if a thunderstorm were brewing up, to release the tenseness of the atmosphere. And she herself? Wasn't she different too? Whereas she and Anna had laughed at silly nothings, Anna was very silent nowadays, and she herself seemed always to be on the verge of tears.

Next morning she astounded them all at breakfast. Just as she was leaving the table she said casually: "I'm going to an engagement party tonight. It's Rosa's. Will you let me in if I'm late, Anna?"

Joseph had already left the house. Moe looked quizzically at Krista. "So we're getting independent at last, are we?" she said. "About time, too. Go out and enjoy yourself while you can, girl. What's happened to your boy friend?"

"It's finished," said Krista faintly.

"I thought so," said Moe quietly. "You're a silly child to let your father influence you. You've been looking peaked these last few days. Make it up with him. Kiss and be friends!" She laughed loudly and slapped Krista on the thigh as the girl came round the table to say good-bye.

"Life's nothing without a boy friend," she called after her. "But don't be late home or Pa'll throw a fit again."

Paul answered the letter in person. When she and Rosa came out of the factory the next day he was there waiting for her. They stood looking at one another until Rosa greeted him with an invitation to accompany them to her party. Paul was taken aback. What had happened to Krista? Here she was actually going to an evening party. She always told him that such a thing was impossible. He felt aggrieved.

"I'm egging her on to revolt!" laughed Rosa. "Just wait until my mother gets on to the subject too!" She saw their discomfiture at this unexpected situation. "I'm not letting Krista off coming to the first party she's ever been known to attend just because you've turned up like this!" she said to Paul. "Come along too. You can talk to her at home."

"I'd hoped to see you," began Paul awkwardly to Krista. "I got your letter, and asked for twenty-four hours' leave."

Krista couldn't say anything. The letter lay between them. She longed to take it back. The sight of Paul had sent all her decisions to the winds.

"Well, make up your mind!" urged Rosa. "We've got to get a move on—it's my party—it can't begin without me!"

"I've got the car," said Paul. "I'll drive you."

The evening opened a new world to Krista. For the first time she entered a home in which she could sense the unity and complete devotion of the family in it. Rosa, her mother, her young brother and her English fiancé John were in perfect harmony. The flat in which they lived was small, in an area which had been devastated and was being rapidly rebuilt; but it was full of books and flowers, and held an atmosphere of quiet happiness which was enchanting to the girl, accustomed as she was to the stormy one of her own home.

And Rosa's guests, all young people who came in to congratulate her, were of a kind whom Krista had never met. They knew a freedom which was denied her. A freedom to go about where they wished and with whom they liked. They all went dancing and rambling, swimming and boating, yet none of them had much money, and all of them worked hard. Before the evening was over she realized that she, too, would not lack for invitations and partners for such recreations if she wished—and if Pa permitted it. At the thought of his insistence on her being home early every night a violent revolt began to take place in her mind. Why shouldn't *she* go out too? Why shouldn't she go dancing and walking and swimming? Why should she and Anna work hard all day and have no fun in the evenings? Was that what Katie, Hank and the twins did now? Did they slip out after Pa was in bed to avoid the fuss he invariably made when *she* wanted to go out?

When she got up to leave—and from sheer force of habit she couldn't bring herself to stay late—Paul got up too. In silence they got into the car and drove back towards the river.

"I'm going to forget your letter," he said as they approached the great bridge. "You didn't mean what you wrote, did you?"

"But I did," she answered wretchedly. "I promised Pa."

"Oh, damn him!" exclaimed Paul angrily. "It's too stupid. How is it you could go to a party tonight? You never have time for me."

"I wanted to see what other people's homes are like. The girls often invite me. This time I determined to go."

"And how did you find it?"

"I loved it," said Krista simply.

"That's how a home should be," said Paul. "If you'd have the courage to defy your foster-father we could have a home like that. But what's the good of talking to you? You seem to think he's God."

They got out of the car and went down to their usual meeting-place, and he pulled her on to a seat under the lime trees. "So you don't want to see me again?" he said. "You meant what you wrote?"

She began to cry. In a bewildering agony of torn emotions she tried to control herself. Through the curtain of tears she saw the barges passing, the patches of light and dark on the shining water, the moonlight catching the froth of foam from the paddle steamers; and in her heart revolved like a gramophone record Moe's words: "You with your child's body that's changing . . . you're the sort that men like all right." Tonight she had seen its truth—and something seemed gone from her. For when those other men at Rosa's had looked at her, had asked her to dance, had clamoured for her favours, she had seen Paul's face, and the quiet amusement on Rosa's. She knew that Moe was right. There would be others even if she gave up Paul. And she hated it—and hated herself because of it. Her feelings were so ravaged that she longed to flee from him and from herself. She turned to him and said violently that she could not see him again. She loved him too much. It was too painful.

He said quietly, "If you send me away there'll be others. D'you think I didn't notice those fellows tonight? Why don't you face the fact that you love *me*?"

She looked away from him to the fast-flowing current, at its urgency, its very life, as it carried the country's trade to other lands where they spoke other tongues. There was something frightening in the remorseless flow of this great river, this wide trade-way from the mountains in one country to the sea in another. In spring when the snows came down from those mountains it overflowed its banks, and this very place where they were now sitting had been deep under water only three months ago. The tow-path in the village had been submerged, and the tram could not run because its lines were under water.

It seemed to the girl now, awakened by this first urgent stirring of the heart and blood, that life was as relentless in its flow as was this river. With one blinding flash of perception she had recognized this piercingly sweet emotion aroused in her by Paul as the thing which they all talked and sniggered about at Moe's table, and over the chain-belt table in the factory. Was it love or this other thing that she felt for him? She didn't know. But whatever it was it was real. The most real thing she had known. "You can't escape from life" was what Rosa's mother had said to her. She had been saying that, even though she was sad that her daughter would have to live in England, her happiness with the man she loved was all that mattered to the mother.

"I do face it," she said at last. "And I'm going to marry you, Paul. If only you'll wait just a little longer. I can't worry Pa just now. Things are all wrong at home. But I *will*."

"You mean that?" Paul was overjoyed. "You *do* love me? You're not kidding me?"

"No," she said gravely. "No, I'm quite sure now. And if Pa won't agree I can get Moe's permission and ask the Court for theirs. Rosa's mother told me so. You see, no one really knows how old I am or what my name it. It's a special case. But maybe Pa'll change his mind so that none of that's necessary."

Krista was alarmed at her sudden decision. But things had been stirring in her mind for some time. Rosa's mother had been the turning-point. She had asked if Moe approved the marriage, and when told that she did, she had said, "It's a mother who really knows. A father is always silly about daughters. I've had to be both to Rosa, so she's lucky."

"And when will you tell him?" asked Paul, kissing her.

"Soon. Perhaps tonight. I'll see how it is when I get back. But I must go now, Paul. *Please*."

"I'll get you a ring—you'd like that, wouldn't you?"

"No. Not yet. We must wait."

"I'll run you home," he said resignedly. "You'll write to me?"

"After I've told Pa that I mean to marry you. I must tell him first." Even as she said it so lightly her heart failed at the thought of his anger. But she would do it. When Paul dropped her, at her insistence, in the shadowed lane a few hundred yards from her home it was raining, and she ran quickly in the direction of the house. But she had said she would marry him. She had clung to him by the river and in the car, and as he drove back along the river he was wildly happy.

X X V

At home Joseph was astonishing the family with a violent burst of energy and interest. He had come back and proceeded to start a tremendous clearing-up campaign, just as he used to do. The boys, surprised and annoyed at the renewal of this custom, obeyed his orders sullenly. He gave them pleasantly but firmly. There was a new ring of authority in his voice as he made Karl and the twins sweep up the falling leaves, the potato-peelings which Moe still flung on the ground, ordered Katie and Robert to wash down the concrete yard, and had the little ones picking up their toys and generally tidying up. The bicycles were all inspected. They were filthy. He had never seen such indolence and neglect. A bicycle was a valuable thing and must be cared for. He soon had them all at work, washing, polishing and oiling their machines.

The children looked at each other in amazement. What had come over Pa? Was it because the silly Elections were over and his beloved "Old'un" firmly in office again? He had been gloomy and concerned about his chances recently. Well, now he was Chancellor again; maybe that accounted for Pa's milder moods and sudden bursts of interest in his family again.

When all this was done he suggested some music, some part-playing. For several evenings now they had sat as they used to do before the advent of Rudi, under the acacia tree practising hard. But some of their former interest had waned. Hank and Katie were now accustomed to the more exciting use of their leisure: so were the twins.

Anna and Krista enjoyed it but their minds were often on their absent boy friends. This evening the first thing Pa had asked when he had come in was the whereabouts of Krista.

There had been a silence; then Moe said that she had gone to an engagement party with a girl from the factory.

"What girl?" asked Joseph.

"Her name's Rosa and she's engaged to an Englishman," Anna replied calmly. "She works next to Krista on the perfume-filling machine."

"How's she coming home?" growled Joseph.

"On her legs," giggled Karl, "or perhaps she'll swim down the river."

His father reproved him sharply. The twins continued giggling happily.

"She won't be late," assured Moe, "she never is."

"She's not here to sing." Joseph was upset. Krista had a sweet, pure voice and a perfect ear.

"I can sing her part," said Robert eagerly. "I can sing just as high."

"Let's call it off then," suggested Hank. He did not want to have to get involved in one of Joseph's concerts this evening.

He and Katie had other plans. It was damned awkward. But Pa was adamant. They were going to practise. Christmas carols were what he suggested.

"In summer weather?" said Moe. "No, Joseph, I draw the line at that. Choose something in keeping with summer. The neighbours will all think we're mad if we sing 'Stille Nacht' or 'Tannenbaum' tonight." For although early autumn, it was still very warm.

Katie loathed the whole business. She had no chance to slip over to the Frenchman's now. Pa watched them like a cat. Why? This evening, for instance, she and Hank were due to meet Leo at an early rendezvous in the ruined shelter. How could they get away? They sat round the table under the acacia and were all relieved when it began to rain heavily.

"In we go," cried Hank, picking up his accordion.

"We'll continue in the summer-house."

"There's not room. Besides, Katie and I are going out." Hank's voice was aggressive.

"Where?" asked Joseph bluntly.

"In the town," said Hank.

"I know that, but where in the town?" persisted Joseph.

"We're going to visit a friend there," put in Katie quickly.

"What friend?" asked Pa.

"Oh, for heaven's sake, Pa, why this inquisition? You've never asked us before what we do or where we go—why now?"

"Because I've been hearing some strange things about the goings-on at night from this house." He looked straight at Hank as he said this.

"We go to some friends in the town, and sometimes we're late home. This blasted village knows everything we do. Why d'you listen to their tales? You know they hate us!"

"It wasn't the villagers who told me," said Joseph quietly.

"Then it was that damned Englishwoman next door," cried Hank angrily. "They're always up late at night and see everything we do."

"It wasn't the Englishwoman."

"Oh, what the hell does it matter who it was?" shouted Hank. "I'm not going to be questioned like that. I pay my way here; I have the right to my own life."

"Then go and live your own life." Joseph's voice was curt.

Hank was startled. Moe was looking at Joseph with a new respect. What was in his mind now? She didn't know what to make of this new mood. She was grateful that he was gentler to her and the children, but on the whole she didn't trust it. She had got accustomed to the sullen silences and the sudden outbursts of temper. Now she would have to fathom this new phase.

The rather tense silence which followed Joseph's retort was broken by a squabble amongst the younger ones. Robert was hit on the head by Karl and retaliated, and in a moment Moe had got up, taken the heads of the two combatants and knocked them together. She always stopped a fight in that way. The uproar had only just died down when two men came in at the gate. One was the policeman who had brought the boys home on the night of the celebration of the international football victory; the other a tall man in plain clothes.

Joseph could not fail to notice Hank's start or Katie's sudden pallor. Nor could Moe. She was used to the policeman coming on the usual visits of complaint about bicycles or hens. But who was this stern-looking man with him?

"We'd better be going, Katie," said Hank, who was already on his feet. But the policeman, after greeting them all, said pleasantly, "No, don't go just yet. Sit down, will you? Are you all here?"

He pulled from his pocket a small narrow black belt. He held it up so that they could all see it.

"Are all your daughters here?" the man in plain clothes asked Joseph.

"My adopted daughter Krista is not here. She'll be in soon," said Joseph. He was bewildered. But he was always polite and careful with the police: he was used to the sharp biting voice of authority. Police were like the officers in the army. One had to obey instantly.

The policeman held up the belt and said carefully, "Have any of you ever seen this belt before?"

There was a silence broken only by the rain which now began to pour down. "We must go in," cried Moe. "Come quick. We'll go into the parlour."

She led the way for the policeman. She noticed with growing fear that the man in plain clothes stayed behind and ushered every member of the family in before him. There were so many of them that there were not enough chairs. This room was seldom used by them all. The photographs of Grandpa and Grandma stared down menacingly at them. Moe hated the stern old couple but was afraid to move them.

They formed a ring, the boys sitting on edges of small stiff, plush chairs, and jostling each other in excitement and fear. What was it all about?

"Have any of you ever seen this belt before?" repeated the policeman. No one answered. Then Robert said quickly: "Yes, it belongs to one of my sisters."

Krista was surprised to find the whole family still up. It was only ten o'clock but they usually went to bed early except at weekends: their day started early. This evening two men were with them in the sitting-room. One was the policeman from the next village—there was none in theirs—whom they all knew. He was a fat, fatherly individual. The second man was in plain clothes. He was young and had keen grey-blue eyes which seemed to bore through you. Everyone was very still. The chairs in this stiff room were as little used as the room itself. Krista had been astonished when Pa had called to her to come in, and was amazed to find them all in here like this.

"What's wrong?" she asked fearfully.

"This is the third one, Krista," said Pa to the men, "but she won't know anything about it."

"About what?" she asked, staring at the uneasy group.

"Oh, some silly old belt," began Anna.

"One moment, please, let us question her." The policeman smiled reassuringly at her and held up a narrow black belt.

"Ever seen this before?" he asked, looking hard at her.

In astonishment she took it from him and examined it carefully. She had seen it before. But where? She recognized the clasp. It was an automatic catch which came undone too easily for safety. An unusual clasp, although the belt was commonplace enough.

She looked up to answer, and caught Katie's eyes hard on her. There was a menace so clear and so insistent in them that she hesitated. Was it the belt from that new frock which Leo had given Katie? Was it? Surely it was too small for Katie. Hank's face held an anxiety which was unmistakable as she looked at it again.

She felt rather than saw the fixed watchful faces of the whole family as she handed it back to the policeman. What was it all?

Why did they all wait for her answer like this? She saw Katie's eyes again and she knew suddenly that it *was* her belt. She took a deep breath. She had lied already. What did another matter? They all clearly expected a denial.

"No. I have never seen it before," she said unsteadily.

"Sure?" persisted the fatherly old policeman. "If you're not sure, don't be afraid to say so. It's important."

Hank's eyes conveyed a warning which was now urgent.

"I have never seen one like this," she said faintly.

"Strange," said the man as he took it from her. "Your young brother here thinks that one of you—he doesn't know which— had a similar one."

"Children say anything," declared Moe comfortably. "How can he know? Can you describe the belt your wife is wearing today?"

The man shook his head, laughing. "But you're wrong about children," he said. "They're very observant."

"What's it all about? Whose belt is it?" asked Krista fearfully.

"Ah", said the man in plain clothes. "If we knew that we'd be nearer to knowing who murdered that old caretaker a few weeks back. This belt was found near his body. Under it, in fact."

"But why should you bring it here?" insisted Joseph. "Why here?"

"Because," said the man slowly, his eyes on Katie who was deadly white, "two youths and a girl were seen, not only near the scene of the crime, but also near *this* house on the night of the murder. But you were all in bed early that night. Your father says so."

He got up. "Well, that's all then. The boy must be mistaken. After all, boys seldom notice their sisters' belts." Robert opened his mouth to speak but Hank growled, "Shut up. You talk too much."

They took their leave after apologizing for the lateness of the hour. They had waited for Krista to come in. And she, looking with foreboding from one taut face to another, knew that she had stepped again into an atmosphere so fraught with fear that for her to tell Joseph of her decision now was utterly unthinkable.

"There are many other families in the village who ride on motor cycles," said Moe, as she saw them out. "You'd better go and ask some of them."

"Of course. It's a routine check," said the plain clothes man politely.

XXVI

KATIE LIVED NOW in constant fear. Always on the defensive, her naturally highly-strung nerves were stretched to breaking point. In her dreams the face of the dead caretaker haunted her, and she would awake terrified and sweating from her unrefreshing sleep. At times, alone in the garden, or sitting by the river, she would have a vision of the tourist's body washed up in the reeds. Whenever she now saw any unusual object such as a tree trunk or a piece of wood caught in the thick reeds her heart would almost stop beating. Furious with herself for her yellowness she was incapable of overcoming these horrible fancies.

It was this wretched baby! Soon everyone would know. She was frightened of that, too. Moe would be all right. She would never turn her out. Moe was kind in spite of her rough tongue. But Pa! He would be angry, as Moe had said. She had never seen him so angry as he had been over Hank's motor cycle. For a long time now, nothing had seemed to move him to such intensity of feeling as Krista. He'd been violent enough over her and her American. She hated Krista. She could scarcely restrain herself from hurting her physically sometimes. Katie was the only one of the family who had resented her adoption.

In her sharp quick mind she knew that she was not loved by anyone. She got on best with Hank. They understood one another well enough and there wasn't even a year's difference in their age. She loved Leo with all the passion of her violent temperament. She had watched with anguish his passion for her fade—then die. He no longer even pretended that he cared at all for her. He wanted Krista now. That was the latest! He had twice asked Katie to bring her along one evening and to get her to join the gang. When, from sheer defence, Katie had angrily refused, he had tackled Hank.

Hank was taken aback at his chief's request, but determined that he shouldn't have anything to do with Krista. The very thought of Leo and Krista maddened him. It was unthinkable. He made no excuses, but merely said bluntly that it was impossible.

"Why?" asked Leo.

"She's different," said Hank lamely.

"That's why I want her," said Leo. "Why should *you* care about her? She's not your sister. She's nothing to you. Why all this fuss about her?"

Hank was silent. She wasn't his sister. That was something which he had just begun to realize. Krista was no blood relation to him. If he wanted her there was nothing to prevent his having her. Nor Leo either. He wondered why the thought of Krista was coming so frequently to his mind lately. Was it because Leo had designs on her? Was it because that young American wanted to marry her? Was it his father's obsession with her?

He had noticed that girls in the village had what was a "vogue" with the lads. If one boy was keen on a girl, then invariably, if she was attractive, others were round her too. Was this what was happening to Krista now? He had heard Anna tease her about the young supervisor who always tried to follow her now, had heard her joke about the way men in the tram were beginning to look at her. He had known Krista as his sister always, but the thought of Leo being attracted to her made him begin to think of her in terms which were not brotherly. He had never been attracted to a girl, never. He was over eighteen: it was time he had a girl. In his rather stupid mind he longed for one because he had some idea that it would gain him greater admiration in the gang.

But the gang did not fit in with Krista. She would be horrified if she knew of it. She was not afraid of him as the younger ones were. He had never harmed her, *never*. He asked himself why, and simply could not find an answer. She had always had something which instinctively made him want to protect her. Something soft, shy, appealing. She was everything a girl ought to be—and never was. When he thought of the girls in the gang they seemed as far from Krista as if they belonged to another sex.

When Leo repeated his request that Krista should be brought along the next evening, Hank refused again, bluntly and firmly.

Leo was accustomed to getting what he wanted. He determined to work on Katie. He called at the house the evening after the row over Hank's new motor cycle. Katie was in the garden and her eyes hardened at the sight of him. He had put her in this vile position. She was carrying his child and he neither knew, nor would he care, if he did know. She looked at his graceful form as he swung across the grass and came to her in the summerhouse where she sat knitting. She seemed to be for ever knitting. She was expected to make not only her own child's garments but all Franz Joseph's jerseys and all the boys' socks as well.

Formerly Moe had spent the early afternoons sitting with her under the acacia, also knitting. It had been pleasant with the radio on and someone to chat to. Now Moe went several times a week to visit Rudi, and when she was at home she went to Carola. Katie had to knit alone. Krista and Anna helped her in the winter, but in the summer they had no time. They had their own things to wash and mend. Now she was faced with the prospect of even more knitting—for Leo's baby. The idea made her so angry that she could scarcely answer him when he spoke to her.

He noticed her angry face and said, "You don't seem pleased to see me." He was piqued. His conceit made him want every woman to desire him. He honestly thought that every woman he met was in love with him—and many were—women much older than he was, as well as younger.

"I'm as pleased to see you as you are to see me", said Katie sourly. "What d'you want?"

She looked into his smiling face and at his pleasantly curved mouth, and longed to poke one of her knitting needles into those deceptive eyes. So pleasant, so attractive; and so utterly ruthless—and she loved him still. That was what made her so wretched. She loved him, really loved him. The Frenchman was all right but it was *still* Leo.

"How's Leila?" he asked.

"Is that all you've come to ask? If so why don't you go along the river to her cottage and ask her yourself?" she snapped.

"Steady on, spitfire." Leo's eyes narrowed. "I only asked. I was thinking that you'll have to do the next job, with Trudi away and Leila out of action."

He was flicking a stick from the willow across the grass as he spoke. Whenever Katie thought of Leo she saw him with a rope, a coil of something which switched and hurt. The willow wand was pliable and he began stripping the bark from it. He called to Franz Joseph suddenly: "Got a piece of string?" And when the child came back with some he made the wand into a neat bow and another stick into a sharpened arrow. Franz Joseph was delighted.

"Leila's better, but her arm's still in plaster and she's watched like a hawk by her grandmother. That doctor was very suspicious . . . he's spoken to the police."

"If she's given anything away—" began Leo in a deadly voice.

"She hasn't," snapped Katie, "but the whole thing was suspicious. They knew her arm had been wrenched—not only the broken one but the other as well. You can't wrench both falling off a cycle."

"Well, that's settled it. *You'll* have to do it."

"When?"

"As soon as Eddie gives the signal. It'll be easy for you now. Hank's got his motor bike. He can bring you in."

"It's going to be damn difficult, that's all I know. Pa's in a very queer mood lately. He watches us, and he'll know if we go out. He's bound to hear the cycle."

"Get Hank to leave it in the summer-house; he can get it over the grass quietly enough."

"All right," she agreed finally, "but I don't like it."

"Where's your lovely foster-sister?" he asked idly, twirling a long grass in her face and infuriating her.

"Somewhere where you'll never be," snapped Katie. "She's sure to be in church, confessing her sins."

"She's the sort I go for in a big way," said Leo smilingly. "The pious ones give me the greatest thrill. I adore piety in my women-folk."

Katie looked at him. Was he serious? She never knew with Leo, that was the trouble. She had a quick brain, but this lad was too sharp for her.

"Not that you'll ever suffer from that," he finished softly.

"Suffer from what?" she said angrily.

"Piety," laughed Leo. "The idea makes me laugh—forgive me dear Katie, but it's too funny."

Katie pulled a knitting needle out of the stocking she was knitting and jabbed viciously at his face. But he was too quick for her and moved his head, while with his hand he seized the knitting needle and broke it in two. Taking the knitting from her he snapped the other needle in the same way and then tore the garment viciously across, unravelling it as he did so.

She looked at it lying at her feet and tried to free her hands; and at that moment Krista came in at the gate. She looked from one to the other but passed on into the house with a brief greeting.

"Why didn't you say something and make her stay here a moment?" grumbled Leo, releasing her hands.

Katie, almost sick now with rage and jealousy, said sharply, "You'd better go. Pa'll be home any minute and he doesn't like you."

"That's just too bad," scoffed Leo, "but I came chiefly to see your lovely foster-sister and I've seen her, so I'll go." He got up. "See you're ready to be on call. You'll get the signal as usual. Hank'll bring you in—there's no need for me to come for you now. It'll be your little foster-sister who has *me* here on tap next."

Furious, she struck out at his grinning face, but he was off, and vaulted over the garden fence with the grace of a trained athlete.

She sat there shaking with rage for a moment, then gathered up the spoilt knitting and the broken needles. Moe was calling her. "Where've you been?" she asked. "Here've I been getting the meal and calling you. What do you *do* with all your time?"

The table had to be laid; Krista was helping with the cooking. Katie took the large pile of plates and began laying them out on the long table. She had an insane desire to fling them all on the floor and run away. But how could she? There was Peppi, and now another one well on the way.

"Take care how you throw those plates about," cried Moe, her mouth full of the stew she was tasting. "They're not potatoes, and go and comb your hair, girl. You look a real slut". She looked from Katie to Krista as she spoke. Krista had the kind of hair which was never untidy. In rain or wind or after sleep it was still lovely. Katie's was heavy and ruffled now from her scuffle with Leo. She looked with dislike at Krista. She would like to have thrown a plate at her. She hated her so much that she couldn't bear to be near her. She carefully laid her own place as far away from Krista's as possible.

The Frenchman had returned from France again. As she stared across the road Katie could see him through the uncurtained windows. He seemed to be alone at the dinner-table, and yet to be talking to a lot of guests. She crossed the road after making sure that no one was looking, and crept up under the side window of the room. He sat there in evening dress with a wine-glass in his hand. Places were laid for a number of guests at the polished dining-table. Candles were lit and there were roses—red ones—amongst the candles. They were red too.

He sat at the head of the table and was making a speech. To whom? She stared into the room but there was no one there at all. Katie knew that his latest housekeeper, a widow from the village, had left long ago. It was late for dinner. She stared, fascinated by the man talking to no one. He glanced round the table at the empty places and then raised the glass in his hand and drank. And all the time he was laughing, laughing in a way that held no mirth. The windows were open and she could hear him. But he was speaking in French. She knew a little. Henri had taught her some. Every time he raised his glass he said, "*À la Mort, à la mort.*" She knew what that meant all right. But the flowery words he used otherwise were unknown to her. She climbed up on the window-sill and suddenly he looked up and saw her.

"*Entrez! Entrez!*" he cried mockingly. "*Enfin une hôtesse!*" He put down his glass and caught her as she swung down into the room.

"Welcome, my dear," he cried mockingly again. "Welcome to the party. D'you like champagne?" He put a glass in her hand clinked his with it, and cried again, "To death."

"What death?" asked Katie, who swallowed the champagne in one draught, and allowed him to refill her glass. She sat down on his right and began picking up food from the laden table and stuffing it in her mouth. He began to laugh again.

"It's funny, really funny," he said. "I'm drinking to the health of a man whose death I caused today. A German. And now my only guest with whom to celebrate it is a German! Oh, but it's funny, it's funny!"

"What man?" asked Katie stolidly. She was eating as fast as she could. She was always hungry and never dared to satisfy her hunger lest it drew attention to her condition, still unknown to anyone but Moe and Anna.

"The man who killed my son," said the Frenchman. "It has taken me all these years to track him down. But it's done. Today he was executed. Dead! Dead! Like my son. My little son whom he shot."

Katie looked at him in horror. She was not in the least shocked that his son had been shot or that he had caused a man to be executed. But she was suddenly terrified for herself. "Yes."

he went on, drinking again and urging her to do the same. "You can't escape justice. It catches up with you in the end. And yet . . . and yet . . . d'you know, Katie, I don't feel any satisfaction that my son is avenged. I vowed to do it. It's done. But what have I achieved? The death of another, and it can't bring back my son! Nothing can do that. But I found it out too late. Too late."

Katie had got up. Her dark eyes were fixed on him as if she were mesmerised. She had a vision of the dead caretaker, his open mouth and staring eyes. "Stop it! Stop it!" she cried. "It's horrible! Horrible!"

She threw her empty glass down so violently that it smashed. She had drunk several glasses very quickly and her head was swimming. She realized that the Frenchman was drunk. Where were his guests? She asked him. "Gone to a better party—to the French High Commissioner's, where I should be," he said bitterly, "but I have a guest. A charming one." He filled another glass and put it to her lips. "Drink, drink to love, my dear. It sounds better for you than death. You're too young to know that they're the same."

Suddenly he picked up one of the bottles of champagne from the pail of ice on the floor and hurled it out of the window. It crashed against the garage wall. He hurled a second one after it, laughing in that cynical mirthless way which frightened even the hardened Katie. She caught at his arm suddenly and prevented a third bottle from following the others. Everything could be seen through the lighted windows. She blew out the candles. The smell of the hot wax was mingled with the heavy scent of the roses. In the darkness his arms found her. She began to laugh. It astonished her that her own laughter sounded just like his—not really laughter at all. And suddenly she knew why she was laughing like this. It was funny, just as he said. That he should be weeping for his dead son, and she for the man whose child she carried but who did not love her. For she was weeping. This strange laughter; what was it but the echo of agonized tears?

XXVII

THE BODY of the tourist had been found. The current had carried it, just as Leo had foreseen, far down the river, until it had stuck in some reeds. The papers said merely, "The body of an unknown man . . . The police are making investigations." The fact that there were no identity papers or wallet, no personal item of any kind on the man, and also that there were injuries to the head, suggested foul play.

Leo read all this in the papers with amusement. There was absolutely nothing to connect *him* with the crime. Of that he was certain. He had thought of everything. He remembered that last wretched business with which he had been connected. His chief—for he had belonged to another gang before he had started his own—had slipped up on the jeweller, and the river police had discovered the body caught in the reeds a few minutes after he had been thrown there. Things had been pretty hot for a time. They had left the man's card, his business card, on him, having overlooked a small pocket. They had taken the keys of his shop from his ring, and were all round there looting the stuff when the police, warned by the river patrol, had arrived. Leo had only been a look-out then, and he had got away at once. The others had been caught there and then. His former chief was still in gaol. Leo had himself been sent to prison, but only for a few months. He had been two years younger then, and nothing had really been proved against him. There had only been the word of the others, who were determined that he should not go free if they were gaoled.

Leo had learned a lot from that slip-up. He had, for instance, made a study of the river and its currents. He knew where *not* to throw a body in. He had gone over the tourist's clothes minutely; he was satisfied that there was no clue whatsoever to his identity. Eddie had said that the man was on a long business trip, he would not be missed in his home town for some time. As to the care-taker, the police were still "making investigations," as the papers always said.

Hank had killed that old man. Hank alone. He had done it unaided, from panic. Leo was keeping that as a hold over Hank, who was becoming too big for his boots. It was time he got a reminder. He had helped cosh the tourist too, but the three of them had worked together over the man—it was a joint killing. Somehow it seemed better when there were several in a crime, it meant that one would not take the consequences alone if caught.

The country had only recently done away with the death penalty. Leo thought this rather funny.

The British in whose zone they were living, for instance, still had the death penalty in their own country. It made the vanquished seem one up in civilization on their victors. There had been a lot of talk when the decision was made. He and his friends were far too clever to try robbing Occupation houses, as so many others did; it meant that they might come up before an Occupation Military Court, and that could mean anything. No, this lad was too clever for that. Leo had a tremendous opinion of himself, which grew with each successful escapade concluded by his gang. He spent a lot of time studying in his own mind the characters of its members. He flattered himself that he was quite a psychologist. When the Occupying troops had first come, he had made friends with some of them. Two of the officers had taught him English, lent him books, given him food and money. He had soon sized them up. They did not like the position they were in. They wanted to be liked. They grew fond of this lad who ran errands for them, sold their cigarettes and coffee for them and generally made himself useful. They found out that he was homeless and had taken him into the Mess as a kind of help to the barman and waiters. This was how Leo had acquired the education of which Hank was so envious. Both the officers had taught him things, and one of the Belgians had taught him French in return for help with his German. He was quick at imitating and intent on taking advantage of every opportunity. He was a boy on his own, alone in the world; his parents dead, his relatives cut off from him by the Iron Curtain. The officers had more or less adopted him while they had been stationed in the district. He had been a good-looking child—he was now a good-looking youth. The officers had gone back to their own country. They still wrote to Leo, and he still answered. He began to laugh now as he thought of their horror should they know what he was doing.

Well, in a way it was *their* fault. They had accustomed him to an easy life. Before they came he had lived from hand to mouth, sleeping in bunkers and thieving scraps from anyone and anywhere. From them he had got used to money. They had always given him a percentage of the Black Market deals he did for them. They had never had enough money. Their pay simply did not cover the luxuries they needed. He had been really upset when they had left to return to their own country. Life had been terribly empty for a time. Then he had taken up with that first gang, and some of the fun and excitement with which his life with the officers had been filled came back to him.

Leo was in Eddie's room in the town reading the papers when he saw the bit about the finding of the body. Of course, he didn't actually know that it was the tourist's, but from the description it seemed pretty obvious. Eddie, when he came in after the evening's work, had a plan all set for the following Friday. A man who had been coming regularly for the last few evenings to drink and sometimes dine at the restaurant had asked him to find him a girl friend. Eddie had promised one for the following Friday.

"O.K.," said Leo, "Katie can do this job. It's her turn. Besides, we've no one else."

"Sorry," said Eddie laconically, "but he wants a blonde, young and innocent. I told him there's a dearth of virgins, but he's an optimist!"

"Well, we can't let that by," said Leo. "Do you mean he's a plum?"

"Right—and ripe for the picking too. We've *got* to find him a blonde. He carries thousands in notes on him."

Leo sat back in an uncomfortable chair and put his long legs on the table. He screwed up his eyes and appeared to think.

"It's a pity that Leila's out of action," said Eddie gloomily. "She's blonde enough, and although a bit soiled she'd pass as new goods all right; she's young enough."

"She's got her arm in plaster still. We went a bit far with the works on her."

"What about getting one of the dolls dyed? What about having Katie dyed blonde?"

"No good," said Leo shortly, "she's got the look of a regular."

"Well then, what about Trudi? Isn't she back yet?"

"No, not until Saturday. Can't you put this deal off until then?"

"No good—he's off again then. Which makes Friday a particularly good night. He's booked to leave early the next morning. Well, he'll just miss his plane; that's all."

"I've got it," shouted Leo suddenly. "The little plaster saint . . . little Snow-white. The father's crowned her with a halo and the whole family are besotted with her. She *looks* the part—and what's more, she's untouched goods."

"How d'you know?" asked Eddie curiously. "Been having a try?"

At the memory of his unsuccessful encounter with Krista Leo's face darkened. He would pay the stuck-up miss out for her obvious revulsion of him. At the same time he would put paid to the refusal of Hank and Katie to bring her into the gang.

"She's absolutely what we want," he went on, ignoring Eddie's taunt, "but it's going to be the very devil to get her."

"She'll never do it if she's really a plaster saint," sneered Eddie. "What's the use of an unwilling decoy?"

"She won't *be* unwilling when I've finished with her," said Leo quietly. Eddie looked sharply at him. He thought Leo had gone to greater lengths with Leila than was wise . . . was he going even further with this girl? Eddie had heard of the adopted daughter of this large family, everyone had heard of her. Wasn't it a bit dangerous using her?

"Leave it to me," said Leo loftily; "the thing's as good as fixed for Friday night."

The following evening he sent a signal for Katie, and when she came to the shelter he put his plan to her. She was adamant. She would not do it. Then, when she heard that Leo wanted Krista for a wealthy tourist, she was mollified. She began to think how the thing could be worked. She hated Krista so much that it would be a wonderful thrill for her to know that the prudish girl whom her father adored, and even her brother Hank was now crazy about was to be smirched and rolled in the dirt.

It would be very difficult to get Krista to the restaurant, even more so to make her decoy the man. She would have to be got there by a trick; no other way would do. What kind of trick would Krista fall for most easily? Suddenly Katie had it. Hank was due at the shelter very shortly. He would have to be *made* to help.

Hank, however, when he did come, refused blankly to contemplate using Krista. He appeared horrified at the idea.

"She'd never agree," he said curtly.

"She isn't going to be asked to agree," snapped Leo, "she's going to be got to Eddie's room. *I'll* see to the rest. There are ways of making people willing. You saw what happened to Leila." He said this with an eye on Hank's horrified face.

"You aren't going to use the works on Krista?" Hank's voice was so shocked that Katie said furiously, "And why not? Why should she get off everything?"

"I won't stand for it. She doesn't belong to the gang. She's never taken the oath. Leila had. She got what she deserved for breaking it. This is different. I won't stand for it."

"Won't?" said Leo in a dangerously quiet voice. "*Won't?* I should think again if I were you. Who's boss of this gang? You or me? I give the orders here and you obey them. And don't you forget it. I can put you behind bars any day I like. Who killed the old buffer? *You.* You alone."

Neither Hank nor Katie had dared to tell Leo about the visit of the policeman with the belt. He had been furious about Hank and the twins having been brought home by the policeman when they were drunk. Hank's face paled at Leo's threat about turning him in for the murder of the caretaker. Katie was white with fear. She saw that she would have to count Hank out on this deal. Jealous as she was of Leo's interest in Krista, she would get her there. She would do it to protect her own skin.

Hank went on ahead to see that the motor cycles were all right. Katie lingered behind. She said to Leo, "He's soft. He's as besotted with her as Pa is. We'll have to think up some way of making him harden up."

"I'll put the fear of prison in him! That ought to outweigh little Snow-White," retorted Leo brutally.

"Get a move on," shouted Hank. He was waiting for Katie. They were to join the rest of the gang in the shelter. Although the others were not in this new deal there were things to discuss.

Leo got the general business over quickly. The gang were sulky. They did not like this new idea of only one or two members being in on each deal. They had all become accustomed to having money. They needed it now. They said so.

"You've got to wait," their leader insisted. "I've got a grand new scheme. Just give me time to work it out. As soon as we've got the cash from this next thing, I'll tell you about it."

He got rid of them. But there was an uneasy feeling that all was not well. Dissatisfied members were no use to Leo. Hank was getting too big for his boots. He'd have to take him down a peg or two. He'd deal with the youngsters later on.

"They're fed up," observed Hank as he and Katie were left alone with Leo in the shelter. "I told you this decoy scheme's no good. It's dangerous and it makes the others jealous and disgruntled."

"Well, that's my business. *I* run this show. And I'm not having any of your soft scruples about little Snow-White getting in the way of a good haul from this old mug. You've got to get the girl for Friday. Understand?"

"But I thought you agreed to count her out."

"I may or may not use her for the mug. It depends on how she behaves to me. She may be so sweet that I'll be as jealous as you are!" Leo roared with laughter at his own perception of Hank's reluctance to bring Krista under the influence of his chief.

"I *won't* do it!" asserted Hank.

"Very well. I will," snapped Katie.

"I don't care which of you persuades little sister to come into the spider's web but she's *got* to be there. Eight o'clock sharp on Friday night. Understand? And if she's *not*, well you know how pleased the police will be to have the killer of the old man named. There's been a lot of outcry in the press because he's still at large."

Katie had been thinking hard. She did not trust Hank. She had a plan. It was simple enough and very clever. Katie knew Krista. Knew that in spite of her own spiteful behaviour to the girl Krista was so innately sweet that she would go to anyone ill or needing her help.

Katie was utterly unscrupulous in what she intended to do. She needed money urgently if she was to do something about this baby. Moe might talk of Katie doing something about it, but she would never countenance what Katie meant to do. Moe loved children. She might grumble about having so many but she liked to have a lot of young, budding life round her.

Once rid of the child there were possibilities. The Frenchman, for instance. He might be induced to take her to Paris. He liked her as she was. No one else did. She wanted passionately to be loved. Had she told any member of her family this they would not have believed her. She had started life off on the wrong foot. She wanted to start again. Without any encumbrances. She had quite a hoard of money hidden away in the summer-house. It was difficult to get there now and count it. Pa was always in the place. Unless she slipped out in the early hours of the morning it was ten to one that she'd find Pa there smoking his pipe. He sat with his feet right over the loose board in the floor. Katie laughed whenever she thought of it.

"Well, I leave it to you," finished Leo in a hard voice. "You'd better not let me down."

The wind was howling, and the branches of the trees swaying against the broken shelter-roof made a strange knocking sound. They listened intently when Leo said suddenly, "Keep still. Listen. I swear I heard someone moving then . . . just outside . . ."

"It's only a branch," whispered Katie a minute later as she peeped outside. "There's not a soul about."

"I'm sure I heard a cough or a choke—like a child makes, then light steps running," insisted Leo.

"Well, what if you did? This is a fairly public path. We're damned lucky not to have been discovered before," sneered Hank, who had never approved of Leo's choice of a hide-out.

"I've found a new place," announced Leo shortly. "You'll be hearing about it next week. Hank, you have a look outside. I have a feeling there *is* someone about."

"Nothing, absolutely nothing," reported Hank scornfully. "Getting windy? Have a drink and forget it."

They sat there for a while longer drinking.

On the way home Katie said to Hank, "You've *got* to fall in with Leo's plans. You're a damn fool to mind about Krista. Fancy you being soft over a girl. Think of those iron bars Leo spoke about. They won't be soft. And you won't see little Snow-White either if you spend the rest of your life behind them."

"Shut up." Hank was driven beyond endurance by her taunts. "Don't forget that it was your belt found under the old man's body. Have you thought of that? What would Leo say if he knew the police have your belt?"

"That blasted little Robert," swore Katie, "I'll pay him out for that."

"I've put the fear of the knife into him already," snapped Hank. "You'd better see that Leila's mouth's kept closed."

"Eddie's done that," said Katie sullenly.

"If you hurt Krista I'll *get* you. Don't think I'm going to stand for it. I'm not. I'll agree to her going there because I've no choice. You'd better both watch out if you hurt her."

Katie said nothing. She knew that Leo would take good care that Hank was prevented from interfering. Leo no longer trusted

Hank. Hank no longer trusted her. And she? She began to laugh. She hated them all. *All* of them.

Anna was in a deep sleep when she was awakened by Robert. His hands and knees were bleeding, his face was wild and almost frantic with fear. She would not wake up. He pulled her long fair hair. He dared not make any noise. Krista slept in the next room with Franz Joseph. Tonight Peppi was there too. He had had to be terribly careful not to wake them when he crept out two hours ago. At last at his shakings and hair pullings Anna woke up, yawning and rubbing her eyes.

"'Tisn't time to get up yet, Moe," she grumbled; then finding it quite dark she said sharply, "Is that you, Katie?"

"No—no—it's me, Anna. Listen, please listen, it's Robert, Anna." The child's voice was urgent. Anna sat up.

"Robert!" she exclaimed in surprise. "Whatever's the matter?"

Since the episode of Robert's back, Anna had looked after him very carefully. She was afraid for his safety. The terror in his voice now alarmed her.

"Quick, quick, listen, Anna. Katie'll be back soon. *Listen.*" And into Anna's incredulous ears Robert poured the story of a plot against Krista. All about a gang. Hank, Katie, and that Leo.

To the boy's excited urgent anxiety Anna seemed slow and dense. She made him repeat everything over several times. She was so sleepy that she just couldn't decide whether she was dreaming it all.

Finally she got out of bed, poured cold water over her face and wrists and sat down with Robert on the bed. He was shivering and whimpering and in a fever of anxiety lest the others should come back before he had explained the urgency of the matter to Anna, and begged her to do something about Krista.

When she asked him how he knew all this he told her that for weeks he had been slipping out at night; following them to their hide-out and listening to them at their meetings. It wasn't only just tonight, he insisted; he'd been there lots of times. The things he began telling Anna were so horrifying that she couldn't believe them. And yet why not? The hut, as the child said, was full of cracks and in many places open to the sky. It was easy enough to hear what was going on inside. They always had a look-out, but he had usually been placed on the tow-path where the entrance of the shelter faced the river. Robert had apparently crept up behind the hut each time, and climbed the tree; hidden in its branches, he could hear most of what they were saying.

He had not been so lucky tonight. The wind had been so fierce that some of what they had been planning had been lost in the sighing of the branches. They had almost caught him tonight. He had slipped, but just managed to grasp another branch and by keeping terribly still had managed to slither down while the wind was particularly wild.

When he had finished whispering to Anna he began to sob.

Anna was so shocked at what he had told her that for a time she could think of nothing to say. She bathed his hands and knees and comforted him as best she could. She knew Katie and Hank belonged to some kind of gang. Hadn't Katie asked her to cut in with them? But that these children, for they were little more, robbed and killed, she hadn't had the faintest idea. Who could, even in their wildest dreams have imagined such a thing? At first she thought Robert was inventing it all, but the look of terror on his face as he implored her to save Krista told her that this part at any rate must have some truth in it. Then she remembered those black gloves . . . and the blood . . . the death of that old caretaker . . . Katie's strange behaviour . . . the police coming with that belt. She questioned Robert further. Yes. He knew all about that; they had killed him. Worse, they said that Hank had killed him, only Hank, and that if he didn't make Krista do this thing they wanted, Leo would either kill Hank or give him up to the police.

They heard the sound of the motor cycle approaching. "Go back to your bed," ordered Anna. She realized with a stab of fear the danger that this child had put himself into. He had given away the only real clue to the police by admitting that he recognized Katie's belt. Of his appalling danger in going out at night she shuddered to think. She hugged him to her, trying to calm him and assuring him that if only he had come to her sooner she could have prevented all this.

"Why didn't you tell someone?" she urged him.

"I was too frightened," he confessed, hiding his face. "They told me when they carved my back that if I opened my mouth again they'd do something much worse to me."

"But you could have told Father Lange," said Anna gently, "that would have been different."

"He guesses some, he's always asking me. Once he saw me out at night. He took me back to his house and gave me cocoa and tried to make me tell him what I had been doing. But I didn't." He finished proudly. "No one's made me tell. Not even Heinz and Hank, and they tortured me."

The one thing which Robert had not been able to hear was the actual time when this thing was planned to happen. The wind had prevented that. When he had been tucked back into bed and she left him, she put on her coat and sat thinking. She heard the motor cycle approaching and later Katie scrambling in the window, and lay down with the sheet pulled right up to her chin, pretending to be asleep. As she heard Katie undressing in the dark she was filled with loathing of her mean spitefulness. She had always known of these traits in her sister, and accepted them, but that Katie would go to such lengths to hurt an innocent girl shocked Anna inexpressibly. She lay awake turning over this hatefull, appalling problem.

How to do something to prevent it happening? And Hank? Anna held no brief for Hank. He was a *murderer*. At least it seemed so. But that was such a nightmare, if it were true, that for the moment she accepted only the fact that Hank was in Leo's power; that he held over Hank's head this appalling threat of giving him up to the police for the crime—whether or not he had done it—if he did not produce Krista. Anna knew that Leo had had his eye on Krista for a long time. She had seen him looking at her in the tram, on the tow-path, in the town. And there had been the episode of her being annoyed by him in the woodland.

What puzzled her was Robert's insistence that Hank did not want to do this thing: that they had said they wouldn't hurt Krista if only he would help get her to Eddie's room. And Robert didn't know where that room was.

What should she do? Warn Krista? No, she would be terrified. Go to the police? Would they believe her? She had only the garbled story of a frightened little boy. But they were already suspicious. They would surely look into the whole matter. Anna shrank from the police. They'd had so much petty trouble from them already. Pa! Should she go to him? He was suspicious of something, that was obvious, ever since the police had come. Since Robert's back had been carved with that vile word, Pa had watched them all whenever he came home. Should she tell him? Or should she tackle Hank—now?

Anna was no coward. Acting on the impulse of the moment she dropped out of the window and went round to the conservatory where he slept. He came at once at her insistent tapping.

"Come out," she whispered, "I must speak to you." Something in her tone made him obey, although he was just getting into bed.

She wasted no time. As soon as he walked round the corner of the house to join her, angry but apprehensive, she attacked him. She knew all about the gang and its activities. She knew about the murders. She saw Hank's danger, knew that he was in Leo's power.

"The game's up," she said firmly, "the police are on to the gang. It's only a matter of time. Unless you go to Pa and tell him everything I'm going to tell him myself."

Hank made a move towards her. His great hands were trembling. "Take care," he warned; "I may silence you."

"What's the good of that?" asked Anna contemptuously. "How d'you think I know all this? I'm not afraid of you."

"Who told you?" His threatening attitude had no effect on Anna. Calm, stolid and forthright she stood there and told him what she thought of him. Her words were pitiless. "And don't think it'll make a penny-worth of difference if you kill me," she ended sharply. "Others know all this. They told me. It's only a matter of time before the police round you all up."

"What am I to do?" Hank was terrified now. Anna was so sure, so absolutely certain of herself. He had not the faintest idea that she was bluffing him.

"Tell Pa the whole thing," insisted Anna. "If you won't then I will."

"Give me until tomorrow night," pleaded Hank.

"All right. But no longer. You tell me tomorrow when I get back from work what you've decided."

"All right," agreed Hank finally. "I'll make up my mind. But what can Pa do?"

"I don't know and I don't care," said Anna fiercely. "But I *do* know that he won't let Krista suffer for your vileness."

She turned from him without a word and went back to bed. She had suddenly remembered that slip of paper in her bag. It bore the address of Paul's present whereabouts. Not so very far away. If she wrote to him "express" he would get it quickly. The proper person to come and take Krista away from all this filthy mess was Paul. She didn't trust Hank. She would write the letter anyhow.

When Paul received Anna's letter he thought he was reading some piece from a cheap gangster magazine. She had had very little time, and she was no great letter-writer. It was terse and to the point. "Krista is in danger from a gang. They intend to force her into it. They have got the means to do this. If you love her, come as soon as you get this letter. Come to the house and ask where she is. I'll look out for you. Don't fail her. Anna."

He re-read the letter. It had a ring of both urgency and sincerity. He liked Anna. She had a solid enduring quality which all the others in that family lacked. She had said that she would help him. Was this her way? Was it some trick? Some way of reuniting the lovers?

At the thought of any possible danger to Krista Paul saw red. What could such a gang be? How could they threaten a girl like Krista; have the means, as Anna said, of forcing her into their power? The gangs round that part of the Rhine were notorious. Paul knew this. They hid in the ruined parts of the Haven. Was this such a gang? That lad Hank—Paul was sure he had a hand in this. He took the letter to his friend Bob.

"Read that," he said.

Bob read it, then whistled.

"What d'you make of it?"

"Dunno. It sounds the real thing to me. This kid's scared out of her skin. Not for herself. For your Krista."

"It's incredible. It must be some trick." insisted Paul doubtfully.

"Maybe. Maybe not. How much d'you care for the girl?"

"She means everything in the world to me."

Bob whistled again. "Looks like you can't ignore this then. It may be a trick, it may be O.K. Let's go see!"

"You'd come with me?"

"Sure thing. *If* we can get off. This border dump's about as thrilling as a Sunday school. We'll take my automobile."

Paul was undecided whether or not to answer Anna's letter. She had sent it express. He had got it the same night. They might get week-end leave and set off tomorrow afternoon. It wouldn't take long in Bob's fast car.

Finally he decided against a telegram. It might attract too much notice. He would send an answer the same way as she had, by express.

"Supposing it's a hoax," he said to Bob as he posted the letter. "Well, we'll have had the trip. We'll have got out of this dump," Bob said cheerfully. "And you'll see your girl."

Would he? Paul began to think. The idea of seeing Krista again was so exciting that he didn't see how he was going to get through the next twenty-four hours.

XXVIII

HANK TOSSED and turned. The night was close. Although all the windows in the conservatory were wide open it was absolutely airless. Accustomed to heaving himself into bed and knowing nothing more until Moe awoke him with the watering-can (if the alarm-clock had failed to do so), he was now wide awake and burning with impatience. Tomorrow would be Friday. Anna had come to him again today as soon as she had come home.

"Well, what about it?" she had demanded in a hard voice. He had stalled. He had some plan for getting the twins to help against Leo in this thing planned for tomorrow. He would see that Krista didn't come to any harm. He had begged her not to warn Krista. Anna was dubious.

"You'd much better go to Pa," she urged.

"Look," pleaded Hank, "it's life or death to me. Can't you see that? If I can fix this without having to tell Pa it'll be the better for us all. I promise you no harm shall come to Krista." He couldn't bear the thought of Krista knowing of his part in the gang.

"I don't trust you," said Anna bluntly; "I'll give you until tomorrow morning. If you haven't done something by then I'll *have* to tell him."

He lay now wondering what on earth to do. How to get the better of Leo in this terrible fix. Leo was ruthless. He wouldn't have the slightest compunction in turning Hank over to the police. And he would get the rest of the gang to lie for him.

They would lie not only from fear, but also for money. The wild thought of making a run for it entered his mind. He was sick of the whole beastly business. He'd gone into the thing chiefly because he was bored. He'd run away!

The thought that if he did so Krista would be left to the mercies of Katie and Leo was so terrible that he simply couldn't lie still. He got up and went out of the conservatory, put on a coat in the lobby, and went into the garden. It was a lovely night, still warm as he entered the summer-house. Even as he went in he smelt the tobacco-smoke and, too late, saw his father sitting hunched up in a corner.

Joseph looked up. "Come in," he said. "It's not often we have any talk together."

Hank was astonished to find his father there, and embarrassed too. Joseph noticed his perturbation. "What's wrong?" he asked, taking his pipe from his mouth.

"Nothing," mumbled Hank.

"Oh yes, there is," said Joseph. "And the police came here this afternoon again. Didn't Moe tell you?"

He did not miss the fear which came into Hank's face.

"I've been looking round," said Joseph slowly, "and I've been thinking."

"What did the police want?" Hank's voice shook.

"The number of your motor cycle."

"What for?"

"How should I know? I've never owned a motor-bicycle. In fact I've never owned an ordinary push one, as you very well know."

"Did they ask to see mine?"

"Yes. Moe showed it them."

"What did they say?"

"Nothing. Just took down the number and examined it. They wanted to know about the licence, I expect. But I *don't* like it. All that business about that belt. It was funny Robert thinking he'd seen it before. He's a bright boy and not usually mistaken."

"Moe never told me about the police coming today," said Hank.

"Why are you so frightened? What's the matter, Hank?" For Hank was shaking now and it was obvious to Joseph that something was terribly wrong. "What's the matter?" he asked sharply again.

For answer Hank put his head in his hands and sat silent. Joseph was thoroughly alarmed now. A sense of terrible foreboding had been with him all day. The priest's words came back to him. He had seen Hank, Katie and that horrible Leo on a motor cycle late at night. But they had denied that it could have been them. The police had come here twice. About that belt found under the caretaker's body, and now about Hank's motor cycle.

"Hank," he said sharply, "Tell me where you go at night. The *truth* now."

Hank drew a deep breath. "Robbing, housebreaking, and murdering," he said in a rush.

Joseph was so astounded that he could only stare. He thought Hank was joking. "Don't be a fool!" he said roughly. "It's no time for joking. I want the truth, I don't want jokes for an answer."

"I'm not joking," said Hank, and there was in his voice that which froze Joseph into horrified acceptance of what he had said. "Robbing, housebreaking and murdering." God. God. What did the boy mean?

"Father." The word burst from Hank. "You *must* help me." And he burst into appalling broken sobbing.

Joseph sat as if turned to stone. Then as he looked at the bent huddled figure of this great lump of wickedness that was his son. A wave of violent anger enveloped him. A red, wild rage seized him. He wanted to choke the evil out of this wretched youth. To take his throat in his hands and shake him like a mad dog and choke him—choke him until there was nothing left but a cry for the mercy he had never shown anyone himself.

But he sat perfectly still and slowly the fury died down. He'd done that recently. And it always worked. He took hold of his thoughts. Anger would not help him. It would only muddle his brain. He needed to get his mind clear. He tried to think of Hank as a small boy. When he had gone away first to join the army Hank had been just such a plump merry rascal as Franz Joseph was now. He'd been such good friends with his son. What had happened? When he'd come back there'd been nothing but violent antagonism between them. Bitter wrangling and sullen jealousy. Looking at him now Joseph could find no point of contact. None. And yet this was his son! Flesh of his flesh and blood of his blood. God, oh God. What was the outcome of this to be? The thing was *real*. A wave of terrible conviction that what Hank had said was true came over him. He sensed it now. The dead weight which had been hanging like a black fear over his head for months was about to descend in a horror far worse than anything he could have imagined.

Putting his hand roughly on Hank's shoulder he tried to control his voice. "It's no use sitting there like that. Tell me the whole thing. I can't help you unless I know the truth. *All* of it. No excuses. Get it out quickly, for God's sake."

Hank raised his head. Joseph, looking at his son in the moonlight coming through the acacia, thought he looked like a crushed creature. Something brought to bay but still alive and dangerous. He pushed the thought from him. This was his son. *His* son.

"I killed a man. The old caretaker. If I don't give Krista up to Leo tomorrow night, he'll split on me to the police. There's no choice. What can I do? *What?*"

Joseph's brain could not take this in.

"Say that again," he said incredulously. "You sit there, *my* son, and tell me you killed a man. How? Was it an accident?"

"No. I didn't mean to kill him. But the old fool resisted!"

"Resisted? Resisted what?"

"The gang, of course. He put up a fight."

"Gang?" said Joseph. "*Gang?* What is this? Tell me what you mean."

"I belong to a gang. Everyone does. Katie got me in. We did housebreaking. On one of the evenings we coshed this old fellow too hard and he died."

"We? Just now you said *I*. Who did it? Answer me. Which of you do you mean?"

"I did it. Alone. That's why Leo has got it on me. He can make the others swear to it. Damn him."

"You, *my* son, murdered an old man deliberately. My God, Hank, how can you sit there and tell me that?"

"Because you've asked me to. And don't keep on harping on the word murder. You've killed plenty of people yourself."

"I? I've killed people? What d'you mean?" Joseph's voice was rising in anger.

"I've heard you talking about the war. The invasions . . ." Joseph looked at Hank in horrified despair. Was his son actually a murderer? A self-confessed one? And what was far worse, an unrepentant one. He simply could not stomach this last justification. That his father had killed. That there was no difference in those deaths.

"Answer me." he said so sternly that Hank straightened up at the authority in his voice. "Did you actually murder this man in cold blood? For money. Or for what? Had he attacked you? *Why* did you kill?"

And then in incoherent, broken sentences Hank poured out the story of the murder of the old caretaker. He omitted nothing once he had begun. As he talked he found at last some relief from the intolerable strain of the last few days. Joseph was spared nothing. The coshing—the rolling of the body under the table—the luring of the tourist—the heaving of the body into the Rhine—the torturing of Leila—and finally the threat to Krista.

At the mention of Krista Joseph cried out in protest.

"Don't bring her into this vile business. She's made of other clay," he said violently. "Leave her out of it."

"That's just what can't be done," groaned Hank. "Leo is determined to have her. If I don't deliver her to him at the agreed time and place he will give immediate information about the murder of the caretaker to the police."

"He'd never dare. Why, he's involved too much himself."

"I tell you he's clever. Damned clever. He makes circles round me. He'll give me up, all right, and get off free himself. The others will swear to anything he orders them."

Thinking of Leo's face that evening when he had looked at Krista on the tow-path, and remembering his cunning, deliberate eyes, Joseph could not doubt Hank's words. He sat there without looking at Hank. He could not. He felt such a revulsion for this son of his that it was all he could do to stay next to him on the wooden seat of the summer-house. At last he said. "Why have you told me this?"

"Because you've *got* to help me, Father. If you won't do it for me, you must do it for Krista. I *can't* let Leo have her."

At something in Hank's voice Joseph looked at him sharply "Why should *you* care? You've killed and tortured; old men, girls, children. Why should you care about Krista?"

"I don't know." Hank's voice was puzzled. "But I do. I mind so much that I can't sleep. I can think of nothing else. That's why I'm telling you this—to save Krista."

"You can do that yourself. Go to the police. Now," said Joseph sternly.

Hank recoiled. "No," he cried violently, "I'd be shut up in a cell for ever. A life-sentence. Leo told me so."

"Then what do you think *I* can do?"

"I thought you could think of something. *Do. Do.* Please, Pa." He asked it as if he were asking for a sweet, as he had done as a child. As if he were sure his father could do something. Perform a miracle perhaps. It was galling to Joseph, who had endured the contempt of this son for so long, to have to undeceive him.

"There's no answer except the police," he said heavily. "You must give yourself up, Hank. God is merciful. He will forgive you if you are repentant."

"God? D'you think I care about God?" shouted Hank violently. "I care about saving Krista from Leo and saving my own skin, that's all. If you won't help *me*, then help Krista."

Joseph was appalled. He questioned Hank at length and the more he learned of the activities of his children the more stupefied he became. When Hank finished he was silent. Too stunned to say a word. He simply could not take it all in. That *his* children went out at night to rob from houses which they had broken into! Went out to decoy and lure tourists to their deaths in order to steal from them! His horror was so great that beside this the infidelity of Moe seemed as nothing.

"The others? Anna, Robert, Karl? Are they all in this?" he said at last.

"Only Katie and the twins."

"The twins are only sixteen!" groaned Joseph.

"I've been doing this since I was fourteen!" Hank's voice was flat.

"Why? In God's name *why*?" shouted his father.

"I was bored in this god-forsaken village. There's nothing to do. Not a damned thing. One miserable cinema open twice a week. In Cologne there was always life. Shops, cinemas, people, plenty to do and see. What is there here? A row of blasted houses full of miserable smug creatures who look down on us. To get into the town we need money. Plenty of money. *You* take a lot from us each week for your damned house. Moe takes some for the food—there's not enough left. So what? There are plenty of people with more than they need. We helped ourselves—to get back what *you* took from us for the house."

"But we must have a place of our own. The house is for you—for you all—so that you won't have to listen to complaints and grumbles about your noise and doings—so that you'll have a place of your own."

"Maybe, but we won't be there by the time it's built. See? We want lives of our own, homes of our own, we resent your taking our wages for *your* house. We went into the gang at first to put back all that money you took from us. Later it got bigger, and bigger. We all wanted more and more."

"And so you murdered!"

"That was an accident—the old man shouldn't have resisted. He'd no right to be there." Hank's voice was resentful.

Joseph looked at him in an agonized dismay. This large lump of evil—for evil he was; what else could one call him?—was his son. God! Oh God! What to do, what to say?

"The tourist, the second one. Was that an accident?" he managed to get out.

"No, that was planned. He had plenty of dough. We were all short of cash after the bargees went away."

Joseph groaned. The world was crashing. If only it were all a nightmare. He'd been having terrible ones lately, but none so appalling as this which Hank, his son, was creating for him now.

"Father." The word which Hank never used was dragged from him now. "Father, you *must* help. For God's sake help to do something about Krista."

"God! I wonder you can mention His name—or Krista's either," cried Joseph.

"I love Krista." Hank heard the words come from his own lips with astonishment. They were true. He knew it now. He loved her. That was the reason for his agonizing fear for her. She was the one thing he loved and cared about. Why hadn't he realized it before? Before he'd got too involved with the gang? He knew suddenly why her face was forever before his eyes. Why he dreamed about her. Felt queer when she smiled at him, when she praised his music. He, Hank, who never cared about anything, loved a girl. The girl who'd been brought up with him as his sister. But she wasn't his sister. That was just it. She was no relation. And he did not love her as a sister.

"You've got to help me, Pa. You must. For *her*," he almost screamed in his excitement.

"Hank," Joseph was hesitant. "Answer me one thing. Are you sorry for what you've done?"

"Yes. I'd give anything to have it all wiped out."

"Then come with me to the police. I'll help you all I can, Hank. We'll go to Father Lange first."

"No! No! Leave him out of it. Father, I *can't. I can't.* Don't you see? They'll shut me up, for the rest of my life. Think of it—to be behind bars!"

"I have been," said Joseph quietly.

"Then you *know*! And I'm young! Only eighteen. I can't, I *can't*," His voice was rising in hysteria now.

Behind bars . . . in a cage. That lion; the lion with the unhappy tortured eyes. Joseph's mind flashed back at the word "cage" to that free day when he'd visited the circus. The whole of his life now seemed to have been entangled on that day. Moe. Krista. Hank. All hopelessly involved. And he had been blind. Absolutely blind to what had been going on here in his own home. His mind had been revolving round himself and the wrong that Moe had done him, and on this new business of the Rearmament and the Peace Treaty. Every night when he'd come home he'd tried to switch his thoughts off all that excited argument and chatter of his workmates on the burning topics of the day. And while he was watching with amazement the blindness of his comrades in approving what could only mean a recurrence of that last disaster, he had been completely unaware of the appalling things which had been taking place in his own family.

He looked at the huddled form of Hank. "There is no other way," he said harshly. "Face it." He felt suddenly an overwhelming pity for this wretched son of his. The anger, disgust and revulsion were swept away for a moment in pity. In the white scared face of the once arrogant, insolent youth he saw the little boy with whom he had once had such a loving understanding.

And then it was dissolved again in horror as Hank burst out, "I could kill *Leo*. Why not? I'm stronger than he is. But he has the gun. I could get a gun too." His voice rose excitedly. "Why didn't I think of it before? I could kill *Leo*."

Hank was sorry now that he had confessed to his father. What a fool he was not to have thought of killing Leo. He would make the twins help him.

Joseph sat very still looking at his son. Then he said slowly, "So you would kill again? You're not satisfied with what you've already done? And you dare to drag Krista into this? More killing, more murders. You wretched boy! Think of your soul. Think of that!"

"I have none. There's no such thing," said Hank flatly.

Joseph recoiled violently. These last words of Hank's horrified him more than his confession to the murders. Hank was beyond all help if he believed that he had no soul.

"May God forgive you," he cried hoarsely. "For I find it hard to believe that you're my son."

"I'm very like you. A chip off the old block, in fact." There was no flippancy in Hank's voice. He was merely stating a fact. "Look at our hands." Hank spread out his large squarish hands. "They are exactly alike. Ask Moe!"

Joseph looked down at his hands, just as he had on that day in the factory when he had wanted to smash them in his comrades' faces. Had he passed on to this son his own blinding fits of temper? Had Hank killed in one of those red rages?

"No, no," he said furiously. "We're not alike. Not at all." The idea nauseated him. Revolted him. And yet? Was it true?

"Father." Hank's voice was pleading now, something Joseph had not heard in it for years. Not since he had been a small boy wanting some special treat. "I could run away. If I can't kill Leo, I could run away. You could wait until I'd got away and then tell the police to save Krista from Leo."

"Where would you go?" asked Joseph remorselessly. "Everywhere you go you'll need identity papers. You'd be found soon enough. With radio and telephones you wouldn't stand a chance."

"With money I could buy new papers."

"Don't be a fool. There's no escape. You should have thought of the consequences of all this before. God! My son to be in such a fix!"

"You *won't* help me then?" Hank got up and faced his father. "You don't care what happens to Krista? You minded enough when that American wanted her."

"Stop it," cried Joseph, goaded beyond endurance. "I'll see that no harm comes to Krista. Go to bed now. You're shivering. Leave me here. I want to think."

"You'll find a way out?"

"There is only one way out."

"I *won't* go to the police. They'll put me in prison. All my life." Hank was hysterical again. "I won't. I won't."

"Leave me now, Hank." Joseph's voice was rough but not un-kind.

The boy stood there staring at his father. Both wanted to make some gesture, some approach. Both felt that this terrible few min-utes could have been the beginning of some new vital contact between them. Hank for the first time since his father's return from the war felt the stirring of something approaching respect and even affection. Joseph felt little now but an overwhelming horror. All his pity had given way again to revulsion. A revulsion so great that he could not bring himself to put out his hand and touch his son. Across the way, from the lighted windows of the Frenchman's house, came the soft strains of his favourite record, "La Vie en Rose." Suddenly the music stopped. The lights went out. Nothing could be heard except a nightjar and in the distance the continuous clanging of the bridge-repairers. Hank turned, his shoulders hunched, and went back to the house.

Joseph sat on. The hours of the night were boomed out in the distance by the great clock. The night-shift worked ceaselessly under the great flares. The bridge was almost finished. It would be ready by Christmas. The moonlight caught the fine delicate threads of a spider's web in a corner of the summer-house and turned it to filigree silver. For a long time he watched a spider ensnare and devour a small moth. The process was like human life, he thought. One was swallowed up, devoured in an inhu-man machine of a relentless turn of events. What to do about Hank? *What?* His instinct was to go straight to the police. But Hank was his son. His own son. Krista was not his daughter, though he loved her above everything. She was good, inherently good. And Hank was bad.

His foot which had been tapping restlessly caught the loose board in the floor. He bent down and pulled it up. Under-neath there was a deep hollow. He put his arm down and drew up two long black heavy things which looked like sausages. They were old black stockings filled with sand in which a bicycle chain was embedded. At first it did not dawn on him what they were. Then Hank's words about coshing the old man came back to him. Here were the terrible weapons with which they had rendered their victims senseless! And made by children! For to him they were but children. Black hooded capes and black jerseys were there in a bundle, and wrapped in one of these which had a faint scent of perfume he found a large packet of bank-notes. They were tied with a blue ribbon. Almost a thousand marks there. Joseph's hair prickled with horror as he touched them. He looked at the things carefully, touching them gingerly as if they were stained by blood. Then he put them all back again, pressed the board back into place and removed the marks he had made in prising it up. He had not really taken in all that Hank had told him. Now he was forced with a violent shock to realize the enormity of it. Here were the visible tools of the gang. Their death weapons! Their loathsome garments in which they hoped to conceal their identities! Katie, too, he had said. And the twins. Yes. There were four sets of these vile things here. Katie had got Hank into the gang. And the twins? Joseph groaned. They were decent boys, or so it had seemed to him, not cruel and bullying like Hank. Just full of animal spirits. At least that was all he had seen. But he had seen so little, so pathetically little. They were strangers. Living in the house. Like lodgers. They paid their way. They harped on that whenever he reproved them. They paid their way . . . they were entitled to a say in everything.

And Krista? Her Botticelli face with its startling purity came to his mind. She must not be allowed to have the slightest contact with this vile gang. The very thought of it maddened him. Why hadn't he allowed that young American to have her? At least she would have been safely cared for and protected from this threat. Moe? Should he tell her? What would be the use? She would protect and excuse Hank and his brothers. She would plan to outwit Leo in some way. No! This was his problem. He sat on, turning it over and over in his mind. When the first streaks of red light lit the sky and the sudden lull from the bridge told him that the night-shift was changing for the early morning one, he got up at last from the hard wooden seat in the summer house. It had taken him hours of torment. But he had made up his mind.

Hank. Krista. Hank. Krista. The two had revolved through his head ceaselessly with each clang from the bridge. He felt like a blindfold justice weighing out the scales. And the issue? Flesh and blood against a stranger. Good against evil. Justice against wrong-doing. When he staggered out of the summer-house, back to his unslept-in bed, Joseph looked and felt an old man.

XXIX

AT HALF PAST FIVE Moe burst into his room. He was lying on the bed, fully clothed, and she saw at once that he was wide awake.

"What's the matter? What's happened? Hank's just come to me in a terrible state saying something about your going to the police, and refusing to help him."

Her eyes in the pale morning light were black pools, her face tense. "You've seen him? When?"

"I've just bumped into him wandering about in the hall. What's it all about? No one seems to sleep in this house." Her eyes went from the unused bed to his unshaven face and crumpled clothes. Fear made her voice sharp. "Joseph, what *is* it?"

He had a strange seared look, like a tree that has been blasted by lightning. Something about his whole stricken posture alarmed her. She resisted an impulse to put her arms round him, furious at this sudden flood of pity. He got off the bed slowly and said mechanically, "Come out to the summer-house. I've something to show you."

"But what *is* it?" she asked impatiently.

"Come," he said roughly and shutting the hall door quietly behind them, she followed him across the dew-covered grass to the summer-house. The birds were noisy, the sun already making golden threads in the grey veils of mist from the river. She stood at the entrance to the summer-house, watched him stoop down and prise up a board, and from the hollow under it draw out the black clothes, the home-made coshes and bundle of banknotes. He turned from the heap and said harshly, "Our children. That's what's the matter. They belong to some vile gang. They wear these! They use them to carry out their crimes. And for *these*!" He thrust out the banknotes. "*Our* children. Yours and mine!" His voice rose. "And we knew nothing of it. *Nothing.*"

The sight of the black garments and coshes shook her. "I knew," she said as calmly as she could. She was apprehensive. He had found out about Hank's coffee racket. It was just like him to go poking about and find their things hidden under the floor.

"You *knew*? And you never told me? You *knew*. And you lied when the police came here that night?"

"Lied? I've never lied. What d'you mean?"

"When the police questioned the children about that belt you said they had all been in bed."

"The belt? What's that got to do with this?"

"But you said you *knew*! Robert was right. It was Katie's belt. They *murdered* the old man."

"Joseph!" The word burst from her. "You're mad!" She began to laugh. Her laughter infuriated him.

"Be quiet! It's you who are mad!"

"I won't be quiet!" she shouted. "You stand there and tell me the children murdered that old man! Are you crazy? Their gang is a black market one. They run coffee from Belgium. Oh, I know it's wrong—but they all work some fiddle now. They've gone without things for years and now they want everything quickly. Hank told me about it. I got it out of him."

"When?" cried Joseph urgently. "When?"

"The night he carved Robert's back," she faltered, terrified at what she saw in his face. For at the thought of Hank's lies to his mother, rage had seized him again. "What's the matter now?" she asked, bewildered. "Joseph, don't be so angry! You must move with the times. All the kids do these things now. They want money! It's the war, and the films they see."

"They don't *murder*!" shouted Joseph. "Your son's a *murderer*! By his own admission. Not once, but twice. And you laugh. You don't believe me. You tell me it's some coffee racket. I tell you, a few hours ago, he stood where you are now, and told me so. Begged me to help him. He's at his wits' end because of Krista. Otherwise we'd have known nothing of this until the police caught up with them."

Moe stood clutching the coat she had flung round her shoulders. She stared speechlessly at Joseph. She saw that he wasn't mad. He wasn't making it up. It was true! In one quick flash of feminine intuition, she knew it. Everything fitted into place. The gloves, the blood, the belt, Katie's apathy and nervousness.

Robert's terror and nightmares. The child knew something . . . and Hank knew that he did. The glibness of Hank's explanation to her, the sullen reluctance of Katie to answer at all. She saw it all now.

"The police?" she whispered through dry lips. "Hank said you won't help him. They're on to him?"

"They will be," he said grimly; "unless he takes Krista for the gang to use as a decoy tomorrow night, Leo is to give him up for the murder of the caretaker."

"Hank told you this?" The disbelief in her voice goaded Joseph.

"He did. Go in and ask him yourself. He seems to have led you up the garden path all right."

"But why? Why did he tell *you*?" He was furious and yet triumphant to sense in her voice that she couldn't understand why the boy hadn't gone to her, rather than to him. She'd have helped him to escape.

"I told you. He's in love with Krista. It's because of her. He asked me to save her from the gang."

At the mention of Krista and of Hank's feeling for her, there was a flicker of an emotion which Joseph couldn't fathom in Moe's face.

"So she's the price of silence? Is that it?"

He was, as always, amazed at her quickness. "Yes," he answered heavily.

"And you? What did you say?" Her voice was unnaturally high.

"There is only one thing to say. Hank must go to the police. Or I will."

"Joseph!" From her shocked incredulity he saw he had been right in his decision not to consult her. Women were hopeless where law and order were concerned. He had known her reaction would be to help Hank to escape.

"What else is there to do?" he shouted, his anger rising again at the scorn and fury in her face. "He admits the crime. He's not in the least sorry. He'd kill again. He said so. That's our son. Yours and mine. He's only come to me because of Krista. He imagines he's in love with her."

"Well, and why not? Aren't you?" She screamed wildly, "It's Krista, Krista all the time. Not Anna, Katie or Carola. Always Krista. You're besotted with her. God damn the day you found her!"

At her reckless insinuation, Joseph went cold. She must be mad. He stared dumbfounded as she went on shouting, "She's the real reason for all this. But you want to take it out on me because of Rudi. You'd go to the police and give Hank up for *her*!" Her eyes went suddenly to the floor to that heap of black garments and she stopped.

"Yes," he said, answering her look. "Katie too, and the twins." She remembered suddenly those threats of Hank's about dragging in all her brood.

"No, no!" she cried frantically. "Not the twins! Not them, Joseph, you *can't* go to the police. Think of them! They're only children. No! Oh no! You'd give them up for Krista?" Her face was incredulous.

"What else can I do?" he said wearily. "They've committed murder! Think of their souls! Think of that. Hank stood there and told me he had no soul!"

She burst into wild noisy sobbing, rising to hysteria. "You'd give away your own flesh and blood for a girl you found in an air-raid! You're unnatural! Vile! A Judas! A filthy Judas! You never loved them. Never! Only that girl and Robert. And now listen, just listen to me. Your darling Robert. Well, he's not yours. Put that in your pipe and smoke it. I hope you'll enjoy it. He's the son of an Englishman! One of the conquerors! Yes, *your* Robert. Now d'you see why he likes to go next door so much? He's the son of a man who gave me food. Food when the kids were starving. But don't think he demanded payment. I gave it. Of my own free will. I liked him. Just as I like Rudi." Her voice had become a shrill harsh monotone and suddenly she was laughing. The sound was appalling in the quiet garden. He took her by the shoulders and shook her violently. The coat fell from her arms and she stood in her thin nightdress. He struck her sharply across the face several times. The laughter ceased. She looked at him in horrified surprise and began to cry.

"Don't take it out on me through the boys." she pleaded, "I know I'm bad. But not Hank and the twins! Not them. Please Joseph. You can't understand. Only a mother can. Please . . ." She had fallen on her knees on the dirty floor and gripped him urgently. He was icy cold from what she had said about Robert, but her sobs unnerved him. For as he looked at her with contempt as she pleaded for her boys he hated her—but at the same time he loved her. She was his woman. There would never be any other for him.

"Get up!" he said roughly. "And listen. Nothing that you've done affects this. I don't care about your whoring. What matters are the children and what we've done to them. Yes, you and me! We brought them into the world, and they're liars, thieves, and murderers. Not only through what we've done, but through what we've failed to do. What does your whoring matter compared to this horror? Go with your blasted men, but you'll not see the children any more. I've been blind. Blind. Blinded to what is right and what is wrong. There's nothing else. Nothing. Everything comes down to that."

"You've been taken up with your damned politics and the wretched house," she cried violently. "All your thoughts have been on that—and on Krista and her American. You've had no time for *us*. If you'd let him have her, none of this would have happened."

"Don't you see that it's all one and the same thing? Our children have lost all sense of right and wrong. Why? Not only because you and I haven't shown them, but because of a bloody Government which encouraged crime and vice."

"People get the government they want!" she shouted hysterically. "Why won't you see that? Governments don't make people good or bad. They're born that way!"

"Like Hank? He's your son and mine." She flinched.

"What are you going to do?" she shot at him stormily.

"There *is* only one thing to do. I've been awake all night deciding it."

"No! No! You *shan't*! Leave it to me. Let me warn Krista. She'll understand. She owes us something."

"No. Hank doesn't want her to know anything about it. That's why he came to me. You keep out of this now. And don't you breathe a word of it to the others. It'll all be settled tonight after I come home." He had taken her firmly by the shoulders and thrust his face close to hers. She stared at him unbelievingly. Was this the man who had been unable to take a decision of any kind? The man who until recently had taken any amount of back-chat from Hank? Who had not protested when she had been regularly visiting her lover?

In the blazing eyes and the firm set mouth she saw the Joseph of before the war. The clamorous male who had had to be obeyed. The hardness and determination in his voice, the grim lines in his face amazed her. For suddenly the dead mists of the past with their cloying doubts and indecisions had been swept away from him. In place of the maze of by-ways was one clear path ahead. An extraordinary strength, like that of a man possessed, re-born from a slow death, overcame the bodily exhaustion from his terrible conflict. He saw the dawn of something like admiration in her face, and at the same time he felt disgust and shame at exulting in having vanquished her; at still wanting to crush and subjugate her. Her body showing through the thin nightdress taunted him. She was still on the floor.

"Get up!" he said more gently. But she did not move.

"The twins?" she cried desperately. "You'll keep them out of it? They're only children." Her hair fell over her white shoulders, her eyes were frantic. He put his hand on her bare skin. It was months since he had touched the satin-smooth body which another man had been enjoying. He pulled her roughly to her feet.

"It's no use. It's too late. What d'you think the police are doing? They're on to it. Why d'you think they've come here twice. They'll come again—you said so yourself."

She snatched up the bundle of notes, recognizing the perfume as Katie's.

"These could get Hank away!" she cried, clutching them. "Money will do anything."

"Give them to me," he said. And at the iron authority in his voice she handed them over. "You can't do it! You can't!" she cried desperately.

"Be quiet. The neighbours are up now. Remember what I said. If you interfere, I'll throw you out! You won't see any of the children again. I'll deal with this when I come home tonight. You're not to breathe a word to any of them." They stood staring at each other, and in that moment both knew that they were bound together by those other lives—bound inexorably, whatever had happened or might happen. Joseph might say that he would throw her out, but he knew and she knew that he wouldn't, for he had mastered her. The long battle with her, with the children, with work, politics, with life itself was all one and the same thing. He had avoided it, by-passed it, shut his eyes to it. But now it was here; and there was no weakening in his determination, no tipping of the one scale against the other. They had balanced.

X X X

KATIE HAD MADE careful plans of her own for luring Krista to Eddie's room, but she was inadvertently helped in her plot by Moe. Moe, agitated and exhausted after the scene with Joseph, slipped on some of the potato peelings which she herself had thrown down, and wrenched her ankle badly. It began to swell rapidly and by midday she was obliged to tell Katie that she wouldn't be able to get to the hospital that afternoon to visit Carola, and that Katie must take her place.

Katie thought her mother looked strange, but she put it down to the pain and annoyance of the foot. When she was sent to the village to do the shopping she rang up Leo from a call-box. He knew about her plan and was delighted at hearing how fate had played into their hands.

"Come straight to Eddie's room from the hospital," he told her. "I'll get off early from the yard and be there waiting for you."

Moe hadn't spoken a word at breakfast. Pa had gone off without any. Hank had seemed distraught and uncommunicative. He had sat there looking at Krista. Katie laughed when she thought how they were going to fool him over her. Anna had been peculiar too. When Katie had asked her what was wrong with everyone, she had replied cryptically that she would soon find out: and she had given Katie the most meaning and unpleasant look.

When Katie went to Moe to get the small luxuries for Carola, Moe was pale and very short-tempered with her. She looked hard at the girl and said, "I don't like your going. Come straight back. I can't get about easily with this foot and you'll have to bestir yourself. Besides, your father wants to speak to you all tonight."

The peculiar tone in which her mother said this frightened Katie. Had he found out anything? Her heart gave a jump, but Moe would not enlighten her about what he was going to say. What a good thing that she and Leo had been able to fix their plan for an earlier time than this. She would be well away with it before Pa got home. She noticed that Moe had been crying, and she was worried. Moe looked older suddenly. As if she'd had some kind of shock. Probably Rudi was getting tired of her. Men were all the same. Katie shrugged her shoulders at her mother's silence. Men! Just wait. She would learn to hurt them as they did her.

"How are you feeling?" Moe called after her. "Are you all right? It's a long way to the hospital; you'd better start at once."

She listened to all the admonitions and messages for Carola, assuring Moe that she would remember them all. Moe looked at her again, as if she were on the point of saying something vital. Then she set her lips firmly and told her to be off.

When Krista came out of the factory with Rosa that evening she was astonished to be approached by a tall youth who got off a motor cycle. His face was vaguely familiar. When he spoke to her she knew suddenly that she had seen him with Leila from the next village.

"Katie sent me," he began politely. "She gave me this note for you." He handed her a piece of blue-lined exercise-book paper which Katie had torn from one of Robert's school books. On it was scrawled in Katie's handwriting:

Dear Krista,

I have been taken ill in the town. Please come with Eddie. I am in his room. He will bring you on his motor cycle.

Katie

Krista read the words slowly. She was perturbed. What was Katie doing in the town? Then she remembered that Moe could not go to Carola today. She had slipped and hurt her foot. It had happened just as she and Anna were rushing off. Katie had at once offered to make the visit. Of course. Katie had been right out to the hospital and on this hot thundery day had been taken ill. She did not hesitate. Turning to Rosa she said quickly, "My sister's ill. I'm going to her now."

She was terrified at having to ride on the back of Eddie's motor cycle. She asked him anxiously if it were far. Couldn't she walk there? No, it was quite a way, replied Eddie. Much too far to walk. It was on the river, on the wharf, some distance from the big bridge.

"Oh, don't be silly," urged Rosa. "It's fun to ride pillion. I've often done it. Don't go too fast. She's not accustomed to it. Be careful."

She watched Krista get up behind Eddie. She did not like him. He was a good-looking boy, but there was something she distrusted in his sardonic, unpleasantly narrow face. There was going to be a thunderstorm. It had been heavy and close all day. Now great streaks of lightning shot across the dark sky and the ominous rumble of thunder startled Rosa. She knew Krista was nervous of thunder storms, and she suddenly felt afraid for her. She had received no answer when she had twice asked Eddie where he was taking Krista. Why hadn't he said? Was it so secret? The first drops of rain began to fall and she hurried away home.

Krista was frightened of thunderstorms but she was far more afraid of Eddie's motor cycle. She got up fearfully behind him as directed, and put her arms round his waist. He was not yet an expert driver. Like Hank's, his machine was a new one. Obliged to stop constantly for the traffic signals, Eddie had difficulty in restarting. The rain kept off after those first few drops, but as they sped on through the busy streets towards the town, flashes of lightning and crashes of thunder terrified Krista. She begged Eddie to stop. They would shelter somewhere until the storm was over. But he laughed. Lightning couldn't hurt them, he scoffed. And what about poor Katie? She was waiting for Krista.

In reality Eddie was cursing the storm. If it did not break soon it would wreck all their plans for this evening. The whole success of the plot depended on the tourist being on that terrace in the restaurant garden. No one would stay outside in a thunderstorm. Tomorrow the man left the country. This was the last chance of getting him.

The sky was now so dark that, although not yet seven o'clock, it was as if it were dusk. Cars had their headlights on. In many windows lights showed. Eddie cursed. It looked as if the evening would be a washout. They reached the house where he lodged. Leo opened the door to them. Beyond him the passage was in darkness. A sudden fear came over Krista at the sight of Leo. A shiver of acute apprehension ran through her at something secretly exultant in his glance as he drew her in. She shrank back at his touch, but he signalled to Eddie to shut the door behind her.

"Where's Katie?" she asked sharply. Her voice was high with fear. What had they done to Katie? Had Leo been hurting her? She knew he was tired of Katie.

"She's upstairs," said Leo soothingly. "She's lying down."

She followed them up the narrow stairs to a small room. Again they closed the door after her. Katie was not lying down. She sat smoking in a chair, her face hard and determined.

Krista looked at her anxiously. "Are you better?" she asked anxiously. "Eddie said you were ill."

Katie began to laugh, a horrible taunting laugh. "Ill? . . . so that's why the little saint came, to help her sick sister. Well, I'm better. Very much better, as you see. And now we want a little talk with you. Sit down."

Krista looked round at the two lads and then at Katie. She was now terrified. "No, no, let's get back if you're better, Katie. Let's get home."

Katie laughed again. "Home? Home? That's just where you're not going, little Snow-White. We've got a little job for you to do first."

Krista turned towards the door. Eddie barred the way. "Please, Eddie, will you take me back. I'm tired. I've got to get home."

"Tell her about the job," said Katie tersely to Leo.

"Come here," said Leo roughly. "Come here, and listen to what I'm going to say."

Krista began to tremble violently and the sight filled Leo with pleasure. He loved it when his victims trembled. He caught her by the arms and drew her caressingly to him. "You tell her, you'll enjoy it," he said to Katie. "I'll enlarge on it if necessary."

In a few rough words, the kind of words Krista had heard but never used herself, Katie made it clear what they wanted of her. Krista was horrified when she took in their meaning. They left her in no doubt but that they would go to any lengths to make her act as a decoy to this foreigner.

"All you've got to do is be nice to him. What's the harm in that?" Leo insisted.

"But why?" she asked, stammering with fear. "Why? Why can't Katie do it?" She knew that this was something Katie could do much better than herself.

"Because Katie's got to go and warn Hank," replied Leo firmly.

"Hank's in danger," said Katie. "This man you're going to meet tonight has something on Hank. Unless you manage to detain him in the restaurant he'll give information to the police."

Krista had caught their interchange of glances. Were they lying? They had got her here by a trick. Katie wasn't ill, never had been. She didn't know what to believe, but she sensed that whatever the reason they wanted the tourist decoyed, it was for a dishonest purpose.

"No, no. I don't like it. It's wrong. What's Hank done? Why should the police want him?"

"So you won't help Hank?"

"Not in this way," said Krista firmly.

"All right then, you silly little fool; we'll just have to make you. This is no joking matter." She turned to Leo. "What's the use of waiting? It's after seven now. We must get there by eight or some other woman will get hold of him."

Katie's words convinced Krista that they were lying. It was all a trick. She remembered Robert's anxiety. How he'd kept on asking her to come straight home. She moved back towards the door again, but Leo caught her by the arm.

"Will you do as we want?" repeated Katie. "It's to help Hank."

"No," said Krista with a firmness that she didn't feel. "Let me go, please." She set her lips together and tried to twist out of Leo's grasp.

"I'm sorry," he said regretfully, just as he had done with Leila, "but it's entirely your own fault. You'll have to be coaxed. Can't I persuade you to change your mind? You're so very pretty."

"Get on with it. Take her arms," snapped Katie to Eddie. "What are you waiting for?"

Leo was torn with conflicting emotions as he gripped Krista's soft arm. The dress she was wearing had short sleeves, her thin arms looked pathetically childish as the two lads each gripped one. Katie sat down in the chair in which she had been sitting when Krista had first entered the room. She lit a cigarette. Then she looked at Krista's frightened face. "Twist!" she shouted brutally. The arms were wrenched violently backwards.

Krista went very white, and tiny beads of sweat ran down her forehead. She set her lips more tightly. Her face was rigid. After a moment her torturers relaxed their agonizing hold, but not their hands from her arms.

"Look," coaxed Leo; "we hate to do this. Remember Leila and her injured arm? She got it because she was as obstinate as you are being. I hope you're going to be more sensible. It would be such a pity to break this little white arm." His voice was soft, almost a caress, he had modelled himself on a film gangster whom he admired. Krista shrank back. She knew about Leila. Moe hadn't believed that story about her having fallen from a motor cycle.

"I won't do it. I can't. It's something wrong you are doing. You can break both my arms, but I still won't," she said bravely.

"Twist," said Katie sharply. "Give her some more."

Eddie had seized Krista's arm again. "Wait," cried Leo suddenly. He had seen the same determination in this frail slip of a girl as there had been in Leila. He admired it. And this girl. She was a peach! Lovely, fragile, something he longed to break yet wanted to enjoy first. He wouldn't have her marked. He was damned if he would. There were other tactics.

"Katie," he said smoothly, "you'd better be going. You must go and do something about Hank. There's not much time." He looked at Krista.

"Hank? What is it he's done?" she asked faintly.

"Only murder," said Leo soothingly. He didn't like the livid bruises coming up already on the girl's arms. Her skin was the fair kind which marked immediately. They would look very noticeable in a restaurant. He asked her if she had a coat. But Krista was beyond answering. Her head had begun swimming alarmingly, the whole room was revolving. She staggered as they released her, then swayed uncertainly.

"Now the little fool's going to faint," snapped Katie contemptuously. "Get her some water, Eddie."

Leo fetched the water. Krista drank some. Her arms were so painful that he had to hold the glass to her lips. She sank down in the chair he offered her. She looked terrible. He didn't like it. "Look," he said coaxingly, running a hand down her limp arm, "I hate to do this. You want to help Hank, don't you? Hank is wanted for murder, and if you detain this man you'll be helping Hank. Now, then, won't you do what we want?"

But Krista could not answer. Her mind was upside down. Was this really true? Was Hank really a murderer? She could not believe it. Her horror was so great that the ability to speak was leav-

ing her. Her mouth was dry, in spite of the water Eddie had given
her. Her head ached. The motor cycle had made her feel sick, and
now, shocked beyond endurance, she collapsed in a heap in the
chair. Her arms were burning, agonizing members of her outraged body. With difficulty she raised one to her face and broke
into heartbroken sobbing. It was Katie's behaviour far more than
the boys' which had so appalled her. She had recognized in her
face such unconcealed hatred that she was terrified.

Leo brought her some more water. "Let's try some schnapps,
Leo," suggested Eddie, "and you rub her arms, Katie. She's going
to look fine in the restaurant with those marks on them."

But at Katie's approach Krista shrank back so wildly that Leo
pushed her away. "We'll have to get going," he said curtly. "The
storm'll break any moment now. We must get her there while he's
still on that terrace. You'd better go ahead, Eddie. You're on duty,
aren't you?"

"There's plenty of time," said Eddie, "I'm not on duty till
eight. It's all arranged. I told you so."

"See to her face," ordered Leo to Katie. Katie opened a powder compact and thrust it into Krista's hand. "Powder your face,"
she said brutally, "and comb your hair. You've got to attract a man.
Think of that, little innocent, a *man*!"

Leo began to give Krista her orders in a low careful voice.
"You can't go wrong if you watch Eddie. He's the waiter there.
He'll give us the signal and then you just walk in and join the
man at his table. All you've got to do is to smile . . . and damn
well *smile*. I'll be watching you, so will Eddie. Just let him paw
you a bit. He'll be pretty well sozzled by the time he comes so he
won't expect you to talk much. Don't let him paw you too much.
I'm reserving that for myself . . ." He laughed in a possessive way
and put his hand on Krista's white face. "Don't be frightened,"
he said laughing.

But Krista was slowly gathering her strength again. This could
not happen. It could not! The Blessed Virgin would surely save
her. She began to pray urgently and determinedly.

"Ready?" asked Eddie, looking at Krista's now thickly pow-
dered face. Katie kept on telling her to use more.

"Some lipstick?" suggested Leo, looking appraisingly at the
curve of Krista's immature mouth. Katie drew a scarlet line across
her lips and held up a mirror for Krista to see the effect.

"Too much," commented Leo. "He likes them inno-cent-looking."

Krista wiped the stuff off with shaking hands. Tears kept drip-ping down the thick powder on her cheeks and forming little channels.

"Oh, stop slobbering," snapped Katie impatiently. "You look hideous. No man will look twice at you except to laugh."

Krista stood up. Her legs felt like jelly. Her head was bursting; like her legs, it didn't seem to be attached to the rest of her body. The thunder crashing on the still air was ignored by the others. It added to her terror. "Oh, Holy Mother, give me strength," she breathed.

"Come along, my dear," said Leo softly. He put an arm caress-ingly round her shoulders. Katie's sharp eyes took this in, but she made no comment.

"I'm not coming with you. I won't!" said Krista quietly. She gripped the back of the chair and clung to it with all her remain-ing strength.

"Why, you wretched little idiot!" cried Katie. "I told you she'd be useless, Leo. I said she'd only make a mess of it." She advanced menacingly towards Krista, who shrank from her. "This is your last chance!" she shouted. "Are you coming? Or do we have to carry you?"

Leo held up his hand. "Listen," he whispered. "Listen." There was the sound of a motor cycle stopping outside, then hurried steps to the door, followed by a loud insistent knocking. Leo switched out the light and threw open the window. Hank was below. "Have you got Krista there?" he shouted. "They're looking for her at home. They telephoned the factory."

"Damn! Damn!" swore Leo. He threw the key of the door out of the window. "Come on up—and don't make such a noise," he called angrily.

They sat in darkness. Krista felt a hard hand on her shoulder. "Keep quiet. Remember," breathed Katie.

Hank came in noisily. "Why in the dark?" he began, switch-ing on the light. Then he caught sight of Krista. In one rapid glance he took in the livid marks on her bare arms, the shocked rigid tear-stained face and her relief at his advent. "Why, you dou-ble-crossing beasts, you liars!" he shouted to Leo and Katie. "You promised me you wouldn't use her." He flung himself upon Leo in a fury. Katie switched out the light again. Through the windows the sudden streaks of lightning across the river lit up the room as the two lads grappled. Leo, taken unawares by Hank's violent attack, lost his balance and crashed backwards. Eddie rushed at Hank with a spanner which he had pulled from his pocket. Hank caught him and threw him across a chair as easily as if he had been a cushion. His strength, always prodigious, was increased by fury. Krista, terrified, cowered down behind a chair in the corner as Hank advanced again at Leo who had now regained his balance. She screamed as she saw the Luger in Leo's hand.

"Take care, Hank, he's got a gun!" she cried warningly, before Katie's hands came down over her mouth. But the sight of the gun had brought uppermost in Krista all her instincts for self-preservation. She began to kick and struggle violently. Katie never dreamed that she had so much strength in her slight body. She forced Krista down again and held her on the floor. Eddie was picking himself up slowly. Hank stood ready for him. "Come any nearer and I'll shoot," screamed Leo, the gun pointed at Hank. "Take his arms, Eddie." But a loud knocking at the front door startled them all. In their excitement they had not noticed the persistent ringing of the bell. The knocks were the kind which proclaim authority. Nobody moved. In the darkness they could hear each other breathing in short, jerky gasps.

"Open up! Open up!" came a stern voice from the street.

Hank moved cautiously to the window, backing away from Leo who still covered him with the gun. He took a rapid look down into the street. "Police," he said briefly. There was such fear in the word that it reached them all. "Lots of them. We've been double-crossed!"

In that brief glance below at the group of police and the cars, he saw for himself the black bottomless pit. Who had given them away? Anna! The thought of his father doing so never entered his head. What a fool he'd been not to have shut her mouth for her. When he'd seen his father this morning not one word had been said, although he knew his mother would have pleaded for him. When he'd caught up with him as he hurried off to work and grasped his arm frantically, saying: "Have you thought of something Pa?" his father had said quietly, "Yes, I've settled it. I stayed up all night. Go off now. I'll see you tonight. Don't worry. It's settled." His father's face had looked so strange. Old, tired and ravaged, but Hank hadn't thought of anything of that. He heard only the calm confidence in his voice.

"Thanks, Pa, thanks," he had said, and had put his hand timidly on his father's arm. But Joseph had brushed it off. Then he had suddenly caught Hank roughly by the shoulders and said, "God help you, Hank. God help us all."

When Hank had got home there was already an outcry going on because Krista hadn't come back from work. She always told them if she was going to be late. Anna, suspicious and frightened for her safety, had telephoned the factory and was told that the door-keeper had seen Krista leave on the back of a motor cycle. Thoroughly alarmed now, Anna regretted that she hadn't warned the girl. Somehow they had always taken it for granted that Krista should be protected and spared all possible unpleasantness. When Hank came in she attacked him at once. Where was Krista? She was anxious for her. Where was Katie? She hadn't returned from the hospital, although visiting-hours ended at four. Moe was furious and apprehensive but couldn't do much with an injured foot.

Hank's immediate thought was that the others had outwitted him. Leo had left the works early, and Katie was also missing. Cutting short Anna's accusations that he hadn't kept his word to her, he dashed off on his motor cycle through the storm. He made straight for Eddie's room. Anna had insisted that he tell her where he was going, and in a fury he had shouted out Eddie's address as he went down the lane with Anna following him. As he rounded the bend to the level-crossing gates he saw an American car approaching. A flash of lightning lit up the face of Krista's friend Paul. Hank did not stop. He was frightened for Krista. Arriving at Eddie's place he saw the light in the window, the motor cycles parked outside, and rushing upstairs had found his fears justified.

Now he stood looking down at all those police. The thought crossed his mind, even in his terror, that Anna couldn't have got on to them so quickly.

"Police!" breathed Katie now. Her face was ashen. Krista could feel her trembling violently. The knocking became more insistent. Suddenly Hank ran to the door, braving Leo's gun. "There's a yard behind which goes down to the river. There's a wall right above the water. Let's make a run for it. Come on."

The knocking now was violent. "Open up. Open up, or we'll smash the door!" shouted the same stern voice. Dragging the struggling Krista with her, Katie followed the lads in a wild rush down the stairs. Krista caught her foot and fell heavily to the bottom of the flight. Katie, who had saved herself from doing the same, hauled Krista roughly to her feet. "Come on, you little idiot. Come on, I tell you." She shouted to the three boys to come and help her. Leo came resentfully back and helped drag the still resisting girl out through the kitchen to the garden.

"Lock the door after you. It'll delay them," cried Eddie. Already the heavy tramp of feet proclaimed that the front door had yielded and their pursuers were in the kitchen.

"Leave the girls," shouted Leo to Hank, who had gone back to help Krista. She was now incapable of resisting them any more. Her breath came in great tearing gasps, her whole body one searing pain from the fall and from the arm-twisting. Her head had a shooting pain which almost blinded her. She did not care any more what happened to her. All she wanted was to fall down and lie still.

Katie released her suddenly and she collapsed in a limp heap on the patch of grass in the yard. Katie raced after the others frantically. "Don't leave me! Beasts, beasts!" she screamed. "Wait for me."

But Leo was already high up on the wall above the Rhine. Hank was trying to scale it, but he was heavier and not as agile as Leo. He caught violently at Leo's foot. Leo, brandishing the Luger, shouted, "Let go or I'll shoot. Let go!"

Kicking wildly at Hank's face Leo freed his foot, and turning, faced them. Raising the gun high so that they could all see it, he stood on the wall outlined against the wild sky. "If anyone tries to stop me I'll shoot," he was screaming.

Hank was still trying frantically to get up on the wall. "Don't shoot!" he cried. "I'm not trying to stop you, give me a hand up!" He caught again at Leo's foot. Leo, kicking viciously at his hands, took aim and deliberately shot again and again. Hank fell back with a terrible cry and collapsed at the foot of the wall. Krista, who had been watching, horrified, managed to stagger up, and in spite of the warning shouts from the police now swarming into the garden reached Hank.

The whole garden seemed filled with police. "Stop him! Stop him!" shouted the man directing them. But Leo, poised on the high wall, outlined dramatically against the stormy sky, began to shoot wildly at the advancing men. Before they were ordered to retaliate he had thrown up his arms high above his head, twirled round, and taken a magnificent headlong dive far out into the river below. They heard the splash as he hit the water. Eddie, at the other end of the wall, followed suit.

Krista sat there, dazed, with Hank's head in her lap. She was frantic at the ever-widening pool of blood. She hadn't believed what Katie and Leo had said about his being a murderer. To her he had always been gentle. She knew he was cruel, but not to her. He was the brother who had given his skin for grafting when she had been so terribly burned. The brother who had protected her at school; fought her battles for her. She held his head between her hands and sobbed.

"I've had it!" he said grimly. "The police have got me. Watch out for Leo and Katie. Katie hates you. She's got it in for you." He gave a sound which was half a choke, half a sigh, and closed his eyes.

But the mists of unconsciousness were closing over Krista too. The world was revolving in coloured patterns, just as it did before she went to sleep. A tremendous sense of peace was coming over her so that when amongst the colours she distinguished the face of Paul she was not in the least surprised. So she often saw him before she went to sleep. When she heard his voice anxiously questioning the large fat policeman whose face was also revolving round in the colours and she realized vaguely that he was actually there, she was not surprised. She had prayed to the Blessed Virgin to save her; and just as the twins and Robert had been sent that time when Leo had thrown himself on her in the woodland, so now the Blessed Virgin had sent Hank, and then Paul. It seemed quite natural somehow that it should be Paul who carried her to a seat when the police were attending to Hank. "I knew you would come. I knew you would come . . ." she kept repeating, shivering violently. Paul wrapped his coat round her but the shaking grew worse. He was alarmed, but the policeman re-assured him.

"Shock," he said decidedly. "She's had about as much as she can take." He pulled the coat back. "Look at her arms," he said grimly.

Katie, who had watched without any visible sign of emotion the shooting of her brother, had not moved to help him. When she saw Leo leap down from the wall and heard the splash as he hit the water she began screaming. "You'll never get him! Never! Never! You're all fools! Fools!"

She kicked and bit the man who had caught and held her, but he did not release her.

"We'll get him all right. Warn the river-patrol boat! Warn the patrol!" shouted the man in charge. A policeman raced out to a car to send a radio message.

"He'll never make it in that current, the storm's made it worse tonight," said the man holding Katie.

"He will! You'll never get him! Never! Never!" she screamed again. She was bitter and angry. He had gone off without a thought for her. He'd only been concerned with saving his own skin. She struggled wildly with the policeman, trying to wrench herself free. "You'll never get him!" She burst into angry bitter sobs.

"Come along now. Come along. It's no use struggling like this. It's all over!" said the man holding her.

Paul stood up with Krista in his arms. She was now quite unconscious. Bob, who had been up on the wall with the police trying to see where the fugitives came up, was concerned for his friend. "Don't worry," he said, "she's probably only fainted."

"I don't think she's hurt," agreed the policeman who had first reached her, and lifted her off Hank's body. "But they'll soon find out in hospital."

"Must she go to hospital?" asked Paul. "Can't I take her home?"

"I'm afraid not," said the man. "She's a very important witness. We shall want you all at the police station."

"But how did you get here?" asked Paul. He had been given Eddie's address by Anna as soon as he reached the house in answer to her letter, and had arrived just after the police.

"We went out to the house. The father came to us this afternoon. We acted as soon as we could," said the man.

At the mention of her father Katie looked as if she could not believe her ears. "You mean to say my father actually blew the gaff to you?" she demanded incredulously. "I don't believe you. You're trying to make me talk."

"You can talk to him yourself at the police station," replied the man dryly, "He's on his way now."

"The swine! The double-crossing swine! What a nice father!" cried Katie bitterly.

"The ambulance is here, they're bringing a stretcher for the boy. The police surgeon will see him before you move him. He's just coming," called a voice.

Below the wall of the yard a great commotion was still going on. Searchlights were now playing on the water trying to locate the swimmers. The storm which had been threatening all evening now broke with terrific violence, and torrential rain was added to the brilliant lightning. There was a shout. Eddie had been caught by the river-patrol. But Leo had got away. He could swim under water longer than any other swimmer Katie knew. She listened intently to all the search directions, ignoring the rain and the storm.

The police surgeon had been examining Krista, whom Paul had laid on a seat under the trees. "Yes, let them take her," he said to the policeman giving orders to the ambulance men; "I think this is concussion of some kind. Did she get a blow on the head?" he asked Katie.

"She may have knocked it when she fell down the stairs," answered Katie indifferently, "But she's not hurt. Not she! I wish she were. I wish she were!"

Katie hadn't so much as glanced at Hank when he was put on the stretcher. Her face was a white mask, her head held high. Only her shaking hands gave her away, and she thrust them into her pockets. She ignored the policemen on each side of her as if they did not exist. Indeed, for her they and everyone else had ceased to matter now that Leo had got away. Outside in the street, in the blinding rain, the police car bringing Joseph turned and followed the ambulance.

XXXI

AND NOW AT last it was quiet. So quiet that Joseph sitting under the acacia could hear the hushing sigh of each leaf as it fell. Tonight was All Souls', and in spite of the mild clear evening a chilled sadness pervaded the garden. The children were in bed. He saw to that himself now.

For weeks the place had resembled a circus, with police, press, photographers and sightseers tramping all over the scene of the now notorious bunker gang case. Nothing had been spared them, either in Court or in the press. Everything had been brought into the open—except the affair of Moe and Rudi. Everyone knew of it, but nothing had been said. Joseph had resented this furiously, had felt it unfair that he should have to take all the blame. For the judge had not spared him. His comments had been scathing; he, like the police, had found it difficult to believe that the father had known nothing of his children's activities. Joseph had now accepted it all as just, as he was accepting the attitude of Moe and many others over his having given away the gang to the police.

He thought of all those glaring headlines in the newspapers: he thought about them all, but about Krista in particular. The story of the unknown girl found unconscious in an air raid had caught the interest and sympathy of the press. She had unwittingly achieved as much publicity as any film star. Photographs of her had been blazoned on front pages with the story of her romance with Paul. Well, he accepted that as well; she loved the fellow, and all he wanted now was her happiness.

The leaves fell, one by one, the slight breeze from the river blowing them on to the grass. Through the thinning branches he could see the lights far up the river. If he stood on the low wall under the tree he could see the twin spires of the cathedral. They were floodlit, two slender silver fingers in the indigo sky. As he stood there looking at them his thoughts were on Hank. On Hank, and that last scene at his death. Joseph had betrayed him to the police, but only after a torment which surely Hell itself could not reject.

Hank was dead. But what of Katie? Katie who had looked at her father without the faintest sign of recognition and at Moe with only the slightest emotion as she had been sentenced. Katie, who was to bear the child of the now notorious Leo who was still at large. And the twins? He could still hear Moe's frantic cries as they had been torn from her clinging arms to be taken away to a reformatory.

It had been horrible ... horrible. A nightmare. But now it was over. But was it? Was anything ever over? Moe had said that for her it had only begun. His hate was dead, he felt only humility and great compassion; but hers had just come to life. She had called him Judas, had shouted the name at him in her violent grief over Hank's death. Couldn't she see that if the boy had survived the shooting he *would* have stood his trial for murder, and spent the remainder of his life behind prison bars? Like that lion. He had noticed the spires particularly on that day when he had noticed the iron bars of the lion's cage. Had the impact of the two things been intentional? A warning? Had it taken Hank's life to force him to face up to things?

Last Sunday they had signed the Paris Peace Treaty. He supposed in time it would go through. The Frenchman had come over and discussed it with him. But he had got over his burning feelings about it and the rearmament which would come with Treaty. He felt now as if he had come into some kind of haven after the racking storm of the last few months, and a measure of calm was slowly returning to him.

Today had been very quiet. No hammers, the scaffolding everywhere empty, the bricks lying idle, the suspension bridge deserted—it was All Souls'. But he no longer resented the building. It was right. Inevitable. It came out of the destruction. A new country, they said, was arising out of the ruins of the old, as birth from death. One should get out of the filth of the past. He looked at the new high cement-wall being erected between this house and the one next door. The British family were packing up to leave and the German owner's first reaction to coming out of prison had been to put up this great wall. But what did it matter to him? He was going to have a house himself. He still couldn't believe it. He'd given up all idea of his dream of building. The children had said in Court that one of the reasons they had joined the gang had been because their father had insisted on their contributions towards a house. What had Hank said to him? That there was no place in this world for dreams. He'd given up the whole idea, and although he had felt apprehensive when the news of the Peace Treaty had come, and again when the owner of the next door house had had his property returned, he had hoped for the best. And now? He fingered the paper in his wallet. The land was his. Building would soon begin.

He had avoided not only Peter but all his workmates during the publicity of the police proceedings. He had imagined their disgust and condemnation. He had bluntly refused to have anything to do with their mass protest meetings against Rearmament although he felt just as strongly about it as they did. He had finished with all that!

So he had been astounded when Peter had sought him out one evening and told him that the men had actually held a mass meeting about him, Joseph! They had decided that he'd had a pretty raw deal and they wanted to help him. The decision had been unanimous, Peter said. They had approached Franz, the builder, and the outcome of it was that the money for the deposit had been found. Found by his fellow workers whom he had treated with surliness and unfriendliness for the last few months. They liked him, Peter said; they actually wanted him as their nominee on the worker management board. He had refused of course—Peter could do that far better than he could—but the fact that the men wanted him in spite of all this horrible business had restored his morale as nothing else could have done. He hadn't wanted to accept the deed. He had refused. But Peter had argued with him, goaded, scoffed and finally shouted at him, "Come off it! Put your bloody pride in your pocket and be thankful. What d'you think I dragged you through all those blasted campaigns for? Hauled you across those frozen plains step by step for? So that you can cave in now? You said you couldn't go on then, but you did. And you'll go on now. You'll live all this down. But not in this dump! Stop all this bellyaching and get on with something new! You've *got* to!"

Peter was right. He was a good friend. One of the best. He'd accepted the deed. But it was for the little ones he had accepted it. So that they should have a better chance—which they must have. On an impulse now he went into the silent house. Karl and Robert slept alone now in the great sun room. It smelt of geraniums, of damp, and was littered with the rubbish boys love. The two truckle beds, empty by the far corner, belonged to the twins. He stood looking down at Robert. He loved this child passionately, as he did Krista. There was a poignant look of sadness on his face even in sleep. He thought of the child's anguish as he had stood sobbing in Court, being pressed to answer innumerable questions about the gang. Robert had suffered something of his father's agony in the scorn and contempt with which he had been regarded for having spied on his brothers and sister. As he looked at the fine clearly-cut features, the high forehead and the sensitive mouth, he thought of Moe's confession flung mercilessly at him. This boy was not his. Well, he had always known it somehow. It made no difference anyway, except to make it more ironical that both the beings he loved most in the world were not his own flesh and blood.

In the other room Franz Joseph and little Peppi slept. They lay together, their arms entwined. For the first time Joseph saw this child of Katie's as something to be loved and pitied. Katie's brat! This was how this baby had always been spoken of. The beauty of his sleeping face with its pathetic vulnerability moved him strangely. Franz Joseph was clutching a little basket tied with red ribbons in his hand. And he smiled in his sleep, laughing suddenly aloud. Hank had looked so like this when he was small. And as he lay dead. His face then had been that of a tired child with all the brutality wiped from it.

He wandered back to the garden. Moe and Anna would be back soon. They had gone to the cemetery with a lantern for Hank. They had waited until it was late so that all the villagers would have returned from their pilgrimages. Hank lay under the dark cypresses beside Moe's old mother. Some of the villagers were angry. They thought that he had no right to be there. But Hank had made his peace with God and was above their petty quarrels now.

Anna had said they were going to visit Krista. She was in the convent with the nuns, convalescing after her concussion. In the spring she would marry Paul. Moe had scarcely spoken to Joseph since Hank's death. Her resentment was still burning in her. A father who had betrayed his own son! She hated him now, hated him. That young man, Rudi had left the village. He'd left as soon as the police court proceedings had become public. Joseph hadn't said a word to her about it, but he'd seen that under the hard pride she'd taken a knock. She'd soon got over her anger with Krista. No, it was only against him that she still felt this furious anger.

He looked round the garden. It was tidier, much tidier. True, there were not so many of them to mess it up. But he was strict now; and since the day when Moe had slipped on the potato peelings not one had been flung down in the yard or garden. The dog, sitting close to his master, suddenly raced away barking to the gate. They were returning from the cemetery. Anna went straight into the house, but Moe came very slowly and hesitantly across the grass to him. She was very pale and he saw that she had been crying. When she was close to him, she said, without looking at him, "I met Father Lange in the cemetery. I am going to him tomorrow."

They were the first voluntary words she had addressed to him since Hank's death, and he saw that she was tremendously moved. He got up and held out a hand to her. "Margarethe," he said very gently. She did not take his hand. For a moment she stared stonily at him; then suddenly something in the taut mask of her face flickered, as if a curtain had been drawn across a window. She put her hands blindly over her eyes and turning from him broke into terrible sobbing.

He couldn't bear the nakedness of her suffering. She seemed to him now as one of the children needing infinite compassion. He turned away in unbearable pity as the sobs grew wilder. There was nothing he could do—yet. She must go through the fire. For him the worst was over. For her it had but begun.

Finis Cologne. November, 1954.

*The following newspaper story by Frances Faviell was originally pub-
lished in 1956, in the London* Evening Standard. *It was part of a series
of articles, by various authors, published under the heading: 'Fact or Fiction? The Answer will be given tomorrow'. Unfortunately we don't have
the answer to the* Standard*'s question, though the piece is undoubtedly
informed, at least in part, by the author's experiences in Germany after
the war, as recorded most notably in her books* The Dancing Bear *and*
A House on the Rhine.

THE RUSSIAN FOR SARDINES

IT WAS Oktoberfest in the Zoo in Berlin and the whole Tiergar-
ten had been turned into a Carnival. East mixed with West for
this occasion. It was easy to pick out the Easterners not only by
their clothes but by an air of uncertain bewilderment.

The small guests for whom I was waiting at the entrance
near the Bahnhof am Zoo were late. I stood there watching the
milling crowds, trying to see Tomas, Gela and Barbel. At last they
came –not running excitedly as most of the children were, but
sedately, cautiously, Barbel, the eldest, with a motherly eye on the
two younger ones.

They waved gaily when they saw me, and, looking carefully
from right to left, rushed across the street to me. "We were held
up! The guards at the barrier made us take a test in Russian!
That's their latest! That's why we're late!" cried Gela.

"Hush! You're talking too loudly!" reproved Barbel anxiously.
Tomas, the youngest, said nothing – his eyes were on the flags and
banners in honour of the Oktoberfest.

The children had come by train from a small village 30 kilometres from Berlin in the Russian Zone. Each of them had a
special pass-card for the occasion.

The zoo was crowded with gay visitors, loud with the canned
music of merry-go-rounds and monster gliders and chairoplanes.
Only the animals in their cages seemed depressed. At every booth
and stall were lotteries and exciting games of skill and chance.
The prizes were not the kind we find in similar fairs in Britain:
they consisted of food for the most part.

There were tins of milk, fish and meat. Kilos of groceries and
Cellophane packets displaying the succulent charms of chick-

ens, ducks and even geese. These last were the very top prizes, we were told, and took a great many vouchers. There were any amount of chocolates and sweets.

The children had East German marks, and although I had money for them they wanted the excitement of changing them themselves at the special kiosks set up for the purpose. They were disappointed at having to give up five of the East marks for each West one.

The gaiety of the noisy crowds, the sunny October afternoon, the music, streamers and balloons everywhere excited them, and we set off to try our luck at some of the many games of chance and skill.

The one we liked best was in the charge of a fat, motherly woman. Set in a huge circular map were all the important towns in Germany. Each person chose a town and received a voucher in exchange. The woman then released a lever which set a ball in motion as in roulette. At whatever town the ball stopped, the holder of its voucher won a prize.

I chose Berlin. When all the other towns had been allotted the ball was set in motion. Breathless we all hung over it. It came very slowly to rest on Berlin.

"You've won! You've won!" the children screamed joyously.

"Try again?" asked the woman smilingly. "Or will you choose your prize first? Here's your prize voucher."

"We'll all try again!" I said.

This time Barbel won on Leipzig. After that Gela on Branden-burg. All of us had vouchers for prizes except little Tomas.

"They are from the East?" asked the woman. When I nodded, she said, "One can tell at once. This Oktoberfest is a special one to help the East. Many of the shopkeepers and large firms have given goods, hoping that the East Germans will win them." She lowered her voice: "And I, for one, see that they do. Come, little Tomas, here's a free try for you. What town will you have?"

The child looked long and carefully. "Hamburg," he said firmly.

I lifted Tomas up to watch the ball. He wore a little green Bavarian hat of felt with a feather in it. His jacket was green with brass buttons. The woman looked at me and then at him. The ball stopped right on Hamburg.

"You've won! You've won!" screamed his sisters delightedly. "Now we've all got a prize."

When it came to choosing the prizes I was astonished at the children's choice. Ignoring firmly the boxes of chocolates held out to them they asked anxiously if the vouchers included groceries. They chose tins of milk, packets of margarine and butter and tins of meat. I asked what I could send their mother with my voucher, suggesting cigarettes or chocolate.

They looked at me with large, serious eyes. "Oh, no. That would be a terrible waste. We need food – not luxuries."

"Well," I said, "what shall it be, then?"

"Sardines! Sardines!" shouted Tomas. "That's what Daddy wants. He's got a bad cough and needs oil."

We got three tins of sardines and Tomas was overjoyed. The kind woman offered to look after the things for us while we tried our luck elsewhere and visited some of the animals.

We then collected our prizes and repaired to one of the many open air cafes for some refreshment. While we were sitting sipping raspberry juice and eating hot frankenfurters I asked the children if they would have any trouble in getting the food back through the East-West check-point. They showed me the labels on every article stating that the commodity was a prize won in the Oktoberfest.

"See? We'll be allowed most of these – not all. It's a special day! We got passes for it. The guards may give us another test in Russian, it's compulsory in our schools!" said Gela. "But it won't be difficult. They'll ask is the names of all the food in Russian – if we know the words they'll let us keep some of them."

"And do you know them?" I asked.

They began reciting the Russian words for each thing in their high childish voices and I saw several people at neighbouring tables looking amused. They knew them all – Tomas was made to repeat each one after his sisters. But when they came to the most important prize – the sardines – they couldn't think of the Russian word for sardines. And neither could I!

We sat there under the golden trees whose leaves were dropping on to the check tablecloth. We thought and thought – but none of us could remember it. Despair was in the children's faces. It was hard to realise that the loss of the sardines would be a major tragedy for them – but it would be. I hadn't a dictionary with me – who would have thought that I would need it? "What is it?" cried Barbel. "I know it quite well – but I can't think of it."

Their faces were so gloomy that I was in despair.

"Go and have a ride on the auto-racer!" I suggested. "Perhaps if I sit quietly I'll think of it."

Tomas and Gela raced off joyfully but Barbel stayed with me. Her high round forehead was wrinkled with anxiety, and I hated to see such a look of apprehension and worry on so young a face.

"Try to think of it, *please*, Tante Frances. If Tomas makes one of his scenes at the check-barrier it'll be awful!"

It was almost time to take them to the station. I had promised to put them on a certain train. There was no time to go hunting for a dictionary.

"What *was* the word? What is the Russian for sardine?" I groaned aloud.

At the next table a rather ugly, big man with high cheek-bones and attractive humorous eyes had been watching us for some time. He was sipping a glass of beer. Finishing it now, he stood up, took the bill from the waiter and after paying it took a pencil from his pocket and wrote something on the back of the bill.

He smiled to himself as he did so. As he passed our table he brushed heavily against me, then excused himself in German.

I looked after him in surprise. It seemed that he had bumped into me purposely. He wasn't a German, I knew that from his accent.

"What a clumsy man!" I said. "I've seen him somewhere before," said Barbel in a puzzled way. "Look Tante Frances, he's left a piece of paper on your plate!"

It was the bill for his beer, and on the back he had drawn in pencil a sardine. Its eye was half-closed in a deliberate wink! Above the fish he had written the word sardine in Russian letters.

I was a little worried, although Barbel cried joyfully. "Of course! Of course! It's almost exactly the same as in German!"

Had he been a Russian? He had been wearing civilian clothes, but he had an air of authority, even importance. Shortly afterwards I saw the children off.

A week later I got a letter from Barbel. It had been opened by the censor but nothing had been deleted. After thanking me for the afternoon, and sending her love to my young son who was in England, she went on: "We got *all* our things through the check-barrier! Weren't we lucky? Not many people got all their food through – but we did. The guards made us tell them the names of everything in Russian. One of them, a big man, seemed to know all about us and our afternoon at the zoo. He kept on teasing Tomas, saying that he knew there were Russian sardines hidden under his hat!

"He and all the other guards kept on laughing as if at some great joke and asking us: "What is the Russian for sardine?" I thought I had seen the big man somewhere before – he wasn't at the check point when we passed through earlier in the afternoon. I've seen him somewhere besides at the barrier – but I just can't remember where."

AFTERWORD

I THINK I was about 11 when I realised my mother was becoming a writer as well as being a painter. I was home from my English boarding school for the summer holidays when my father suggested that I should not disturb my mother in the mornings as she would be working. … At the time I was upset as my mother had never seemed to worry if I disturbed her.

My mother was born and grew up in Plymouth, Devon. She was the fourth of five surviving children born to Anglo Scottish parents. Named Olive, she showed her innate independence at an early age by insisting she be called Olivia. She showed early talent as an artist and in her late teens won a scholarship to the Slade School of Art, then still under the direction of Henry Tonks. Her tutor, and later good friend, at the school was the painter Leon Underwood.

In 1930 she married her first husband, a Hungarian academic, whose work took him to first Holland and then India. But they separated while there (and later divorced). She then stayed on for three months in the Ashram of the great Indian thinker and writer Rabindranath Tagore. Travelling on her own, painting and sketching, she visited other parts of India including Assam and for a few weeks lived with the Nagas, a primitive indigenous people in northeast India. On her way back to England she travelled via Japan and then China – still painting and sketching – until she had to flee Shanghai when the Japanese invaded.

On her return to England she lived in Chelsea, then a haven for artists, and earned her living as a portrait painter. She met my father, who had recently resigned from the Indian Civil Service, in 1939, and they were married in 1940 after he had joined the Ministry of Information. Bombed out during the Blitz, as portrayed in her last book, *A Chelsea Concerto*, they spent the rest of the war, after I was born, in the Home Counties before returning to Chelsea in 1945.

When the war ended my father was recruited to the Control Commission of Germany and became a high ranking official in the British administration, first in Berlin, negotiating with the others of the four powers on the organisation of the city, later in the British zone of West Germany.

We joined him in Berlin in early 1946 and it was here that my mother encountered the Altmann family. It was her experiences with them that inspired her to start writing her first book, *The Dancing Bear*, which movingly describes Berlin in defeat through the eyes of the defeated as well as the victors.

Each of her books, whether non-fiction or fiction, were inspired by an episode in her own life. By 1951 we had moved to Cologne and it was here that her second book, the novel *A House on the Rhine,* was conceived, based around migrant families (from the east of Germany) she had met and helped.

Subsequently, she published another novel, *Thalia,* based on her own experience in France before the War when she was acting as a chaperone to a young teenager for the summer. Her final novel *The Fledgeling*, about a National Service deserter, was also based on an actual incident.

My mother was diagnosed with breast cancer in 1956 though I did not know at the time. At first radiotherapy seemed to have arrested the disease. But then two years later, it reappeared. She fought the disease with courage and humour, exhibiting the same clear sightedness with which she had viewed life around her as a painter and a writer. She died just after *A Chelsea Concerto* was published, in 1959.

In her books as in her life, my mother had an openness to and compassion for others and, when she saw an injustice or need, would not be thwarted by authority of any kind in getting something done. But as she always pursued her causes with charm as well as firmness, few could deny her requests for long.

John Richard Parker, 2016

FURROWED MIDDLEBROW

CPSIA information can be obtained
at www.ICGtesting.com
Printed in the USA
LVOW07s1051081017
551665LV00025B/1131/P